Cuba: the second decade

Ciudad, Habana

Prov. Habana

Pinar Del Rio

Matanzas

Cienfuegos

Villa Clara

Sanct
Spirit

Isla De Pinas

Edited by John Griffiths and Peter Griffiths
for the Britain-Cuba Scientific Liaison Committee

Cuba:
the second decade

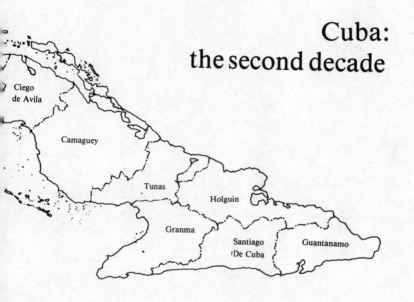

Writers and Readers Publishing Cooperative 1979

Published 1979 by Writers and Readers Publishing Cooperative,
9-19 Rupert Street, London W1V 7FS, England.
Designed by Pat Kahn
Typeset by F.I.Litho Ltd.

Printed and bound in Great Britain by Billings and Sons Ltd.
Guildford, London, Worcester.

ISBN case 0 906495 00 8 paper 0 904613 75 5

Contents

Preface

This book aims to introduce the reader to various aspects of life in contemporary Cuba. It attempts to fulfill, in part, some of the widespread demand in Britain today for information about Cuba, particularly for up-to-date information. It also suggests other sources for further information.

It is written for the general reader though, as the emphasis is on presenting a picture rather than a polemic, students may well find it an accessible resource. Many of the essays try to put together two kinds of reports: a sense of day-to-day experience of life *and* an account of the underlying social political and economic structures. In no way does the book pretend to be a comprehensive picture of Cuba in the 1970s. The different chapters and sections simply reflect the spheres of expertise of certain members and associates of the Britain-Cuba Scientific Liaison Committee.

This book was not written collectively, therefore the writers of individual chapters do not necessarily agree with all the views expressed in other sections.

Acknowledgements

The Britain-Cuba Scientific Liaison Committee would like to thank all those people who donated or loaned money so as to make publication of this book possible.

We are grateful, too, for assistance and information provided throughout the 1970s by numerous members of the Cuban Embassy in London. Roberto Carbajal, Miguel Alvarez, and Sandra Alvarez were especially helpful in providing information and illustrations for this book.

PHOTO ACKNOWLEDGEMENTS

P. 1 COPROFIL, Cuba. P. 18 Joey Edwardh P. 53 Prensa Latina. P. 101 John Griffiths. P. 110 Susan Clifford. P.121 Rodney Mace. P. 131 Joey Edwardh. P.153 FMC. P. 171 John Griffiths. P. 182 *Cuba Internacional*, March 1971. P. 198 *Cuba Internacional,* May 1971. P. 214 David, in *Recopilación de Textos Sobre Nicolás Guillén*, Casa De Las Americas. 1974. P. 223, 228 Chris Rawlence/John Griffiths. P. 235 John Griffiths. P. 247 John Griffiths.

VISITA DE LEONID I. BREZHNEV ENERO 28 A FEBRERO 3 1974

Cuba: the Second Decade

John Griffiths and Peter Griffiths

Few observers of the Cuban Revolution in 1959—or many of its participants, for that matter—could have foreseen the development, less than twenty years later, of the global influence of Cuba and its policies. Cuba is now sending considerable numbers of teachers, constructors, doctors and nurses, to aid other developing countries, and military personnel—to Angola and Ethiopia, for example—to defend and assist others in the consolidation of their revolutions. It has become a nation whose interventions in world affairs are decisively helping to change the balance of forces. For a country—still poor by 'developed' standards—of less than ten million people, the continuing fight for its own development against difficult odds is remarkable enough. But that Cuba should stretch her slender resources by going to the aid of several African countries, as well as Vietnam, Syria, the Yemen, and neighbouring countries in the Caribbean, such as Jamaica and Guyana, is astonishing and unique.

In many ways, Cuba's internal and external struggles are part of the same process. The growth in her assistance to other countries has only been made possible by the strengthening of her economy and the increased security and confidence of Cuban society as a whole. The economic growth of the 1970s is a tangible result of the sacrifices, efforts, and commitment to development of the Cuban people throughout the 1960s. The popular support in Cuba for acts of international solidarity is part of the high level of political awareness generated by the practical experience of struggling out of underdevelopment and constructing a socialist society. This political consciousness is now being utilised and enlarged even further with the development of a system of popular, participatory government in Cuba.

The political ideal of international solidarity has been a firm component of Cuban foreign policy throughout the past twenty years. In the early 1960s, when the momentum of the revolution was quickened by the commitment to a socialist path, links with other liberation movements were established. During this period Cuba supported a variety of liberation organisations in Latin America; provided arms and medicines for the emerging Algerian Revolution, and sent construction and medical teams to Vietnam throughout the period of the war with the USA. The short-lived, progressive military government in Bolivia, the Peruvian government, and Salvador Allende in Chile, could all count on Cuban support. Advisers on political and military matters assisted in a number of African countries from the early 1960s. For example, Che Guevara and a number of Cubans, experts in the armed struggle, were active in the Congo at this time. And links with African resistance movements have been maintained and in many cases reinforced. In Angola, the early contact with leaders of the MPLA (Popular Movement for the Liberation of Angola) has matured into whole-hearted military support for the government led by them. After a commitment to the Eritrean struggle for autonomy, Cuban support has been forthcoming at a developmental and military level for the revolutionary government of Ethiopia, following the seizure of power that opened the way to a socialist transformation of that country.

It is precisely because of this military involvement with the Ethiopian and Angolan revolutionary governments that Western attitudes, especially those of the USA and Britain, have hardened towards Cuba. The military support for Angola, for example, came as something of a shock to the Pentagon who had regarded it previously as beyond Cuban resources. In September 1975 there were about one thousand Cubans advising the Marxist MPLA and training its army (FAPLA). By February 1976 15,000 Cuban troops had arrived in response to the invasion of Angola in October 1975 by South Africa in open support of the FNLA (The Front for the National Liberation of Angola) and covert operations by the United States. Cuba again sent reinforcements to counter the threat of UNITA (The National Union for Total Independence in Angola) which was supported by China, Zaire and the USA. By September 1977 Cuban troops in Angola numbered 19,000.[1] They were not only there as a reaction to the increased participation by South Africa, Zaire and the United States. They were there because of Cuba's long standing and intense relationships with other Third World countries and her commitment to their liberation.

To demonstrate and to reinforce Cuban solidarity with governments and liberation movements in Africa, Fidel Castro visited a number of African countries in March 1977, among them the 'Front Line' countries. He also visited Ethiopia and Somalia and, in an attempt to bring about a reconciliation over disputed territories, arranged a meeting between Mengistu Haile Mariam of Ethiopia and President Siad Barre of Somalia that was later held in Aden. Unfortunately the meeting did not lead to the hoped-for reconciliation and Cuba, along with other countries, was forced to decide which of the countries it could continue to support. With the Somalian invasion of the Ogaden, all Cuban assistance was removed from Somalia, and by June 1977 some 400 medical and military advisers were in Ethiopia. They were joined later by Cuban troops who were to assist in the joint action against the Somalians, who retreated from the Ogaden in March 1978.[2] On the question of Eritrea, the Cuban Government has consistently maintained its position that the dispute with the Ethiopian government is an internal matter. Cuban troops have not been used against Eritreans and there is considerable evidence that Cuba has sought (and is still seeking in the Spring of 1978) to bring about a reconciliation of differences between the two sides.[3]

Cuba is currently supporting other African countries, such as Mozambique and Guinea-Bissau, with economic, medical or military assistance; a position consistent with her long-held relationships with these countries. The possibility of further military assistance in support of South African and Rhodesian liberation groups has not been ruled out. When questioned by a British journalist in February 1978, Cuba's Vice-President Carlos Rafael Rodriguez spoke of the 25,000 Cuban troops active in African countries—the total strength of the Cuban army is 110,000—and went on to stress the responsibility held by the various liberation organisations: 'Revolution cannot be imported and exported. It's up to the movements themselves.' But at the same time he left no doubt as to the continuing support of Cuba for Africa's liberation, stressing Cuba's independence with regard to foreign policy decisions:

'Cuba will go on giving the African liberation movements the help they need, with or without the co-ordination of other countries. It will be according to what *we* decide.'

There is, of course, close co-ordination in Africa between Cuba and the Soviet Union, as Carlos Rafael pointed out:

'It is obvious that we have a close relationship with (them). But when we first sent troops to Angola we did not rely on a possible Soviet participation in the operation. We started it in a risky, almost improbable, fashion with a group of people packed in a ship and in those British Brittania aircraft of ours.'[4]

Cuba's relationship with the Soviet Union is obviously an important one, and operates on a number of levels. The Soviet Union, and, increasingly, Cuba have contributed largely to the making of the new picture of world forces in the 1970s— the strengthening of world socialism through the creation of new socialist governments; the continuing rever- berations of the US defeat in Vietnam; and the end of Portuguese colonialism in Africa. The visit of Leonid Brezhnev to Cuba in January 1974 was a significant gesture underlining the strength and importance of the relationship between the two countries and of the Soviet Union's commitment to Cuba. By the time of that visit Cuba had already become a member of the Committee for Mutual Economic Assistance (COMECON) in July 1972, and had made new long-term agreements with the Soviet Union which included deferring payment of existing debts until 1986. These are to be repaid, at no interest, over the following twenty-five years. The Soviet Union has also agreed to further short-term credits, at a low rate of interest, as well as to higher prices for Cuban sugar and nickel.[5]

The relationship between the two countries has been strengthened in other ways. According to US intelligence reports, the volume of Cuban/Soviet trade has grown threefold in the 1970s. From a figure of US$1.2 billion in 1972 to US$3.5 billion in 1975.[6] It is likely that this trend will continue, given the signing of a new five-year economic agreement with the Soviet Union. This covers the period 1976-1980 and provides for a 250% growth in Soviet/Cuban trade as well as for the installation of Cuba's first nuclear generator and a small steel mill.

The price Cuba pays the Soviet Union for oil, necessary for virtually all its energy requirements, has been indexed to the price of Cuban sugar for the period. Such an agreement, given long-term agreed prices, is of enormous help to a country planning its development. Cuba's first five-year plan (1976-1980) was framed after consultation between JUCEPLAN, Cuba's planning agency, and GOSPLAN, its Soviet counterpart, so as to further facilitate the co-operation between the two countries.[7] Cuba's economic integration with the Soviet Union and the other member countries in COMECON has been further reinforced by the dramatic fall in the price of sugar on the world market in recent years, and the consequent loss of hard currency for Cuba. This is in marked contrast to the situation in 1973-74 when sugar reached its highest level ever on the world market. Then, trade with non-socialist countries (Japan, Canada, Latin America and Western Europe) increased enormously.

The percentage of imports from the West increased from 17% in 1972 to 41% in 1975. On the basis of Cuba's financial strength, stemming from the temporary windfall of high sugar prices and a reputation for always meeting its foreign debt obligations, credits were offered from Spain, Canada, Argentina, France and Britain.[8] By September 1976, however, the picture had changed. The price of sugar had crashed to a miserable 8 cents a pound, drastically cutting off Cuba's main source of hard currency and with it the possibilities for continuing high levels of imports and credits from the West.

Characteristically, Fidel Castro openly reported the grave consequences of the fall for Cuba's short-term development plans at the 16th Anniversary rally of the Committees for the Defence of the Revolution (CDRs) on September 28th 1976.[9]

In addition to the strengthening, albeit temporarily, of economic relations with the rest of the world in the 1970s, Cuba also restored or reactivated many of the diplomatic links which had been closed off during America's diplomatic offensive against her in the 1960s. In July 1975 the Organisation of American States (OAS)—a body that had consistently reflected the foreign policy of the USA—under pressure from Mexico and Venezuela, lifted sanctions against Cuba, so permitting member countries the individual right to re-establish diplomatic relations. The OAS were merely legitimising what was already happening; Allende in Chile re-established relations with Cuba as one of the first acts of his government; Peru similarly restored diplomatic relations in 1972; Argentina in 1973; Venezuela in 1974; Colombia in 1975. Cuba was beginning to come in out of the diplomatic cold. The long-term economic and political consequences of this upturn in diplomatic activity between Cuba and the rest of Latin America appeared, at the time, to usher in more optimistic times for continental co-operation. Unquestionably Cuba has an important role to play in Latin America, given her high level of technological development, her political influence in the world, and her firm links to the rest of the continent by history, language and culture. However, recent events in Latin America —especially the continued slide of countries to the Right—hold out very little hope in this direction in the near future.

In the Caribbean too, Cuba has strengthened diplomatic relations—particularly with Jamaica and Guyana. Both countries have politically progressive governments who wish, despite destabilisation attempts, to develop closer links with Cuba. The threat to Western domination of the Caribbean is clear: Cuba is a highly educative example. Its internal revolution is a constant model for the transformation of other countries, *and* Cuba is actively demonstrating *in those countries* the social benefits of the particular path it has taken. The Conference of Caribbean Churches described Cuba's involvement with Jamaica at the beginning of 1977:

'Cuba has provided Jamaica with a wide range of assistance in educational, agricultural, health, trade and other sectors. They constructed a series of micro irrigation dams; built the most modern secondary school the country owns—at a cost of $4 million—to educate 500 students with accommodation for boarding; established a pre-fab housing plant to produce building materials for a new township; trained more than 160 Jamaican youths in building construction in Cuba, where an additional 250 are currently being trained in the same field; provided scholarships in deep sea fishing, language studies, and sports as well as making available 14 doctors to improve the efficiency of the Jamaican health service.'[10]

These benefits had all resulted from the United Commission for Economic, Scientific and Technical Co-operation set up between the two countries after Michael Manley's visit to Cuba in 1975. Both Fidel Castro and Michael Manley have spoken of their shared history, experiences and proximity, and of the advantages in mutual assistance. This is how Manley expressed it when speaking on television in Jamaica in November 1976:

'Cuba is our nearest neighbour, shares with us great dependence on sugar, is home to many of our migrants, has a long history of friendly relations with Jamaica, and, most importantly, shares our dream of struggling to change the present world economic order which condemns the poor to their poverty for the rest of time.'[11]

A similar agreement exists with Guyana. Guyanese students have university places in Cuba; Cuba has assisted in the development of Guyana's fishing industry and Cuban doctors help run a hospital close to Guyana's border with Brazil.[12] The newly-forged links between Cuba and the rest of the Caribbean reflect a new consciousness among the people of the Caribbean as much as the emergence of Cuba from its enforced isolation.

All these are tangible proofs of the failure of US policy to blockade and isolate Cuba and have directed American attitudes towards the possibility of a 'rapprochement'. There was no chance of this while Richard Nixon was President. Nixon was regarded by the Cuban leadership, and the Cuban people generally, as a criminal because of his belligerence in Southeast

Asia. In the Cuban press the 'x' in Nixon was printed as a swastika. The closeness of his relationships with Cubans in the United States, like 'Bebe' Rebozo, precluded any gesture towards Cuba on his part. His dislike of Fidel Castro and the Cuban revolution, which he communicated to President Eisenhower in 1959 and which influenced all subsequent US foreign policy towards Cuba, remained as intractable as ever. Henry Kissinger echoed this intransigence when he asserted that no small Latin American country was going to dictate American foreign policy. Under President Gerald Ford, however, the US government was more flexible in its attitude to the Cuban revolution and was forced to recognise Cuba's increasingly important role in world affairs. So, in 1974 and '75, informal talks began on the possibility of restoring diplomatic and economic relations.

President Carter also showed himself to be more sympathetic. He came under considerable pressure from sectors of his own party, who admired many of the social achievements of the Cuban revolution and who found the lack of relations anachronistic. Also, there were clear mutual advantages to be gained, as the Anti-hijack Agreement, signed in 1972 between Cuba, Canada and the USA, had shown.

By September 1977 Cuba and the US had moved closer to re-establishing relations, with officials in Havana and Washington respectively setting up 'Interest Sections'—offices to represent their country's interests abroad. Many more steps, however, along a very difficult political path, are needed before full mutual recognition will be achieved.

In the meantime the process of changing long-held attitudes about the other country is under way in both the United States and Cuba. After twenty years of completely negative reactions, the possibility of collaboration in such areas as sport, the arts, tourism, etc. marked a dramatic turnabout. Cuban sportsmen and women competing in the US; a tour by the Cuban National Ballet; even the apparently trivial act of lifting the ban on the sale of Cuban stamps to US philatelists— all these represent significant changes. The Cuban people are being shown as human again—not as supermen or as satanic forces to be checked at every turn. American television and the press have been given access to Cuba, even to Fidel Castro himself, as in the case of the historic and lengthy interview by Barbara Walters for ABC in 1977.[13] In April of the same year agreement was reached on a 200 mile fishing zone. US senators, like George McGovern, have made visits to Cuba for informal talks and observation, and so have increasing numbers of academics, journalists and business men. US tourism is once again under way, too, with charter flights out of New York, as well as regular flights from Canada, bringing not only interested North Americans, but much needed hard currency.

These positive moves have not been made without obstacles. In the US, pressure from Cuban exile groups, the Mafia, and Right wing political organisations, as well as from reactionary groupings in the government itself, has to be resisted constantly. Despite the fact that the sabotage of a civilian Cuban airliner off Barbados in October 1976, with the loss of 73 lives, was linked, as were all previous attacks, to the US Central Intelligence Agency, the anti-hijacking agreement between the two countries still stands.

Given the geographical proximity of Cuba and the US—Florida being just 90 miles away—it seems absurd *not* to establish economic and cultural, as well as diplomatic, relations. Both countries could benefit from trade with each other. The Cuban leadership have made no secret of their desire to obtain US technology, for example. Potential trade figures have been estimated at US$350 Million in the first year and US$1 Billion in the third and fourth years.[14] However this trade is not so crucial to Cuba's development that the US can use it as a lever in negotiations about other parts of foreign policy. The reluctance of the US government to recognise this point has caused the process of 'normalisation' to slow to a snail's pace. When that stumbling block has been removed, others wil still remain: the question of 'compensation' for US assets expropriated; the US base which still exists at Guantanamo in Cuba; the recompense for the US inspired sabotage of Cuban property; etc. There is little question that full diplomatic relations will be restored eventually, but, as Fidel Castro has indicated, the process could well take many years.

The changes wrought by the internal politics of Cuba in the 1970s have been as dramatic as the foreign policies. The period, aptly characterised by Fidel Castro as 'a phase of intense legality' has been particularly marked by the process of institutionalising the Revolution. A new, socialist, Constitution has been formulated, debated and adopted by the Cuban people. Popularly elected assemblies of *People's Power,* at local, provincial and national level, are now operating throughout the country. As a result, decision-making and the organisation of the economy have been decentralised. The roles of the main organisations have been clearly defined and enhanced. And the Cuban Communist Party (PCC) has held its first, truly revolutionary, Congress.

The new political, administrative and legal structures embody the socialist values that emerged from Cuba's experience of revolution in the 1960s. They reflect the new consciousness and confidence of Cuban people, and mark a dramatic break with the structures of the early years of the Revolution: the centralisation of the economy and of decision-making in general, and the concentration of power in the hands of a few members of the revolutionary government, able to govern by decree.

Why did all these developments occur in the 1970s? A glance at statements and speeches by members of the Revolutionary Government throughout the 1960s reveals their preoccupation with the question of institutionalisation. However, they were clearly not going to act precipitately. In 1965 Che Guevara, a decisive influence on the direction of the Revolution, referred to this topic in his essay *Man and Socialism:*

'The institutionalisation of the Revolution has still not been achieved. We are seeking something new which will allow a perfect identification between the government and the community as a whole, adapted to the special conditions of the building of socialism and avoiding to the utmost the commonplaces of bourgeois democracy transplanted to the society in transformation. Some experiments have been carried out with the aim of gradually creating the institutionalisation of the Revolution *but without too much hurry.*'[15]

At the time this was written, the Revolution was still gaining momentum, feeling its way towards the development of socialist consciousness out of the old political disorder—an immense task. Immediately prior to the Revolution, during

Batista's second period of office (1952-59), there were no democratic structures to speak of. He took power by force, and by the time he was ousted, had corrupted, or added to the stagnation of, the whole political and legal system. In 1959, when the Rebel Army took Havana, the state apparatus was in tatters. Fidel Castro indicated some of the problems of establishing a new order when he said in 1971:

'Some vestiges of the bourgeois state remain even now in Cuba. It is quite possible that some of the organisation we created was even more bourgeois than the old bourgeois state. Our Revolution made greater progress in the political field and in the field of mass organisation than in that of creating an apparatus to replace the old bourgeois state, with all its ministries and so forth.'[16]

The group that had taken power for the people in 1959 had taken with it the responsibility to represent their interests. Its success over the Batista regime had, after all, been entirely dependent on mass support. It immediately took on the cause of the formerly oppressed of Cuba: the working class and the rural peasants, as well as exploited groups like women and blacks. With the militants of the Cuban Communist Party, the leaders of the Revolution were the only credible political force in Cuba, and the only source of trustworthy administrative expertise. Many people who possessed political experience and education had either fled the country, were about to do so, or were opponents of the Revolution. Cuba was threatened by counter revolution internally, which was aided and abetted by the external aggression of the USA, in the Bay of Pigs invasion and in other acts of aggression and sabotage. The mass of Cuban society had been denied direct political power, and access to such rights as education, for so long, that it could not realistically take on significant, long-term, political and social responsibility and planning, except through its leadership. So it is not surprising that political power was centralised.

This centralisation was focussed through Fidel Castro. His exceptional abilities as leader, his military experience and political credibility, made him the only choice. He had the support of the masses and managed to remain in tune with them. In *Man and Socialism* Che Guevara writes of the 'dialectical unity' between Fidel and the mass:

'What is missing (*in 1965*) is a more structured relationship with the mass. We must improve this connection in the years to come, but for now, in the case of the initiatives arising from the top levels of government, we are using the almost intuitive method of keeping our ear open to the general reaction in the face of the problems that are posed. Fidel is a past master at this; his particular mode of integration with the people can only be appreciated by seeing him in action. In the big public meetings one can observe something like the dialogue of two tuning forks whose vibrations summon forth new vibrations each in the other.'[17]

In the 1960s other priorities—developing the economy, developing the security and the strength of the revolution through mass organisations, developing resistance to external aggression, developing an educated people—became reasons why political power was not immediately handed to those unused to wielding it. In retrospect, all these reasons which appeared at the time to be adjustments to immediate necessities, can be seen as necessary preparations for the development, in the 1970s, of sophisticated political structures in which the entire population of Cuba could participate, knowledgeably and fully.

The most pressing problem was that of economic development. Cuba only really began to develop after 1959 and the problems were monumental. With the US inspired blockade of Cuba, even the most minor bottlenecks and setbacks became exaggerated. Access to hard currency was difficult because of US pressure and, even when it was obtained, the obstacles to using it, created by the United States, were often insurmountable.

Throughout the 1960s most of Cuba's trade was with the socialist camp, primarily the Soviet Union, with whom a massive balance of payments deficit accumulated. It was the desire to break out of that indebtedness that provided the impetus for the Ten Million Tons 'Zafra' (sugar harvest). Sugar was, and still is, Cuba's most important export. It was the only sector of the economy that could be expanded rapidly in the 1960s to meet the pressing need to pay for Cuban imports; especially imports of fuel, since there is no coal or hydro-electric power to speak of. Under-utilised plant in the sugar sector could be made more productive; output could be expanded with very little investment—in contrast to nickel, for example, where huge investment in foreign technology would be necessary; and the harvest could be lengthened.

The 10 Million Tons target was not reached. There were problems of new machinery; transportation; in some provinces too much rain affected cane yields, in others too little; inefficient managers and inexperienced workers cut into productivity. The revolutionary government shared the responsibility for the failure. As Fidel Castro admitted: 'The administrative apparatus and the leaders of the revolution are the ones who lost the battle.'[18] The dislocation to the rest of the economy was enormous and was also admitted, with not a little pain, by Fidel Castro, who asked that the set-back be turned into a victory.

The failure to reach the target of 10 Million Tons marked the start of the second decade of the Revolution, and was responsible for a number of positive effects. In the short term Cuba *was* able to meet its financial commitments through increased revenues from sugar. For the long-term it launched a revaluation of the shape and direction of the Revolution. The roles of the mass organisations and their relationships with the revolutionary government were re-examined in the light of the discovery of administrative short-comings during the *Zafra*. The critical scrutiny they all received resulted in the new political and social structures developed in the mid-1970s.

In stressing the effects of dislocation and newness, the continuity of experience should not be forgotten. The struggles for survival on the economic, ideological and political fronts in the 1960s were in large part responsible for the improvements achieved in the 1970s—the real economic advance and the consolidation of political strength inside and outside Cuba. At the heart of all the economic advances were the sacrifices of the Cuban people. Their greater political awareness, commitment and confidence flourished within the revolutionary process itself, and were hardened by the rebuffing of external attempts to destroy it. During this time the revolutionary government refrained from devolving administrative power until after the people had experienced socialism in action at some length.

It became necessary at the end of the sixties to review the work of the mass organisations. These organisations would, after all, be essential elements in the creation of more democratic participation in the State. First, the Trade Unions. These had all but disappeared by the end of the 1960s, in part because Che Guevara, seeing their purpose as confined to the conflicts between workers and capitalists, had questioned the necessity for their existence in a socialist society. By 1969, there was little effective representation of workers' interests. This certainly contributed to the high levels of absenteeism at that time. Industry's 'invisible men' were constantly exhorted to reappear, but there was still a fall in production.

So the necessity to strengthen and extend trade unionism throughout Cuba was clear, long before the important CTC Congress in 1973 when the roles of the worker and the trade union were discussed and defined. At this Congress a shift of emphasis away from moral incentives to work was clearly articulated. Over-emphasis on moral incentives was part of what Fidel Castro has called the 'idealistic mistakes' of the 1960s, when the Cuban people were attributed with a communist consciousness even though the period was one of transition to Socialism. That such a consciousness did not exist was revealed by absenteeism in particular. A greater stress on material incentives—to each according to his/her work— became an important step in improving production and productivity and, with them, the standard of living of all.

Although material incentives have been re-emphasised, moral incentives have not been completely displaced. Vanguard workers are still elected as 'Heroes (or Heroines) of Labour', and a moral dimension to material incentives remains in the allocation of resources to communities in areas where the farms or factories exceed the norms laid down. Scarce goods, like refrigerators and televisions, are allocated according to a worker's economic contribution and his/her contribution to society as a whole.

Both moral and political considerations arise in selection for the PCC, which has grown substantially in membership. In October 1965, when the PCC was created from the various revolutionary groups then in existence, membership stood at

50 thousand; by 1970 the figure had doubled; in 1974 it was almost 187 thousand; and by 1975 was nearly 203 thousand out of a population of around 9 million. The increase in membership was seen in Cuba as an important part of the democratisation of the PCC through a wider representation of all sectors of society, as well as a significant measure of the institutionalisation of the Revolution. The First Congress of the PCC, held in Havana on 17-22 December 1975 was one of the high points of this process.[19]

The Congress opened up the Party, making it accessible to the masses and breaking down its somewhat elitist image. Like the Constitution and the Family Code previously, the programme of the Party was debated throughout Cuba, a process which involved almost half the population at over 100,000 meetings. The greater accessibility of the Party is demanded by the very special role it has to play in Cuban society now; it is described in the Constitution as 'the supreme directive force of society and the Cuban state', with the role of 'organising and orienting the common efforts for the realisation of the construction of socialism and advance towards communism'.

The First Congress affirmed this new, socialist, Constitution, which defined the roles of the various groups in society as well as the rights and duties of individuals, and which was endorsed two months later, in the referendum of February 1976, by 97.7% of the electorate. The Congress also made visible the institutionalising process. New political-administrative structures and new provincial divisions were agreed, to be implemented in 1976. The six old provinces, dating from the time when Spain divided the island with a ruler into roughly equal portions, became fourteen new ones, each of a size to make more manageable the new decentralised system of economic and social control.[20]

This move towards decentralisation has been given its greatest expression in People's Power (*Poder Popular*), a form of government which gives substantial responsibility to the province and municipality for the running of health and education, a range of goods and services, transport, housing, sport, and tourist outlets. Other concerns still come under central control, either because of their strategic importance (for example, nickel, sugar and banking) or to ensure standardisation (as with the education curriculum). Democratic control and accountability are at the heart of the new system. Delegates are elected for regular periods of office, and must account for their performance to their constituents as well as to the next tier of command—local to provincial, provincial to national. If their performance is not satisfactory, delegates can be re-called and, if necessary, dismissed. The work of People's Power is inevitably closely enmeshed with that of the Party, Trades Unions, Women's Federation, CDRs, etc. It is still too early to assess its efficiency and its effectiveness in democratising decision-making. Preliminary judgements suggest that in parts of Havana, for example, there has been considerable invigoration of the administration of a wide range of services under People's Power local control. What *is* clear is that this bold experiment in popular participation is a logical outcome of the political experience and educational attainments of the 1960s.

REFERENCES

1   'Operation Carlota' by Gabriel Garcia Marquez in *New Left Review* No. 101/2, Feb/April 1977.
2   *Observer*, London, June 26 1977, p.6.
3   *Observer*, London, April 30 1978, p.7.
4   *Observer,* London, February 26 1978, p.14.
5   *Granma*, Havana, January 14 1973, p.2-3.
6   US Central Intelligence Agency Research Aid, *The Cuban Economy Statistical Review 1968-76.* ER 76-10708, Washington, 1976.
7   *Granma*, Havana, January 14 1973. p. 2-3.
8   Gonzalez, Edward and Ronfeld, David, *Post Revolutionary Cuba in a Changing World*, Rand Corporation, Santa Monica, 1975. p.60-61.
9   *Granma Weekly Review*, October 10, 1976.
10 *Caribbean Contact*, January 1977.
11 Quoted in 'Setting Its Own Course' by Shepherd Bliss in *Cuba Review*, Vol.III, No.1, April 1977, p.20.
12 *Granma Weekly Review*, November 16 1975.
13 Complete text in *Granma Weekly Review*, July 17 and 24 1977.
14 *New York Times,* October 4 1977, p.10.
15 Guevara, Ernesto, *Man and Socialism*, Instituto Del Libro, Havana, 1968, p.12.
16 *Fidel in Chile*, International Publishers, New York, 1972, p.83.
17 *Man and Socialism,* op.cit., p.6.

18 'Report on the Sugar Harvest' in *Cuba in Revolution*, Eds. Bonachea, Rolando and Valdes, Nelson, Anchor, New York, 1972, p.296.
19 *Granma*, January 4, 1976, p.9.
20 The full text of the new Constitution is found in *Cuba International*, Havana, No. 102, March-April 1978.

People's Power

Cynthia Cockburn

THE NEW POLITICAL AND ADMINISTRATIVE SYSTEM IN CUBA

When Fidel Castro described in 1970 the intentions for electoral democracy in Cuba he used a phrase that is characteristic of revolutionary Cuba and of few other societies. Decision was to be put into the hands of the masses so that 'the revolutionary process may become a *formidable school of government* in which millions of people will learn to take on responsibilities and resolve problems of government.'[1] The importance to us all of Cuba's initiative in introducing electoral government as an integral part of a socialist and revolutionary process is difficult to overestimate. Socialists everywhere, whether they live in capitalist and imperialist countries or in bureaucratic workers' states or in newly liberated territories are bound to be seeking answers to the question: how can a revolutionary process be at one and the same time based on a sound socialist economy, secure against internal and external counter-revolutionary threats *and* democratic?

MAKING A NEW CONSTITUTION

The 'school of government' foreseen by Fidel Castro and other revolutionary leaders was a system of popularly elected assemblies from local to national level. They gave this the name *Poder Popular*—People's Power. On January 2, 1974, Raul Castro, head of the Revolutionary Armed Forces, first announced the forthcoming 'experimental' introduction of People's Power in Matanzas Province. Matanzas borders Havana Province and the main town, Matanzas itself, is about sixty miles east of Havana City. Although the Matanzas elections were called experimental, it was made clear at the outset that they were experimental only as to methodology—a firm commitment had already been made within the Communist Party of Cuba and the Council of State to bring People's Power to the whole of Cuba within a few years.

The situation was explained by Fidel Castro as follows.[2] The Rebel Army had to take power in 1959 and begin the task of making the Revolution. But 'our revolutionary state has had its provisional structure for many years. The Revolution was not in a hurry to endow the country with definitive state forms. We didn't want to create some temporary expedient but rather to build solid, lasting and well-considered institutions that would respond to the realities in the country....The revolutionary process now has enough maturity and experience to take on this task and bring it to fulfilment.'[3]

The creation of *Poder Popular* is only one of a really important series of concurrent projects embarked on since 1970 by the Cuban leaders and people. After the failure of the ambitious sugar production plan in that year there was a period of urgent reassessment and a recasting of economic plans and political processes. Basically there seemed to be a choice at that point to go forward by authoritarian and bureaucratic means, with stricter work discipline and material incentives to productivity, as urged by the USSR; or to look for a way to get higher productivity that relied on moral incentives and greater mobilisation and participation of the mass of the people. The latter is known to have been Fidel Castro's preference. The result was a little of the former, but more importantly a renewed commitment to mass participation, which is much more characteristic of the Cuban Revolution to date.

A number of key decisions were taken over the following

two or three years. To draw up a Constitution—including provision for elected assemblies as the supreme authority in the country. To redesign the provincial boundaries and to decentralise the administrative functions of central state bodies. To involve the rank and file of the Party more, and in particular to hold a first Congress of the Communist Party of Cuba. To go over to a Five Year planning system in place of the annual economic planning of the past. And to set up new planning bodies and create a new *Sistema de Dirección de la Economiá* to 'train, prepare and educate the people in an economic awareness they now lack'.

Although all these innovations were inter-related, it is the Constitution that had the most striking effect on political life. The way it was brought into being is descriptive of decision-making in Cuba. A Mixed Commission of the Communist Party of Cuba and the Government was set up in October 1974 and briefed to draw up a preliminary draft constitution 'completely suited to the socialist character of our society'.[4] The Commission presented the draft for discussion to the Political Bureau and the Council of Ministers. Then it was presented in the press, through the state bodies and the directorates of the social and mass organisations for the people as a whole to consider. The draft was discussed article by article in the mass organisations at grass-root level, in work places, the universities, schools and the units of the armed forces, in the period up to September 1975. Six and a quarter million votes were cast in meetings of organisations of the masses (total population of Cuba is nine million). It was reported that if we except only children, all the rest of the citizens of Cuba took part directly and personally in the examination of this document.[5] Five and a half millions of votes were cast in favour of it in its published form; 16,000 voters proposed modifications and additions which were supported by more than 600,000 participants in the various assemblies.

To understand the meaning of electoral democracy in Cuba it is important to understand also the political infrastructure of the country, because *Poder Popular* has not been introduced merely to decentralise the existing central state organisms, to fill a vacuum at local level. It rather gives one new task to the myriad mass organisations that already exist.

These popular bodies are the basis of Cuban society. *Poder Popular* will forge an additional link between them and top-level decision making.

The proletariat in Cuba is usually defined as the industrial, agricultural, intellectual and other workers, the members of the Revolutionary Armed Forces, students, small independent farmers and women working in the home. These groups are integrated with each other through overlapping membership of one or more of the mass organisations that are articulated down to very local levels. They include the workplace organisations (*sindicatos*), the National Association of Small Farmers, the Federation of Cuban Women, the Union of Young Communists, the Federation of University Students, middle and primary school children's organisations, and the units of the armed forces which also serve as political organisations because of the high level of awareness and discussion maintained in them and their close contact with people out of uniform.

Most important of all the mass organisations however are the Committees for the Defence of the Revolution (CDR) which have 4.8 million members, eighty per cent of the population over 14 years of age. The CDRs date from 1960 and were formed as an urgent necessity to guard against counter-revolutionary activity. They are a very complete, convivial and inclusive form of political organisation. There is normally one CDR for each block in a city, sometimes for each street, or for each small suburban area. Sometimes, in the countryside, they bring together no more than seven or eight family *nucleos*. Each CDR has a sign over the door of the meeting place, which is normally the room or flat of the current president. Originally defensive, they have gone on to practical responsibilities such as beautifying and cleaning the area (each household contributes a person, typically on a Sunday morning), doing night watch duties over the local grocery store, administering innoculations and routine cancer tests and blood donation. The CDRs are co-ordinated upwards into regional organisations. These distribute ideas for discussion and pass comments onward to government, because the CDRs' most important role is that of providing a forum, open freely to all, for the discussion of speeches, decrees, draft laws. Speeches in Cuba have a special significance. Fidel Castro is unusual among national leaders in making speeches less to dramatise power than to inform people, to take them step by step through current events at home and abroad, analysing problems and policies, and thinking aloud about the future. The CDRs and other mass organisations thus have rich material to work on and know that views expressed within their meetings will be passed back to the leadership and listened to. The degree of mass mobilisation, informedness and organisation that is so striking in Cuba is largely due to the mass participation enabled by the CDRs and other bodies.

Discussion of the Constitution resulted in 'feedback' on a huge scale. The proposed amendments were publicly reported and considered; some amendments were made and reasons given for rejecting others.[6] The Constitution was put to the First Congress of the Communist Party of Cuba in late 1975. Then it was made the subject of a public referendum in February 1976. Over 90 per cent of the adult population turned out to vote. Ninety-seven per cent voted in favour, in secret ballot.

The Constitution replaces the much-amended and largely irrelevant Law No. 1940, which dates from the pre-Revolutionary period but was still technically in effect. The new document is clearly for public use and avoids legal jargon. It deals with basic socialist rights and duties (no person may employ another etc.). It covers the main points of domestic law, published in more detail as the Family Code (no discrimination against children born out of wedlock, equal rights for men and women within the family etc.). It instituted the system of People's Power.

The Commission had been given a phrase of José Martí, the 19th Century intellectual and freedom fighter, as a guide. 'I would wish that the first law of our republic be the elevation of Cubans to the full dignity of mankind.' The brief to the Commission had continued 'only under socialism can the full dignity of mankind be achieved. Not in slavery, with the bestialities against slaves and the vices of the slave-drivers; nor in feudalism with its relations of servitude and vassalage that impose a constant humiliation on the serfs; nor in capitalism, with its exploitation which engenders unemployment and extreme misery leading to the degradation of the human being, can the lofty wish of Martí be achieved. Only when mankind has been liberated from slavery, from serfdom and from exploitation can the first law of the Republic really be the elevation of Cubans to the full dignity of mankind.'[7]

Till the introduction of *Poder Popular* there had been no elections in Revolutionary Cuba, though the mass referendum mechanism had been used. (Incidentally, the reference of specific issues to the whole population through referenda is still provided for in the new Constitution.) Now there were to be elections throughout Cuba by the autumn of 1976; 'revolutionary elections, something better than bourgeois elections' Fidel Castro said, and drew a laugh from the audience. But it was more than a joke. The elections were revolutionary in that they were the first ever held in the whole history of Cuba that were carried through without intimidation, without guns or bayonets, the ballot boxes attended not by thugs but by the children—the Pioneers.

EXPERIMENT IN MATANZAS

The new system of government provided for under the Constitution is based on 169 Municipal Assemblies, covering the entire area of Cuba. They include urban *municipios* and the old rural *seccionales*. Above the Municipal Assemblies are fourteen Provincial Assemblies. And in Havana there is the National Assembly of People's Power (NAPP) whose character is defined in Articles 67-70 of the Constitution as follows: 'the NAPP is the supreme organ of power in the State. It represents and expresses the sovereign will of all the working people. It is the only organ with constitutional and legislative power in the Republic. It is made up of deputies elected by the Municipal Assemblies of People's Power in the form and proportion established in law. It is elected for a period of five years.' The NAPP elects from among its members the Council of State, whose President will be the head of government and of State, and an executive Council of Ministers.

The experimental developments in one of these fourteen provinces, Matanzas, had, as announced by Raul Castro, gone ahead even while the Constitution was being formulated. In May 1974 a special Commission had been set up to organise in Matanzas elections that would ensure 'that the masses may be permanently, institutionally incorporated into state and administration so that the people may form a direct part of the organs of the state, fully identified with it as a socialist workers' state, deeply democratic and revolutionary'.[8]

Constituencies. The first step in introducing *Poder Popular* in Matanzas was to draw up maps of constituencies. This itself was a process of careful study. The number of inhabitants per constituency varies according to the density of population, from one member per 500 population in the thinly populated rural areas to one per 1000 in the centres. The aim was to keep them small, so that the representative could really be known to electors and keep in touch. The second criterion was to design more or less meaningful entities with which people could readily identify.

In drawing up the constituency map the CDRs and, in areas where small independent farmers predominated, the *bases campesinas* were used as building blocks. A constituency could be one or more of these territorial units. A constituency would also be the whole or part of a large residential institution, such as a military base or a pre-university boarding school in the country, which would have its own candidates and comprise an electoral 'college' of its own. No *municipio* was to have fewer than 20 constituencies. And each constituency would elect one member to the assembly. So a Municipal Assembly would normally have a minimum of twenty and more commonly around 50 members.

Workers, students and householders were active at this stage drawing up a Register of Electors. Those qualified to vote or stand for election were the whole population over sixteen years of age, excluding certified mentally ill and condemned criminals, and anyone who had stood for election in the disreputable election immediately prior to the overthrow of the Batista tyranny.

Nomination. The nomination meetings were organised by volunteers, in each Committee for the Defence of the

Revolution or *base campesina*. Each of these mass organisation units was able to nominate one candidate for the constituency election. There would thus normally be three or four candidates to choose from—but in exceptional areas where the constituency comprised only one base organisation, then two candidates would be nominated from this one, to ensure that an election would be held. The basic competition, therefore, in the Cuban electoral system, is between little territories, each represented by their base organisation, rather than between political parties. For example, the nominee of the *San José Street* CDR, the *Maceo Avenue* CDR and the *Che Guevara Base Campesina* together making up one constituency, might compete for the honour of representing on the Municipal Assembly the area covered by all three.

The first meetings called by the base organisations were to choose a person to preside over the nomination process. A quorum of 50 per cent was all that was needed at such meetings, but in fact in Matanzas an average of 72 per cent of the voting population turned out at this stage. The presidents thus elected were then given a three-hours-a-day six-day training course in election procedure, by people themselves prepared at national level. There were thus by election day a corps of local people, numbering several hundred in Matanzas province, already well versed in the processes of People's Power. They acted subsequently as teachers and guides to the people as a whole.

Then came the nomination meetings. Again the quorum was 50 per cent, the turnout 73 per cent. The 'president', now well briefed, described the procedure that would be followed and answered questions. Speeches were made in favour or against anyone whose name had been put forward. Then there was a vote by a show of hands. The person then being nominated as candidate for that base organisation would be the person receiving half-plus-one of the total votes cast. If necessary a second vote would be held between the top two contestants in the event that neither polled more than 51 per cent first time.

The elections. Every family *nucleo* was then circulated with biographies of the candidates emerging from the base organisations. In Matanzas Province there were on average between four and five candidates for the electorate to choose from on election day: 4712 candidates of whom 1014 were elected.

The quality of the members of the Municipal Assemblies is clearly vital in this new system of government. This is the only *direct* election in *Poder Popular*, since these members later elect from among themselves the provincial and national deputies. That is why there was a continual emphasis that 'the selected *compañeros* must possess the revolutionary qualities of hard worker and good neighbour, and must be a genuine representative of our values.'

The result of the Matanzas elections, held on Sunday June 30, 1974, were later analysed by Fidel Castro, as reported in *Granma*.[9] Of the 1014 successful candidates for membership of the eighteen Municipal Assemblies in the Province, 46% were members of the Communist Party of Cuba, 13% were members of the Communist Youth organisation, 41% were at the time studying on full or part-time courses, 20% had primary education only (i.e. no higher than 6th grade). Only 3% of the members (7% of the candidates) were women. Fidel Castro commented particularly on the fact that less than half of the members were Party people. He read it as a good indication, he said. It showed the democratic spirit of the elections and he would not have wished to see anything different. The Party was properly a vanguard, it was selective. The mass organisations of the base were full of dedicated and magnificent workers who were not Party members. The people, not the Party, were to govern the country.[10] He also commented at length on the very low proportion of women elected, which he believed to be evidence that the Revolution had not advanced sufficiently, and called for a quicker emergence from the 'injustice and prejudices of the past'.

Accountability. In People's Power it is not intended that elected members will 'take power'. First of all, they are subject to immediate recall at any time. Their electors can dismiss them and call for a new election if they are dissatisfied with their representation of the people's interests. Members must attend three-monthly 'rendering of accounts' meetings to report back on government policy and their own activities. At these meetings they hear criticisms from their electorate about their own performance, and can have their mandate withdrawn by a vote of no confidence. In Matanzas at the first of such meetings several members were indeed withdrawn and new elections held. The reasons mainly amounted to 'abuse of power'.

The Municipal Assemblies constituted through these elections are the highest state authorities over matters germane to their district. They are intended to lean on the initiative and 'fullest participation' of the population and to act always in strict co-ordination with the social and mass organisations. Their meetings are to be open to the public always, with very unusual exceptions bearing on personal matters or state secrets. They sit for a term of two-and-one-half years.

The upper tiers. Provision was made in the Constitution for Provincial Assemblies, covering areas such that the electorate of one representative would be approximately 10,000 people. The electorate for the National Assembly delegate would be three times that number. The role of the provincial authority with regard to the municipal was to be to guide, control and audit them and to generate a comprehensive view of developments and activities in their area. The Provincial Assemblies were to be capable of relating on equal terms with the provincial delegations of the strong and experienced central state ministries. These had been deployed in six old provincial areas and were themselves undergoing re-organisation as the provincial map now changed to fourteen.

One of the first tasks of the newly elected Municipal Assemblies in Matanzas therefore was to elect from among their number the delegates to the Matanzas Provincial Assembly. In Matanzas they also voted in 1974 for intermediate-level Regional Assemblies, but these were later omitted from the national system in the interests of avoiding bureaucracy. The upper tier elections in Matanzas produced a membership differing somewhat in composition from that of the Municipal delegates taken as a whole. The representation of militants was higher (75% were Party or Communist Youth members compared with 41% among Municipal delegates.) They were more highly educated (only 7% were below 6th grade as against 20%). Women did better too—with 7% at regional and 16% at provincial level, as compared to 3% in the

Municipal Assembly.

THE PRACTICAL TASKS OF PODER POPULAR

The management work of the assemblies is supervised by an Executive Committee. The first meeting of any Municipal Assembly was therefore to elect such an executive, of five members, to take responsibility for the day to day administration of the authority. The process of election involves a new *ad hoc* body called a 'municipal commission'. The commission has quite a vital role to play. It is put together from representatives of the municipal branch of the Party, the Communist Youth and each of the mass organisations. It puts forward a list of those delegates its members see as possible candidates for the executive—and there must be 25% more candidates than offices, so as to allow for choice. The Assembly may reject or propose modifications to the commission's list of candidates, and then goes on to vote for the executive team. The candidates are elected to the separate positions of president and secretary (paid full-time professional posts) and vice-president (who may also in some circumstances be paid), and to two remaining seats which like the run of seats in the Assembly are non-professional, unpaid and part-time.

The situation would be bound to arise in which a person elected to executive office at the municipal level later found her- or himself elected to the provincial executive. Provision is therefore made for a by-election to be held in such circumstances at the lower level. But it was felt to be undesirable that the best, most able, most revolutionary members be 'creamed off' for higher level duty for lack of competent provincial candidates when their real place was close to the people, actually handling the greater part of the state business which rests with the bottom tier. For this reason the list of candidates prefered by the provincial commission for the executive elections may contain co-opted individuals. These outsiders, though selected by the commission, would of course be subject to voting by the elected assembly.

In this way 'the necessary and logical elevation of the best representatives of the people to the burdens of higher office will not be braked or impeded and, on the other hand, the real daily and constant representation of the inhabitants of each constituency at the heart of state power will be maintained.'[11]

The job that the *Poderes Populares* have been elected to do is rather more diverse and complicated than that done by local authorities in a capitalist economy. Like them, they administer reproductive services such as education, housing, and health. But they have *productive* tasks too. In Cuba, where production is social, the local authorities have to handle much of the activity that in a capitalist society falls to private business. Take Matanzas Province as an example. There is a population of half a million and an area of 12,000 sq. kilometres. No fewer than 5,597 units of service or production (that is, one for every hundred inhabitants) were handed over for administration by People's Power. Of these, by far the greatest part, 4,984, went to the bottom tier, to *municipio* or *seccional*. People's Power was meant to be a very local business.[12]

'The essential criterion is this: all the units of production and service that work for the community, that's to say for the locality, ought to pass to that locality...'[13] The Municipal Assembly gets all the units whose impact is mainly at that level, the Province likewise. In no case is a relationship between an organ of People's Power and a central state body to be one of subordination, it is intended to be a partnership. But five strategic functions remain with the centre: deciding norms, procedures and methods; deploying technical experts; training and deployment of specialist cadres; research and development; and planning and statistics. Fidel Castro emphasised in speaking to the people of Matanzas that *Poder Popular* does not mean that every locality can set its own prices, decide its own school curriculum—quite the contrary. Such norms and standards have to be national because they are intended to ensure absolute equality between Cubans.[14] In addition to the five strategic roles of the central state, certain enterprises are also to be administered centrally, even though they will certainly be *located* in the territory of a particular local authority: the merchant and fishing fleet, banks, railways, mines and basic industries are examples.

It should be emphasised that, somewhat apart from the

administration of central ministries, which themselves have a departmental planning function, there exists in Cuba a national economic planning system, administered by JUCEPLAN and the Institute of Physical Planning. The whole of Cuba is mapped into Plan areas. The national plan determines for instance the concentration of certain agricultural, mining or manufacturing sectors in certain territories, the large scale movements of population, the building of the many new rural settlements, the location of the big new *secundaria basica* schools, the schools-in-the-fields.

Before the introduction of *Poder Popular*, major policies evolved by interaction between the top and the bottom. They were discussed in detail by the leadership and these discussions carried into the mass organisations and to individuals through the press and TV. At the bottom, every man, woman and child was asked to put energy into implementing, being a living manifestation of, this economic development. But in the middle connecting the two, the decision-making remained purely technical and reserved to the central state planning teams. The central planning system and that of *Poder Popular* are now intended to fuse. It was pointed out, however, in speeches and articles on the Matanzas experiment that the *Poderes* were being asked to carry through programmes for 1975 that they had had no part in planning.

Central proposals had, however, been published for a scheme of operational directorates that, with certain variations, would be appropriate for all Municipal and Provincial Assemblies.[15] At provincial level twenty were proposed, ranging from 'nurseries' to 'posts, telegraph and printing'. At municipal level there were to be ten, rather broad-based, directorates: education; culture and sport; health; distribution and catering; local industry and commercial services; collection of root crops, fruit and vegetables; social 'assistance' and 'prevention'; internal administration; and economics. This latter seemed designed to have a key liaison role, collecting statistics about its area and passing them for aggregation to the higher tier. These directorates were to have managers or *dirigentes*, who would be fulltime paid staff on the payroll of the local authority.

During the period before the introduction of *Poder*

Popular the only gesture towards local administration had been the existence of a *national* 'local service', the National Commission of Local Authorities (CONAL) which supervised a number of municipal authorities that were responsible for certain urban tasks such as refuse disposal, street cleaning and the running of cafes, repair workshops etc. These municipal authorities were not elected, but appointed by government. When the transfer of responsibilities to *Poder Popular* occurred, these CONAL units went first and formed 'reception nuclei' for the remainder. Fidel Castro in his speech gave an example of the kinds of units passing to *Poder Popular* in Matanzas. While certain units of strategic significance, he said, would remain under central administration, including the sugar factories and the massive tourist complex at Varadero beach, the Municipal Assemblies would take responsibility for two transmitters from Radiodiffusion; the cinemas of the Central Cultural Commission; bookshops from the Book Institute; repair workshops from the Ministry of Internal Commerce; biscuit and bread bakeries; ice, flour and other food factories; a printing works; garages and petrol stations from the Ministry of Transport; hospitals and polyclinics from the Ministry of Health; and all of the very many schools. He described what he meant by the participation the people would henceforth have in their local enterprises. 'Today the community receives hospital services, but it has nothing to do with the working of the hospital or clinic, whether it works well or badly. That is to say, the strength of the people is not applied to the working of the hospital.' As for the factories, now it would not only be the workers and administrators who would be concerned with production, but the local community, who are also consumers.

IMPLICATIONS OF CHANGE

Many of the new measures being proposed in Cuba, and the English words used to describe them, have a familiar ring as part of the rhetoric of bourgeois social democracy: grassroots involvement, participation, power to the people. Forms of government, however, are historically specific. Where the state organisations are the counterpart of a capitalist mode of production electoral democracy has a specific role to play in preventing working class threats to the continuance of that mode and 'participatory democracy' can be little more for working people than a new challenge, a new terrain of class struggle. In Cuba, on the other hand, as Blas Roca put it, 'our people voted long ago for this power by fighting for it, with sacrifice and bloodshed.'[16]

In 1976, following the Matanzas experience but before the first national elections, there was much discussion of the hopes for *Poder Popular* and the immediate problems attending its introduction. In the short run there would inevitably be disruption and discontinuity in services and production units, and uncertainty in the division of responsibility and the working relationship between the two levels of local power and between the *Poderes Populares* and the central ministries. It would take time for paid officials to learn how to co-operate with members of elected assemblies, and for these delegates to find a role for themselves in local affairs. It was expected there might be a shortage of experienced staff in certain locations. More seriously, would the disturbance cause a set-back to production, on which Cuba's economic existence hangs? Against these worries people were asserting reasons for optimism. Cuba has proved its almost unbelievable capacity for sustained and rapid change. The adjustments involved in *Poder Popular* would be made through the very practised mechanisms that had effected earlier changes: the mass organisations. The Cuban working class is politically experienced. The new elected delegates would have known years of experience in organisations at the workplace, in the CDRs, in the Party. And paid officials would have a similar political background.

The long-run challenges to *Poder Popular* are of a different kind. A decentralised administration of the greater part of the state's production and service activities could be less cost-efficient than strongly centralised sectoral administration. Fidel Castro mentioned the need for vigilance on this score.[17] Bureaucratisation, red tape and over-staffing, was another risk warned against by Raul Castro.[18] Provincial and Municipal Assemblies could become little hegemonies each asserting its rights and powers.

A further risk for *Poder Popular* is illustrated by an interview with a provincial delegate from Matanzas.[19] Asked what questions people were bringing to the three-monthly 'accounting meetings', he gave as examples complaints about non-delivery of root vegetables, breakdown in supplies of ice, the lack of choice on the menu of the local cafe and the poor standard of maintenance in a local school. Most were topics of consumption. In the Cuban situation where everyone is keyed into discussions of *production*, it may be that the participation of the masses in local government might become typically a channel for consumer complaints and might therefore lead to difficulties for society in keeping levels of consumption suitably modest and demand quiescent during the period of consolidation of the economy.

Again, an assembly could become a focus for separatist feeling in a region with very strong character and interests. Fidel Castro warned the people of Matanzas against localism. 'Don't forget' he said 'we are one indivisible republic, organised not anarchic, socialist not capitalist.'[20] The assemblies could equally well become nurseries for political faction. A revolutionary socialist constitution necessarily precludes any question of alternative platforms that might re-introduce a person's right to employ others, or to buy and sell land and property in a private market. But it is conceivable that the local assemblies could become the prize of competing tendencies within the socialist context and this, while it might be necessary in the event of a leadership becoming repressive, could also weaken the solidarity and shared purpose needed in the face of imperialist threats from without.

If such dangers were recognised in the shift to electoral democracy, there were stronger countervailing reasons for going ahead with it. The practical gains, in a contradictory way, are inherent in the very risks. First among them is convenience of administration. As the economy grew more complex decentralisation became an imperative. *Poder Popular* would 'permit a more direct link between management and the base, it will facilitate rapid communication and a better understanding of actual situations. It will ease the taking of decisions and the control of execution.'[21]

Decentralisation, however, could have been achieved without electoral democracy. Why elections? There was apparently no popular pressure for early elections and the leadership made it clear that it was no obeisance to foreign bourgeois opinion.[22] One reason is that the existence of the new assemblies will provide for more direct flows of information between the Council of Ministers and the masses, to supplement, though not replace, the present informal process of consultation by means of the mass organisations. As the economy grows, and the population too, as the standard of living rises, a government that is responsible for production and consumption as well as services has increasingly complicated communication requirements.

A second advantage may be, eventually, a more comprehensive and co-ordinated approach to development at the local level, comparable with the special efforts currently being made by 'community development' teams in the scores of new rural settlements in which formerly scattered peasants are now coming to live. Local assemblies could become a peripheral co-ordinative mechanism for all the different sectors of the economy to mirror the over-all view of JUCEPLAN at the centre. Third, the consumer opinion role of the local 'accounting meetings' may become an appropriate socialist means of promoting a rational development of variety and quality in consumer goods and services.

It is not the practical advantages of *Poder Popular* however that are most emphasised in discussion in Cuba. The impetus most strongly apparent is simply that of principle—the revolutionary idea. In Cuba the Revolution is a project that engages the efforts of leaders and workers alike. To Fidel Castro, it is apparent from all his speeches, marxism-leninism means democracy; it means people's power. No-one is better prepared to carry forward the revolutionary project than the people of Cuba. If certain risks and problems are encountered on the way—worse have been overcome in the past.

The creation of a firm structure for the state, based on electoral democracy, was 'an irrefutable necessity, a historical moral obligation to this generation of revolutionaries...

'Today we need a socialist constitution, one that corresponds to the character of our society, with the social conscience, the ideological convictions and the aspiration of our people. A constitution that reflects the general laws of the society we are building, the deep economic, social and political transformation being worked by the Revolution, and the historic achievements of our people. A constitution in short, that consolidates what we are today and helps us to become what we want to be tomorrow.'[23]

REFERENCES

1. Quoted by Enrique Mesa in *Granma*, May 28, 1974.
2. *Informe Central,* Primer Congreso del Partido Comunista de Cuba, 1975.
3. All quotations from Cuban documents are translated from the Spanish by myself and should not be taken as official.
4. *Gaceta Oficial*, Government of Cuba, October 23, 1974.
5. *Informe Central*, as above.
6. See Blas Roca in *Granma*, January 14, 1976.
7. *Gaceta oficial*, Government of Cuba, October 23, 1974.
8. *Gaceta Oficial*, Government of Cuba, May 6 1974.
9. *Granma*, July 28, 1974.
10. The Communist Party of Cuba is given the following status in the Constitution (Article 5): 'the organised marxist-leninist vanguard of the working class, the superior guiding force of society and state, organising and steering communal efforts towards the construction of socialism and a communist society.'
11. This quotation and much other material I have drawn from Enrique Mesa's useful analyses of *Poder Popular* in *Granma*, May 28 and June 28, 1974.
12. *Gaceta Oficial*, Government of Cuba, October 24, 1974.
13. *Granma*, July 28, 1974.
14. Ibid.
15. *Gaceta Oficial*, Government of Cuba, October 24, 1974.
16. *Organos de poder popular,* Documentos Rectores para la Experiencia de Matanzas, Editorial Orbe, Instituto Cubano del Libro, 1974.
17. *Granma*, July 28, 1974.
18. *Granma*, December 24, 1974.
19. *Granma*, May 16, 1975.
20. *Granma*, July 28, 1974.
21. *Informe Central*, as above.
22. *Granma*, July 28, 1974.
23. *Informe Central*, as above.

Political Consciousness in Cuba

Antonio José Herrera & Hernan Rosenkranz

It is well known that Marx and Engels, basing their analysis on the experience of the Paris Commune, conceived the Socialist State as a form of *direct or participatory democracy*, in opposition to the *representative* system of bourgeois democracy. This State would consist of political organs which would assume executive and legislative functions under the direct control of the proletariat. The proletariat would be able to nominate and dissolve these as and when necessary. The debate as to whether or not such a form of direct democracy has been established in allegedly socialist countries continues. In post-revolutionary Cuba, its leaders maintain, the State has always represented the *interests* of the proletariat in the form of a dictatorship exercised against 'counter-revolutionary' elements from within and outside the country. This *dictatorship of the proletariat and the peasantry* has been exercised by the revolutionary vanguard without the participation of the lower classes, even though these sectors have amply demonstrated their support for the Revolution. From the very beginning the leadership has taken the initiative in creating forms of mass mobilisation, such as the Committees for the Defence of the Revolution (CDRs).

For the purposes of the following exposition, we can conveniently define the State as 'that agency in the division of labour which has the power of coercion over all other agents in the society'.¹ In capitalist societies, this form of coercion attempts to ensure that the social agents fulfil the roles assigned by the division of labour corresponding to an economic organisation based on private property in the means of production, and a determinate form of control over the production process and distribution of the social product. A notable feature of societies organised in this way is the manner in which economic organisation seems to acquire autonomy.

Through a determinate form of ideological obscuration, the dominant groups have been able to exclude the questions relating to their material power base from the arena of political discussion. Thus, such questions as those relating to control of the productive process, the property rights embodied in capital accumulation, and the use of the social product, are largely ignored even though they constitute the *real* base of society. In the expressive terms employed by Balandier, politics appears as a 'mere power-trick' which can thus be *ritually contested* without putting the material foundations of the dominant classes' power into play.²

By contrast, in socialist societies, the coercive power of the state seeks to ensure that the social agents fulfil roles within a division of labour corresponding to a form of socialist property in the means of production. The retention of the State as an 'agency of coercion' in the international division of labour is required at least until the threat of imperialist aggression has ceased and an increased development of the forces of production has taken place. This appears to be the understanding of the Cuban leadership, which also seems to believe that a previous period of internalisation of socialist roles is necessary in order to create a new political culture. Only then would the Cuban people themselves be able to assume direct control of the economy and the State.

Socialist democracy then, could be built once the remains of *bourgeois* political culture had disappeared. After the Bay of Pigs invasion, when Fidel Castro publicly recognised the socialist character of the Cuban Revolution, Osvaldo Dorticos, then President of the Republic, explained why the Revolution had to wait such a long time before it was able to qualify itself as socialist:

'....for a large part of our population—we say it with absolute frankness—even for a large section of our workers, the social-ist ideas which are the revolutionary ideas for our historical epoch, cause astonishment merely by the mention of the name...(so it was that)...the people which united behind this revolutionary transformation of our economy, one fine day discovered or confirmed, that which it applauded and which it supported, and which was the great historical conquest of the Cuban people, that Revolution which was making so many changes, was a Socialist Revolution'.[3]

Therefore, the argument alleged that the dominance of *bour-geois ideology* had rendered the historic interests of the working class and the peasants *opaque*, and that without the full perception of these interests it was not possible to establish a socialist democracy. Twelve years later, summarising the history of the Revolution, Fidel explained that, once Batista had been overthrown, nevertheless:

'it was necessary to commence a great battle, on the ideological terrain, and in the political sphere. It was necessary to finish with bourgeois and imperialist culture because, at the end of the military struggle the enemy possessed very powerful wea-pons; it possessed economic weapons and, at the end of the day, those of the military forces. And our people threw itself into that political and ideological battle, to confront cultural backwardness, illiteracy, and ignorance, until it developed the solid revolutionary and socialist political consciousness that it possesses today'.[4]

The experiment in popular participation termed 'Popular Power' (*Poder Popular*), which culminated in 1976 with the opening of the National Assembly of National Delegates[5], actually began in the Province of Matanzas, in 1974. Undoubtedly however, the antecedents for this process lay in the decentralising measures carried out after 1970. Fidel Castro had stated towards the end of that year that it was 'impossible' for the Council of Ministers—the superior organ of government—'to direct and co-ordinate this apparatus (the State). For this reason it is necessary to create a structure of a political character, in order to co-ordinate the different sectors of social production'. In 1972, the Council of Ministers was reorganised, and an Executive Committee was created comprising eight ministers, whose task was to co-ordinate and control the ministerial activities previously carried out by Fidel himself.

On the other hand, it is widely known that at the triumph of the Revolution, there were three political organisations which had fought against Batista: the 26th of July Movement, the PSP (Communist) and the Revolutionary Directory (Directorio Revolucionario). Once the first of these organisations had been purified of its bourgeois-liberal elements, the Cuban leaders proposed the fusion of these organisations into a single party. In 1961, after overcoming bitter resistance, the Integrated Revolutionary Organisations (ORI) were created, which grouped all the organisations under the control of the Communist Party (PSP) chief Anibal Escalante. However, Escalante did not delay in trying to use his position so that his party might assume control of the Revolution, a move which was blocked by Fidel in his famous denouncement of sectarianism in March 1962. At the end of this year, the ORI was replaced by the Single Party of the Socialist Revolution (PURS), and this became the new Communist Party of Cuba in 1965. This party assumed the full political control of the country. The State and the Party became the same thing. The party assumed elitist characteristics while the mass organisations, with the exception of the CDRs, virtually did not exist.

Nevertheless, at the beginning of 1971, winds of change began to blow over the Party. Attempts were made to separate the Party from administrative functions, to rid it of its select character, and to redistribute tasks more evenly through the ranks. Finally, in December 1975, the Party resolved to encourage the development of popular participation and to give over politico-administrative functions to the new political institutions.[6]

Before 1970, practically the only possible form of participation was through the CDRs, which fulfilled the most diverse functions, such as ideological preparation, education, sport, cultural demonstrations, voluntary work, public health, urban reform, produce distribution, etc. After 1970 the Cuban Central Trade Union (CTC), and the National Association of Small Farmers (ANAP) gained greater dynamism and helped to stimulate great public debates on the Family Code and the Socialist Constitution.[7]

By 1975, the Cuban leadership undoubtedly supposed that 'socialist' roles had already been internalised, owing to the spread of the culture of the 'New Man', the principal architects of which had been Fidel himself and Che Guevara. The Cuban vision of the New Man is based on the necessity of, on the one hand consolidating the revolutionary process in a country where the development of the productive forces is still at a low level, and on the other of carrying out the task of preparing a people to live under socialism.

The culture of the New Man was introduced between 1964 and 1968, and once again between 1970 and 1973, when, as might be expected, the questions concerning material incentives and the role of the mass organisations were reconsidered. The main accounts of this cultural vision are to be found in Che Guevara's *Socialism and Man in Cuba*, and Fidel Castro's speech presented on the 26th of July 1968.

Among the values commended are generosity, the spirit of sacrifice, responsibility, austerity, internationalism, and the capacity for criticism and self-criticism. The most important ideological apparatuses which spread this political culture, are the two principal mass organisations of the country: the Central Trade Union and the National Association of Small Farmers. Periodic discussions take place inside these organisations on topics which range from Marxist theory to the political and social significance of Popular Power.[8] The mass communications media are used to good effect, without on the other hand neglecting the contribution made by such novel media as comics, or those of a more traditional type such as folklore. The following passage is an example of the latter, featuring an argument between two singers and poets (representing a famous old tradition of the 'twenties) in which one (Santana) defends the *idealist* conception of the world, while the other (Lumindoux) favours the materialist vision:

Santana(the idealist):

You deny then, songster,	*Entonces niegas, cantor*
with your new theories,	*con tus nuevas teorias*
that the world was created	*que el mundo surgio*

in 6 days	*en 6 dias*
by the hands of the Creator?	*de manos del creador?*
Is it not true that the	*No es verdad que el*
great Lord	*gran senor*
in less than a week	*en menos de una semana*
made the sky, the rich earth,	*hizo el cielo, la tierra lozana,*
the night, the aurora,	*la noche, la aurora,*
the sea, the animals,	*el mar, la fauna,*
the plants,	*la flora,*
the first human couple?	*la primera pareja humana?*

Lumindoux (the materialist):

This world already fathomed	*Este mundo ya sondeado*
by investigations,	*por las investigaciones,*
was formed not in a few days	*no en dias, sino en millones*
but in millions of millions	*de millones se ha formado*
Not by a mythical God	*No por un dios increado*
but by evolution	*sino por la evolucion*
when the combination	*en la que una combinacion*
of atoms founded	*de atomos dejo fundida*
the earth, and life arose	*la tierra, y surgio la vida*
by the Law of Transformation.	*por la Ley de Transformacion.*[9]

The Party, together with the mass organisations, prepares study materials, lecture recommendations, texts of Fidel Castro's speeches, etc. In additon, seminars, conferences, radio and television programmes, newspapers, and magazines, serve to internalise the roles required by socialist society.

At the same time as this ideological infusion of roles takes place, the means of direct popular participation are being developed. These comprise both indirect participation, through the election of representatives to the various commissions of the mass organisations, and direct control, especially of the local productive process.

The following is a sample from the survey taken in Cuba between June and October 1976, with the object of measuring the degree of popular participation prior to the beginning of the Popular Power experiment.[10] The survey covers aspects of political culture in Cuba; the actual presence of the people in

the learning of that political culture; and the extent of participation in the decision-making process which results from
putting this political culture into practice.

POLITICAL CULTURE

In relation to those concepts or values which guide political activity in Cuba, we would like to emphasise the following:
the notion of democracy, the image of the leader, and formal
political knowledge. The first two of these are directly related
to the problem of popular participation, and the third, although more general, will nevertheless serve to evaluate the
efficiency of the internalisation process.

The notion of democracy

Tables A and B show the idea which the sample respondents have about democracy. In the first Table it can be seen
that 303 respondents, or 85% of the total, 'defend their points
of view in discussions regardless of whether the others (even the
leader) hold different opinions'. Nevertheless, in Table B, 66%
of the respondents said that 'when discussions are taken to a
vote there is always, or nearly always, complete unanimity'.

Table A: Opinions of Cuban workers and peasants from the Habana
Campo and Habana Ciudad Provinces, on the behaviour of their
companions in discussion meetings. 1976

Question: Do they defend their points of view regardless of whether
the others (even the leader) hold different opinions?

	WORKERS						PEASANTS						Total workers & Peasants	
	Non-Leaders		Leaders		Total		Non-Leaders		Leaders		Total			
	No	%	No	%	No	%	No	%	No	%	No	%	No	%
The Majority	115	86	37	77	152	83	121	87	30	91	151	87	303	85.5
Some yes, others no	19	14	11	23	30	17	18	23	3	9	21	13	51	14.5
Total													354	100

Table B: Opinions of Cuban workers and peasants from the Habana Campo and Habana Ciudad Provinces, on the results of the motions on which they vote. 1976

Question: Is there unanimity?

| | WORKERS | | | | | | PEASANTS | | | | | | Total workers & peasants | |
| | Non-Leaders | | Leaders | | Total | | Non-Leaders | | Leaders | | Total | | | |
	No	%	No	%	No	%	No	%	No	%	No	%	No	%
Always, or nearly always	92	68	30	63	122	67	87	62	27	82	114	66	236	66
Sometimes	33	25	17	34	50	27	53	38	6	18	59	34	109	30
Never, or nearly never	9	7	1	3	10	6	0	0	0	0	0	0	10	2
Total													355	100

The apparent contradiction which arises when comparing the two tables, indicates one of the most important features of democratic proceedings in Cuba. Everything appears to indicate that Cubans understand democracy not as the 'free circulation of ideas', but as a mechanism to achieve a *majority consensus* of opinion. Therefore, as evidenced by the Tables, it would appear that the discussion is more important than the vote which follows, since here there is generally an attempt to overcome divisions in order to produce a consensus of opinion. The vote then is no more than a formal legitimation of what is decided in the preceding discussion.

The typical image of the leader

In order to obtain an approximate idea of what is considered to be the typical leader at the present time in workers' and peasants' organisations, respondents were asked to select from a number of variables, those which best explained the election of the leader of their organisation. This section of the survey also represents an attempt to detect whether or not there is a tendency toward elitism or clientelism in the criteria used for leader selection. In fact, the answers given for the variable that we thought would indicate elitism, were not quantitatively important enough to justify analytic consideration. For example only 4% of the respondents considered that the leaders of their organisation were elected because of 'friendship or favouritism', and only 5.7% due to knowledge of Marxism.

The reasons selected are more 'noble' in character. As can be seen in Table C, for the peasants the more important ones are 'responsibility', 'work experience', 'revolutionary history', 'best worker' and 'cultural level'. For the workers the order varies and 'best worker' assumes the first place followed by 'responsibility', 'work experience', 'revolutionary history' and 'cultural level'.

Table C is organised so that the peasants appear in two groups corresponding to the type of economic organisation in which they participate. The first group is bracketed under the heading 'Integrated Plans' (referring to an organisation where the individual parcels of land are integrated into 'State Collective' and the peasant therefore resembles an agricultural worker); while the second group appears under the heading 'Specialised Plan and Peasant Association' (where the peasant, in the strict sense of the word, has property/possession rights over the land). The reason for making this distinction is to show the important differences in the responses of workers and peasants. As we saw, the workers chose 'best worker' (*mejor trabajador*) as the more important value in electing leaders. The peasants however put the same value in the fourth place. On the other hand although the workers place 'revolutionary history' as the fourth value and the peasants as the third, the former outnumber the latter in its selection. Undoubtedly 'best worker' and 'revolutionary history' have a more 'genuine' revolutionary connotation than the other values and they seem to be favoured more often by the workers than by the peasants.

According to our analysis, these differences are not explained by the variables of age, sex, social background, militancy, or education, but rather seem to be related to the differences in the material conditions of production and the reflection of these at the level of the 'social relations of production' characteristic of workers and peasants. This interpretation is supported by the fact that those peasants who are more similar to workers in terms of their social relations of production (i.e. those of the Integrated Plan) are also more similar to workers in their response patterns.

A brief conclusion from the evidence seems to suggest that the Cubans know that they ought to give priority to the values

Table C: Typical leader image among Cuban Workers and Peasants from the Habana Campo and Habana Ciudad Provinces 1976.

	Workers		*Peasants*						*Total*	
			Integrated Plans		Special Plans and Peasant Ass.		Total Peasants			
Variable	No	%	No	%	No	%	No	%	No	%
Responsibility	116	64.1	38	84.4	96	75.0	134	77.5	250	70.4
Work Experience	93	51.4	22	48.9	87	67.9	109	63.0	202	58.9
Best Worker	126	69.6	17	38.7	34	26.5	51	29.5	177	48.8
Revolutionary History	87	48.1	21	46.7	54	42.1	75	43.2	162	45.6
Cultural level	16	9.4	11	24.4	34	26.5	45	26.0	61	17.1

of the New Man, rather than use criteria of a possibly elitist character. Nevertheless it would appear that the workers have assimilated those values of revolutionary connotation better than the peasants.

Formal political knowledge

A considerable number of variables covered this theme in the survey, but here we will only deal with those related to knowledge of some international figures with a relevance to Cuban life and history.

The respondents were asked about the nationality and political position (and/or their ideas) in relation to the Cuban Revolution, of thirteen personalities who in one form or another are associated with Cuba's history or present international policy.

As can be seen in Table D, there is little doubt that the workers and peasants sampled have responded positively to the attempts of the Cuban leadership to broadcast detail of the present international position of the Cuban Revolution. We recorded the results shown there and found out that 57.4% of the workers and 40.6% of the peasants, representing 49% of the total sampled, knew the nationality and political position of all thirteen persons in line with the Cuban Government's official view. If Mao Tse Tung (whose situation was unclear at the time of interviewing) is excepted, the figure rises to 62%.[11]

Table D: Nationality and Political Position (and/or their ideas) in Relation to the Cuban Revolution of a Group of International Figures, according to Cuban Workers and Peasants from the Habana Campo and Habana Ciudad Provinces. 1976

Name of Personality	Correct Nationality-Friend		Correct Nationality-Enemy		Other*	
	No	%	No	%	No	%
Salvador Allende	342	96.3	1	0.3	12	3.4
Gerald Ford	2	0.6	325	91.5	28	7.9
Mao Tse Tung	38	10.7	257	72.4	60	16.9
Leonid Bresnev	335	94.4	1	0.3	19	5.3
Simon Bolivar	289	81.4	2	0.6	64	18.0
Ho Chi Minh	332	93.5	4	1.1	22	6.4
Sekou Toure	271	76.3	2	0.6	82	23.1
Nguyen Thi Binh	310	87.3	3	0.8	42	11.9
Abel Santamaria	343	96.6	0	0.0	12	3.4
Valentina Tereshkova	334	94.1	0	0.0	21	5.9
Mariana Grajales	345	97.2	0	0.0	10	2.8
Luis Corvalan	334	94.1	0	0.0	21	5.9
Agosthino Neto	342	96.3	0	0.0	13	3.7

* Other includes: Incorrect Nationality-Friend, Incorrect Nationality-Enemy, Don't Know or No Response-Friend, Don't Know or No Response-Enemy, Correct Nationality-Don't Know or No Response, Incorrect Nationality-Don't Know or No Response, and simply Don't Know or No Response in both cases.

Participation in study circles

Study Circles or groups are the most important mechanism for the transference of political culture. As suggested by the high degree of value and role internalisation revealed in the previous section, the attendance rate in the Study Circles is very high. According to the sample, 90.7% of the respondents 'always or nearly always' attend the Study Circles, and only 8.4% reported that they attend 'sometimes' or 'never or nearly never'. Also, 86.8% 'always or nearly always' actively intervene in the study sessions; 96.3% 'always or nearly always' receive the group leader's explanations when they ask for them, and 98% study the material given out in the Circle at home, or in the CDRs (53.8%), in the Circle and at work (14.4%), or only in the Circle(29.1%).

Apart from the high overall levels of attendance, the peasants appear to give greater attention to the Study Circles than do the workers. Thus, the peasants obtained a 'score' of 2.73 discussions attended out of a possible maximum of three, while the workers only managed 2.50, or 10% less.

The reason for this difference perhaps lies in the results of our examination of Political Culture, where the peasants were found to come below the workers on such indicators of a revolutionary connotation as the values used to select leaders, and the level of formal political knowledge. Owing to this discrepancy, it would appear that the Revolution has insisted rather more on political education for the peasants than for the workers.

PARTICIPATION IN DECISION MAKING

We wish to terminate this study with an attempt to determine up to what point the internalisation of the roles and values which together make up Cuban political culture, has resulted in a true process of participation in the decision-making process. In the following sections we will try to:
1) determine the frequency with which assemblies involving workers and peasants take place;
2) reveal the real level of participation in these assemblies by the sample correspondents;
3) discover which area of participation, according to correspondents, signifies the concretisation of the relation.

Frequency of assemblies involving workers and peasants
According to information obtained from the Organising Secretaries of the CTC and the ANAP, assemblies involving workers and peasants take place in the work centres at least once a month. These assemblies, apart from dealing with matters arising from production, involve discussion of such problems of relevance to the worker and the peasant as, for example, the institutions of Popular Power.

For the three months preceding the survey, there was, in addition to the Regular Production Assemblies, at least one meeting in each work centre of the first Assemblies for the

Election of Delegates to the Popular Power. Our statistics indicate that almost 65% of the respondents attended all meetings, and the rest participated in at least one meeting.

The level of participation in assemblies by Cuban workers and peasants. As an indication of the real grade of participation, 284 respondents, representing 80% of the sample, said that they 'always or nearly always' made a personal intervention in the assemblies, and another 20% said that they did so 'sometimes'. Asked to comment on the level of participation of their companions, 83% of the respondents said that 'most times' they did make interventions.

The location of the most important areas in the decision-making process. Table E is fairly self-explanatory. It brings together a series of activities which the workers and peasants indicated as being the most important areas of their participation in decision-making. This is the result of a 'content analysis' made on an 'open' question, where respondents were asked 'to mention the most important themes, affairs or matters which are discussed and resolved in your organisation with the direct participation of the workers or peasants'. It follows therefore, that all the affairs and activities mentioned in the Table were suggested by the workers and peasants themselves, demonstrating the extent of the interest which they have in the decision-making process.

The fact that the workers' responses were much more evenly distributed among the various areas of participation selected, in comparison to those of the peasants, requires a more detailed analysis, but what can be observed here is that, although the overall level of participation is high (3.82 activities out of a possible maximum of 5), the situation which appeared when considering the Study Circles is reversed, since participation is 10% higher among workers than among the peasants. Perhaps this could be taken as an indication that despite the effort by the leadership to raise the political awareness of the peasants to the level achieved by the workers, the latter will continue to be the most advanced class in Cuban society.

Table E: Decision-Making Activities in which Cuban Workers and Peasants from the Habana Campo and Habana Ciudad Province Participate. 1976

WORKERS			PEASANTS		
Activities*	No	%	Activities	No	%
Production Plan[1]	173	95.0	Production Plan	165	95.2
Education[2]	104	57.1	Topics C. de E.	131	72.7
Voluntary Work[3]	98	53.8	Education	86	49.7
Topics C. de E.[4]	91	50.0	Absenteeism	61	32.5
Emulation[5]	69	37.9	Voluntary Work	45	26.0
Absenteeism[6]	53	29.1	Emulation	40	23.1
Saving[7]	33	18.1	Mass Organisation	34	19.6
Political Calls[8]	24	13.1	Political Calls	24	13.8
Health Plan[9]	23	13.0	Health Plan	14	8.0
Cultural Affairs[10]	21	12.0	Cultural Affairs	14	8.0
Mass Organisation[11]	11	6.0	Saving	1	0.5
Others[12]	24	13.1	Others	21	12.1

1. Is the arrangement and implementation of the different stages of the work process. Based on a preproject by the State, the workers together with their leaders, or the Base members in the case of the peasants, prepare a project and a final plan. The plan covers the whole year but is checked at monthly intervals.
2. Concerns the formal educational courses prepared by the workers and peasants to ensure that their companions attain the minimum level of sixth grade of scholarity.
3. Productive and non-remunerated work undertaken outside of normal work hours, and which despite its voluntary character must also be planned.
4. Many of the matters discussed in the Circulos de Estudio, are also discussed or put into practice in the regular Production Assemblies.
5. A mechanism through which two workers or work centres are related—based on the better achievement of production target. This is not a simple form of competition but more as the word 'emulation' suggests, a form of mutual assistance.
6. The problem of labour indiscipline, preventive measures, sanctions, etc.
7. Concerns saving of raw material as well as energy.
8. Proclamation of solidarity with international movements, government's policies, etc.
9. Hygiene of the work place and workers' and peasants' health.
10. Programmes include theatre, music, history groups, etc.
11. Concerns the discussion of the work done by the Executive at the base level.
12. Includes: the vanguard movement, innovator movement, etc.

The evidence obtained from this 'measurement' of the

political behaviour of the workers and peasants interviewed, suggests a high degree of internalisation of the values and roles which, according to the official Cuban leadership, will characterise the new political culture. In addition, the development of the 'decision-making mechanisms' is part of a parallel system of popular participation.

Both processes seem to be fairly successful in achieving their desired result. Their 'legitimacy' as a means to construct socialism is a separate question. What the Cuban revolutionary leadership has officially stated is that these 'decision-making mechanisms' provide a real possibility for direct producers to participate in the control of the productive process. If this is the case, then one can say that socialist social relations of production are in the process of emerging in Cuba. The Cuban workers could become not only *owners* of the means of production through the agency of the State acting on their behalf, but could also have direct *possession* of these through the 'decision-making mechanisms' to which they have access, and which their political preparation disposes them to use. If this accurately reflects the current situation in Cuba, the organs of Popular Power constitute genuine embryonic forms of popular democracy, appropriate to a socialist socio-economic formation.

REFERENCES

1   This definition is taken from Robert Dahl and Charles E. Lindblom, *Politics, Economics, and Welfare* (Harper and Brothers, New York, 1953).
2. See also Anthony Downs, 'An Economic Theory of Political Action in a Democracy', in *Landmarks in Political Economy*, ed. Earl J. Hamilton et. al., (The University of Chicago Press, 1962), p. 562.
2   Georges Balandier, *Political Anthropology* (Penguin Books, London, 1970), p. 41.
3   Osvaldo Dorticos Torrado, Conversation in the Ministry of the Revolutionary Armed Forces on the 14th of June 1961, in *Los Cambios Insitucionales y Politicos de la Revolucion Cubana* (Biblioteca Nacional Jose Marti, Cuba, 1966).
4   Fidel Castro, Speech delivered on the 30th December 1973, to close the military manoeuvre at the 'XV Anniversary of the triumph of the Revolution', in Marta Harnecker, *Cuba, Dictadura o Democracia?* (Siglo XXI, Mexico, 1975), p. 10. This book is a well documented investigative work about popular participation in Cuba.

5   According to Law 1269, which inaugurated Popular Power in the Matanzas Province, these are organs which possess 'faculties for the exercise of Government, for the administration of production and service facilities, for the commissioning and carrying out of constructions and repairs, and in general the promotion of all the activities required for the satisfaction of the social, economic, cultural, leisure, and educational needs of the community, within their competency.'

6   The Cuban Communist Party has itself given a clear account of the different types of activities which it undertook during the transitional period and subsequently under socialism, in other words, while it was *entrusted* with the control of the State, and afterwards when it withdrew from this role. The second General Secretary of the CCP, Raul Castro, claimed that after the creation of the Organs of Popular Power, the principal task of the Party would be the ideological direction of Cuban society, while the Popular Powers would be left as the sole authority with the jurisdiction to create compulsory rules and mandates. In other words the Party would guide, while the Popular Powers governed. See Raul Castro's speech delivered at the closure of the Popular Powers seminar, which took place in Matanzas on the 22nd of August 1974. *Organos del Poder Popular* (Instituto Cubano del Libro, Cuba, 1975), pp 62-63 .

7   According to the information collected by Antonio Jose Herrera in February 1976, concerning the Referendum by which the Cuban socialist constitution was adopted, the constitutional project was preceded by a process of discussion involving nearly 6,200,000 persons, approximately 5,500,000 of whom voted in favour of maintaining the project without modifications, and 16,000 suggested modifications, which were supported by some 600,000 persons.

8   Both in the CTC and in the ANAP these discussions take place in the Study Circles, which are without doubt the most important mechanisms for political instruction which exist in Cuba. There are 25-30 people in each group, usually one per Peasant Base and up to two per Trade Union Section, where the average number of members is 50. The meetings, which are led by a discussion leader, democratically elected from among the members of the group, take place once a week for one or two hours.

9   *El Indio Nabori, Santana y Lumindoux* (Cuba: DOR-PCC, 1974), p. 5.

10   The sample is part of the fieldwork programme which Antonio Jose Herrera carried out in Cuba between January and November 1976. The selection of the sample universe, which comprised only the Habana Campo and Habana Ciudad Provinces, and likewise that of the final participants, was made on the basis of a 'two-stage stratified random sample'. The interview technique used was that of 'collective interviews with a previous individual questionnaire'. Out of an initial selection of 186 workers and 180 peasants, 182 workers and 173 peasants were interviewed.

11   The complexity of Mao's case is a result of the following circumstances: on the 5th of April 1976 the Cuban Communist Party, responding to an attack by the Chinese delegate to the United Nations who accused Cuba of being responsible for the intervention of South Africa in Angola, condemned the 'Maoist clique in the Chinese leadership' for its policy of solidarity with the counter-revolutionary movements in Angola, and with the fascist dictatorships of Latin America. This statement marked the beginning of a denunciation of 'Maoist deviations', unprecedented in the history of the Revolution; until this

time Cuban allusions to the Chinese problem had been few, and in no case were the attacks directed at Mao. Also, before the survey was completed the Chinese leader died, and consequently his revolutionary past acquired greater prominence. Therefore, for some of the respondents, at the time of attempting to classify him as 'friend or enemy', it was not clear which was most important, his 'revolutionary past' or his recent 'phase as an ally of imperialism' to use the words of a peasant from Artemiza.

Economy in the 1970s

Chris Logan

Problems of underdevelopment do not disappear overnight even if the aim of a government is to ensure social equality throughout the period in which an economy is transformed. The Revolutionary Government of Cuba made an early pledge to launch programmes necessary for leading workers and peasants into a new life, free of the evils of capitalism which they had known so well. Such a society of necessity required a transitional phase before socialism was to be achieved. During this transition, economic development was to be stressed: efforts would be demanded equally of all and sacrifices would be shared by all. Such a policy is in marked contrast to that of most Latin American countries, particularly Argentina, Brazil, and Chile where the accumulation of capital is achieved by the impoverishment of millions for the benefit of a small minority. Cuba enjoys real growth rates of income year after year, while at the same time her population has at least its basic requirements met in food, housing, health and education.

As a consequence of the defeat of Batista and the subsequent confrontation with United States imperialism, Cuba's revolutionary leadership found that it was in control of an economy which could only with difficulty meet the majority's needs. These needs were the major causes of discontent amongst the workers and peasants, since the previous regime had done little to satisfy them or even recognise their existence.

The Cuban government led by Fidel Castro, however, had promised to raise general living standards by eradicating poverty and unemployment. Throughout the sixties Cuban economic policy tried to find a way out of the dilemma of transforming a sugar-dependent economy forming part of an imperialist world system into one which was responsive to the broadly-defined requirements of the majority. Under the best of circumstances such a task would be formidable, but the particular situation faced by Cuba was such as to make the necessary transformation of the pattern of production and consumption even more hazardous.

Firstly it should be remembered that Cuba in the pre-revolutionary period earned up to 80% of her foreign exchange from exporting sugar. The United States was her main market. Annual quotas for exports of sugar to the U.S. thus played not only a major role in determining foreign trade income but also, given the great dependency upon exports, the overall prosperity of the economy. Apart from sugar, tobacco and cigars were also exported, as was nickel. Previous attempts to get away from overspecialisation on the one crop had failed. There are many reasons for this failure to diversify the economic base of Cuba's economy but two should be singled out as being of major significance: lack of capital and the implications of a trading relationship with the U.S. for a small nation.

Such industry as did exist under Batista was either government subsidised or the result of direct foreign investment, mainly American. The U.S. direct investment meant, of course, a high degree of foreign managerial control over many sectors of the economy, into which a total of $1000 million had been poured by 1959.

The second important factor limiting Cuban prospects for diversification away from sugar and hence increased levels of income and employment was the presence of United States products on the local market. As a condition for gaining access to the American market Cuba was obliged to give 'most favoured nation' treatment to imported goods manufactured by the corporations. Such goods, particularly consumer items, industrial raw materials and machinery were priced far below the level at which any local enterprise could compete. With a small internal demand, limited by the receipts from the sale of quota sugar to the U.S. and hence conditional upon access to cheap U.S. manufacturers, and no real prospects for exporting any new products, a vicious circle of dependency had grown up.

Thus the prerevolutionary economy was in a state of permanent crisis. Some shifts in production did occur, as local industry began to produce basic consumer commodities, but by and large the picture was gloomy: 'By the single standard of average income, the island's economy stagnated during the entire sixty years leading up to the 1959 revolution. Income per head (in constant prices) averaged $201 annually in 1903-1906, $216 per year in 1945-48, and about $200 in 1956-58. Between 1950 and 1958 total production increased at an annual rate of only 1.8 per cent while population growth was 2.1 per cent per year. Hence, average income declined every year by 0.3 per cent!'[1] The option of increasing sales of sugar did not exist for the market is a highly unstable residual one subject to wild fluctuations. In times of poor demand the only effect of making more sugar available is to push prices down further on the commodity exchanges. To produce for stock is expensive, and to speculate is too risky a development strategy for a government.

Consequently Cuba was a society which was highly stratified with a few very rich, an urban middle class, and a large mass of low income workers and peasants. Amongst the latter, unemployment and poverty were particularly severe, as the planting and harvesting of sugar cane only took up five months of the year. O'Connor estimates that the island's sugar mills were owned by eighty-three individuals, of whom roughly one half were Cubans and one half North American. 'Cuban economic stagnation and underdevelopment before 1959 was attributable to the cartelisation of agriculture, monopolistic industrial organisation and practices, and the subordination of the Cuban economy to the United States economy' he concludes.

Faced with this situation the Revolutionary Government attempted in the early sixties to engage in a major diversification of the economy. In the face of obstacles—created by U.S. corporations and their government—the Revolution swung further to the left, ultimately abolishing capitalism and private property as the basis of economic, social and political life. Blockaded by the United States Cuba turned to the Soviet Union for credit and a mutually beneficial trade agreement, which included a barter agreement for sugar. The sugar crop in 1961 was a record in recent history, and, given that the U.S. had abolished her sugar quota, new barter agreements were drawn up with socialist and other countries. In the light of these events a two-pronged strategy of development emerged in Cuba as a means of introducing socialism: agricultural output and employment was to be increased in order to satisfy the nutritional needs of the people and industries were to be set up to provide basic commodities which otherwise would have to be imported. Sugar would finance this transformation together with soft, i.e. low interest, loans and credit obtainable from the socialist countries and other sympathetic nations.

The history of subsequent developments in the sixties has been extensively covered by others, so only brief reference will be made to those aspects of Cuban economic policy which represent a continuation or reaction to such developments. A fundamental commitment to redistributing consumption between the various strata in Cuban society still exists, together with the need to create full employment and increase output through accelerated programmes of capital investment. From the beginning the Revolutionary Government had favoured the rural peasants and labourers when allocating new investment, both productive and in health, education, and current consumption. Urban workers were equally guaranteed minimal needs, but emphasis was always on bringing up the standard of living of the poorest sections of the community by positively discriminating in their favour. Differences inherited from a class society are only eliminated slowly, however, as Fidel Castro affirmed on outlining the government's intention to move still further towards an egalitarian society; equality in the satisfaction of needs is the product of a highly developed society, not of one in which the productive forces and the material base are still being developed![2]

In order to reduce these differences in consumption levels the Cuban planners are taking a series of measures which are continuously developing in the light of results judged by a 'pragmatic mixture of needs and ideology'. Development is aimed at achieving an egalitarian distribution of consumption within the two constraints of guaranteeing full employment and continued capital accumulation. Such new capital investment is designed, of course, to ensure future surpluses for redistribution in order to raise future living standards. The earlier attempts at industrialisation through rapid import substitution met with very mixed results. By 1962 it was decided to give priority to agriculture in development plans. A target was set to produce 10 million tons of sugar, other targets being set for cattle and dairy farming, citrus fruits and similar agricultural products. In the early years of the Revolution there were a large number of unemployed available to cultivate hitherto idle land and make better use of resources previously used wastefully. But the very success of Cuba in achieving full employment and increasing output, while reducing differentials in consumption meant that new tactics would be required to increase output further. As David Barkin observes, the strategy was for 'future growth to be based on the reorganisation and mechanisation of the economy; agricultural technicians, machinery operators and personnel possessing industrial skills of all types, were urgently needed to allow the setting up of new processes and productive plants and to replace low-productivity human toil with machinery'.[3]

The Cuban economy's growth had not been very great in the first five years of the Revolution, averaging only an annual increase of 1.9 per cent in gross social product between 1961 and 1965—an outstanding achievement, nevertheless, if one takes into account the deliberate disruption caused by external forces. Industrial output grew by 2.3 per cent over the same period starting, as we have noted, from a very narrow base. By 1966-70 both economic indicators registered a much greater improvement with gross social product growing at an annual average of 3.9 per cent and industrial output attaining an annual average growth of 7.3 per cent. In the years 1971-75, further increases in production are recorded, gross social product growing by more than 10 per cent annually whereas industrial output rose by 9.5 per cent over this five year period. Clearly the revolutionary process was consolidating itself, with appreciable progress being made in changing the island's basic economic structure and the standards of living of large sectors of the population. Table A indicates the benefits conferred upon the rural regions as compared with Havana over the period 1953 to 1972.

Table A: Distribution and Increase of monetary income by family according to areas within Cuba: 1953-72.

Areas	Increase 1953-70	Distribution of monetary income in relation to national average	
		1953	1972
National	108.3	100.0	100.0
Havana	106.6	114.7	113.2
Rest of country	113.7	89.4	94.0

Source: National Bank of Cuba, National Income and Expenditure Survey, 1952-53. Juceplan National Survey of Incomes. October 1973.

This vast improvement in the living standards of the previously impoverished is only partly indicated by the data given above. Free education and medical care are available to all as 'social goods' and do not therefore appear in *monetary* income estimates. Equally significant is the fact that the whole of the male population was now brought into employment and that the number of women at work not only increased substantially, but the type of work open to women changed radically for the better. Unique amongst Latin American countries, Cuban development favoured the peasantry and agricultural workers against the town dwellers. Indeed there has been a net movement of population out of Havana as a result of a deliberate policy to develop industry and services in the secondary cities. Other welfare indicators also pay tribute to the success of the redistributive measures. Infant mortality, for example, has fallen by around a half to 27.4 per thousand births while average life expectancy for the population has risen to seventy years, with the mortality rate falling from 36 per thousand in 1964 to 29 in 1970 and an estimated 27 per thousand by 1975.

Such improvements in general welfare and income needed to be accompanied by greater labour productivity if they were to be sustained. The revolutionary leadership never failed to stress the relationship between efficiency, output and the general socialist aims of the Revolution: 'Productivity is from now on and always the fundamental question in our country,' says Fidel Castro, echoing Che Guevara's earlier declaration that 'everything, however you analyse it, comes down to one common denominator: the increase in the productivity of labour, the fundamental basis for the construction of socialism and indispensable premise for communism'. In order to build up the economic base, Cuban planners firstly tried to improve the productivity of agricultural employment. Such a choice was consistent with the overall aim of ensuring full employment at the same time as continuing to favour the least privileged. Agricultural surpluses would be expected to provide the necessary foreign exchange for acquiring industrial plant and know-how for further diversification of the economy. This strategy was outlined in the early sixties and has continued to be operative in the seventies forming as it does the basis of the impressive growth figures quoted.

The efforts to increase output in the sugar industry led to a watershed in Cuban planning. Having set a target of a 10 million tons sugar harvest (*Zafra*) for 1970, all efforts were concentrated on achieving this level of output. As all the world knows, the concentration on a single industrial target—that of sugar output—did not lead to the target being attained but rather resulted in a shortfall of some 1.4 million tons. This in itself would not have been so bad had it not been for the fact that the concentration upon the sugar industry to the exclusion of other sectors of the economy also led to a fall in industrial output and investment. Labour was drafted out of factories, mines and other sectors of agriculture to aid in the harvesting of sugar cane and its delivery to the mills, with a consequent disruption in output. Cuba was still a one product economy, and the reverse suffered by the relative failure to boost sugar output in order to reduce the trade imbalance with the Soviet Union was felt at all levels in society. Fidel Castro gave a characteristically courageous and honest review of the country's situation in a speech—the famous 'autocritica'—in which he did not hesitate to take a proportion of the blame for 'the failures in revolutionary leadership'. However, equally characteristically, a slogan was formulated which expressed confidence in the Cuban people and its leadership's ability to learn from mistakes: 'We will turn the setback into victory'.

In order to improve the performance of the economy 'a

new series of measures were generated, emphasising, above all, the involvement of the masses in economic management, in identifying the problems of our economy, in greater administrative thoroughness, which are today developing with promising success'.[4]

As a sequel to the basic rethinking of priorities and procedures the economy began to improve slowly, despite a fall in sugar production to 4.8 million tons in 1971. Output in other sectors of the economy rose, yet the underlying economic situation in Cuba did not improve although personal consumption went up by six per cent. The reason was that foreign exchange receipts fell even lower than in 1971, reflecting the drop in sugar output and the reduced demand for nickel associated with a cyclical slump in the steel industry. During the 1970 *zafra* nickel was a 'preserved' industry which was not called upon to release manpower for cane cutting because of its balance of payments contribution. The extremely high nickel prices prevailing during the steel boom of that year had slumped equally dramatically, hence the same level of output yielded lower returns in 1971.

After the trauma of the 10 million tons sugar harvest, the recovery of industrial output was spectacular in some cases and encouraging overall. Delayed or postponed projects were completed and carefully laid sectoral development plans formulated. Light industry output rose by some 20 per cent, the construction industry grew by 25 per cent, and there were very substantial increases (41.2 per cent) in the production of building materials notably cement, and in the related output of the metals and metal products industry (41.5 per cent). Apart from sugar, output also fell in the tobacco and cattle rearing sectors of agriculture. The need to meet export commitments for Cuban cigars led to severe reduction in the internal consumption of tobacco. More serious, however, was the decline in the dairy herd and meat cattle population, thwarting any hope of increasing meat protein consumption and that of milk and dairy products. Milk in Cuba is mainly reconstituted from powdered milk imported at a great cost in dollars (around $30 millions in 1971) from Britain and Western Europe.

The response of the Cuban revolutionary leadership to this crisis was to stress the need to have a correct attitude to work.

In May 1971 Fidel Castro gave a speech in which he outlined the fundamentals of economic strategy of the Revolution. Particular emphasis was put on the maximum use of the labour force, and on the role of wages and prices at this stage of economic growth. Given that all wealth comes from work there could be no one who refused to work at all under socialism. A law against vagrancy was passed, but even before it came into effect on April 1st, moral pressure had induced 101,000 persons formerly unemployed, to register for productive work. A Revolution which met its obligations to educate the 40 per cent of the population under the age of sixteen, which gave pensions to those whose right to retirement it had created, should equally be able to see, said Castro, 'the only just road and the only way out, that of the duty to work and the battle for productivity'.[5]

Only by a concerted and conscientious effort on the part of the workforce could any of the broader goals of development be met. A developing country trying to build socialism faced backwardness in its productive forces and labour productivity. These contradictions between aspirations and reality required a major effort by all if they were to be successfully resolved.

In 1971 the sugar harvest fell to less than 5 million tons. Two years of drought had been followed by a rainy summer which coupled with the absence of a cold period meant that the sugar content of the cane remained low. Clearly if any long term economic development was to be feasible the pressing problems of the sugar industry had to be solved. Thus a major effort was made to reduce the uncertainties in the volume of sugar obtained in each harvest. The fetishism of targets was abandoned in favour of a determined effort to increase output in absolute terms by increasing sugar yield and labour productivity, and reducing the effects of vagaries in the weather. In order to achieve such a desirable situation it would be necessary to mechanise cane harvesting, to increase the sugar yield of cane by the introduction of new varieties, to promote growth by the use of fertilisers and to increase irrigation. Such a programme would lead to vastly improved labour productivity while at the same time making sugar output more reliable, hence stabilising foreign currency earnings and producing a steady flow of funds for further industrialisation and increased consumption. A measure of the significance of such a policy would be the reduction in the number of manual cane cutters required, from 310,000 in 1972 to around 50,000 in 1980, according to the Minstry of Sugar's estimates. Mechanical cane cutting by harvesters required reorganisation of canefields so that cutters could gain access to canefields of a size which justified their use. Irrigation equally required investment and both procedures demand greater skills than possessed by those who cut cane by arduously wielding a machete.

Mechanising cane loading into wagons for subsequent delivery from the fields to the sugar mills has been achieved relatively easily. It has proved more difficult to design machines similar to combine harvesters for cutting cane. The cane becomes tangled in the fields and has to be stripped of unwanted top growth. Early attempts with adapted Russian cane cutting combines in the run up to the 1970 harvest were unsuccessful so a major research and development effort had to be made to design machines capable of operating under specifically Cuban conditions. Such has been the development of engineering know-how and maintenance skills that the 1975 sugar harvest employed more than 1000 combines which cut 39 per cent of all the cane harvested. A plant to produce 600 combines a year by 1980 has been built which will certainly greatly facilitate harvesting. Each machine replaces 56 cane cutters, eventually relieving 100,000 manual cane cutters in total. The area under cane has been increased to 1.6 million hectares and the number of manual cane cutters has fallen to 170,000 at the same time as the output of sugar has gone up steadily since 1973. Progress has been considerable. In order to continue the process the 1976-80 Five Year Plan—the first to be attempted—views a continuation of mechanisation as an essential means of ensuring, in conjunction with other measures such as irrigation, selection of high yield cane varieties and the increased application of fertilisers, that the Plan's target of between 8.0 and 8.7 million tons of sugar be met by 1980.

In order to ensure that the sugar harvest will become more reliable, irrigation is particularly important as a means of maintaining adequate crop growth. By 1980 the area under cane cultivation should rise to 1.7 million hectares but the role of irrigation is as important as increasing the area under cultivation, as a means of increasing output. The impressive dam building programme, which to date hàs increased the dam capacity of Cuba a hundred-fold since the Revolution, is to be continued and new plants are to be built for manufacturing pipes, sprinklers and other necessary irrigation accessory equipment. In August 1977 Fidel Castro opened one such plant with an annual capacity of 2,300 kilometres of tubing and 193,200 sprinklers. Fertiliser production has also increased very rapidly as a vital means of raising sugar and agricultural output generally. In 1975 Cuba had a total fertiliser production of 750,000 tons, which with fertiliser imports led to a level of application which had effectively trebled that attained in the sixties and is in the middle range of developed countries per capita production of plant nutrients.

Apart from the mechanisation and irrigation programmes, other industrial developments have been closely linked to the need to raise agricultural productivity and output. Particularly important has been the construction industry which is involved in building not only dams for water storage and hydro-electric power generation but also roads, bridges, silos and many specialist sheds required by modern dairy and pig farming practice. In 1975 alone as part of the drive to increase milk production, 270 dairy complexes were built with a capacity for 58,700 cows. Over the whole period 1971 to 1975 the annual increase in construction expenditure was 27.0 per cent in agriculture, the leading sector being educational building (72%) followed by industry (25%) and housing (19.5%).[6]

Such a great increase in output requires a parallel growth in the basic industries: those that produce intermediate products and raw materials. Specially important in this context are the cement and steel industries. These two sectors have grown rapidly, as is to be expected in a country undergoing a sound and rapid transformation linked to the development of a modern agricultural sector and the provision of greater welfare through housing, schools and hospitals. Cement production doubled after 1971 to reach 2 million tons by 1975, and the growth of steel was even more spectacular. In particular, over the same period the output of deformed steel bars rose by 150 per cent and that of steel rods by 135 per cent while common steel products registered an increase of 169 per cent. Overall growth in the years from 1971 to 1975 averaged an annual 23.5

per cent. Steel is a basic requirement of not only the construction industry, where its use goes hand in hand with that of cement, but also in mechanical engineering where it is a basic raw material. Indeed steel output has increased tenfold to 305,000 tons since the Revolution and the future of such basic industries as steel and cement is seen as very significant by Cuban economic planners. The five year plan for 1975-80 is based upon further industrialisation, with concommitant improvements for both the standards of living of workers and their working conditions. In order to ensure the sound development of the economy investments are to be made which will set a firm base for future development. A key sector which will have a major impact on future wealth creation will be the iron and steel industry, according to plans whose gestation period extends to 1985. As Fidel Castro outlined this plan he stressed its significance:

'This is the largest investment we have ever undertaken in our history and will mean a decisive boost to the future development of the country's machine industry. In its first stage, which we expect will be completed by 1985, it will be able to produce 1.4 million tons of liquid pig iron which will be made into billet and rolls to cover the needs of Antillana Steelworks: 410,000 tons of hot rolled plates and bars; 200,000 tons of cold rolled plates; 110,000 tons of tinplate, and 50,000 tons of galvanised plates.'[7]

Another development of great importance for Cuban foreign trade and the economy generally is the increased investment in nickel in which the country has a comparatively long run international advantage given the extent of its reserves of nickel-bearing minerals. Under present plans the existing nickel production capacity of around 36,000 tons will almost be doubled by the construction of a new plant, with some technical assistance and financial credit. This increased production will find a ready market in the socialist countries and, albeit still hindered by the American blockade, in developed, industrialised Western Europe. The grade of nickel offered by Cuba is preferred by those who operate electric furnaces for producing stainless steel. Stocks are held in depots in Europe and marketing at good contract prices should bring in much-needed foreign exchange. By strengthening its position as a supplier of nickel, and ultimately stainless steel, to the world's markets Cuba has achieved a signal success and has consolidated on the progress made in the sixties. The U.S. had abandoned the two nickel plants, even going so far as to sabotage one, confident that their operation was beyond the Cubans' technical reach. Indeed in the early years of the Revolution there were only four metallurgists in the whole country. Nevertheless by dint of hard work and judicious application of operating knowledge and experience, not only were the plants brought to their current full operating capacity, doubling their pre-revolutionary output, but also technological improvements were made. It is against this background that further additions to nickel capacity can lead to legitimate expectations of further benefits to be gained from new investment.

All industrialisation processes and increases in the standard of living of broad stratas of population require great amounts of energy. This is the case in Cuba as much as in any developing country. Unfortunately Cuba is also almost wholly dependent on energy imports with which to run her new factories, to light houses and roads, to pump irrigation water, to power motors etc. There is some production of oil in the coastal region around Matanzas, and there are vast peat bogs as yet unexploited as well as hydroelectric power, but around 80 per cent of energy requirements are imported. Since the blockade the major sources of energy, crude oil and coal, are imported from COMECON, the oil coming almost entirely from the Soviet Union. Electricity generation increased by 255 per cent from 1959 to 1975 in which year 6,500 million kilowatt hours were produced. The majority of the generating stations are fed by imported oil refined in Cuba's three refineries and supplied as fuel oil. Equally the needs of other energy-intensive industries are met by imports, particularly coal for the nickel smelters and for the cane-carrying part of the railway system. Some fuel economy is made in sugar mills by burning bagasse but the residual products of the sugar industry, although readily combustible, have other uses as valuable industrial raw materials.

The situation facing Cuba on the energy question is

typical of that facing many Third World countries, particularly the sugar islands of the Caribbean. However, because of the close relationships that exist between members of the Council for Mutual Economic Assistance, COMECON, Cuba has been to some extent insulated from the fivefold increase in oil prices that has occurred since October 1973. The Soviet Union has decided to trade oil eventually at world market prices but to raise its price less dramatically for fear of the disruptive consequences for its economic partners in COMECON, which for the last five years include Cuba. Accordingly one of the major problems affecting the external financial stability of developing countries and its repercussions on their internal growth rate is absent. Hence the positive growth rates recorded in Cuba over a period which has been characterised by recession, crisis and general decline in living standards throughout the capitalist world, with the non-oil producing countries being particularly hard hit. Nevertheless although Cuba has a positive growth rate, shown by the real increases in the production of physical goods and services, the planners have revised their targets downwards, mainly because of the fall in the purchasing power of exports. Lower export revenues can finance fewer imports of spare parts and machinery from the capitalist countries, which have increased threefold on average. Fidel Castro in his 1978 forecasts given in a speech to the National Assembly on December 24th 1977 put the position succinctly:

'In 1976 our growth rate was 3.8 per cent and in 1977 just over 4 per cent not including the trade sector. In 1978 it will be 7.8 per cent in spite of the serious international situation.... Suffice it to say that we are using nearly nine million tons of oil, or rather fuel,...and by 1978 we will consume about 9,500,000 tons of oil. At present world prices the bill for this would come to 800 million or 900 million dollars. By exporting sugar to the capitalist world at present prices, based on a market for Cuba in the capitalist world—of course this market does not and will not exist—at the present prices, five million tons would bring us just over 800 million dollars. It would barely be enough to pay for the oil, let alone all the food, raw materials, equipment and other products the country must import.'[8]

The strategy of industrialisation must continue, however, he stressed. Excess capacity must be diverted to exports, in paper, in textiles, in cement, and all sources of export revenue maximised. The current generation must do the hardest work, to accumulate capital, to consolidate and diversify the structure of the economy. The beneficiaries will be future generations. Rather than fritter away all the efforts of the last twenty years on consumption, the transformation process must continue at even greater sacrifice. This solemn message recalls the early days of the revolution when Cuba faced the grim prospect of being economically strangled or destroyed by direct military intervention. Now times have changed somewhat but the grim realities of trying to get away from underdevelopment and dependency into self-sustained economic growth persist. The fall in receipts from foreign trade has led some projects to be shelved, others to be slowed down; but equally other investments made in the recent past are now coming into full production. It is this situation which is behind the expected rise in growth in 1978, and if only Cuba can remain on course, the plans for increasing trade with the socialist countries should grow into the 1990s. The people, through their institutionalised participation in the political process, must become the arbiters and defenders of this intelligent policy.

Summing up, Cuban economic policy in the seventies is the outcome of lessons well learnt from the attempts to break out of the vicious circle of underdevelopment in the sixties. The revolutionary leadership, the planners and the people themselves have achieved a greater rate of growth and experienced notable increases in social welfare. If a comparison is made with any other Latin American country the obvious conclusion is that the broad masses of the people are immensely better off under the Cuban model of development. Whether such a model could be simultaneously pursued by all such countries begs the question: where would the initial transfers of resources come from? But that is not usually the level at which the debate takes place; rather detractors talk of more abstract, supposedly better, liberal economic virtues which when contrasted against reality are patently not delivering the goods. There is no mass starvation, no unemployment of any significance, no idle land, no major class inequality in Cuba.[9] The seventies have seen the institutionalisation of planning in Cuba, a greater drive for economic rationality and greater productivity of labour fulfilling the expectations of a sympathetic observer who wrote at the beginning of the decade:

'In this regard, the prospects are highly promising but whether that promise would be fully realised is very much a matter for Cuba's economic planners. The economic apprenticeship of Cuba's leaders has been, as was recently noted by Dr. Fidel Castro, both a long and a costly one; and this recognition is of itself a cause for optimism and perhaps a precondition for more productive planning and employment in the future.'[10]

Taking a broader perspective and being a little speculative, Cuba's economic prospects could improve even more if some sort of rapprochement could be reached with the United States. At present such an eventuality would seem unlikely but normalisation of relations could solve some of the more acute problems. Oil, for example, could be obtained from the U.S. refineries, or from those located in neighbouring Aruba and Curacao, in exchange for sugar and nickel. Pragmatically Fidel Castro has recently invited visiting U.S. businessmen to put up suggestions for cooperation, joint investments and even direct investment. Such a policy makes sense for Cuba needs advanced technology and access to large markets with freely convertible currency. It remains to be seen whether the U.S. can bring itself to concede that Cuba has sovereign rights as a nation in an interdependent world and act accordingly. Whatever the outcome, however, Cuba is developing its economy, consolidating the gains made earlier in the Revolution and changing the structure of agriculture and industry the better to pursue its broader societal goals. This is the achievement of the Seventies: one which contrasts markedly with other Third World countries' experience and would seem to bode well for the future.

REFERENCES

1   James O'Connor, *The Origins of Socialism in Cuba*, Cornell University Press, 1970, p. 17. This author points out that over this whole period there were wild sugar-induced fluctuations in real income. As the average size of families declined and income per head remained stagnant the effects of lack of real economic growth were not so noticeable at the aggregate statistical level.
2   Castro, May Day 1971, cited in *Granma*.
3   David Barkin, 'La redistribución del consumo en Cuba', *Cuadernos de la Realidad Nacional*, Universidad Católica de Chile, Santiago. No 13, July 1972, p. 77.
4   Dr. Osvaldo Dorticos, President of the Republic in a speech to the 2nd Congress of the Young Communists Union, 3 April, 1977.
5   *Cuba Ecónimica* summary of Castro's May Day 1971 Speech. *Economía y Desarrollo*, Instituto de Economía, Universidad de La Habana July-Sept. 1971. p.179 et seqq. Later in August 1977 Fidel Castro said at a graduation ceremony: 'Socialism is what really has enabled everybody to study without limits. In order to make studying universal in an underdeveloped country, from an economic point of view, it was necessary to make work universal.'
6.   *Economia y Desarrollo* No. 33, Nov-Dec. 1976. 'Cuba Economica'. p. 211-223 gives a complete 1971-75 survey of levels of output and rates of sectoral growth.
7   Speech by Fidel Castro at inauguration of Holguin cane harvester plant, reported *Granma* English language version, Havana, August 14, 1977. p. 2.
8   Speech reported in *Granma*, 1st January 1978.
9   Some recent visitors to Cuba report that unemployment has arisen for the first time since the Revolution. Estimates given are 50,000 out of work. However, Social Security payments ensure that the individual does not suffer materially as in the rest of Latin America.
10   B.H. Pollitt 'Employment plans, performance and future prospects in Cuba' *Prospects for Employment Opportunities in the Nineteen Seventies*. ed. R. Robinson and P. Johnson. London, HMSO, 1971, p.72.

Extracts from the Main Report to the First Congress

Fidel Castro

There are events in the great political processes that are of truly historic importance. One of these is the 1st Congress of the Party, whose work we are beginning. To us has fallen the privilege of living through a culminating moment in the revolutionary life of our homeland. To reach this point, innumerable sons and daughters of the Cuban nation belonging to various generations have had to sacrifice their lives. Many have given their lives for the noble cause of independence, justice and the dignity and progress of our people. At this moment, our grateful memory goes back primarily to those who suffered, fought, and died in the wars of liberation for independence, in the ignominious conditions of neocolony, in the fight against the last tyranny, and in consolidating and defending the Revolution. This Congress, which is now beginning its work, would never have been possible without their ideas, their efforts and their blood.

From the glorious days of La Demajagua until today, revolutionary banners have been handed down from generation to generation. Today, our Party is the depository of these banners and, with them, of the best revolutionary traditions, the heroic history and the most radiant ideals of our homeland.

It is of singular importance and political interest within the framework of Latin America and that of the world revolutionary movement that this Party, the leader of a socialist revolution in a country on the continent of America, is now holding its first Congress. Proof of the high esteem that the revolutionaries of the whole world have for our people, for the political process in this country and for its vanguard Party comes from the numerous and representative delegations which the brother Communist Parties and other outstanding revolutionary organisations from all the continents have sent to this Congress.

We salute all of them with feelings of fraternal affection. For this honour, which goes beyond the merits of our modest contribution to the world revolutionary movement, we are profoundly grateful. It is a great incentive which will strengthen our revolutionary commitment. Not for a moment do we forget that without international solidarity, without the support given to the resolute struggle of our working people by their class brothers of the whole world, and especially by the great people of the Soviet Union, in the face of a powerful, ruthless and aggressive imperialism, which has been the virtual master of the destinies of the peoples of this hemisphere, it would have been possible for the Cuban revolutionaries to die heroically, like the Communards of Paris, but not to triumph.

In the 1965-70 period, the nation concentrated its main efforts on reaching a 10-million-ton sugarcane harvest by the final phase of that period. This policy was outlined due to an imperative need. Our population was growing and consumption increasing; this, together with the country's economic development, demanded important increases in exports. The effort was exceptional and was justified, both from the moral and practical points of view. It was necessary also, somehow, to compensate for the lack of a trade balance with the Soviet Union, which was a basic duty to the people so generously helping us. This endeavour was one of the most noble and enthusiastic undertaken by our people in this period of the construction of socialism. Nevertheless, it could not be achieved. Industrial investments were not yet yielding fruit. Great imbalances in the rest of the economy were caused by the pressing problem of the labour force required in ever growing quantities for the sugarcane harvests, in circumstances in which the mechanisation of the harvest was being delayed for technical reasons. There were also shortcomings in organisation, and inadequate direction and economic management methods. Reality proved to be more powerful than our intentions. It was necessary to rectify this situation and give up the achievement of this objective for some years. This, however, could not have been possible without the understanding of the Soviet people, who accepted reduced quantities of sugar during 1972-74; who did not diminish the growing deliveries of raw materials, food, fuel and equipment to Cuba; and who also raised the prices of our exports, thereby improving the terms of trade.

It is necessary to point out that, in the first ten years, attention was not centred on economic work. In this first period of the Revolution survival in the face of imperialist subversion, military aggressions and the ruthless economic blockade commanded the nation's main efforts. For years we had to keep over 300,000 men under arms to defend the country. To this was added the need of cutting sugarcane by hand, when the army of unemployed, which under capitalism had helped to take in the harvests, had disappeared due to the new opportunities for employment opened up by the Revolution.

Even though the blockade subsisted and still subsists, over the past few years the nation has been able to concentrate on economic development problems in a climate of relative peace. At the same time, there was a reduction of more than 150,000 men in the country's defence and growing mechanisation and productivity in sugarcane harvests which helped to reduce the number of canecutters. With this force freed for construction, agriculture and industry and adequate political and economic measures taken in time, our homeland has made progress at a remarkable rate in the past few years. These results would have been unquestionably better if we had shown greater ability, if our methods of managing and directing the economy had been more efficient.

During the revolutionary period the country has made notable advances in many fields. The merit of this progress lies in the fact, that while the United States, a powerful country with vast military, economic and political resources, has done everything possible to strangle the Revolution and to reestablish its corrupt, exploitative and opprobrious system, our people have not only resisted and emerged victorious, but have accomplished, in these difficult conditions, magnificent deeds.

CONSIDERATIONS ON THE ECONOMY

When we started our revolutionary activity and the concrete problems were confined to overthrowing the tyranny, taking over power and eradicating the country's unjust social system, the tasks ahead in the economic field seemed to be much simpler. In fact, we were highly ignorant in this field. The problems that the country was to face, starting with a high degree of underdevelopment of the productive forces, scarcity of natural resources, dependence on agriculture and foreign trade, lack of technical and administrative cadres, social upheavals and innumerable social needs in sight, to all of which would be added a ferocious imperialist blockade, were far more difficult than we could have imagined.

Furthermore, we live in a world where a large part of the trade of the underdeveloped countries is carried out with western capitalist countries. These are the traditional buyers of our raw materials and products, who dictate the conditions of brutally unfair terms of exchange. Exporters of coffee, sugar, cocoa, tea, solid ores and other products have to sell their goods at ever lower prices and buy machinery, materials and equipment from the developed capitalist world at ever higher prices.

The increasingly acute crisis of this sector of the world economy also adversely affects the economies of other nonindustrialised countries to a great extent. The problems of oil and energy, with their present exorbitant prices, make the situation much more complicated. The socialist camp does not yet have the productive and trade capacity to compensate for the destructive effects of this situation on the economies of the underdeveloped countries.

In short, our economic programme for the coming five years is being worked out in the midst of an acute economic crisis that adversely affects a large part of the world. Our sugar production, which has secured satisfactory and profitable prices in the Soviet Union — a country to which we export a sizable part of our sugar output — does not enjoy the same situation with regard to a similarly large share that we have to necessarily sell to the capitalist area. Prices which a year ago were as high as 60 cents a pound are now below 14 cents a pound — that is, less than 25 percent of the earlier price. It is impossible to make exact forecasts concerning the possible evolution of prices during the next five years. Apart from nickel, tobacco and fish — which make up a small proportion of our hard currency earnings— sugar accounts for most of our hard currency earnings.

After the Congress, our country will have a five-year plan for economic development for the first time. As the basis of this plan, we know exactly how much sugar we will be sending to the USSR in this five-year period, at what prices, and which consumer goods, raw materials and producer goods will be coming in from that country. In more or less similar terms, we also know how much sugar will be exported to other socialist countries, the goods to be received in return and their prices. However, the prices of sugar exports and those of the goods that we must buy in the capitalist countries remain unknown.

At the beginning, we aspired to work on a rather ambitious economic plan for the coming five years, because we were aware of the many needs we had and of the marvellous things we could do if it depended only on our will, our energy and our creative effort. We ardently want many more houses for our people than those we have built at present, more schools, hospitals, day-care centres, means of transportation, cultural and recreational centres, consumer durables, garments, food, etc. Of course, we want many more industries and productive facilities in the cities and in the countryside, because they constitute the material basis for the people's living standard. The stability and the development of our economy, for that reason, also allow us to make a greater contribution to international solidarity and to the world revolutionary movement. We wish at the same time the total and most rapid triumph of the construction of socialism in our country.

But no country can advance beyond the limits set by the objective factors. Something else can be added: not only our country, but the world as a whole is beginning to face formidable obstacles in the limitations of traditional energy resources; the gradual depletion of mineral reserves; environmental pollution; the remarkable population growth; and the shortage of food. Naturally, these problems are aggravated by the uneven development of the nations, the fabulous squandering and waste of natural resources by capitalist consumer societies. They have instilled into the minds of large human communities material life patterns, habits and customs inherent in the social system they represent—where the superfluous rules over the essential, the mercantile and exploiting spirit rules everything and man is brutally alienated and morally ruined—all of which are incompatible with the rational and adequate solution of the material and spiritual problems of the human being. Such habits also clash with the relatively limited resources that nature and its environment provide man with, above all when one thinks in terms of a just and equitable distribution of the benefits of civilisation and progress of all mankind.

Thousands of millions of human beings still live in the greatest poverty without electricity, running water, medical care, clothes, shoes, food, adequate housing and education, while a handful of developed capitalist countries squander more than 50 percent of the world's resources. That is why capitalist societies can never provide the material life pattern for an advanced social community. Neither will there be any solution to these pressing human problems except on the basis of socialism on a world scale.

If the doctrines of Marx, Engels and Lenin had not truly proved that the capitalist social system was historically bound to disappear as a result of the laws that rule the evolution of human society, one would come to the same conclusion by a simple arithmetical and logical analysis of the world's limited natural resources, population growth, the squandering and disorder inherent in capitalist society, the inescapable consequences of all this and the need to find rational solutions for mankind's pressing problems.

We would be deceiving our country if we got our people to believe that, as the masters of our own destiny in the economic and social spheres, free from imperialist tutelage, we would have boundless access to wealth and abundance of our society.

The first limitation is the natural resources of the physical environment themselves where our people live, to which is added the agricultural basis from which we start, the cultural and technological development achieved and the objective and subjective difficulties of the world in which we live.

But there is also a limitation of a moral nature: even if that were possible, a people cannot afford to think only about its own material well-being, disregarding the problems and difficulties of other countries of the world.

In the shaping of our communist consciousness, the raising of the material standard of living is, and should be, a fair and noble goal of our people, to be attained through dedicated work, in the natural environment in which we live. But at the same time we should be aware that this environment is limited; that each gram of wealth has to be wrested from nature by effort;that material goods are created to satisfy the real and reasonable needs of the human being; that superfluous things should be discarded; and that our society cannot guide itself by the absurd concepts, habits and deviations with which the capitalist production system has infected the world.

This becomes even more reasonable, considering that our country started off from great poverty, the masses lacking the most vital essentials. That is why we should never give way to excessive ambitions, out of line with our Revolution's real possibilities and moral principles.

Socialism means not only material enrichment but also the opportunity to create a great amount of cultural and spiritual wealth for the people, to form a man with deep feelings of human solidarity, free from the selfishness and meanness that vilify and oppress the individual under capitalism.

We should never encourage a squandering spirit, the egotism of wanting what we do not rationally need or the vanity of luxury and unwholesome cravings. We should never fall into the vulgar mentality and stupid vanities of the capitalist consumer societies that are ruining the world. Our duty is to concentrate all our energies and means—which are limited—on the creation, with due priorities, of the wealth and the services that will ensure a gradual improvement of the material and cultural base of our people and at the same time, allow us to think, act and fulfil our obligations as citizens of a new world.

ECONOMIC DEVELOPMENT IN THE COMING FIVE-YEAR PERIOD

By analysing our possibilities realistically, it is proposed to the Congress that our economic development should proceed at an annual average rate of about 6 percent over the next five years. This is not an exaggerated figure; it is even below the rates of the 1971-75 period. But our base is already higher. Six percent of 100 is not the same as six percent of 160. This means that in 1980 we will have a gross social product 34 percent higher than in 1975. In only eleven years, the country's economy will have doubled.

It also should be taken into account that, according to socialist methodology, only material production is considered in the growth percentages. Services, such as education and public health, are not included in the gross social product, as they are in the capitalist countries. Otherwise, our growth estimates up to now and in the coming five-year period would show much higher figures, for the abundant resources and the material and human investments that the Revolution has dedicated to these activities are well known.

The possibility of achieving such growth in the next five-year period within a world situation in which many countries—excluding the socialist countries—are undergoing stagnation or are declining in their economic production, is highly satisfactory for our Revolution.

The bases upon which the five-year plan period will be formulated are laid down in the guidelines for economic development in the five years from 1976 to 1980, which will be submitted to the Congress. We may add that they have been made according to a conservative criterion and that they are based on realistic possibilities.

The Preparatory Commission of the Congress has been very careful in seeing that all the commitments endorsed by the Party are fulfilled. In any case, an effort will be made to have the objectives overfulfilled rather than taking the risk of having any decisions adopted by the Congress later unfulfilled. The Party's word should be sacred, and we all have the duty of seeing that it is so.

The industrialisation process in the country will be significantly accelerated in the coming five-year period. During the first years of the Revolution, there was no alternative but to concentrate on agricultural production. At this stage, the closest attention will be given to agriculture, but the main emphasis will be on industrialisation.

Contracts have already been signed for most of the factories to be set up in this period, and the rest are being negotiated. This industrialisation programme does not yet solve many of our difficulties, but it will mean an important advance.

Among other objectives, the directives include the raising of sugar production by from 35 to 40 percent, so that by 1980 stable volumes of production of between 8 and 8.7 million tons of sugar should be attained. As will be seen, it is a lower target, but it is much more realistic than the one we set ourselves in the previous decade for 1970. Pertinent investment will be made to restore, consolidate and broaden the installed facilities, including the reconstruction of several sugar mills and the construction of new sugarcane facilities.

Ten plants for the production of proteins from molasses for animal feeds, with an approximate capacity of 10,000 tons each will be completed. The system of mechanical bulk and sack handling of sugar will be completed. The programme for automating the production process will continue, and productivity in this branch will increase by more than 40 percent.

The generation of electric power will go up by over 35 percent. New thermo-electric units with a total capacity of 900,000 kw, at present under construction or under contract, will be put into operation. In only five years, the capacity of new facilities will be equal to almost three times that existing before the Revolution.

The national electric-power grid will be interconnected by means of 220,000-volt lines. The construction of the first 880,000 kw atomic-power station will be undertaken. This has been guaranteed by an agreement with the USSR.

In the chemical industry, oil refining capacities will be enlarged, and the construction of a new refinery will begin.

The production of nitrogen fertilisers will increase considerably, and work on the construction of a new plant will begin.

The production of new glass containers will be expanded, and a new factory with greater capacity will be built.

Paper production will increase, and its quality will be improved. Existing plants will be enlarged, and the construction of a new combine, with a capacity for 60,000 tons of pulp and

80,000 tons of paper, will be undertaken.

Tyre production will be raised, and a new factory of great output capacity will be built.

The two existing nickel plants will be remodelled and their capacity increased, and two new 30,000-ton factories will be built under agreements, one with the USSR and the other with the CMEA (Comecon).

The output of nonferrous metallurgy will be raised by at least 90 percent.

The production of corrugated bars for construction and other purposes will grow by 75 percent, for which the necessary investments are already being made.

Technical and economic studies will be completed, and work will begin on the construction of an integrated iron and steel plant. A 45-percent increase in labour productivity will be achieved in ferrous metallurgy.

A modern plant for the production of agricultural implements will be completed, and a cane-harvester plant will be put into operation, to reach a production capacity of 600 units a year.

During the five-year period 9,000 buses will be produced in the two already constructed plants, and the production of other means of transportation will be increased.

Investments will continue until a production capacity of 100,000 TV sets and 300,000 radios a year is reached.

Two large modern cement factories, which will raise production capacity to over 5 million tons, will be completed and put into operation.

The production of structural materials and prefabricated elements will be doubled.

Three new modern textile plants will be built, two of which are already under contract, and the existing production facilities will be considerably amplified by way of enlargement and modernisation.

The new facilities of the furniture industry will be put into operation.

New pasteurising plants and plants for processing yogurt will be built.

Two new flour mills are to be built and put into operation during the period.

Seven candy factories, already purchased by the country; a glucose factory; and various other factories for producing oatmeal, flour and corn flakes, will soon be started.

By 1980 there will be a fish catch capacity of 350,000 tons, thus doubling the present output.

The fish-processing industry will be mechanised and its production considerably increased by the installation of a newly-constructed plant with a processing capacity of 60,000 tons a year.

Some new wood factories are to be established using bagasse as the main raw material.

Two modern print shops are to be built and put into operation.

This enumeration does not include all the projects in the industrial field, although the most important ones are included, several of them having already been implemented or contracted.

Special attention will be given to agriculture. In the next five years, no less than a million hectares of new land, including grazing areas, will begin to be cultivated. Labour productivity is to increase by 35 percent over that of 1975.

Sugarcane has to be supplied to correspond to the above-specified sugar production. This means that the plantation area has to be increased up to 1,700,000 hectares, or almost 127,000 caballerias.

In 1980, 60 percent of the cutting has to be mechanised. Sugarcane planting for the new mills is to begin.

The citrus programme is to be carried forward.

Rice areas are to be definitively established and developed, special attention being given to technical matters to ensure that the population's consumption is met from national production.

Tobacco production is to be increased, and a programme to better the coffee plantations is to be carried out.

Root and other vegetable production is to reach 1,500,000 tons by 1980—that is, almost 50 percent more than in 1975.

Milk production by that date is to be raised by 80 percent over that of 1975.

Cattle raising is to be developed, improving its structure and the number of productive cows.

Egg production is to reach 2,000 million units a year, and the amount of poultry procurement offered for sale is to go up approximately 85 percent over the present 40,000-ton level.

Pig production is to reach 80,000 tons live weight, almost double the present figure. Much attention will be paid to technical matters: seed quality, veterinary service efficiency, plant protection, soil study and watering systems.

The program of reforestation will continue.

In transportation, one of the tasks will be to standardise cargo throughout. Passenger railroad transportation is to be increased and improved by new equipment. Steps are to be taken to achieve the best possible service by the various transport facilities. The maritime transport and port operation requirements stemming from foreign and sugar trade are to be satisfied by new port facilities and by enlarging and mechanising the country's main ports. Inland freight transport will be extended. Between 900 and 1000 km of the Havana-Santiago de Cuba railway will be rebuilt to meet speed, efficiency and safety requirements. Air freight transportation is to be increased.

Tremendous advances will be made by installing 1800 km of coaxial cable to improve and ensure our internal communications. The telephone network is to be extended and colour television introduced.

In keeping with economic programmes, investment and construction are to increase considerably. The volume of investments is at least to double the figure for the previous five-year period. Approximately three fourths will be assigned to the productive field. Hundreds of industrial projects will be carried out.

Over a thousand agricultural facilities are to be built: dairies, hog-breeding centres, poultry farms, etc. Hydraulic construction will be continued at the fastest possible pace.

For further educational development, during the 1975-80 period no fewer than 800 school facilities will be constructed to accommodate at least 400,000 students at the junior and senior high school level, as well as numerous facilities for higher education, hundreds of elementary and day-care centres and research facilities.

By 1980 the number of houses under construction will be at least double that of 1975. Likewise, during that period over a hundred new hospitals and polyclinics will be built.

Work will be undertaken to develop ports.

The construction of the National Highway and the highway and road network will be continued. Work on the infrastructure and the building of additional railroads for the Central Railroad System will be completed.

The construction of a network of warehouses for the national economy will be started.

The necessary humanitarian facilities, such as homes for the aged and the physically handicapped and special schools for mentally retarded children, will be included in the construction programme.

The construction of hotels—started during the preceding five-year period—and commercial facilities, movies, theatres, libraries, sports centres and other social facilities which the country needs, although not given priority due to our limited resources, will also be envisaged in the construction plan on a modest scale. During this period educational facilities, hospitals, polyclinics and day-care centres will account for much of the bulk of our construction plan for public building projects. We are sure that after 1980 the country will have the means to give an adequate impetus to the aforementioned works.

Construction work will also include aqueduct and sewerage development to improve the present network and to start new ones.

The maintenance of the country's economic and social facilities should receive the utmost attention.

In principle, industrial and, in general, economic works should have top priority in the investment plan.

Industrial development will carry great weight during the five-year period. Just the already decided-upon investments to be made in this field will amount to 3,877.7 million pesos. Of this figure, 2,660.5 million pesos are for external supplies, 60 percent of which have already been contracted. Out of the total investment, 48 percent are channelled into the basic industries sector, totalling 796.2 million pesos; and 14 percent into the construction sector, totalling 547.8 million pesos.

In the development of material production and services the utmost attention should be given to quality.

We have omitted reference to many other activities whose

enumeration would make this report endless. It is gratifying to think that our Revolution has created the conditions for these achievements, that, in spite of the fact that they have been conceived with the necessary prudence, they are nevertheless outstanding and have the necessary backing.

Agriculture and Rural Development

J.R. Morton

Agriculture has always been central to the development of the Cuban revolution. There are many reasons for this, economic, social and political, but the original reason was historical. The Cuban Revolution could not have succeeded without the support of the peasants. The poorest peasants forced into the hills by rapacious latifundists were the people among whom the guerillas had to operate. It was these people's decision to back the nascent revolution against the authorities which was crucial, and the leaders of the Cuban Revolution have never forgotten it.

The first Agrarian Reform Law was the first major act of the new revolutionary government on coming to power. It expropriated the latifunda from the major landowners without compensation, distributed part of them to such peasants as were landless and set an upper limit to the amount of land which could remain in private property.[1] The second Agrarian Reform Law further restricted maximum holdings and guaranteed the security of the peasants landholding in perpetuity.[2] The first Law was the initial cause of the break between Cuba and the USA and led to a split in the government between liberal reformers and revolutionary socialists. This split was resolved, in the summer of 1959, by a march of hundreds of thousands of peasants to the capital to support the Law.

Limited in natural mineral resources, Cuba was dependent on agricultural development for economic progress. But peasant small-holdings (minifundism) are as inefficient a form of agriculture as rich absentee landlords (latifundism). Economic progress of the nation and social·progress of the peasantry was dependent on persuading the latter to revolutionise their ways of farming and of life. After some setbacks in the 1960s, through the 1970s there has and continues to be enormous effort put into the transformation, and it is still far from complete. Much of the 30% of cultivable land still privately owned is split into individual smallholdings.

There could be no question of forced collectivisation on the Stalinist model, either in the intentions of the Cuban Government or in practice. The Cuban Revolution depends on the support of the peasantry and attempts to coerce them would undermine the government rather than increase production. But it is hard to convey the impression gained in visiting Cuba that the rationale for decision-making is not so calculated. From an early stage in the revolutionary war, the leaders emphasised that the violence of the means of revolution could only be justified by the morality of its ends, which must be reflected in the morality of the fighters. In this seemingly old-fashioned morality a pledge given must be honoured. Fidel Castro reiterates in every speech to a mainly peasant audience that 'it is up to the peasants' and that 'their decision will be respected. Only on the basis of persuasion and respect of each peasant's free will can such change be effected' (Speech to Republica de Chile production cooperative, 31 May '77). The physical evidence of the honouring of this pledge is sometimes comical, with the smallholding of the thatched hut, palm trees and goats of the recalcitrant peasant who would not join standing in stark contrast in the middle of a highly organised state collective dairy farm. Sometimes even the access roads bend to get round his property. Where, for example, a peasant must be moved from his land for the construction of a dam, he is offered in exchange an equivalent smallholding of another peasant who has chosen to join the collective.

A major aim of the Cuban revolution is to provide in the countryside the amenities necessary to a full and civilised life for the peasantry. But this requires a voluntary change in their life-style which produces a difficult paradox for the Cuban authorities. The older peasants may have seen their fathers and grandfathers forced off their smallholdings by the latifundists.

Indeed many of them will have suffered this fate themselves and be slow to come round to giving up the one surety that they feel they have against future starvation. Yet the young adapt readily to new ways and are unwilling to give up films, television and sports grounds for the life of their fathers in a thatched hut without electricity, running water or transport. Cuba cannot afford a drift from the land, yet their policy of education will encourage it, unless they can persuade the peasantry to transform rapidly.

In other ways, the voluntary policy has had economic advantages. It has meant that all changes are 'totally dependent on the small farmer's understanding of the advantages of modern methods in agriculture and that modern methods will advance society and hence benefit himself and his family'[1] (*Main report to the 5th Peasant Congress,* 14 May '77). With this approach the imposition of an *overall* bureaucratic plan for collectivisation is impossible. Proposals for collectivisation must be seen by the peasants as means to improve agricultural production. Hence they must differ according to the forms of produce that have been and can be grown in different parts of the country. Nevertheless there are two major forms of collectivisation, peasant cooperatives and state farms, known in Cuba as 'state plans'.

State plans developed first. The latifundists used their lands in two ways, as large sugar plantations worked by migrant seasonal labour and as extensive cattle ranges patrolled by a few paeons. Thus when these lands were expropriated large tracts to which there were no natural claimants fell into the hands of the state.

Sugar was an obvious candidate for state plans. Today only 19% of the sugar delivered to the mills comes from the private peasant sector, and this source has never been the most important. Sugar was an agrobusiness before the revolution. The problem for the revolutionary government was, and to an extent still is, to transform the mode of production. It would obviously be anathema to a socialist government to depend on a pool of unemployed for seasonal labour, and in any case the distribution of land to the peasants has done away with the pool. For a time the harvesting of sugar cane had to depend on brigades of volunteer labour. Though this may have been good for the political consciousness of those involved, gangs of office workers and students were neither efficient, nor even always safe, at wielding sharp machetes. The requirement, which Cuba is rapidly achieving, is to mechanise sugar production, particularly harvesting, to the point that the work force can be reduced to relatively few full-time professionals who are expert not only as cane-cutters, but in all the jobs in the cultivation of cane.

Plantations in hilly land connected to distant mills by an ancient and decrepit rail system have been scrapped and replaced with plantations of new varieties in flat lowland situations close to the mills and suitable for mechanical harvesting. Although some advantage was taken of the Australian experience in the design of harvesting machines, these have mainly been developed *de novo* by collaboration between Cubans with a knowledge of cane and Russian engineers who had never before seen the crop. Monsters with two great augers like the probosci of giant insects from a sci-fi movie, the machines' impact on the total harvest is still small, but they are now being produced in Cuba at a considerable rate. Meanwhile the improvement in the productivity of cane-cutters supplied to ANAP (the small farmers organisation) from about 1700 to 2700 kilos per man has enabled the work force to be cut from over 40,000 to under 30,000 in the five years up to 1977.

The removal of the sugar-cane to the plains freed upland areas for other uses, allowing the move away from sugar monoculture with its economic and possible epidemic disease disadvantages. The ranch lands were still available. And a considerable area of previously uncultivated land was cleared, to the extent that despite all the various building projects undertaken by the revolution, the total agricultural land has remained so far constant at about 6,600,000 hectares. (1 hectare = 10,000 square metres = 2.47 acres).

The other major area for the use of some of this land in state farms was in milk production. Prior to the revolution Cuba was a net importer of foodstuffs. The dairy cows of the peasantry might produce two litres per day if they were Brahman (a Zebu cow) and much less if Criollo (a degenerate beast of Spanish origin), barely enough for the peasant's own family. The problem was aggravated in the 1960s by the success of the revolutionary government in reducing infant mortality. A modern dairy industry was desperately needed, involving the construction of plants for cooling and pasteurising milk and for cheese, yoghurt and butter production, and a service to control disease in the herds as well as the milk itself. Only a state farm system could produce the transformation fast enough.

There are other problems to the creation of a dairy industry than the production of better cattle and the means of processing the milk. In Cuba the most important is the dry season. Because of the massive deforestation of Cuba, and other Caribbean islands, for timber since the 19th century, the boundary between the continuous rainfall tropical climate and the seasonal sub-tropical has moved from the middle of Florida to south of Jamaica. Cuba now has a winter dry season which may last from November to April, and the natural grasses which have evolved are more noted for their ability to survive this drought than for their nutritional value. The land of the dairy plan is therefore being transformed through irrigation and the sowing of new varieties of grasses. Two of these have so far been introduced, Star grass and a Coastal Bermudan cross. The irrigation is mostly small scale. The geography of Cuba leads to short runs of rivers to the North or South so that provision of water for large areas from a single major dam is seldom possible. In any case the construction of such projects consumes time and scarce engineering skills. Instead quite small mountain streams are impounded by minidams using mostly local materials and producing reservoirs often no larger than a few hectares in extent.

The change in scenery as a result of these developments is striking. The contrast between the open ranch or sugar plantation and the individual peasant plots dotted along the stream valley is gone. Instead, below the minidam, are fenced fields of green sward of almost 'home counties' neatness interspersed with whitewashed dairies and, perhaps, a cheese factory. Above everything, in place of the thatched huts of the peasants, is the new hilltop village. It is positioned so as not to waste valuable agricultural land and consists of a water tower, perhaps a dozen four storey blocks each of about 20 flats equipped with refrigerator, washing machine and so forth, and a village centre with a few shops, a polyclinic (health centre), usually a bar selling beer, soft drinks, coffee and ice cream, often a small cinema and, most importantly, an elementary (primary) school. These villages provide the basic level of new social organisation in the countryside. Far from collectivisation by trinket bribery, the ethos behind this transformation is to combine the agricultural workers into a unit of a size where the drudgery of peasant life can be removed by the economic provision of electricity, water, transport, education, health welfare and the means to live a community life. On the slopes below the village are the communal vegetable fields, largely cultivated by the children and old people, providing for the needs of the villagers and usually for some surplus for sale in a manner analogous to the peasant cooperatives.

Similar primary units of social organisation associated with a particular form of agricultural production are being evolved for other rural industries, whether state or cooperatively owned. Such speed of social transformation by education and persuasion, but not compulsion, is without parallel. The secondary level of rural organisation is equally functional, composed of the secondary school, usually a high school in the countryside, the local hospital, and in the case of a dairy plan the veterinary centre, the artificial insemination laboratory and so on. In reviewing the way in which the animals are supplied to the dairy farms, a similar *functional* hierarchy rather than a chain of command will become evident. Thus the advent of People's Power which appears as a sudden change in political organisation to the outsider was already inbuilt in the structural changes that have been developing in rural Cuba.

Although most of the early development of facilities for testing farm animals had been achieved with help from Eastern Europe and particularly the U.S.S.R., the best dairy breeds are largely confined to N.W. Europe and N. America. The first cross (F_1) of Canadian Holstein on Brahman proved extremely successful in Cuba, having a fair heat tolerance and a production of around 10 litres per day rising to 20 or more in some individuals. The first importation of 25-30 Canadian Holstein bulls was used mainly for the production of these F_1s, so that milk and dairy products are now fairly freely available in Cuba, and, for example, 13,128 mainly F_1 cattle provide for the 500,000 people of Matanzas old province (*cf.* 2,700,000 dairy cows for the 49,200,000 people of England and Wales— *MMB Breeding and Production report 1976-77*). A single national elite herd of pure Holstein cows is served by frozen semen of tested bulls from Canada to provide bulls for progeny test in Cuba. This test was originally based on a parameter system whereby the lactation yields of daughters of the bull were compared to target figures. With the development of improved populations of cattle this has been changed to the system of comparing heifer daughter yields with those of their contemporaries in the same herd, as used in Canada and, with modifications, in Britain. These contemporary comparisons from pure and crossbred herds are combined, and recently the first proven Cuban-born bulls went into commercial service.

The hope of producing a heat-resistant Holstein similar to the Cuban Charolais (a beef and traction breed derived from the French Charolais early this century) has proved unattainable. Even first backcross 3/4 Holstein suffer from heat exhaustion and commonly have to be herded back into the shade by 10a.m. Further, because of this lack of heat tolerance their milk yields are by no means uniformly superior to the F_1s. Instead a synthetic Holstein-Brahman breed will be formed, to be called the Siboney, after the original Amerindian inhabitants of Cuba. The precise constitution of the synthetic is as yet uncertain but seems likely to be 5/8 Holstein 3/8 Brahman.

The whole dairy herd is bred by artificial insemination (AI) with pelleted frozen semen. It can thus be centrally controlled by the National Directorate of AI, which although responsible for all AI work, has concentrated to date on dairy cattle. The bulls are held in centres in each old province; that in Havana contains 143 bulls in varying stages of rearing, testing or on stud, of which 104 are Holstein. According to their test performance and history of use, the National Directorate designates the semen of each bull for use in an elite herd or in one of the 'plans', in this case administrative collections of a score or so of dairy units. The provincial centre which holds the semen checks for inbreeding dangers and delivers the semen. The plan administrators oversee the reproductive life of their cows and investigate any problems. And each dairy unit, which is larger than most English dairy farms, with between

100 and 300 cattle, carries its own inseminator. There thus exists the overall control of breeding policy which has many times been shown to be essential for a successful animal breeding programme.

There are problems with the use of complete package deals, such as the Canadian dairy herd evaluation system. This gives as much emphasis to the conformation as to the production of the daughters of bulls on test, which the Cubans rightly consider a mistake. Yet they do not want to drop all selection on conformation for fear of allowing degeneration of such genuine features as sound jaw structure, legs and udder. There is continuing debate about the extent to which one should tampér with such package deals which are known to be functional in their entirety.

But another aspect of the Cuban animal breeding system which worries some Europeans is probably not a problem at all. This is the fear that the centralisation that the Cubans have applied to cattle breeding and wish to extend to the other farm species, may lead to bureaucracy and inflexibility. The counter-balance to such tendencies lies in a willingness to throw responsibility back on the people, as much in the small scale of dairy farms as in the large scale of People's Power. In Matanzas old province the policy of collecting the best cattle into elite herds was modified to leave one or two outstanding cows and their daughters on the dairy units in which they were detected, to encourage the farm workers' pride in their stock and to train them in the management of high yielders.

The ideology behind this decision was that the revolution in Cuban agriculture must be as beneficial to the life of the ex-peasant as it is to the nourishment of the general population. But the practical result will be that when the dairy farms of Cuba are populated by improved stock they will be run by workers of high motivation and skill. If the experience of British dairy farms is relevant, this will be vastly more important than the maximisation of genetic progress.

For reasons similar to those put forward for dairy cattle, there is a need to develop alternative modes of production to the peasant smallholding or even the agricultural cooperative for all animals. Although the peasants, collectivised or not, continue and are encouraged to keep backyard hens and pigs, and even in drier areas goats, for their own needs, these provide no surplus for the rest of the community. The pre-revolutionary practice of keeping pigs in the backyards of city tenements is now forbidden; understandably so in a tropical country. The contribution of excess production and retirement from the peasants' herds of milch cows and yoke oxen is still important in trying to satisfy the Cubans' voracious appetite for meat, but is clearly insufficient in quality and quantity. Advances in the catch of fish and the farming of shellfish have not yet been matched by a willingness on the part of the Cuban people to change their meat-oriented diet. So state enterprises exist for the improvement of production in all meat animals with the possible exception of goats, although for reasons of priority these are far behind the dairy plans.

Modern methods of poultry production, whether for eggs or meat, require the production of 'hybrids' between special strains whose performance is relatively invariable and on average better economically than that which can be achieved by normal backyard chickens. These special strains have been developed almost exclusively in the United States. Fortunately, it appears that the U.S. political embargo on exports to Cuba was no more successful than the British, supposedly veterinary but actually protectionist, embargo on imports from the U.S. Trials of the various crosses amongst the imported strains have now been completed at the vast poultry centre at Cacahual on the outskirts of Havana city, and the centre has been split into research and production divisions to facilitate the routine production of improved 'hybrids' for the various state chicken enterprises.

To date there has been maximal expansion of the dairy herd in Cuba, so that its contribution to beef supplies has been limited to unwanted males. Most of the remaining beef has been supplied by pure-bred Cuban Charolais, which have been selected since 1968-69 for daily gain, efficiency of food conversion and weight for age by performance test from 90 days to 400kg, which the Cubans now feel may be too low relative to the optimum slaughter weight.

As dairy cow numbers become sufficient, their excess reproductive capacity must be used for beef production. This can be done using dual purpose breeds: indeed some British scientists claim that with its rapid growth rate the Friesian/ Holstein is a dual purpose breed, but there are doubts about its efficiency as a converter of food to beef. The Cubans have done some work on the more genuinely dual purpose Brown Swiss, which they have selected on a combination of the criteria used in Holstein and Charolais. But a number of econometric studies, particularly from Edinburgh, have shown that selection for beef characteristics in the dairy, or dual purpose, herd is inefficient unless the price of a kilogram of beef increases from about 8 to about 12 times the price of a litre of milk. In Cuba there is great priority placed on every form of provision for children. The value of milk relative to beef will therefore be greater in Cuba than Western Europe and the argument for the alternative strategy of selecting a beef breed for crossing onto the surplus dairy herd even stronger. With this in mind the Cubans have started trials crossing Charolais, Hereford, Zebu and Holstein x Zebu F_1 bulls onto their dairy cows. The Zebu and particularly Holstein x Zebu bulls are unlikely to be the answer, since there will be little or no boost in performance from cross breeding. The Hereford crosses have proved particularly heat-sensitive, which might have been foreseen from Canadian results suggesting that their success in that country may be due to efficient winter heat retention. The Cubans report less trouble in calving the offspring of Charolais inseminations than has been the experience in Britain with French Charolais, so that there may be no need in Cuba for a small efficient beef producer such as the Hereford. But the evidence favouring three breed crosses for the production of a large calf crop suggests that the Cubans will have to try some other imported breed.

The developments described in the model dairy plans are costly in time, labour and materials. The area of ranch land taken over from the latifundists or produced by clearance of upland sugar plantation or simply of previously uncultivated land is far too great to permit similar developments throughout. The beef herd then has to be reared largely extensively on unimproved ranch land. The winter gap in grass production can be mainly filled by the use of sugar byproducts such as molasses, bagasse and ensilaged sugar cane tops with the addition of new strains of Torula yeast as a protein supplement, sometimes grown in the molasses which are to be fed to the beasts. But the limits to the development of such things as farm roads has produced a demand for more and better horses for riding the range. Partly because he was never as under-privileged as the subsistence peasant and partly because his job has remained unchanged, the paeon seems less affected by the revolution. Such traditional scenes abound as the old hand instructing the young in the niceties of throwing a lariat. But efforts are being made to improve the ranch-hand's principle 'tool, his horse. This has consisted largely in upgrading the local Criollo breed, which the Cubans describe as small, lazy, slow and lacking in stamina, by crossing with English thoroughbred. While this has improved these characters, there is no genetic selection for them. Instead there has been selection for repro-ductive normality in the Criollo mares, and when this was relaxed, a severe drop in conceptions by AI resulted. The lack of direct selection for the desired characteristics stems from the difficulty in measuring them. If the need for working horses is not transitory, Cuba might become the one remaining country where racing could fulfil its original function, the performance testing of potential breeders of future work horses. A nice sideline of the horse-breeding industry has been the production of ponies from Welsh and Shetlands imported from Canada. This started from a suggestion from Fidel Castro that the horse breeding industry should produce riding ponies for Cuban children, but has developed with the idea of providing an alternative tourist attraction to Cuba's endless miles of perfect beaches.

Lack of properly defined objectives hampered also the development of pig breeding in Cuba in the 1960s. This came from the loan of a team of East European experts who defined their objectives in strictly European terms. From 1970, the simple aim was laid down of increased pig meat without excess fat. The Cubans would have liked to couple this change with a centralised organisation similar to that in dairy cattle. But the reduction in conception rates and litter size through the use of frozen boar semen makes this impossible. The pigs are there-fore bred in thirteen regional centres in each but one of the new administrative provinces, as a result of pure-bred performance tests in paddocks for growth rate and backfat thickness. At any one time two breeds from two centres are compared at the national progeny testing centre, in 3 litter groups of 2 males, 1 castrate and 1 female per sire, individually fed on a semi-restricted diet, and tested for growth rate and backfat thickness and % prime cuts in the castrates and females. The absence of efficiency of feed conversion (e.f.c.) as a criterion of selection is glaring, and this is being rectified for the boars at the national station, but its introduction to the 13 genetic centres is having to await planned new testing accommodation. Until this is available and a form of index devised to take account of the e.f.c. of the castrate and female at the national station, it might be preferable to use the latter entirely for testing boars for this criterion.

The Cubans use a 3-breed cross for their production pigs, with Yorkshire as the maternal grandam, Landrace as the maternal grandsire, and for the final sire the Duroc, which is used for this purpose throughout the Southern U.S. and is known for its heat resistance. The use of Yorkshires as maternal grandams is surprising to a European. The reason for it is partly simple availability and partly high prolificacy under Cuban conditions; but the Cubans have not yet considered piglet output per sow food input, the acid test in which the breed might be expected to rate less well. The Scandinavian Landrace initially suffered from the heat, as might have been foreseen, since they are the purest domestication of European wild pig, and one reason for the import of Asian pigs into Europe in the 18th century was to cope with the heat of deforested Mediterranean countries. Improved management techniques have now overcome this problem, but, automatically raise another. Cuba rightly sees the pig as a coverter of humanly inedible by-products, such as citrus pulp from the juice factories and swill from the tourist centres, into food. So that when the Cuban pig population finally recovers from its infection with a virulent virus introduced by the C.I.A. in 1971, one would expect the pig farms to be scattered through the country in relation to the availability of those by-products. Will it then be possible to maintain the high standards of management necessary for the Landrace breed?

This difficulty is part of a more general doubt which stems from the influence on Cuban animal improvement programmes of the English geneticists Preston and Willis. They encouraged the testing of animals under excellent conditions including high energy, high protein concentrate diets, even if their offspring use, as in Cuba, largely forage and by-product foods and simple accommodation. It is supposed that any loss of progress through specific adaptation of the selected strains to the good conditions will be more than offset by the rapid generation turnover possible with the high quality foods. Although there are theoretical objections to this approach, it must be admitted that few practical problems have arisen from it in Cuba.

In contrast to the organisation of the sugar and animal industries into state farms for reasons of economics and logistics, many other crops are for equivalent reasons best left in the direct control of the peasants, although all surplus produce is sold to the state. We have seen that while owning 30% of agricultural land the peasants only contribute 18% of the sugar cane crop while owning more than a quarter of the livestock in Cuba the consumption of animal products by the general population depends but little on these herds. On the other hand the peasants produce more than half of the fruit and vegetables and practically all the tobacco and coffee. These are crops where traditional knowledge and care are worth more than any amount of state organisation. The coordination of production and the interchange of information with state agencies is carried out by ANAP, the small farmers' organisation.

Tobacco for the manufacture of Cuban cigars must be picked, handled, selected and cured with particular care. Although the export market in Cuban cigars is small in relation to that in sugar, given the present depressed market in sugar, the cigars provide valuable foreign exchange. Tobacco cultivation is so labour-intensive that even in a well organised cooperative only about 1-1/2 hectares of tobacco per peasant couple can be grown. (The tradition dies hard that the men are responsible for the tobacco crop and the women for the vegetables except when tobacco needs extra labour). The state's contribution to tobacco farming has been limited to the provision of some improved varieties which have helped with the modest increase in yield of a little over 1% p.a., and the replacement of thatched curing sheds with ones roofed with corrugated iron; the main purpose of this is to cut down the population of scorpions.

Coffee is a problem crop. It is exceedingly tedious to harvest. It cannot strictly be considered a vital necessity requiring the injection of scarce state funds to increase yields. Yet there is probably no limit to the number of small cups of strong sweet coffee that a Cuban will consume given the chance. During the recent world coffee shortage, Fidel Castro refused the offer of a free consignment of coffee from Angola so that no-one should misconstrue the motive for Cuba's military help to that country. The Cuban people must have been proud but at the same time a bit sad. Coffee will grow in poor hilly conditions where little else is favoured — much of Cuba's being now grown on the heights of the Sierra Maestra. So the policy has been to encourage anyone who has a small piece of otherwise unpromising land to put it to coffee. Even the main AI Station near Havana grows a crop for its own use between the offices and the bull pens.

Vegetables, such as potatoes, cocoyams, beans and including maize or rice for human consumption, and fruit such as bananas, mangoes and oranges, have long been staple crops of the Cuban peasant for his own consumption with some surplus for cash sales. In Cuba, as elsewhere, vegetable and fruit production is often as efficient on relatively small as on large land holdings, although the very small fenced fields of the uncollectivised peasant obviously obstruct efficient cultivation. Once one advances beyond the level of one man and a spade, some form of combination of labour, whether exploitative or cooperative, becomes essential.

It is in these areas that the movement for the formation of peasant cooperatives, also known as agricultural societies, is being encouraged. An attempt at such a movement was made directly after the revolution before the state plans got properly under way, but it was abandoned when it was realised that the political consciousness of the peasantry needed to be raised before the system could be made to work. Some of these early cooperatives were so only in name, the reality being the employment of landless by landed peasantry, and the bedrock of Cuban socialism has been from the start the outlawing of private employment. Even in some model cooperatives there remain problems for which various experimental solutions are being tried; in how, for example, the tractor driver is to be genuinely integrated into the cooperative. The general principle of operation is that while ownership of the cooperative is divided by shares among those who contributed materially to its creation by the pooling of land, livestock, implements or whatever, distribution of its proceeds are equally to all who have contributed a full year's work.

In mid-1977 the first of the new agricultural societies, the 'Nueva Cuba' of 270 ha. worked by 30 families celebrated its 10th anniversary by paying the final instalment on a 50,000 peso loan secured from the state in 1970. (1 Cuban peso = 1 U.S. $) At the same time the 43rd cooperative, the 'Republica de Chile' of 580 ha. worked by 135 families was inaugurated. It can be seen that development of peasant cooperatives has been cautious after the early failures. But it is now felt that the time has come to push forward and it is planned to increase them to about 3,000 over the next few years. Since in rural Cuba a family of five is the norm, simple calculation shows that if this plan is achieved it will comprise roughly 20% each of the population and the cultivable land in the country. It is then easy to see why the cooperatives are urged to become firstly self-sufficient, apart from some interchange of products where certain lands favour certain crops, and secondly to produce some surplus for the general population. A major topic of discussion among the peasant representatives has been the way in which the peasant society will contribute to 'social expenditure'. It is indicative of the Cuban approach to socialisation that, far from imposing levies or tolls on the peasants, they are themselves presented with the ethical problem of how to pay for the education, health care and so on that they receive.

State encouragement to the formation of cooperatives comes in the form of direct investment and credit to the societies, and it has been made clear that the degree of state aid will be determined by the needs of the people not the potential return on investment. Direct aid mainly takes the form of provision of the infrastructure, roads, electricity and water, including dam construction. Loans are made for the cooperatives to acquire machinery, piping and so forth for irrigation, new seeds and fertilisers and the materials for the construction of new housing, although in this last case state construction workers will help with the project until such time as the peasants have trained themselves to take it over. Because of this scheme for housing construction and because the peasants themselves recognise the value of building on non-productive land, some of the new cooperative villages are coming to be very similar to the hilltop villages of the dairy plans, while others have combined modern and traditional skills to produce, for example, an elementary school constructed of concrete and glass but thatched with palm leaves.

State aid to the peasantry is concentrated on the new cooperatives rather than on the still uncollectivised section. In part this is to encourage collectivisation, although a more potent encouragement seems to come from the community development officers, usually women, whose job it is to explain the plan to the peasants. But the practicability of aid to the collectives is more important. It is no good providing minidams if individual small farmers are going to argue over the costs of the main irrigation conduits. Little is achieved by state construction workers demonstrating new building techniques if there is no peasant organisation to continue the work.

Principles of self-help, self-sufficiency and voluntary labour spread agricultural production much wider than the classes traditionally associated with it, and are indeed some of the tools used to weld Cuba into a unitary society undivided even into the classes of peasant, worker and intellectual. Two cases may exemplify this.

The surplus fruit and vegetables from the peasant community do not supply all the needs of the towns. These are filled from state market gardens on the outskirts of the major conurbations. On many occasions, but particularly during official holidays such as the celebration of the anniversary of the victory of the Bay of Pigs, office workers flock to these fields to harvest the produce. When there is no holiday but labour is needed in the fields, in theory the few colleagues remaining in town cover for the volunteers. In fact it is unwise to attempt to find any government official in his office at such times. It is perhaps hard to appreciate that voluntary work in the fields could indeed constitute a celebration in a true sense. But with the help of guitars, drums, the odd bottle of beer or rum, and the infectious enthusiasm of the Cubans it seems easy.

The second example concerns the agricultural work of the high schools in the countryside. These provide many of their own food requirements from smallholdings attached to them and worked by the students, but they contribute importantly to national production of fruits. Citrus fruits in the form of juices in particular provide a means of selling sugar at a reasonable price, and can be used for this in much greater quantity than is provided from the surplus of peasant production. The fruit yield from secondary schools is thus a real contribution to Cuban exports, and incidentally the original source of the citrus pulp which is used to fatten pigs. A project that the Cubans hope to develop is to use the ground below the citrus groves for rearing sheep. Perhaps shearing will be the next item to add to the school curriculum.

Throughout agricultural development and the social transformation of rural Cuba runs a skein of sheer practicality, which could hardly be in greater contrast with the pragmatism of Western social democracy. The difference would seem to lie between the affirmation and the denial of idealism, and the greatest difficulty in this description of developments in Cuba has been to pass on this sense of idealism and the moral commitment to social progress.

REFERENCES
1. The first Agrarain Reform Law of May 1959 had been drafted by the guerilla army in the Sierra Maestra in October 1958. It limited land holdings to 30 *caballerós* (= 402 hectares = 993 acres) and up to three times this area for holdings of high yield and efficiency.
2. The second Agrarian Reform Law of October 1963 expropriated all forms larger than 5 *caballerós* (= 67 hectares = 165 acres) and gave a staunch guarantee that any further changes in the agricultural ownership system would be *strictly voluntary.*

Computers

Chris Lazou

Before describing computer developments in Cuba it is necessary to examine briefly some of the strategic implications of computers in modern society. What sets computers apart from many other technological inventions is the fact that, like the human brain their function is to control the many interlinked components of a system. Computers have an input facility, the ability to do calculations, a storage, and an output facility. The system which a computer can control could be a simple washing machine, an information retrieval system for car licences, a payroll system, an automated factory control system, a space exploration programme, a model for the evaluation of energy resources, or a model for assisting in the economic planning of a company or a country. The thousands of applications to which computers can be put, makes them unique and opens a whole vista of possibilities; their fast calculation capacity of up to 50 million additions per second makes it possible to solve in a few minutes problems which would have taken scientists several thousand years to compute manually.

The impact of computers is perhaps greatest in the field of storing and retrieving information. Information is the prerequisitive to knowledge and access to this information provides the potential to make informed decisions for control, be it in the field of economics, transportation, or society as a whole. Governments, and technocrats controlling these accumulated data banks, can abuse them for their sectional interests as is being discovered in Western developed countries. But computers can just as easily be put in the service of the people.

In a society like Cuba whose objectives are the planning of the nation's material and human resources for the improvement of the people's lot, computer data banks provide central planners with immeasurable opportunities. Fast access to real data from the field allows them to respond promptly to problems arising and to apply tuning decisions on the economic model they are working with. Performance analysis of previous plans and current performance can be used to make projections which are in turn used to develop new economic models. The importance of computers to society can be assessed by the annual national expenditure in this field. For example, Britain currently spends over a billion pounds annually on computer systems.[1]

It is the awareness of this strategic element which has influenced the Cuban leadership, as far back as 1967, to invest in the new technology[2]. In order not to be caught in the vicious circle of dependency, by relying on developed countries for such an invaluable and critical tool in their economic strategy, Cubans have taken the next step. That is to develop and manufacture their own minicomputers. Like many industrial products, computers contain components made by a variety of manufacturers. The dominance of the electronics industry by U.S. interests has meant that practically all computers produced in the West have not been accessible to Cuba. More than that, the U.S. has kept hardware out through its trade blockade. This constraint in access to computer technology, is one factor in Cuba's decision to develop its own machines, but it does not appear to have been the overriding factor, as Cuba had access to Soviet computers, which could have served the purpose It is likely that the Cubans have understood the economic importance of computers and the long term strategic benefits in creating a technological infrastructure to support such an industry. Whatever the short term agonies of diverting scarce resources to new long term ventures, the benefits of this all-embracing technology were clearly manifold.

Cuba is poor in natural resources. It has substantial deposits of nickel, zinc and copper sulphate ores, but it is short of energy fuels. Thus the development of a scientific and technological base, has a bearing on the most important resource Cuba has: manpower[3]. In this respect an analogy can be made with another island, Japan, which also lacks natural resources but has exploited human resources in her phenomenal postwar industrial development. Japan's current utilisation of computers stands third in the World behind the USA and the USSR[4]. Computer applications in Japan encompass every walk of life. Investment in computer technology is high in Japan, and relatively speaking, so is it in Cuba. In 1969, the figure stood at 15 million pesos.

History of data processing in Cuba

Data processing equipment, in the form of keypunchers, verifiers, sorters, collators, reproducers, interpreters and accounting machines, were imported into Cuba by private companies from 1929 onwards. Most of the installations were in the private sector and the market was dominated by IBM. During the first year of the Revolution, 1959, IBM Cuba introduced the first digital computer in the island, an IBM RAMAC 305. This machine was never utilised due to lack of trained personnel. IBM Cuba was then nationalised and all its technical staff left the island.

On taking power, the Cuban leadership was already committed to industrialisation. In addition it decided to diversify its agriculture in an attempt to liberate the Cuban economy from being dependent on sugar. Unfortunately this strategy had to be modified in the early years of the Revolution and the industrialisation programme postponed. This became necessary as national effort was needed to solve the immediate problems of keeping industry going and to counter the dislocation effects of the U.S. trade blockade. For a country whose whole industrial infrastructure was dependent on U.S. manufactured machines, the unavailability of spare parts caused great damage to production capacity.

By 1967 the tide in the battle for survival had turned round sufficiently, and the Cuban leadership started developing new plans for the future. By now the Cuban leadership was convinced of the need to use computers to co-ordinate planning and resolve the organisational problems confronting the Cuban economy. It was apparent that effort by one section of industry was often wasted due to lack of an organisational infrastructure at management level, necessary to integrate advantageously the components in the production process. Alternatively, extra production became a storage headache insteading of bringing expected benefits in development. In short, the problem was identified as underdevelopment in the management field, and steps had to be taken to rectify this deficiency.

In response to this need for scientific management, a number of decisions were made in rapid succession. Firstly the Central Directorate for Electronic Calculators was created under the Central Planning Board (JUCEPLAN); and later renamed as *Plan Calculo Nacional*. At the same time under the auspices of Havana University two other computer institutions were set up: *'El Centro de Estudios de Informatica y Systemes'* (CEIS) and *'El Centro de Investigaciones Digitales'* (CID). The latter is a research centre and played an essential role in the development and manufacture of computers in Cuba.

Cuba has bought some computers from the West, built from exclusively European technology. As early as 1968 it purchased an 8K memory Elliott 803B and two 16K memory SEA4000. During 1973-1976 the French company CII has delivered 2 IRIS 50 machines and 8 small IRIS 10s, linked in various configurations to one of the IRIS 50 computers.

Centro Investigaciones Digitales (*CID*)

'I am a third generation Cuban Computer. My name is CID 201-B and I was built at the Digital Research Centre of the University of Havana' *Granma* (September 19, 1974.)

CID started in 1969 employing 5 engineers and a mathematician. By 1976 it had grown to an institution employing 300 staff. The Centre's aims can be summarised as follows:-

1. To initiate research, design and produce minicomputers.
2. To make interfaces, and peripheral equipment.
3. To evaluate peripheral equipment bought from abroad.

4. To provide a computer service to various institutions.
5. To produce the basic software for minicomputers, operating systems, compilers and application packages.
6. To train both hardware and software students in collaboration with the University of Havana.

By 1970 CID produced a prototype small computer which was named CID201. Production of this machine continued until 1972 and 20 units were built. These were used mainly for process control in sugar refineries and other factories. At the same time a parallel development had produced a bigger and faster time-sharing machine with different memory characteristics named CID202. Also by 1972, a bigger and faster version of the original machine was developed and named CID201-B. More than 100 of these machines are now in production in the industrial, economic and educational fields. Up to now DTL technology has been used for interfaces and hooked on the machines, paper tapes, magnetic tapes, discs, lineprinters, card readers and cassettes. Peripherals are bought from Canada, Japan, France, Bulgaria, Czechoslovakia and other Eastern European Countries with quite often incompatible interfaces. British firms with their dependence on American components are still complying with the U.S. economic blockade.

In 1975 a new programme was initiated which culminated in the production of a medium size computer, the CID 300. As well, by 1976 CID were looking into the possibility of producing micro-processors. The Cubans already assemble small calculators using Japanese microprocessor chips.

In addition to its computer developments at home, Cuba has been involved in the development and production of a new range of Ryad mini-computers. The new Ryad is a unified system produced jointly by the Eastern European (COMECON) countries and production of this system was started in 1977.

Apart from the above hardware developments, the Centre is responsible for the production of basic software, and the training of operators, programmers, and maintenance engineers. The operating system is for batch streams, but an educational interactive system for secondary students has been implemented which is capable of servicing 8 teletypes at a time. They have also implemented the following languages: LEAL,

FORTRAN IV, COBOL 65, ALGOL 60, SNOBOL and an educational language called LINGO[5].

Table A: Characteristics of the CID-201-A and the CID-202*

Specification	CID-201-A	CID-202
Memory type	Magnetic core	Magnetic core
Memory capacity	4096 words	8192 words
Cycle time	1.5 microseconds	1.5 microseconds
Word length	12 bits	16 bits
Instructions set	59 instructions	200 instructions
Additions per second	25,000	50,000
Peripherals:		
Teletype	Yes	Yes
Paper tape read	Yes	Yes
Paper tape punch	Yes	Yes
Cassette Recorder	Yes	Yes
Auxiliary storage	240K words	240K words
Multiprogramming	No	Yes
LEN 1 language	Yes	Yes
LEAL language	Yes	Yes
Development data	April 1970	July 1971

* Two new models have since been developed. The CID-201-B which is a larger and faster version of CID-201-A. It has a 32K 12 bit memory and was developed in 1972.
In 1976 the CID-300 with a 64K 16 bit memory and 1 microsecond cycle time was in operation.

Source: 'Computadora CID-201-A' and 'Computadora CID-202' Centro de Investigacion Digital, Universidad de la Habana, 1972. CID presentation to the author, Havana September 1976.

Their educational repertoire consists of training some 300 operators and programmers a year plus around 100 Computer Maintenance Engineers. They also have some M.Sc. students in Computer Science, whose studies are supervised by visiting Professors from the Universities of Montreal and Toronto in Canada.

In addition to the 300 permanent staff, the Centre is assisted by 300 students from the University of Havana. They help in the implementation of both basic software and application packages. The students are an integral part of the work-force and the Centre considers their work invaluable. The innovation of student participation in productive work runs through the whole educational system in Cuba, from junior schools to Universities. This is not done just for economic reasons or because of shortage of trained staff but as a deliberate attempt to change the structure of the educational system. In simple terms, Cuba is attempting to forge a stronger link between education and work. For example, computers are assembled by students at the Lenin Vocational School.

Computer Usage

As stated previously, a socialist economy allows the centralised processing of all national economic data by computer. Already a computer network is under development spanning the whole of Cuba and Cuban institutions are applying computers to monitor progress in many fields. Application programmes in many diverse fields such as education, banking, public health, livestock production, sugar production, shipping, transportation and electric power systems are already in use .

As an indication of how far they have progressed since 1969 in integrating computers into all aspects of their economic life, the Cubans are now actively looking at the social effects of computers on their society.

Cybernetic economic model

A centrally planned and controlled economy lends itself naturally to the application of cybernetic systems. Cybernetics is defined as 'the science of effective organisation' and deals with laws of complex systems that are invariant not only to the transformation of their fabric, but also of their content. It does not matter whether the system's content is neurological, automotive, social or economic.

The concept of a fully automated economy, espoused initially by Beer[6], was in the process of implementation in Chile's copper industry at the fall of Dr Allende's government and quickly terminated afterwards. That Beer believed in the viability of the cybernetic system designed for Chile is well documented. Cuba was aware of the Chilean effort and there are indications that they are following a similar model.

Orlando Carnota Lauzán, from the University of Havana, has stated the Cuban intention to automate the economy completely and has described a national computerized system for economic management (*Sistema Nacional de Computacion para Direccion de la Economia*)[7]. The core of a national computation system lies in coupling of the modules in an island-wide network. Lauzán has also supplied information on the basic specifications for the telecommunications hardware and transmission speeds. On my visit to CID in September 1976, I was shown a map of Cuba with the network marked on it. The problem-solving units of the network are indeed CID minicomputers but the teleprocessing interface equipment was under construction in the Central Telecommunication Laboratory of the Ministry of Communications. The completion of this network would provide the necessary linkage for the national cybernetic model.

The Cuban involvement in automated systems is enshrined in Article 95 of the state law enacted in 1976, which provides the legal foundations of Ministries and other organisations of central state administration:

Article 95. The National Institute of Automated Systems and Computer Technology is the agency in charge of directing, carrying out and supervising the implementation of the policy of state and government regarding central automated control systems and computer technology, and, to this end, it has, in addition to the common duties, powers and functions set out in Article 52 of this Law, the following main powers and functions:-

a) to draw up, establish and supervise the implementation of a single set of methodological principles, to set up central automated control systems in such a way as to insure that their elaboration and implementation are founded on a technical and economic basis;

b) to draw up, together with the other state agencies and the local organs of People's Power, and to propose the plan for the introduction of automated control systems and computer techniques to the Central Planning Board and, once approved, to supervise its implementation;

c) to set up integrated central control systems of high economic efficiency, to set standards for the use of computer technology and supervise their implementation and to organise a technical service in keeping with the said technology;

d) to organise a network of data processing centres for collective use with a view to more efficient use of equipment;

e) to advise the Council of Ministers on setting up or closing data processing centres and automated systems drafting centres under the jurisdiction of central state administration agencies;

f) to foster and provide guidelines for the development of the manufacture of electronic computers, peripheral equipment and materials used in computer technology.[8]

Towards an information society

Computers and electronic automated systems are basic building blocks of an information society, a society which has telecommunications as its kingpin. Such a society can release the majority of the labour force from routine, backbreaking and soul-destroying tasks to engage in more creative activities. This assumes that machines are put foremost in the service of man and not used to make money for a small section of traders in a consumer society. Cuba with its socialist mode of organisation, is well placed to reap the benefits of a computer-based information society, and to improve its people's quality of life.

REFERENCES

1. R.H.W. Bullock, Deputy Secretary in the Department of Trade and Industry. Proceedings of Datafair 77, sponsored by the British Computer Society.
2. Dorticós O. 'Desarrollar cultural, científica y tecnicamente los cuadros administrativos', *Economía y Desarrollo*, No. 20, 1973, pp. 26-57.
3. Fidel Castro, Speech to commemorate the 10th Anniversaty of setting up the Technological Youth Brigades.
4. Kaoru Ando, President of the Fujitsu Institute of Computer Science, Japan. Proceedings of Datafair 77, sponsored by the British Computer Society.
5. R.Delgado Ysla, *Control Cibernetica Y Automatizacion Cuba Abril-Junio 1975*. Ano IX, 1102, pp. 22, 29.
6. S. Beer, *Cybernetics and Management*, English University Press, London 1967.
7. Carnota Lauzán, 'La aplicacion de las computatoras en el campo economico y social en un pais en vias de desarrollo, Cuba'. *Economia y Desarrollo, no 9,* January-February 1972.
8. Text of the law on the organisation of Central State Administration, *Granma* 19.11.76.

Urban and Rural Planning

Michael Edwards

The pre-revolutionary background

The deformations wrought on Cuban economy and society by the successive colonial and neo-colonial exploitations were reflected, as seriously as in other spheres of life, in housing, settlement patterns, and transport.

The traditional peasant house (*bohio*) offers some good qualities—principally, in being adapted to the climate—but it is invariably without sanitary services and also lacks privacy. In the past, rural housing was also a problem with regard to accessibility: the scatter of dwellings made access to good jobs, education and other services impossible for much of the population.[1]

In 1959, land was almost entirely in private ownership. The speculations on urban fringes and prime coastal sites made the few public sector initiatives costly or ineffective, raised the costs of infrastructure, and produced a straggling openwork city form. The underdevelopment of industry, limited in most places to the immediate processing of the island's primary products, was reflected in the spread of small towns.

Industrial underdevelopment was also indicated by the low-tonnage shipping needed to transfer those products from small Cuban ports to the USA. Havana was the only port capable of taking long-haul ships. In addition, the national transport network was poor. Thus, when the US blockade made Cuba switch from trade with the Americas to trade with Europe, the Soviet Union and Canada, the pressure on Havana's deep berths and on trunk roads and railways became overwhelming.

Havana had been pre-eminent in Cuba with regard to tourism, education, hospitals and professional services, and was one of the western hemispheres main centres for gambling and prostitution. Although Cuba was already more urbanised than most Latin American countries, migration from country to towns remained heavy and was associated with shanty settlements on the city periphery. The other noteworthy form of migration was the seasonal movement of workers to the sugar cane and other plantation areas for harvesting; the plantations (*latifundias*) mostly owned or financed by US capital, having earlier displaced populations to cities and to the hills.

Early revolutionary reforms

The revolutionary campaign of the 1950s had land reform as a major campaigning issue, and indication that the peasant base of the struggle was as crucial as its twin, the proletarian base. Within the first two months of the new revolutionary government, Urban Reform legislation ordained large cuts in housing rents, ranging from 50% in rents below $100 per month to 30% for rents over $200.[2] Under-occupied and abandoned dwellings were identified and reallocated; private speculative building was rapidly eliminated; and tenants were enabled to become owners of their dwellings by making payments (not exceeding their previous rents) over a five to ten year period. The conception of ownership was transformed in that owners were not able to bequeath their houses, and only in special cases did their offspring have priority in the reallocation of property. By 1972, 75% of households owned their houses and 10% more were in the process of buying them.[3]

A very strong emphasis on rural development has characterised much of the post-revolutionary period, despite some important policy changes.[4] Havana grew rapidly in the years immediately after 1959, but has expanded subsequently at a rate slower than the national population—a remarkable achivement when contrasted with the disastrously high rates of growth in other Latin American capitals. Most of the urban growth has been in cities of over 20,000 (especially those just under 100,000 in 1966) and in very small settlements in the countryside.[5] The proportion of the population regarded as 'urban' thus grew from 50% in 1953 to 60% in 1970; while the number of people living in dispersed dwellings or in settlements of less than 200 dwellings fell in the same period by 13% of its 1953 magnitude, and has continued to fall.[6]

Contemporary policy and practice

The location of activities and the links between them are central to Cuban economic planning. This is partly a political momentum caused by the increased expectations following the substantial peasant involvement in the revolutionary struggle; partly it flows from the severe spatial inequalities (between regions and between neighbourhoods) before 1959; partly it reflects the importance and growth of agriculture, mining and, more recently, tourism in the economy. All three of these industries are impossible to plan except by taking land and locations as the starting points.

The other important provision of the early legislation was the establishment of the Junta Central (then, Nacional) de Planificacion (JUCEPLAN), the central agency for planning and guiding the economy. JUCEPLAN had, from the first, powers and responsibilities over land use and the location of activities, and came under the general direction of the Council of Ministers. It has responsibilities for the preparation, co-ordination and monitoring of plans and for related research and statistics. It receives draft bids from the ministries for their sectors, reconciles them in the light of priorities laid down politically (paying special attention to balance of payments implications) and makes consistency checks. Up to 1975, plans were made on an annual basis, but from 1976 they have been on a five year cycle.[7]

It would be wrong to see this planning process as simply a

top-downwards system of edicts, even before the re-organisation of 1976/77. In effect it has been a dialogue between (a) the Council of Ministers, articulating national objectives in relation to the process of intense discussions taking place in the mass organisations and Party organs, and (b) the producing sectors responsible for state enterprises (since 1963 virtually all non-farm activity and about 70-80% of agriculture) and representatives of the non-state farmers. Here, too, there are chains of discussion down through the provinces to the individual establishment.

This dialogue takes place against a global model of the economy maintained by JUCEPLAN, comprising related conditional forecasts for each sector with special attention to exports and to the import content of production and final consumption.[8]

Since 1976/77 the planning system has been changing in accordance with the new constitution of the country and the 'institutionalisation' of social and national life around the new elected assemblies. From the point of view of spatial planning, the importance of these changes lies in the decentralisation of control and the new politics of decision making.

As the management of locality-serving activities passes to the municipalities and of region-serving activities to the provincial assemblies, conditions are created where local populations can bring their own needs and priorities to bear directly on planning decisions. It is clear that major resource allocations, price and wage determination, work norms and product standards will remain 'central responsibilities', and much depends on how this bland phrase is interpreted in practice. For instance, will the national 'standard' size for new villages be rigid? Or will assemblies and their staffs be able to vary it to fit their own settlement patterns, terrain and transport networks? In the field of housing, will experiment be possible in the size distribution of dwellings or in the balance between private and collective open space?

The reconstitution opens up a uniquely exciting prospect for the integration of economic and social development (and its expression in the built environment) under democratic control, at three levels—the municipality, the province and the nation.

Many people in the underdeveloped (and the developed)

world will be watching to see if Cuba can reconcile national planning with consumers' sovereignty through mass political involvement.

The articulation of national development in space

The Construction Sector's Institute (previously Department) of Physical Planning (IPF) is responsible specifically for the 'articulation of national economic and social development in space' (this being the phrase the planners use in describing their work). The Institute's early responsibilities were limited to designing and executing major port and industrial projects[9] but have recently expanded vastly.

The IPF national office coordinates and sets norms and standards for lower level offices; it brings together resource bids for JUCEPLAN; it gives methodological advice to its branches; it gathers and processes planning data; and in a few cases it designs and executes major projects (e.g. ports and the large tourist development at Varadero). Perhaps most important of all, it prepares and maintains the National Physical Plan. This plan is an extraordinarily impressive feat. Its preparation and maintenance have probably only been possible for a country at this stage of development because of the intimate state involvement in the whole economy and the centralisation of each sector's control. The preparation of the plan involved technical staff of IPF moving over to work with the staff of the agricultural and other key ministries, so that a truly joint understanding could be reached about the technical potential and the development priorities of each part of the island.

In the framewerd of this plan the provincial and local IPF offices prepare regional and local plans and special projects. These plans themselves have not, at least up to 1976/77, been the subject of much public discussion. They are regarded as one dimension of the realisation of national objectives—the creation of a socialist, and ultimately of a communist, society, the socialisation and expansion of production, the maintenance of exports, the linking of work and study, and so on. It is these *objectives* which are continually the subject of speeches, media coverage and popular discussion in Party groups and mass organisations. The extent to which spatial planning issues will themselves become the subject of political discussion in the elected assemblies is not yet clear. However, it was clear in 1976 that mass organisations are heavily involved in local discussions, decisions and action during the *implementation* of plans—indeed they are essential in that process.

Urban and rural planners appear to be using 'techniques' which are simple, even rudimentary—partly because planners are few and scope for specialised work limited, and partly because appropriate techniques hardly exist. Much attention is paid to how the costs of providing services vary with the scale of provision and with the size of catchment populations for the facilities which settlements are deemed to need.[10] It is probably in the transport field that most effort is needed for the development of techniques. Cubans show great interest in international developments in transport forecasting and planning methods, but are only too well aware of how inappropriate much of this work is in a country where most freight movement and all prices and fares are planned; where the vehicle stock is largely in public ownership; and (most important), where the location of activities can be decided at the same time as the planning of links between them.

Within this planning framework the priorities in development to date have gone to construction work on irrigation and farm building, ports, transport, education, health and industry, with housing taking only a subsidiary position. And, of course, construction as a whole has been competing with huge non-capital spending in industry and social services. The limited resources devoted to housing have been backed up by careful attention to the full use of the available stock and by imaginative devices to make the available skills and materials go as far as possible. There appears to be very little 'leakage' of materials from planned production—so little in fact that quite urgent repair and maintenance work on some older buildings has been impossible for long periods. The resulting net disinvestment in old housing stock is now of concern to the Cubans.

The transformation of the territory

The National Physical Plan embodies analysis of soil and

hydrology, climate, established uses, proximity to ports and industry, to consumers and to workers. Alongside the Land Use Plan is a perspective plan for settlement which, *inter alia*, envisages the whole population being in concentrated settlements by the mid-1980s.[11]

The main device for implementing these national plans is the Territorial Plan covering a few hundred square km with functionally defined boundaries. The majority relate to state agricultural 'plans' and by 1976 some 363 had been prepared for agricultural areas, covering about 28% of the total area thought suitable for such treatment[12] [13].

The main implementing agency is DESA, the construction division which deals with farm buildings, roads, water and settlements. DESA appoints a community development officer for each plan, usually a woman, and always someone with at least primary schooling and with local political experience. Her first job is to contact all the households affected and explain the plans to them, and the option each household has of joining in (and having housing and job priority) or remaining on their peasant holding or a close substitute. The proportion of families wishing to join the plans is apparently high and can exceed the available places; but there are still non-joiners, and their plots are very obvious in the landscape: small plots with mixed crops and thatched *bohios* in the middle of extensive state farms, fenceless except where there are animals.

The impetus to rural settlement transformation appears to be threefold, deriving

a.   from the needs of the new agriculture and the need to avoid long journeys to work on the farm;

b.   from current estimated thresholds for provision of services in each settlement—food and clothes shop, cafe, day nursery, primary school, small clinic (usually run by a young doctor doing her two year's field training), social centre, bookshop, Party office and sometimes a cinema; (Such a service is currently held to require a settlement of 280 dwellings.)

c.   from the need for a physical and social framework for the development of political life. (Each settlement elects its own small council as well as having the normal branches of mass organisations. Living together in a village and managing some of the collective facilities is clearly a contribution to the political self-education of the rural people.)

By 1976, 335 of these small new communities existed, with a total population of 135,000.[14] Progress with these, as with other plans is reported back by a network of 600 IPF staff for a six-monthly update of the plans. Parallel flows of production and employment data are received by JUCEPLAN via the ministries and it appears that this formal monitoring system (alongside the political feedback-through mass organisations) contributes to Cuba's capacity to identify failures quickly, acknowledge them and respond. Much of what is happening in the country is truly experimental, and central and local officials, and many ordinary workers, appear to carry in their heads a lot of up-to-date evidence on the successes and problems which their work is encountering in practice.

As a result, new settlement planning has changed in various ways in the decade or so of the programme's life. At the outset, housing was predominantly in single-family structures. Now—for explicit economic, ideological and consumer-preference reasons— it is being built as low-rise flats. At the outset there was a degree of private cultivation; now it is collective. Settlement sizes have been adjusted and various other changes made.

No account of rural transformation can omit the central role of education, particularly the secondary boarding Schools in the Countryside. These schools, which now accommodate 300,000 children, are an integral part of the rural economy.[15] The children, who live at school all week and return to their parents at weekends, provide a lot of the labour required for the more labour-intensive crops and make use of practical problems arising on the farm as part of their scientific education. The schools are often related to teacher-training colleges and primary schools and these in turn all have their own direct production tasks.

Production criteria do not, however, dominate the entire countryside. Substantial areas are set aside informally for tourism or designated specifically as

either a. National Scientific Reserves. Under the care of the

Academy of Sciences and the Institute of Botany, these are closed to the public and open only for research.

or b. National Parks. There are now ten of these and a new marine national park is being planned. They are sacrosanct areas, with public access by foot or horseback permitted, and corresponding closely to the UN definition of a national park.

or c. National Tourist Areas. These contain traditional agriculture, established settlements and even some industry, but all are subject to very stringent aesthetic controls on building. They correspond roughly to the British National Parks.

or d. National and Historical Monuments. These are smaller sites and areas of special historical interest or of great beauty.

Rural transport is improving as the rural road network expands and as the bus fleet and taxi system grow. The demand for movement is buoyant. Trunk road trips, for example, increased from 14.3 per head per year in 1962 to 40 in 1974.[16] One of the significant consequences of the rapid nucleation of settlement is that growing demands for movement can much more easily be met.

Housing and planning problems in established towns

Whereas the new rural settlements are all built by the formal construction sector, much urban housing is the product of the voluntary labour of the microbrigades. Urban housing problems remain severe, however; it is there that the poor maintenance of old buildings has had its worst effects. Falling family size and the absence of growing numbers of young people—at boarding schools, at college and in the army—help to relieve the worst overcrowding. The expansion of nurseries for young children also relieves some of the stress at home. But the problem remains pressing, especially in Havana.

The other main problem of the cities is transport. Demand for movement is vast compared with twenty years ago. The modern Cuban family would typically consist of two or three workers and two school-children, all of them members of mass political or youth organisations with weekly meetings. The workers are likely to be attending evening classes and may be active in sport as well. Demand for transport is thus not just large, but complex. The consequences of this high demand and the limited services currently available are seen in the acute overcrowding of buses, the very busy service of individually hired and shared taxis, and the long bus queues. Fortunately, Cuban streets are rarely choked by private transport, though the number of cars is increasing. City plans will ensure that, in the long run, the residential areas are easily served by good bus services, and that work-places and other destinations are distributed in convenient sub-centres. But urban transport is likely to remain a problem in the next decade.

REFERENCES

1. Fuller accounts are in Comite Cubano de Asentamientos Humanos, *Los Asentamientos Humanos en Cuba*, Havana, Ins. Cub. del Libro, 1976, and M. Acosta and J.E. Hardoy, 'Urbanisation Policies in Revolutionary Cuba'. *Bull. Brit.-Cuba Sci. Liaison Cttee.*, ¡, 1975 (reprinted from Geisse and Hardoy, eds, *Latin American Urban Research, Sage*, 1975).
2. Ibid.
3. Banco Nacional de Cuba, *Development and Prospects of the Cuban Economy,* Havana, 1975.
4. Report presented to the first congress of the Communist Party of Cuba, December 1975: English version in *Granma*, December 28, 1975 and January 4, 1976.
5. Acosta and Hardoy, op. cit.
6. Banco Nacional, op. cit.
7. JUCEPLAN, *La planificacion economica en Cuba*, Santiago do Cuba, 1968.
8. Ibid.
9. Acosta and Hardoy, op. cit.
10. Use is made of the 'threshold analysis' techniques associated with Koslowski and others.
11. It is clearly understood that the date of achievement of this objective may be distant. It appears that the perspective plan is essentially a hypothetical proposition out of which consistent and feasible parts are drawn for inclusion in specific short term plans.
12. The citrus area of Victoria de Giron is such a territory and is described in *Granma* weekly review, 1976.

13.   The data are from R. Saladrigas, 'Experiencias de Cuba en la Planificacion Regional y Urbana', in *Vivienda*, Mexico, 1976.

14.   Comite Cubano ..., op. cit.

15.   Report, op. cit.

16.   Report, op. cit.

Housing

Rodney Mace

In the decade or so prior to 1959, housing conditions for the mass of Cuba's rural and urban working class were generally appalling—even the government grudgingly admitted that. The 1953 housing census reported:

—only 43% of the population lived in acceptable conditions;
—15% lived in totally uninhabitable conditions;
—62% of all dwellings had thatch roofs and earth floors;
—42% had no electricity; and
—65% had no piped water.

Sanitation, except in the bigger towns and cities, was more or less non-existent; leading, for instance, to high rates of intestinal parasites, especially among the rural population and in the 'viviendas precarias' (homes which squatters constructed from waste materials). The government did nothing. In the cities, especially Havana, the speculators in hotels and casinos made a killing.

When the Revolution came to power in January 1959 there was an explosion of production and creative activity in construction as the new legislative frameworks were introduced. In March 1959, as a first important step, rents across the board were cut by half (up till that time in Havana, for example, three quarters of all homes were rented). The Urban Reform Law of

I am indebted to Dave Harding for some of the information and ideas and the diagrams for this article.

October 1960 finally broke the power of the parasite landlord class by enabling tenants to become owners of their own homes within a 5-10 year period; the rent being paid to the state in the meantime. By 1972, 75% of all households in Cuba owned their own homes for their lifetime.

In August 1961 Fidel Castro outlined the problem posed by housing in the new conditions. Initially, he said, 'no matter how many new projects were suggested there was always enough wood and cement to carry them out, and enough people anxious to work.... But now it is not the same; there are an enormous number of projects and the available cement, wood and construction equipment are not enough to go around.... Priority will have to be given to factories and to other centres of production... after factories come other things.... schools, hospitals, aqueducts. We could produce 100,000 houses... but we cannot do it because then we would remain without factories and schools. I have confessed here that I was one of the leading promoters of uncoordinated projects.... But now I propose to be one of the great defenders of planning.'[1]

In these early years pre-revolutionary housing forms, noticeably the house with private garden, made a brief appearance in some numbers. But these were soon to be replaced by the five-storey walk-up apartment block surrounded by open space held in common. The acute difficulties of construction activity in the countryside provoked early experimentation with forms of pre-fabrication, in an attempt to ease the problems of both transportation and on site work. At the same time, the trade embargo forced Cuba to adopt almost wholly concrete and cement products—which fortunately it possessed the raw materials for—in nearly all its house construction. Other materials like hard and soft woods, glass, ceramic and metal wares were in desperately short supply, as were the materials for household furniture and effects. The five storey walk-ups had the important added advantage that they significantly increased personal comfort by taking advantage of the cooling crosswinds.

Priorities in the construction sector soon became very tightly drawn. A primary emphasis was put on infrastructural work linked to the agricultural sector—the construction of dams and the development of the rural road system. In the provision of services priority was given to educational construction at all levels, and to improvement of public health facilities. Essential industrial building and the improvement of port facilities were other key areas. Housing took a decidedly secondary position.

The limited national resources to be devoted to housing production ensured that location of new stock was very carefully considered in relation to production and employment growth points. The emphasis on redistribution of resources to the rural areas remained, but was more selectively carried forward and linked to a drive for rationalisation and mechanisation in agricultural production. By the end of the decade, despite the limited resources, radical spatial transformations had occurred in many settlements in the countryside. A census report in 1970 shows 250 villages built by the revolutionary government, with a regrouping, on a voluntary basis, of the local population. These are now categorised as urban settlements, because of the high level of associated services and facilities provided. Construction of housing in the urban areas was strictly limited; there were growth points linked to essential industrial development, such as the new town of Nuevitas (construction of port facilities) and the 'rural city' of Sandino but, by way of contrast, production in Havana by the Ministry of Construction came almost to a standstill between 1966 and 1970.

Against this background of limited resources the drive to develop a new practice in housing went ahead. Major investigations into the current state of the housing stock and its expected life was begun. The search to develop new forms of construction, and to develop a consistent supply of materials for the industry continued, both now made more urgent with the onset of the blockade. There was a large investment programme in the production of cement as the primary building material; several newly constructed plants were opened in the late 60s, and, as a result, output in 1970, at 2.4 million tons, stood nearly 3 times higher than that of 1967.

In the design of new forms of housing construction there were tensions between a variety of needs. On the one hand there was the continuing ideological debate around the form that housing in a socialist society should take, and the role it could play in consolidating or retarding social transformation. On the other hand there were technical pressures; the need to develop techniques of assembly that could be easily used in the countryside, that would increase productivity in a sector short of labour, but which also could be operated without too high a demand for skilled labour.

Throughout the years 1964-70 the Cuban leadership conceded publicly that they were not tackling, and could not tackle, the need for new housing construction. In 1965 Fidel Castro remarked that the housing problem was something 'that the Revolution has not even begun to deal with seriously'. A year before he had outlined the scale of work to be done at the National Builders Congress: 2 million houses by 1990, with an average annual production of 80,000. A more detailed forecast at about this time saw production rising from 12,000 units in 1967 to 40,000 the following year and up to 70,000 in 1969.

Fig. 1.

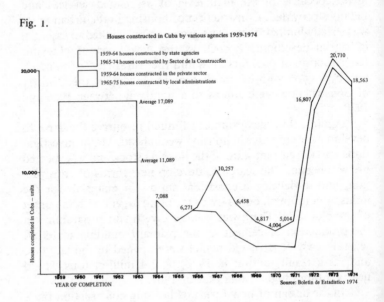

Houses constructed in Cuba by various agencies 1959-1974

Fig. 2.

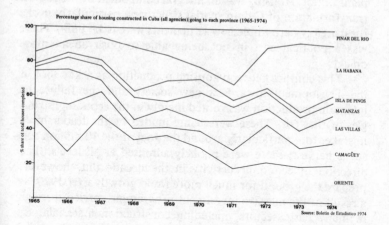

Percentage share of housing constructed in Cuba (all agencies) going to each province (1965-1974)

Source: Boletin de Estadistico 1974

Fig. 3.

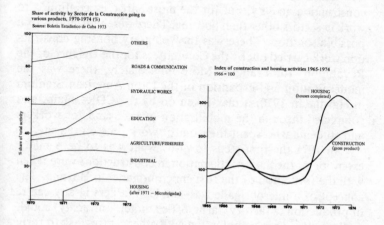

Share of activity by Sector de la Construccion going to various products, 1970-1974 (%)
Source: Boletin Estadistico de Cuba 1973

Index of construction and housing activities 1965-1974
1966 = 100

The problem was not simply one of meeting production plans or not. Housing was an integral component of the radical transformation of Cuban spatial structures, particularly in the rural areas where whole new settlements were to be built. There was a political cost in not being able to push ahead more quickly.

This conflict between housing production as a key tool in the development towards a new society and the failure to maintain production was rooted mainly in the economic struggles of the '60s. These were compounded by the leadership's mistakes too, particularly around the goal of the 10 million ton sugar harvest; these were publicly admitted at all levels. The direction of economic activity in the decade did, however, prepare the ground for much more rapid growth after 1970, as a result of the massive investment programme carried through in many basic sectors, including construction materials. By 1970 the increased output of building materials and the development of industrialised techniques in particular, provided for a new expansion of housing activity.

The key problem in expanding housing activity in 1970 was the acute shortage of labour.[2] New permanent construction brigades were formed to meet a general increase in construction activity, but for the most part they continued to work in sectors other than housing. There were indications of a possible solution. There was the voluntary housing construction work carried out by the Committees for the Defence of the Revolution, for example. More immediately, there was the modernisation and expansion of the Latin American Stadium in Havana in 1970; a task taken on by the CDRs again, and completed through the mobilisation of thousands of workers and students who spent their out-of-work time on the site.

In 1971 the first steps towards what was to be a major extension of the mass participation in constructions were taken with the formation of the first 'microbrigade' in Havana. The concept of a microbrigade was simple. Workers in any centre of production (a factory, farm, office, hotel, university) could, on their own, or in combination with other centres, ask to form a brigade to construct housing to meet their work centres' current needs. A brigade would usually consist of about 30 workers, seconded from their normal jobs to work on housing construction and supervised and taught by two or three experienced building workers. Secondment would last from 1-2 years depending on the nature of the project. In the meantime production levels in the work centre would be maintained by the other workers there taking on 'plus-trabajo'—extra work at weekends or evenings—to cover for the brigade members' absence. Housing constructed by the microbrigades would be allocated to workers at the work centre; allocation would be decided upon at general meetings and would be based on a mixture of factors, including immediate housing need and general merit of those applying, assessed on work performance, political activity and other indicators. New homes did not by any forms of prior right go to those who had built them.

The microbrigades offered the possibility of increased, essential housing output without diverting scarce labour resources from other sectors. The costs to production in the sectors from which the brigades were drawn would be minimized by 'plus-trabajo'. From their first formation in Havana, the growth of the brigades was rapid and they quickly assumed the full weight of responsibility for increasing housing production in the early years of the 1970s.

In 1971 a government survey showed that microbrigades were already involved in the construction of 10,082 housing units. Havana, which was to absorb 70% of this figure, had 218 brigades working by September 1971.[3] By 1973 there were over 1,000 brigades spread throughout Cuba and in 1975 and 1976 annual output from nearly 1,200 microbrigades with a labour force of over 25,000 workers was expected to top 27,000 units.[4] The weight of microbrigade output in national housing construction can be seen in the fact that during 1972 and 1973 they accounted for an average of 65% of all houses built in Cuba.[5]

An initial focus of microbrigade activity was on construction in urban areas, and particularly in Havana. The 1971 survey shows Havana taking a dominant share of microbrigade planned output and from a figure of under 500 units in 1969 production of new housing had risen to a peak of 8,500 in the one year of 1973.

A major construction site in Havana was the Alamar project, started in 1971 and by 1974, occupying 84 microbrigades with a work force of 2,700. On the Alamar project as in other integrated schemes, microbrigade activity was not confined to housing alone; the brigades were responsible for construction of schools, clinics, sports centres, and some small industrial plants.[6]

Microbrigade teams were able to draw on the continuing development and the increase in output of the industrialized building industries. A number of techniques had been put into production which were particularly suited to brigade conditions; they required a relatively low level of skill in assembly, used a minimum number of different designs, and worked with small, light prefabricated units which made fewer demands for heavy on-site equipment. The 1971 survey shows only 13% of microbrigades using the heavier Gran Panel system of prefabrication (a system based on a Soviet type). Seventy-seven per cent of the work was carried out using the E14 and E15 systems: light, small panel units, or by traditional building methods (bricks were coming back into production), while 10% were using a more recently developed light Sandino panel system.

The expansion of housing construction through the new organizational form of the microbrigade was only one facet of a general increase in the amount of construction activity within the economy of the early 1970s. The gross product of the Sector de la Construccion rose in 5 years, between the low point of output in 1970 of 200 million pesos, to 891 million pesos in 1974. Overall construction output increased at an average rate of 28% a year in this period.

Housing activity did, however, take an increased share of this expanding construction output. As fig.3 shows, between 1970 and 1973 the heavy emphasis on infrastructural work (hydraulic works and roads and communication) and construction linked to the capital investment programme in agriculture and industry is sharply modified. By 1973 housing activity and educational construction took nearly 40% of total production. The value of housing units finished in Cuba tripled in the one year between 1970/1 and tripled again in the following year before settling to a slower rate of increase in 1972/3. The shaded section of the share going to housing shows the importance of microbrigade output after 1971 in carrying this rapid expansion forward. The result in terms of numbers of units finished can be seen in fig.1—a rise between 1970 and 1973 to an annual completion of around 2,000 units—with the period through 1976/7 showing a steady increase in output above this figure.

The outstanding difference in the location of newly constructed housing after 1970 was the move back to building in Havana. With the early microbrigade activity centred on Havana, construction jumps from a negligible amount in the late 60s to a peak of over 8,000 units a year in 1973; in that year Havana province absorbed 40% of a much increased national output. The decision to reverse the previous explicit full stop on new housing construction in Havana, appears to have been taken for two main reasons: firstly, in the face of a possible actual deterioration of housing conditions due to the worsening state of much of the older housing stock, and secondly, in the light of a broader policy view that there would be a return to a steady growth of the city in the near future.[7]

Given the increased scale of national output the absorption of a larger share of housing by Havana did not prevent an increase in units finished in every other province in Cuba between 1970 and 1971. Las Villas and Camauey registered particularly large surges forward in house production. And, as well as the return to construction in Havana, the priority remained the restructuring of settlement patterns in the rural areas, with the continuing growth of new centres of population in integrated development schemes. By 1976, 335 such rural settlements had been built or were under construction in Cuba, with a total population of 135,000, and with each settlement enjoying a full range of collective facilities and services.

Over a third of these new settlements were linked to sugar production and another 25% to cattle farms, with the majority of the locations (68%) in the three provinces of Las Villas, Camaguey and Oriente. Changes in the nature of the agricultural production under the revolution necessitated other linked construction programmes in the rural areas. With the sugar harvest now relying, for up to 80% of its labour force, on the movement of voluntary workers to the countryside during the cutting seasons, hundreds of hostels were built to cope with this temporary population. Similarly, the 'schools in the countryside' demanded a massive construction effort in themselves. As these residential schools had a direct effect on urban housing, by helping to reduce overcrowding there, they should be counted as a positive part of the overall housing gain.

Even with the relative upsurge in the housing programme that began in 1971 Fidel Castro was to remark in 1975, summing up the achievements and problems of the revolution in his speech to the 1st Congress of the Cuban Communist Party, that housing was a sector where 'we have not been able to do very much', despite, as he also noted, the 'magnificent efforts of the microbrigades' in recent years.[8] A backlog of problems still remained to be met in 1975. To tackle them it was hoped that housing production would expand steadily throughout the rest of the decade, within the planned slower rate of growth of the economy, to reach 80-100,000 units a year by 1980. The continuing difficulties of diverting still scarce labour resources to build a permanent construction force around housing would mean that in this period the micro-brigades would continue to carry the main weight of the construction effort.

What then, in summary, is it important to note about developments in housing in Cuba since 1959? Firstly, socialist economic and spatial planning are the objective basis for success. Secondly, the mass of the population must be given the means to see that housing is both a political and technical question. The undoubted success of the voluntary rural re-settlements and the microbrigades are ample witness to this. Thirdly, new housing forms appropriate to these fundamental changes only emerge quite slowly.

REFERENCES

1. Edward Boorstein, *The Economic Transformation of Cuba*, Monthly Review Press, New York, 1969, p.117.
2. For a full discussion of housing production and other areas of construction activity see Robert Segre's *Diez años de arquitectura en Cuba revolucionaria* Havana, 1970.
3. *Boletin Estadistico de Cuba,* 1971.
4. *Granma Weekly Review,* 21 December 1973.
5. An estimate from figures in *Boletin Estadistico de Cuba,* 1973.
6. For a discussion of the Alamar project see Tony Schuman's 'We don't have the right to wait,' *Cuba Review,* Vol.v.No.1.
7. *Boletin Estadistico de Cuba,* 1974. For Havana, *La Habana—Transforma-ćion Urbana en Cuba,* Coleccion: Materiales de la Cuidad. Barcelona, 1974.
8. *Granma Weekly Review,* 28 December, 1975.

How Old People Live

Joey Edwardh

Little has been written about the quality of life of old
people living in societies where socialism is the dominant
ideology. This article describes and analyses the life pattern of
a group of old people living in two Havana neighbourhoods
and considers how the proclamations of the Cuban constitution are articulated in the form and structure of today's Cuba
to provide appropriate services and opportunities for old
people.[1]

The constitution, in declaring that food, shelter, health
care, education, and work are basic human rights, has established "the concrete components" of human well-being within
the Cuban state.[2]

The number of elderly in Cuba is a significant group. The
increasing size of this age group is attributed to the advances in
medical science, public health, sanitation, and industrial technology, which, when made available to the Cuban population
in general, have altered drastically the country's morbidity and
mortality rates. The proportion of Cuba's population over 65
years of age has grown to approximately eight per cent of the
total population in 1976 and it is estimated that it will increase
to eleven per cent by 1980.[3] The number of elderly is large
enough that to provide adequately for them takes a substantial
commitment of both human and material resources as well as
significant societal changes.

The Old Ones

The outlook of old people in Cuban society is the product of complex interrelationships based on social class, sex, race ethnicity and religion. The old reflect the same divergent attitudes and life styles found in the total population. However, they share the common bond of growing old, and their life experience is grounded in a radically different social and political system, that of neo-colonial and capitalist Cuba. At the time of the triumph of the 1959 Revolution, most members of this age group were in their fifties with only a limited number of working years left before retirement. Of the old people that I interviewed, most retired in their early sixties on a pension.

The importance of marriage as an institution is reflected in the life patterns of the thirty elderly who made up the group of interviewed. Approximately three-quarters of those interviewed are married. With the exception of one single person, the remaining individuals in this group are widowed, separated or divorced.

Children are very important to the family life of older people and three-quarters of those interviewed have children. Older people tend to live in a multi-generational family unit, particularly after the death of a spouse. Three-fifths of the old interviewees share in the experience of being a grandparent.

Most of the people interviewed are white, and on the whole, this racial mix reflects the pre-revolutionary socio-economic position of this area which would have been identified as one of middle income. Blacks were excluded from a neighbourhood such as this because of their poverty and the racist attitudes so prevalent in pre-revolutionary Cuba.

Roman Catholicism has left a myriad of traditions, values and beliefs in Cuba's social fabric, even though revolutionary Cuba is officially atheistic. The religious heritage of Cuba is reflected by the number of old respondents who classified their religious orientation as Roman Catholic. It is interesting to note, however, that a number of individuals felt they had no religion, and of the total number of individuals interviewed, there was one Protestant and one Jew. Two individuals, while considering themselves Catholics, participated actively in an

Afro-Cuban religion called *Santería*.⁴

Most of the old people in the sample are healthy and able to participate in their daily home life and that of their community. The five handicapped individuals who are suffering from advancing chronic illness, such as heart disease, diabetes, and arthritis have limited physical ability but they can still participate in life around them. Three individuals are essentially housebound as a result of advanced heart disease. And finally, the one individual categorized as bedridden is dying of cancer and in need of constant supervision and care.

For the most part the educational achievement of the old interviewees includes some elementary school education. Only four individuals—all males—completed the North American equivalent of high school. One man had a university degree.

Most of the elderly in both study areas are retired urban workers. With the exception of a pharmacist and two accountants, male occupations generally can be classified as custodians, salesmen, truck drivers and chauffeurs while the women were housewives, saleswomen, seamstresses, cigarette factory workers, secretaries and teachers' aides. Most of the women who worked tended to be either single or married without children. Economic necessity rather than cultural norms placed these women in the labour force.

In pre-revolutionary Cuba, this group of old people, who average 73 years of age, had access to amenities available only in urban areas. They were literate and employed in a country that had suffered from ubiquitous poverty, illiteracy and unemployment along with a myriad of other problems associated with underdevelopment. They were not owners, but labourers selling their only asset, their labour, for a wage.

The Neighbourhoods

The old respondents live in two neighbourhoods located within Polyclinic Pasteur's service area. This area, constructed during the late 1930s and 1940s, is a residential area of mixed single and two-family dwellings, along with a number of two- and three-storey walk-up apartment buildings and a few tenements.

The neighbourhoods are pleasant. Statues of José Martí, the apostle and great philosopher of revolutionary Cuba, dot the landscape. Large trees shade the clean streets. Traffic congestion, with its impatient drivers and noise, is limited to the major avenues, Diez de Octubre, Via Blanca, and Santa Catalina which border the area. As most residents do now own cars, the neighbourhood streets are not defined as hazardous paths by area residents.

There are constant outside activities: people chatting on porches, others engrossed in playing their games of dominoes, neighbours walking to and from basic services interspersed throughout the area, and children playing in yards and on the streets. Basic services, grocery stores or *bodegas*, pharmacies, laundry services, banks, churches, daycare centres, elementary schools, a post office, a polyclinic, a dental clinic, and bus stops for various routes are located within easy walking distance of each resident's home. It is obvious that those services necessary to daily living are spatially accessible. Although some of these amenities were located in the study neighbourhoods prior to the Revolution, others have been added in recent years, for it is the policy of the present Cuban Government that both old and new neighbourhoods be provided with basic amenities. People here walk without fear to locales where friends and neighbours gather and talk while doing errands. For old people, these spaces are important centres where personal concerns, daily events, and foreign affairs are discussed.

It is difficult to assess these neighbourhoods as typical without a social area analysis of the city of Havana. However, this section is about average, according to Orlando Larrinaga, Polyclinic Pasteur's sanitary engineer, who monitors the environmental conditions in the area. He stated that "average" is not his word but a descriptive category developed by the Ministry of Public Health to describe the quality of a number of environmental factors, such as housing, roads, sidewalks, sewers, atmospheric contamination, basic hygiene, and sources of water and food. He felt that conditions were not optimal but certainly they were not bad.

"Average", according to Orlando Larrinaga, "means that the houses might need paint or have cracks in the walls or floors but the housing stock is far from uninhabitable." Furthermore, Larrinaga stated, "average means that some of the *bodegas* do not have refrigeration for food. There are regular bus services. The people are neither underserved nor overserved.''

Environmental Support

One characteristic distinguishing the lives of Cuban old people from their age peers in western industrial societies is a sense of security, both psychological and physical. In their own words, these old people describe a physical and social environment in which basic security needs of human beings are met. Old people, like all other Cubans, benefit from the fundamental reorganisation and provision of services wrought by the socialist Revolution. At the micro-spatial scale of home and neighbourhood, a number of conditions exist which enhance the quality of life of old people.

Safety   The old people interviewed felt respected in their neighbourhoods. Day or night, they are not afraid to be on the streets of their neighbourhood. Capturing the feelings of many, one old woman said, ''My neighbourhood is very good, it is tranquil, I know everyone and everyone knows me...we are like a big family. There is nothing to be afraid of.'' One old man, when asked how he felt about walking on the streets, was puzzled and replied, ''I often go out to run errands and never have any problems.'' Two older women reiterated the thoughts of those who have poor health. One felt ''no fear of walking in the streets but I can't walk more than a block because I am weak and afraid of falling.'' The other responded that she ''feels fine on the streets, but for health reasons I am not on the streets after dark...I'm not afraid of anything; it's just that I can't see very well without much light and might fall.'' Three individuals did comment that they were afraid of the dark and didn't like being alone at night regardless of where they were. But for Cuban old people the personal vulnerability and fear associated with movement on the streets which drastically curtails the physical mobility of the elderly in many of the larger cities in western industrialised societies is, for the most part, a memory of another time.

Home Space   Home space is an individual's personal territory.

It is a bounded space, a place of privacy, a place to be oneself, a place where an individual can imprint his life experience and regulate his social interaction. It is that place where memory, special objects and loved ones are, if not physically, at least psychologically near. The interview sites, in the homes and apartments of older people, introduced the researchers to this special realm of the respondents' private selves. The meaning of this place to their sense of self and indirectly to the quality of their lives emerges not only from our observations but also through their own words and activities.

What is the economic relationship between the respondents and their home space? For the most part, the pattern is similar in both study areas with the majority of people being home owners. For the others, the rents are inexpensive and are set at ten per cent of the total family income. Regardless, whether an old person owns or rents his home, it is that private space where an individual's existential experience can be articulated. In their homes, the old interviewees pursued house maintenance activities along with other meaningful hobbies. Many old women sewed in their free time while others worked in their small gardens. Work in the garden not only keeps the older person outside but also occupies much leisure time. One old gentleman had fenced in part of the backyard in which he raises goats and chickens. Moreover, he grows a spice, *ajo de la montagne*, a species of onion which augments the flavour of any cooked dish. Banana plants grow next to his work shed. The animals were in excellent condition and he stated proudly that it takes a great deal of time and hard work to maintain them. While it occupies much of his leisure time, he raises these animals as an additional source of food. Piles of perfect miniature sea shells in a myriad of colours are scattered over the backyard patio. His wife creates "genre" scenes of everyday life using the colourful shells instead of paints, pastels or other media more common elsewhere. These shell paintings are sold to tourists.

Most of the old interviewees do not cultivate a garden in the same manner as this gentleman, but it would be negligent to ignore the garden as a place to potter. A number of individuals without yards had created plant gardens on their balconies. One old woman mentioned that she loves her plants and that she uses her balcony with her plant garden as a place to sit and rest in the afternoons and also as a comfortable and peaceful place to chat with her friends. One seventy-five year old man simply stated, "I work in the garden to be outside. I work slowly because of my health...At my age it is proper work for an old man."

Their homes are places where the old people can gather with family and friends. Because of the warm climate and tropical architecture much visiting occurs outside on the front balcony or patio. Another factor which probably encourages the use of outside areas for entertaining and being with others is that the space available in homes must be shared with other family members.

Old people in Cuba did not appear to concentrate on the maintenance of their home space as an end in itself. This could be the result of a number of factors:

1. Private property which the old person can maintain, enhance and sell for a profit no longer exists in Cuba. The property, in this case the home of the old person, is respected as his, and on the death of this individual, that of his family, if the family is living in the home. If no family member survives the old person or continues to live in the house, it becomes the property of the state.
2. The availability of unlimited consumer items to cultivate a competitive home decorator market no longer exists in Cuba.
3. Construction materials, such as cement and paint, are rationed and not always easy to acquire. Those wishing to remodel or renovate their homes must apply to *Poder Local* (since January, 1977 these functions are now assumed by *Poder Popular*) for construction materials.
4. The ideological orientation of the society is not to the individual but to the collective. For example, fewer home decorator consumer goods are available because the limited foreign exchange is being spent on the software (polyclinics) and the hardware (industrial equipment) necessary for the development of Cuba.
5. Cubans spend a significant amount of time outside their home working, and in their neighbourhoods participating in

the activities of both the Committees for the Defence of the Revolution (CDR) and the Federation of Cuban Women (FMC).

What are the dwellings of the old people like as places in which to live? The building material used for the construction of all the homes is plaster. During the interviews, it was noted that the walls and ceilings in two of the houses are in a state of deterioration. Two more houses have walls which are visibly cracked. In the rest of the units throughout the study areas, the walls, ceilings, and floors are in good condition. Cosmetically, at least seven of the houses needed painting to lighten and freshen up the interior. In the eyes of the old interviewees, thirteen homes need to be repainted. The comments of three old people summarize the situation of the majority. "The apartment is going to be painted outside but it has been nineteen years since my flat was painted. I am embarrassed that it has been so long and now, well, I simply can't afford it." Another couple emphasized that they are "very satisfied with their home although it needs to be painted." All conceded "paint cost a lot and was not easy to get."

All the residential units except two have their own complete bathrooms. Both are located in homes in study area 1 and appear to be the result of two different situations. One house is about to be extensively renovated and the other is an old servants' quarters which has no separate bathroom. The old woman who continues to live in the servants' quarters of an old mansion converted into a primary school, uses the school's showers and bathroom facilities.

One-half of the old people indicated that they did not have a telephone; although all commented that they could use their neighbour's telephone with no difficulty. To the old people, the importance of the telephone as a communication device to facilitate continuing contact with old friends and relatives, cannot be underestimated. It also provides immediate access to emergency services.

Radio and television provide critical sources of information and entertainment for all old people, but particularly, for those less able to interact with various societal organizations and institutions because of poor health and other factors.

While it appears that a number of old respondents do not have televisions, four are, in fact, owners of old American television sets that are broken. (The United States' economic blockade against Cuba prevented the importation of American made parts for all the American consumer products in Cuba. This has created a significant problem for the Cuban people, since Havana, as an American colony, was constructed with an infrastructure based upon American goods which, after the revolution in 1959, could not be replaced.)

All households have their own kitchen facilities, in which gas is used for cooking by the majority. While all households have a stove (burners) for food preparation, twelve have ovens. Sixteen of the twenty households have refrigerators. Food blenders and washing machines are not widely distributed.[5] Laundry is washed by hand or taken to one of the nine laundry facilities located in the area.

Relations with Neighbours The following rather typical quotations describe the role of neighbours and neighbouring within the lives of the old respondents.

...well, I see my neighbours often, almost daily, and certainly at the meetings of the CDR and the FMC. It seems that if I haven't seen one of my neighbours for a few days, we tend to spend hours catching up. There is so much to talk about. I keep my door open when my neighbours' children are in the street so that I can watch them. You know I have been watching them grow up. I know when my neighbours are home since I know most of their work schedules, and of course, I know those who are retired like myself. Also, I can tell when they are in because I can see the windows open, see lights, or hear voices. I know that my neighbours would help me if I needed it—that they would run any necessary errands for me.

...I go to the synagogue with my neighbour. If any of my neighbours are away, I water their plants and generally look after things. I occasionally pay the light bill for our apartments when no one is home and we settle up later. I know that they would help me if I needed any little thing like getting to the doctor.

...we help each other...we borrow things from each other—sugar, salt, eggs and other *boberias* (little things). My door is always open to them.

...my neighbours always pick up *Bohemia* (a popular Cuban magazine) and other reading material which they share with me.
...I go and visit with my neighbours when I have nothing to do or when I feel that I want to talk.
...once in a while I look after the children of my neighbours when their parents cannot be home immediately after work.

...we work together each Sunday morning to clean up our neighbourhood. We sweep the sidewalks and pick up any garbage.

...oh, my neighbours are welcome to use my telephone whenever they want...the door is always open.

...my neighbour's daughter does my hair.

...my neighbour's refrigerator is broken so she keeps perishable goods here.

...we feel that all of our neighbours would help us if we needed it. We could expect help in any way except economically...we are all concerned with what happens to each other and help each other mutually. For example, since I am a retired pharmacist I give one neighbour her daily injection. Our neighbours know we have applied to leave Cuba to join our only daughter and her family in El Salvador. No one is hostile to us choosing to leave. Although we want to be with our daughter, we will miss Cuba because it is so familiar; it is our country; and we will miss our relatives and our friends.

...everyone in our building has a television; however, if it should be broken they are welcome to come and watch TV in our house.

...when my son, who was living in Miami with his family, died seven years ago, all my neighbours, everyone, came and paid their respects. People were very supportive.

...my next door neighbour has a very old mother so if she is going out she lets me know so that I can look in on her.

...we all talk and exchange news at the *bodega*.

...we get together for coffee and chat.

...I have lived next door to one family for thirty-four years. Their four children were like my own but they left Cuba at the time of the revolution. We miss them but keep up somewhat through corresponding...oh, it has been difficult for their mother. She misses them so much. I see many of my neighbours every day when I am out. We stop and chat but we don't visit all day because each person has work to do at home. I know when my neighbours are home, because I know the schedule of those who are retired and don't work, and the hours of those who work. My neighbours will help me if I need help. They will share their telephone; drive me somewhere in their cars. If someone needs help the neighbours will try to do their best and so will I.

Old people, like their neighbours, have many interests. In Cuba today, museums, parks and beaches are easily accessible and free to all. Movies are inexpensive and those interested can easily attend a less crowded matinee performance. However, many of the elderly commented that their television is their source of information and recreation. Many of them read *Granma*, the daily Communist Party newspaper, and at least one of a number of Cuban magazines like *Bohemia* which can be purchased locally at a minimal cost.

For old people living on a pension, dining out in one of Havana's many restaurants is expensive, even prohibitive. None of the old respondents viewed joining friends and family for dinner in a restaurant as a recreational alternative. Most of the elderly had not taken a vacation since they retired for they have neither the money nor an organized opportunity to do so.

While the majority of the old interviewees consider themselves Roman Catholic, only one-third attend church at all. Churches are open and easily accessible; however, the Church is no longer a center of social interaction and activity. Much of the focus of activity today in Cuba is at the neighbourhood level in the mass organizations.

Mass organizations in the Neighbourhoods—the Committees for the Defence of the Revolution and the Federation of Cuban Women.

Retired Cubans can channel their skills and energies into the work of the Committees for the Defence of the Revolution (CDR) and the Federation of Cuban Woman (FMC), both of which operate at the smallest scale of spatial organization in Cuban society, the urban block. On the block, the CDR and FMC are headquartered in a neighbour's home. These organizations are indispensable to the functioning of socialist Cuba. Since the CDRs and the FMC are located in every neighbourhood, they have the ability to reach into every Cuban's home and confront old ideas, superstitions and prejudices. Many neighbours with varying levels of commitment and capacity can be incorporated into the myriad of tasks attended to by these organizations. In addition, families as a whole can share in the activities of both groups.

The participation of old people guarantees them a meaningful role in Cuban society along with continued contact with others. Their existence at the neighbourhood level prevents the growth of that group of isolated elderly so common in other countries. It is not possible to remain barred behind locked doors, defenceless and poor in a Cuban neighbourhood. Members of the CDR and FMC know if anyone is alone and if help is needed. They not only offer psychological and physical support as neighbours, but also refer the individual to special agencies for assistance.

One-half of the old interviewees are members of the CDR, whereas, approximately one-third of the old women are members of the FMC. In both cases, this is less than the national statistics which indicate that 80 per cent of Cuban women over 14 years are active in the FMC. As an example of the role an older person can play, one seventy-one year old man, honoured as an outstanding member of the CDR, describes his involvement in his block committee.

"I participate in all the activities of the CDR. Each week there is something to be done. I am responsible for collecting primary materials from my neighbours so that this material can be recycled. It saves Cuba a great deal of money. I am also working on a neighbourhood census to determine where we are losing and wasting water. We are trying to solve our water shortage. Also, every month, I attend a study circle. And, even at my age, I still take part in guard duty. Whenever there is a national holiday or special event, I participate in the block mobilization and celebration. I also work voluntarily in the neighbourhood butcher shop to help out.''

While a number of older people choose not to participate as *cederistas* (CDRs) or *federistas* (FMCs) they often share in their neighbourhood organizations' preparations for national celebrations and special activities. As new patterns of commitment and involvement are established in revolutionary Cuba, the new generations of old people will most likely be more active since their experience and orientation, like that of the rest of the population, will be very different.

Family Life

A complex support relationship, whether from a sense of duty, social pressure, or affection exists among older people, their adult children, and their grandchildren. Family members offer support ranging from money, household chores, shopping, transportation, care during illness, and most important, love and companionship. Obviously, much of this assistance is dependent upon propinquity. Approximately one-half of the old respondents live with their spouses or with their spouses and children in a multi-generational family where they participate actively in the running of the home and the care of grandchildren. The majority of those not living with their children have daily contact, or at least, several varied contacts or communications a week with their children. The family life of these old people is reciprocal, intense and very active.

There are those who have children living outside of Cuba. While approximately one-third of the interviewees have some of their children living abroad, most continue to have at least one child in Cuba. Needless to say, the separation of parents from children and grandchildren has caused much personal anguish. For the most part, these relatives chose to leave Cuba soon after the revolution and relocated primarily in the United States; however, a few went to Central American Republics where they found work with large American corporations.

The importance of family is revealed not only by the quantity and quality of interactions occurring between old people and their adult children but also through their own words. The old respondents articulated the meaning of 'family' and made it very clear that no other human relationships replaced that of family bonds regardless of the support provided by the society outside the home. "Those who have family are not alone" is the predominant sentiment expressed. Human problems endemic to ageing, such as widowhood and loss of relatives and friends through death, are viewed as struggles that are mitigated by the love and support of family members. As one old woman emphasized, "one's tragedies and how one faces them depends on one's family situation." Another augmented this sentiment by her comment, "In Cuba we get so much help that if, on top of this help (polyclinic etc.), we have our families, we are fine. If old people have their families, they don't feel alone or lonely; they have loved ones to help resolve any difficulties."

Relations with children and grandchildren consume a great deal of the older person's time and energy. One elderly man mentioned that he was able to help his daughter by walking his grandchildren to school each morning and each afternoon returning to their school to pick them up. Then they usually go to his house to watch some of the late afternoon children's programmes on television. One elderly woman while describing a typical day depicted herself as family oriented.

"My relationship with my children is good. Each day for my daily outing I walk over to the house of my daughter. I regularly eat my meals with them. Each day we visit, eat together and shop together. My three grandchildren live for me. They are adolescents and are at school. In the afternoon, they stop by my house on their way home from school."

Another old woman's grandchildren are home each weekend since they are *becados* or scholarship students at two secondary schools in Havana. She commented, "I worry a great deal about dinner and what I can prepare that is good and different for them. You know, we have a magnificent relationship for their mother has always worked. I really raised them."

A seventy-eight year old woman described her life with her multi-generational family. She lives with her daughter, son-in-law and two grandchildren.

"My relationship with my children is divine. They take care of me. My daughter works across the street in the *bodega*. Whenever I am bored I go across the street and sit. I can watch her work and also visit with neighbours. I help in the house particularly with meals because it seems like we all eat at different times. My grandchildren have such varied activities and operate on different schedules that I give them their major meals at different times. My grandchildren and I have an excellent relationship. There is nothing they wouldn't do for me. I am so proud of them—of all my family."

The form and quantity of parent-adult child interactions, however idiosyncratic and complicated, suggest some patterns. Children appear to provide:

1.   a multi-generational setting where the old person continues to feel useful. They actively participate in the running of the house and the raising of the grandchildren. Because of their pensions, old people contribute to the financial solvency of the family. They are not reduced to mere dependence.

2.   companionship and psychological support. The adult child acts as both a confidant and companion.

3.   transportation. The family helps the older person use the ubiquitous public transportation system.

4.   access to basic services. Although the homes of the old respondents are located near basic services, children and grandchildren constantly run various errands, such as, picking up prescriptions, buying magazines, and helping with specialty shopping.

5.   security during sickness. All the old interviewees feel that their children will help them through an illness. If they do not have children, the respondents are confident that they can rely on other family members, such as, siblings, nieces and

nephews for care and assistance.

6.   an opportunity to assume the role of a grandparent. Old people respond enthusiastically to this rewarding role. The emotional involvement should not be underestimated as a fulfilling factor in their lives. The bond between grandparent and grandchild is built through family ties, love, trust and tolerance. Grandchildren bring both a memory of times past and a hope for the future. They are an extension of self who will live in a world the grandparent will never know.

7.   occasions to spend special holidays, birthdays, and anniversaries with the family. In addition to these special days, Sunday seems to be a 'family' day when older parents, children and grandchildren come together to visit.

However, family life is changing in Cuba for new norms, such as those expressed in the Family Code, suggest a new concept of family life. Women are working, children are in school and family members are involved in volunteer work in the countryside. The traditional role of the elder parent is also changing. However, in whatever manner old people maintain relations with their families, they do so with a sense of dignity and self-respect. Families are not beset by the need to provide the necessities of life for their old parents. The responsibility of the younger family members is that of affection and emotional support.

Work, Income and Pensions

In Cuba retirement at age 55 for women and age 60 for men is voluntary. Forced retirement, whether insidious or explicit, is not a part of the older Cuban's experience as it is for the elderly in many western industrial countries. The Ministry of Labour is developing a method by which older workers will be able to participate in the production process according to their desire and ability. For example, older workers, instead of retiring, may decide that they have the energy to work three days a week. This would allow them to maintain their contact with work centres and work peers, and at the same time, give them a mechanism by which they continue to contribute to the nation's productivity. Thus older people retain their self respect and their value to society.

The present Cuban government guarantees old people a pension upon retirement. At this time, Cuba's pension policy is being re-evaluated by the Ministry of Labour. In the meantime, pensions are fifty percent of one's previous income, and in the case where the individual's past income was very low one will receive the minimum guaranteed pension of 60 pesos a month. The pensions of the interviewees range from 60 to 100 pesos a month. On the whole, these Cuban old people find their retirement income is not satisfactory. 'It doesn't reach to the end of the month' is the ubiquitous comment of most of the elderly. The old ones have difficulty replacing consumer items because of their cost. In addition, medicine, taxis and entertainment are, in general, considered expensive. However, unlike their age peers in other societies, they do not have to purchase the necessities of life through the private market. In addition to free health care, housing is inexpensive and if an elderly individual pays rent it is approximately 10 percent of his income. Food and some items of clothing are rationed and sold at low prices so that it is available to everyone. If any population group, children, pregnant women, old people, and persons with special diets, has a greater need for a commodity, it receives an additional quantity on the *libreta* or ration card.

Health care

Those interviewed in Cuba were unanimously pleased with the changes in the health care system initiated by the revolution. Representative of the responses was the comment "it is a magnificent system." All the old people interviewed were within easy walking distance or a five minute bus ride from both a polyclinic and a dental clinic. It is at the polyclinic that the old respondents, their families, and their neighbours receive complete out-patient care.

Dr. Raul Diaz Padrón, Director of Polyclinic Pasteur, describes the organisation and delivery of care to those within the polyclinic service area. He comments that the polyclinic's approach to health care is environmental. That is to say, to maintain an individual in optimal health is to be concerned with the biological, psychological, social and environmental problems in a person's life.

Individuals and their families have access to a medical team—a pediatrician, an internist, an obstetrician-gynaecologist, and a nurse—who work in a particular geographical section of the polyclinic service area.[6] All people see the same doctor or medical team whenever they visit the polyclinic. People, young and old, are not only able to establish a degree of intimacy with their doctor but also at the same time be assured of continuity of care. This out-patient care is supplemented by home visits from one's physician under the polyclinic's programme of *dispensarizada*, which monitors the health status of selected population groups. This home care is available for those under one and over sixty-five years of age, and those suffering from chronic and communicable diseases and acute pathologies. Moreover, if there is a problem specific to a polyclinic's service area, it can be addressed under this programme. In addition, a psychiatrist, a psychologist, a social worker, and a sanitary engineer are available to work on any defined needs within the service area.[7]

It is from the polyclinic that old people are referred to more specialised services. If an emergency occurs, the respondents state that they would go either to the emergency room of a hospital or telephone and wait for a visit from a doctor who staffs an emergency room. Medicines can be purchased at nationally fixed prices in neighbourhood pharmacies, but medicines are often relatively expensive for those living on a retirement income. However, those with income below a mimimum of 25 pesos per person in the family receive free medicine from social assistance.[8]

The old people feel that they have no difficulty obtaining access to medical care or that they have any reason to be displeased with the quality of care they receive. One elderly man mentioned that he and his wife "have no problems getting medical care at the polyclinic and that we leave the polyclinic satisfied, having enjoyed good service." Most agree that all their health needs are being taken care of. This point was emphasised by one elderly man in his statement: "the polyclinic offers very good services and won't let us let our health go."

Institutional care

Factors, such as, poor health, living alone, inability to maintain one's home and the need for companionship may motivate an old person to enter a home for the aged. In Cuba, the provision of services within these homes is the responsibility of the government. All medical and dental care, chiropody, physical therapy, medical aids, food, shelter, clothing, toilet articles, barber and beautician services, and recreation are provided at no cost to the residents. Furthermore, the pensions of the old residents are theirs to be put in the bank or spent in any manner they wish. Pensions are not usurped by the home to pay for costs, but quite to the contrary, provide income so that old people can purchase 'those little things that matter.' Some examples might be coffee at a baseball game, lunch with a friend, a taxi to a friend or relative's home, books, or a pair of stockings.

The Cubans are devoting increasing resources to homes for old people. There are currently 48 old age homes in Cuba. Some 44 additional old age homes are being built, to be completed by 1980. These homes are planned within the guidelines of the Ministry of Public Health where the focus tends to be on the needs of the elderly largely as patients. While such homes may be the most efficient and least expensive ways of providing high quality, specialised care for the elderly with extensive needs, they separate old people from their communities.

Whether Cuba's elderly want especially contained environments like these is open to question. This research indicates they may prefer to live out their years in neighbourhoods dotted with familiar friends, and favourite locales. Furthermore, in so far as the Cubans' national goals include integrating people of various ages, sexes, races and backgrounds into one socialist society—old age homes may tend to isolate rather than incorporate the elderly into this process.

The Funeral

In some western industrial societies the cliché is—old people can't afford to die. Inability to pay for one's funeral and the fear of leaving such bills to others is yet another insecurity resulting from the financial insolvency of the elderly. However, in Cuba, the exploitation of the funeral industry has been stopped. Funerals are provided for by the state through government owned and operated funeral homes.

All people grow old. As an old person, one shares some common experiences with one's elderly peers. Widowhood, the death of friends and relatives are losses suffered by all old people. Furthermore, changes in one's health and in one's relationships to the productive process affects all old people's definition of self. However, the old people of socialist Cuba in the two neighbourhoods studied, do not share the poverty, and the physical and psychological insecurity of the majority of old people in western industrialised societies.

REFERENCES

1.   The data for this article is based on numerous discussions with public officials, providers of services and representatives of mass organisations. In addition, a number of months was spent observing and participating in all the activities of three homes for old people. I then worked outside of the ,institutional settings and conducted twenty three hour interviews with old people living in two neighbourhoods within the service area of Pasteur Polyclinic. Furthermore, I am not trying to argue that the interviews are based on an acceptable, statistical sample from which concrete generalisation can be made. Rather I attempted to reduce bias and arbitrariness by selecting a random number of old people to interview in each study area. The polyclinic has a record organised by block of persons over 65 years of age who attend the polyclinic. Because of the organisation of Cuban society, it is the exception that would not be registered and receiving health care through the polyclinic. Of the 319 old people residing in study area 1, 261 or 82 percent were registered with the polyclinic. Correspondingly, of the 379 old people living in study area two, 358 or 94 percent were registered with the polyclinic. I sequentially sampled the polyclinic record to generate a list of 20 persons in each area. From this list we interviewed 10 persons in each neighbourhood.
2.   Carolee Bengelsdorf, 'A Large School of Government,' *Cuba Review* Vol. VI, No. 3 September, 1976, pp. 3-18.
3.   Interview with Dr. Carlos Font Pupo, National Director of Social Assistance, Ministry of Public Health, and Juana Monterde Ricardo in charge of Social Services, Ministry of Public Health, September, 1976.

4.   For a discussion of Santería see Alice Hagelman 'Santería in the Black Experience,' *Cuba Review*, Vol. II, No. 6, January 1973, p. 16; Fernando Ortiz, *Los Bailes y El Teatro de Los Negros en el Folklore de Cuba*, Habana, Ediciones Cardenas y Cia, 1951, p. 197; and Wyatt MacGaffey and Clifford R. Barnett, *Cuba Its People, Its Society, Its Culture*, New Haven, Conn., Human Relations Area Files, Inc., 1962, p. 206.

5.   The following list of prices for selected household appliances was collected during numerous browsing marathons in various government department stores in Havana during November 1976,

Radio-	80-100 pesos	Stove-	250 pesos
Television-	650 pesos	Hot Plate-	80 pesos
Record Player-	450 pesos	Blender-	100 pesos
Refrigerator-		Washing machine-	230 pesos
small (Cuban)	650 pesos	Sewing Machine	160-250 pesos
large (USSR)	850 pesos		

(1 peso = US$1 approx)

It is my understanding that scarce electrical appliances are distributed to the general population through work centres. CTC (Confederation of Cuban Workers) locals situated in any work centre with at least twenty-five workers. Workers, eligible to purchase these goods through the department stores and other retail outlets, are selected or approved by their work peers in workers' assemblies. The criteria used by the workers or an elected committee of workers, depending on the size of the workcentre, to evaluate the request of a worker for a consumer item are the following:

   1) need
   2) amount of volunteer work performed
   3) attitude and contribution to the workcentre
   4) rate of absenteeism
   5) educational development and advancement

6.   In Cuba, gerontology and geriatrics is not available as a course in medical schools, or university departments of sociology and psychology.

7.   Polyclinic Pasteur offers services to approximately 36,229 area residents. During 1976, the polyclinic doctor/patient ratio was as follows:
   one pediatrician to 1000-1200 persons under 15 years of age
   one internist to 2000-2500 persons over 15 years of age
   one ob-gyn to 2000-2500 women over 15 years of age

Furthermore, these ratios are amended as experience and need dictates. Polyclinics which are not teaching polyclinics where doctors are also studying employ the doctor/patient ratios of:
   one pediatrician to 2000-2300 persons under 15 years of age
   one internist to 3500-4000 persons over 15 years of age
   one ob-gyn to 3500-4000 women over 15 years of age

8.   Interview with Marina Pujot, Social Worker for Polyclinic Pasteur, December, 1976. Furthermore, *Principales Leyes y Resoluciones De La Seguridad Social 1959-1971* states that the quantity of retirement income is determined by the following rules:

1) for the first 25 years of service one retires at 50 percent of one's average income calculated over the individual's last five years of effective service.

2) for each year of service in excess of 25 years of service, one's retirement income is augmented by 1 percent a year for workers in category 2. Category 1 is work in normal conditions while category 2 is work in dangerous and noxious conditions.

The law also states that no individual should receive a retirement income of less than 38 pesos a month or more than 250 pesos a month. By 1976, the minimum retirement income had been raised to 60 pesos a month.

Social security is presently reevaluating the adequacy of the present retirement income.

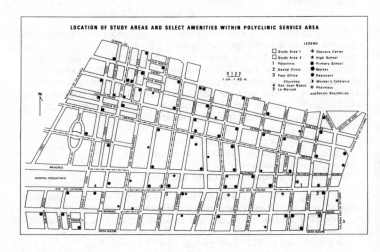

LOCATION OF STUDY AREAS AND SELECT AMENITIES WITHIN POLYCLINIC SERVICE AREA

Women & Family in Cuba

Cynthia Cockburn

On February 14, 1975 the Cuban Council of Ministers enacted Law No. 1289, El Codigo de Familia—*The Family Code*. Besides its importance in ending once and for all the concept of bastardy—'all children are born equal'—it was significant for devising juridical norms for relations between husband and wife, parents and children.

Some months later the First Congress of the Cuban Communist Party passed a resolution on the equality of women. Thesis and Resolution were published in 1976 under the title *Sobre el Pleno Ejercicio de la Igualidad de la Mujer*—referred to below as *Women's Equality*.

This essay discusses the two documents in the context of the situation of women in Cuba in 1975.

A historical process

Revolutionary Cuba is a country where a rapid pace of change is the normal and expected way of life; but the year 1975 was one of surpassing political activity. The new constitution was drafted and discussed; the electoral system of People's Power was in trial operation in Matanzas Province; a new Five Year Plan was in the making; the Family Code reached the statute book; and the first national Congress of the Communist

Party was called. The 'woman question' is a thread that can be traced in the themes of all these documents and discussions. The Constitution proclaimed 'women will enjoy equal economic, political and social rights with men' (Article 43). In the new socialist legality gradually being constructed to replace the exploitative or irrelevant laws of the imperialist bourgeoisie the Family Code was a key component. And the First Congress of the CP debated the progress of women toward equality. It was a moment for reviewing the achievements and shortfalls of the Revolution in this as in other fields.

The position of women in Cuba in 1975 or 1976 was incomparably better than in 1958 or years before. Under the old laws women had featured less in their own right than as the property or appendages of men. In the peasant and working-class poverty of the pre-Revolutionary period hundreds of thousands of women lived a life of domestic misery. Of those who worked outside the home many were maids to the bourgeoisie, many more were prostitutes whose clientele were American armed forces and tourists. Within Cuban society 'machismo', characteristic of all pre-Revolutionary Latin America, pervaded the culture. In urban bourgeois and neo-colonial circles women were sexual objects, valued for their decorative appearance and skills of household management and little else. Women had little control of the course of their own lives; the powerful Catholic Church forbade contraception.

Transforming bourgeois into socialist *human* relations was arguably a more difficult task than transforming property and *production* relations (and it was not unrelated). Women however had been in the forefront of the struggle against imperialism. Women were among those who attacked the Moncada Barracks in 1953. They were active in the 26 July Movement, organising resistance in the cities, and many were imprisoned and tortured. A handful fought in the Sierra with the Rebel Army. The prospect for Cuban women therefore was as much improved as the prospect for the working class of Cuba from the moment the Rebel Army entered Havana in January 1959.

When the Cuban Revolution affirmed its socialist character in May 1961 the rights of women began to be consciously sought and formally established. The Federation of Cuban Women (FMC) was set up in 1960. The dismantling of capitalism itself removed many forms of female exploitation. There was no more advertising: female sexuality would no longer be used to sell products. (This was something I enjoyed about Cuba perhaps more than anything else: a holiday from being abused on posters and hoardings, in cinema and TV commercials.) In a country with no unemployment there is no female under-employment: many women have gone out to work, many more are wanted at work. The principle of day nursery provision in Cuba is that it must be *free*. 'Society profits from the work of every woman' Fidel Castro said in a speech in 1966. 'It profits to the same degree that permits women to receive full wages, without having to utilise a part to pay expenses such as a day nursery.' Abortion too, is free and available.

Where do we stand?

The Congress paper on *Women's Equality,* while it confirmed dramatic progress since 1959, was toughly self-critical. Concern was voiced over persistent discrimination and inequality of many kinds in practice, that socialist principle had not yet had time to erase. Many aspects of women's lives were touched on. The paper urged 'an eradication of the tendency to make women an object of exhibition as is current in capitalist society' and also touched lightly on sexual practice: 'socialist moral principles are identical for all citizens and so it is unjust to apply different criteria in evaluating men and women and in analysing the so-called "moral problems" in sexual relationships.' The sexual practices of a man and a woman, who may have sex with whom, who has responsibility for whom, should be judged by the same values.

The main focus of the paper however was on *women and work*. Women, though half the population, were only a quarter of the workforce. The figure of 600,000 women in work outside the home was considered insufficient—both because the labour power of those still at home was needed by society in industrial, service and agricultural jobs, and because women at home were bound to be cut off to some extent from participation in the Revolution. Many young women were dropping out of work when children were born, in spite of the Maternity Law (giving paid rest periods for childbirth) and Resolutions Nos. 47 and 48 of the Ministry of Labour (1968) which had aimed to guarantee equality of opportunity for women in jobs and protect them from unsuitable occupations. Second, a survey of 250 working women showed that, since they were also still heavily involved in domestic activities, their average working week ("double shift") amounted to 88 hours, no less. Women were working between 11 and 12 hours a day even at weekends "because of the build-up of housework." Although a further 400 day nurseries were promised in the forthcoming Plan period, only 654 existed in 1975, serving 48,000 families. The remaining working mothers depended on relatives and neighbours to look after their pre-school children, mainly the women of an older generation. (The decision to delay the building and staffing of nurseries was a painful economic choice. The Revolution had to give priority to secondary and primary education.)

At work, while women were pre-eminent in administrative work (67.5%) and represented about half the technical and service workers, they were a mere 12% of production workers (obreros). Data from the 1970 Population Census confirmed that an important cause of the low entry of women into production jobs was lack of technical qualification—someting that educational plans would with time put right. However, of those in the paid workforce, women represented only 15% of managers (dirigentes). This failure of women to get promotion or appointments to more skilled and responsible jobs was *not* something that could be laid at the door of education. Working women on the whole could be shown to be marginally better qualified than male workers (Central de Trabajadores de Cuba Survey 1974). Much had to be due to remaining "discrimination and prejudice". The Resolution called for a drive to awaken the consciousness of both men and women on this issue.

The role of women in political activity was also less than equal to that of men. Only 13.2% of the membership of the Communist Party were women. Among the office holders (dirigentes) of the Party at local level, while women represented 22% in the Young Communists (UJC), by the time they reached the Party proper they were no more than 2.9%.

The life of a working mother in Cuba (and this is my own observation) leaves little time for sleep. It begins with housework and child-care, extends to an uncompromising paid job (and people give extraordinary amounts of their time and energy to their work in Cuba as a conscious effort for the Revolution), and includes an expectation that she will attend evening courses and political meetings of mass and social organisations. Then, between 1974 and 1976, the new system of local electoral representation known as People's Power was introduced. This involved the election of scores of thousands of delegates. Again there was a call for women to come forward and play a full and proper part, as organisers, electors and candidates. Reading this appeal it is impossible, as an observer, not to feel: very well, but now surely is the time to examine coolly the question of *who does the domestic work in Cuba*. The question did in fact become an issue after the experimental elections in Matanzas Province.

Family and Housework

In the poll for the assemblies of People's Power in Matanzas Province few women were returned. At municipal level only 7% of candidates had been women; fewer, a mere 3%, got elected. They did a little better at regional level. It was disappointing. Fidel Castro said in a speech afterwards, "The result demonstrates just how women still suffer from discrimination and inequality and how we are still culturally backward, how in the corners of our consciousness live on old habits out of the past."[1]

After the elections, in April 1975, a survey of 635 men and women was made in Matanzas province to investigate the reasons for the poor performance of women. The reason most commonly cited for not voting for a woman was "the responsibility women have for domestic work and care of husband and children". People still spontaneously think "woman cares for man and child" rather than "people look after each other".

It is in the light of these facts that the Cuban *Family Code* takes on such importance, because it deals boldly with the nature of marriage and the sharing of responsibilities for home and child-care. The equality of women is established in the Code under several different titles. First, she has equal property rights. The economic base of matrimony in Cuba now is "the joint property of goods". Salaries, wages, pension and other income obtained by husband and wife during marriage belong to both, and so does anything bought with this income, with few exceptions. Individually they may own goods acquired before their marriage or from inheritance, though the right to hold·or inherit private property is of course strictly limited by the Constitution. The legal concept of the family as a system for ownership and inheritance, that gives a livelihood to so many lawyers in capitalist countries, is a thing of the past.

Secondly, a woman has equal rights and no more than equal duties in the home. "Both partners must care for the family they have created and each must cooperate with the other in the education, upbringing and guidance of the children according to the principles of socialist morality. They must participate, to the extent of their capacity or possibilities, in the running of the home, and cooperate so that it will develop in the best possible way." (Article 26)

"The partners must help meet the needs of the family they have created with their marriage, each according to his or her ability and financial status. However, if one of them only contributes by working at home and caring for the children, the other partner must contribute to this support alone, *without prejudice to his duty of co-operating in the above-mentioned work and care.*" (Article 27) (The italics are added by me; the masculine possessive pronoun is that of the official translators of *Granma*. In Cuban Spanish it would not necessarily have been sexually-specific.)

"Both partners have the right to practise their profession or skill and they have the duty of helping each other and cooperating in order to make this possible and to study or improve their knowledge. However, they must always see to it that home life is organized in such a way that these activities are coordinated with their fulfilment of the obligations posed by this code." (Article 28)

Divorce is obtainable on equal grounds by men and

women and the over-riding formulation is liberal: "Divorce will take effect by common agreement or when the court determines that there are factors which have led the marriage to lose its meaning for the partners and for the children and thus for society as a whole" (Article 51).

Parental authority will normally be given to both parents over the children and both will remain responsible for supporting them. The court will decide with which they will live. A partner (man or woman) who doesn't have a paying job at the time of divorce may receive temporary alimony for his or her *own* support, from the other.

(This is quite apart from the question of alimony for support of childen and other dependents which is also dealt with at length in the Code, and which illustrates the allocation of responsibility for the welfare of non-earners in Cuba between state and family. I should perhaps add at this point that this does not set out to be a full review of the content of the *Code*. There are, for instance, long sections on guardianship of children and on the definition of kinship which I do not touch on here.)

The problem of housework/childcare as a constraint on women joining the paid labour force is thus a central preoccupation of both the *Code* and *Women's Equality*. The latter, apart from calling for a deep change of consciousness in both men and women, proposes many practical developments to help make women free to engage in work outside the home. They include: holiday and weekend playschemes for children; extending opening hours for laundrettes, shops, repair services, etc.; industrial developments in food manufacture, domestic labour-saving devices, non-iron fabrics etc.; extending gynaecological and childcare clinics to night-time hours; making more provision for part-time jobs, piece work to be done on an outwork basis, and a five-day week.

The Intentions for Men

British feminists with whom I have discussed these developments in Cuba have raised two questions. The first concerns the engagement of men in domestic work and child care. They point out that if men do not in reality take on, in as many cases as women do, the daytime care of their young children or of sick and old relatives, then the practical aids (sought in *Women's Equality*) such as extended shopping hours or industrial piece-work at home, will deepen rather than cure women's inequality because they will make it yet more feasible for her to carry on the double shift. The second shift will become less manual, less physically tiring, but it will remain every bit as demanding and constraining.

In *Women's Equality*, while men are urged to "take up their domestic responsibilities and recognise that manhood is not incompatible with the care of children", it is more often "all the family" that are called on to "help the woman". The new provisions are specified in many cases as assisting the woman (la mujer trabajadora) rather than *the man or woman* who cares for young children. If equality of the sexes is to become a reality overnight, many men would be obliged to leave paid work. Attitudes to production would need to change. People are already urged (in *Women's Equality*) to see that women are not penalised in *emulación*[2]—the thrust for better and better work performance—by their domestic tasks. But *emulación* would need to apply also to domestic work. The accolade of Labour Hero would need to reflect not only exceptional achievement out at work, but by men and women working at home and in the community too.

Women's Equality portrays domestic labour as unproductive and brutalising. Lenin is quoted: "thoroughly unproductive, nasty, dulling, brutalising and exhausting tasks". This is the way housework is typically characterised by men who are newly threatened with it. There is of course nothing intrinsically brutalising about domestic work. In fact most men and women recognise that life as the inmate of an institution where you *cannot* choose food and cook it yourself, decorate and repair, care for children, is the ultimate sterility. What is unsocial about housework is its privacy, lack of recognition and discriminatory allocation.

A necessary corollary to men engaging in more work inside the home is that more men should engage in 'caring' employment outside the home. As the economic situation allows for more community provision, will men take on the care of the sick and old? Will men, for instance, be trained and employed in the forthcoming 400 infant nurseries? At present such a suggestion is greeted with surprise and doubt—but things move fast in Cuba.

It is a hard fact that Cuba has been fighting and continues to face an economic struggle for survival: production has to be given priority. If men, who at present tend to be more highly qualified than women, fall back into part-time work to care for children they will release into the workforce women usually less qualified and skilled then themselves. It is only as nurseries become more abundant, women become more highly skilled and capable of economic production, as the humanising effects of socialist education of boys and girls begins to filter through and as threats to the economy are overcome that the ideal of equality of rights and duties in the home, prefigured in the *Family Code*, can begin to become a reality.

The Future of the Family

The second point raised by men and women here with whom I have discussed the *Family Code* has been the nature of the family in a socialist society. The arguments went something as follows:

The Code is prefaced by a definition of the family (and this means marriage) as "the elementary cell of society", "the centre for relations of common existence", meeting "deep-rooted human needs in the social field". In codifying the family the way it does, is there not a risk of enshrining it?

In capitalism the family has economic and ideological functions *for* capitalism and, because that mode of production is exploitative, such family functions are too. The family performs ideological and economic functions in socialism too, this is abundantly clear from the *Family Code*, but because the socialist mode of production is not oppressive neither do these functions oppress. On the other hand, there are characteristics of the family that are common to contemporary capitalist societies and the new Cuba. We all share a history of patriarchy. In both societies the private nature of family relations nurtures dependence and creates exclusiveness. This does not diminish as women become more educated and men and women more equal in marriage. The primary loyalty to the pair bond continues. Indeed in capitalist societies often the 'best' marriages are seen by those within them as providing mutual support in an alien or at least challenging world. We place mutual care very high in our list of priorities because we cannot rely on care, love and purpose existing in the long term outside the family home. In this way the nuclear family in capitalism *unfits* its members for co-operation in a wider political community. At worst, through the destructive power of sequestered and often disguised emotional relationships, as psychiatrists have shown, the family can destroy its members.

In the competitive and anarchic world of capitalism the individual needs the refuge the family represents and is obliged to pay the cost. In socialism, though, the world beyond the nuclear family home is more supportive and benign. Do personal relationships need to be codified? If they do, should not homosexual relationships and households be recognised? Is the nuclear family formalised in the Code not already made superfluous by Revolutionary developments in Cuba?

What it is important to remember, however, is that the institution of the family existed in Cuba—with out-dated and harmful assumptions embedded in it from Catholic and colonial days. Clearly it had to be reshaped, urgent modifications of principle and practice were needed. The *Family Code* spells out these new norms and it was welcomed by 98% of the people. It was widely discussed in all the political and mass organisations for many months before it became law.

It is also a fact that these very political and mass organisations engage the individual in Cuba in society outside the family, dilute the privatising effects of the family, to an extent it is difficult to imagine within our own society. Imagine for instance an organisation such as the FMC that involves more than 2 million housewives and other women in discussion and organisation around feminist issues. Imagine a system such as the network of Committees for the Defence of the Revolution and their rural equivalents which cover all Cuba, street by street, and in which most households participate, organising mutual help, mini-clinics, shared street cleaning, political discussion. Above all, the assumptions of the new generation are much more collective than those of their parents. A high proportion of children in Cuba are educated as weekly boarders in mixed schools in the countryside where they farm as well as study. Most children are active in the evenings and weekends as Pioneers, go on group holidays and so on. The adult, particularly the woman and mother of coming generations, is likely to be progressively less dependent on the marriage relationship for social existence and political expression.

In the same way that economics and land reform has developed toward socialism through successive pieces of legislation since 1959, so too the social structure given shape at present in the *Family Code* is likely to see continual development.[3]

REFERENCES

1. The president of the Federation of Cuban Women, Vilma Espin, said in an interview in *Granma* 29 Aug 1976: "The Party has been very careful to make clear that what occurred in the first experience of setting up organs of People's Power in Matanzas, when the percentage of women elected was minimal and the participation of women in general in the process leading up to the elections limited, must never happen again." The FMC redoubled their efforts in the weeks before the national elections. Unfortunately I do not have the local results but a hand count of the national Deputies shows women as around 20% of the total. There appear to be three out of forty-five in the Council of Ministers.
2. The term *emulación* is used in Cuba to mean not competition, but acknowledgement of one's own skills and achievements, of their value to the development of the Cuban Revolution, and a willingness to help others to learn.
3. This paper evolved in discussion with other women, some with first hand experience of Cuba, and active in the women's movement in Britain.

Fidel Castro's Report on Education, 1976

Summarized by Peter Griffiths

A SUMMARY OF ACHIEVEMENTS AND PROBLEMS

The Cuban government is at present having to face new kinds of problems as a result of the successful developments in education. After a period of great expansion in educational resources and in students' expectations of education it is having to recognise that money for education is not infinite. So, difficult decisions are having to be made on how best to distribute resources, at a time of increasing demand for Intermediate and Higher Education and how to face students whose expectations with regard to jobs it may be impossible to fulfil.

1976 was an important year for education in Cuba. For a start, there was the adoption of the Constitution of the Republic of Cuba, following a year of national discussions—at schools, workplaces, and public meetings—and a referendum.

On 30 August, the Ministry of Education described as the "best ever" the results at the end of the 1975/76 year, in Junior and Senior High Schools in the countryside, Vocational schools, schools for the training of Elementary School teachers, and the Polytechnic Institutes. So when, on 1 September 1976, Fidel Castro started to speak on education at the opening of the new school year at the inauguration of the General

Maximo Gomez Vocational School in Camagüey, it was no surprise when he set out some of these achievements—though he did not stop there. It was an important speech, for he gave a complete picture of the state of Cuban education. He described advances made and provided current facts and figures. But he also gave a frank analysis of some problems and outlined ways of solving them. What follows is a digest of the main issues raised in the speech. The whole text is to be found in English in *Granma* Weekly Review of 12 September 1976.

Fidel started with the three main indices that, *up till now*, have measured progress in Cuban education—attendance, drop out rates, and promotions.

School Attendance

6 - 12 year olds	98.5%
13 - 16 year olds	78.3%
	(cf: 74.9% in 1974/75)

A remnant of discrimination could be found in the figures for 13-16 years olds. In some areas non-attendance of girls was three times that of boys, and this was put down to girls being kept at home to do various domestic duties. Fidel made an appeal for the end of any residual attitudes that assumed education was not as important for girls as for boys.

Dropout Rates   (i.e. percentage of students who enrolled but were not on the particular course at its end).

	Completion	Dropout
Primary	98.0	2.0
Junior High	93.3	6.7
Senior High	96.6	3.4
Teacher Training	94.4	5.6
Technical/Professional	83.3	16.7
Adult Education	81.6	18.4

Promotions (i.e. percentage of students passing their grade examinations)

Primary	97.3
Junior High	96.1
Senior High	95.9
Technical/Professional	96.2
Teacher Training	99.7

Standards for promotion have risen. In the past, you could fail in two subjects in the grade and still pass. For 1975/6, students who failed in more than one subject were not allowed to pass. From 1977 every single subject will have to be passed. In spite of the increasingly high standards, there is an expansion of demand at every point in the education system beyond the primary stage (for instance, at present there are 700,000 students in Intermediate Education, and there will be about 1,000,000 by 1980). And this expansion has brought new problems.

In 1975/76, the total number of students in intermediate education (12-18 year olds) *increased* by over 100,000. Before 1959, the *total* number of students there was under 80,000. As the number of post primary students is growing rapidly still, there is a problem of providing facilities for them. A new building programme to provide 90 temporary schools to supplement the intermediate building programme has been instituted. Already it is impossible to send all students to Junior High Schools in the countryside or to polytechnic institutions and so some city children are being educated as day students— and more will have to be in future. More schools and polytechnics will be needed in the cities, too.

The huge expansion in number of graduates from Junior High Schools will not all be catered for in Senior High Schools. Most will have to go elsewhere for their specific work training; some will go into teacher training; some to polytechnics to train as technicians or skilled workers. Everyone will have a right to continuous education, but as there won't be enough places for all in Senior High Schools, there will be two ways of acquiring this education. One will be for the minority who will follow the "Normal Study Programme": this means they will be admitted to Senior High School, after some form of selection process, and educated in preparation for further study in Higher Education—that is, not in a specific form of production. For the majority, there will be 'Guided Studies' programmes, whereby workers, intermediate technicians etc. will have an opportunity to follow up their own specific interests through Adult Education courses so that in the long term Cuban society generally will benefit.

It will soon be impossible for all university graduates to be placed in the sort of work that they traditionally expect. Cuba has need of a specific number of teachers, doctors, engineers etc. and the time will come when Cuba has enough. A reserve will be added for the benefit of other countries—Castro mentioned specifically Angola's need for technicians—as clear an indication as you could find of the high priority placed on international solidarity by the Cuban government.

In Teacher Training, there has been a large growth in numbers and an increased standard of entry. In 1971 there were about 100,000 teachers in Cuba; in 1976, 150,000—that is 50% growth in 5 years. The teachers are better educated now too: standards of entry are being raised from Sixth Grade to Ninth and Twelfth Grade.

With regard to Adult Education, Castro referred to the overcoming of the problem of massive illiteracy (1 million adults in 1961) and spoke of the new campaign for adults launched by the Central Organisation of Cuban Trade Unions (CTC). This is the 'Fight for the Sixth Grade', i.e. an attempt to get *all* adults to achieve a Sixth Grade education. (Posters exhorting this are a familiar sight in Cuba.) In 1976 a further 140,000 workers, denied the opportunity previously, passed the Sixth Grade examinations.

The total number of students in Cuba at all levels is 3,320,000 (Autumn '76), that is, over a third of the population.

Educational expenditure is now 961 million pesos. In 1958 before the Revolution it amounted to 11 pesos per head of the population—in 1976 it was 102 pesos.

Another of the main emphases of the speech was the importance of physical education. Castro spoke of the achievements in sport and physical recreation and the increased investments in that area. There has been an increase in the numbers of those training to be P.E. teachers, for instance. He urged an increase in the use of existing resources such as swimming pools. Surprisingly, given Cuba's Olympic successes, there has been some drop in participation in sport in 1975/76 compared with the previous year. He pointed to the achievements of Cuba's national sportsmen and women, but reminded the gathering that sport is for the benefit of all.

In speaking about the *future* of education in Cuba, Fidel said that efficiency would no longer be measured by the statistical indices of attendances, drop outs and promotions, as the country will soon be at the limits of growth in those areas. Improvèments will have to be measured in terms of other, *qualitative*, increases. These will be seen in the higher qualifications demanded of teachers; better text books; improved programmes of educations, as advances in pedagogy, science and technology are incorporated; and better school building. He urged that any remnants of subjective problems (leading to, say, non-attendance or punctuality) be got rid of by emphasising the importance of education for all students and workers, and by teaching children positive habits and attitudes towards school.

This is what the Constitution says about education:

Article 8. The socialist state:
b) as the power of the people and for the people guarantees
    —that no child be left without schooling, food and clothing;
    —that no young person be left without the opportunity to study;
    —that no one be left without access to studies, culture and sports;

Article 50. Everyone has the right to an education. This right is guaranteed by the free and widespread system of schools, semiboarding and boarding schools and scholarships of all kinds and at all levels of education, and because of the fact that all educational material is provided free of charge, which gives all children and young people, regardless of their family's economic position, the opportunity to study in keeping with their ability, social demands and the needs of socio-economic development.

Adults are also guaranteed this right, and education for them is free of charge, with the specific facilities regulated by law, by means of the adult education programme, technical and vocational education, training courses in state agencies and enterprises and the advanced courses for workers.

Article 38. The state orients, foments and promotes education, culture and science in all their manifestations.

Its educational and cultural policy is based on the following principles:

a)   The state bases its educational and cultural policy on the scientific world view, established and developed by Marxism-Leninism;

b)   education is a function of the state. Consequently, educational institutions belong to the state. The fulfillment of the educational function constitutes a task in which all society participates and is based on the conclusions and contributions made by science and on the closer relationship between study and life, work and production;

c)   the state must promote the communist education of the new generation and the training of children, young people and adults for social life. In order to make this principle a reality, general education and specialised scientific, technical or artistic education are combined with work, development research, physical education, sports, participation in political and social activities and military training;

d)   education is provided free of charge. The state maintains a broad scholarship system for students and provides the workers with multiple opportunities to study with a view to the universalisation of education. The law establishes the integration and structure of the nation system of education and defines the minimum level of general education that every citizen must acquire:

e)   artistic creativity is free as long as its content is not contrary to the Revolution. Forms of expression of art are free;

f)   in order to raise the level of culture of the people, the state foments and develops artistic education, the vocation for creation and the cultivation and appreciation of art;

g)   creation and investigation in science are free. The state encourages and facilitates investigation and gives priority to that which is aimed at solving the problems related to the interests of the society and the well-being of the people;

h)   the state makes it possible for the workers to engage in scientific work and to contribute to the development of science;

i)   the state promotes, foments and develops all forms of physical education and sports as a means of education and contribution to the integral development of the citizens;

j)   the state sees to the conservation of the nation's cultural heritage and artistic and historic wealth. The state protects national monuments and places known for their natural beauty or their artistic or historical value;

k)   the state promotes the participation of the citizens, through the country's social and mass organisations, in the development of its educational and cultural policy.

Article 39.   The education of children and young people in the spirit of communism is the duty of all society. The state and society give special protection to children and young people.

It is the duty of the family, the schools, the state agencies and the social and mass organisations to pay special attention to the integral development of children and young people.

The contents of the Constitution will, of course, become part of the content of education. Furthermore, some parts of it indicate very precise jobs to be done by the schools:

Article 41.   Discrimination because of race, colour, sex or national origin is forbidden and is punished by law.

The institutions of the state educate everyone, from the earliest possible age, in the principle of equality among human beings.

Education

Douglas Holly

As with everything else, the educational practice of Cuba is comprehensible in full only in the context of the country's special experience of colonialism. The Americanisation of the society, which began in the early years of this century, never completely penetrated the school and university system. Fragmentary and inadequate as it was, the educational apparatus then was Spanish-colonial, or more accurately, Spanish-colonial-revolutionary. The 19th century liberators from Spanish rule were themselves culturally—and often ethnically—Spanish. Today the most revered figure in Cuban schools and the man considered as a father of the nation is José Martí. Quotations from his educational writings—he was a considerable pedagogical theorist in the 19th century liberal tradition—are used as slogans to greet visitors in Cuban schools, and few institutions are without a bust or a portrait of the great man. This cultural hegemony of the Spanish-European tradition is widespread and permeates the world of art as well as *belles lettres*, but its educational aspect was long enshrined in the University of Havana, the oldest foundation in South America.

All this is not to deny the fundamental changes in outlook introduced by the Revolution, merely to contextualise them. The educational aspects of Cuba's political regeneration have been brought about within a framework which was, in origin, European rather than American, and the openness of Cuban schools to a renewed European influence is related to the cultural tradition. It is worth remembering that contemporary Soviet, East German and Polish practice, for instance, has much deeper affinities with this cultural-historical tradition of continental European education than with either our own or that of the United States. This is something which these countries share with Cuba at a much deeper level than that of official ideology. A visit to the superb Gallery of Contemporary Art in Havana serves to underline the 'European' affiliation of Cuba's intelligentsia: in visual art there is a remarkable interfusion of Parisian, Spanish colonial and native tropical. If, consequently, the architecture of Cuba's new *escuelas en el campo* and modern housing developments have a nearness in spirit to the best in East Germany, this is certainly not because of any ideological dependency, conscious or unconscious: it springs from a common cultural root.

Whatever the traditions, however, and whatever the aspirations, the educational apparatus which the *fidelistas* took over in the early 1960s was patchy and elitist. The 19th century liberal principles of the *liberadores* had faded under the impact of American casino imperialism, leaving a few academic schools in the main cities feeding the university, and even fewer technical schools supplying the rudimentary industrial needs of the foreign-based sugar economy. The needs of the colonial economy for literate workers were restricted: neither the *latifundias* nor the sugar plantations considered literacy important. As a consequence the mass of the people, whether of Spanish or African origin, were illiterate in 1959. Elementary schools, where they existed at all—mainly in urban areas—had a very sporadic attendance rate and very early drop-out, so that, even where the basics had been begun at school, they were usually forgotten by the time children started work. The education system, in fact, existed to serve the needs of a very restricted Cuban upper class, almost exclusively Spanish in origin. Paradoxically it is from this privileged élite that many of Cuba's revolutionary leaders have been recruited in the twentieth century, culminating, of course, in the *fidelistas* themselves. The University of Havana has an honourable tradition of providing heroic and altruistic champions of the people—albeit very much against its will. It is fitting that the usually futile revolt of these young intellectuals, sickened by the plight of the ordinary people and the decadence of the pinball society, should have its eventual triumph in the initiative taken by Fidel Castro and his companions of the *Sierra Maestra*.

The more specifically educational aspect of this triumph has been the establishment of virtually universal literacy since the revolution—starting with the famous Literacy Campaign of 1961, in which it is estimated that over a million adults were taught to read. The drive for literacy has formed an important part of revolutionary Cuba's educational effort, emphasising the importance not just of schooling in a conventional sense, but of *adult* education. In Cuba it is not just the children who go to school: symbolically—and to an impressive extent literally—it is the whole nation. Perhaps the most moving thing to witness in the new Cuba is the genuine enthusiasm of ordinary Cubans to 'win the Battle of the Sixth Grade'—i.e. to reach a standard equivalent to graduation from elementary school. It is an important aspect of the new assertion of self-respect so evident everywhere in the country, and so startlingly at variance with what could have been predicted of the pre-revolutionary society, with its widespread decadence and despair.

Socially the 1961 Literacy Campaign was a deliberate exercise in national unification. The young, mainly white high school graduates, went out from the cities to teach people of all ages, mainly black, in the countryside. But they also *learnt*, learnt to share the privations of the people and learnt what it meant to assert that the nascent revolutionary culture was based on the success or failure of the sugar harvest. Far more than from lectures or classes in political education, a whole generation of the intelligentsia of Cuba learned materialism at the cane-roots, so to speak. The present educational establishments of Cuba, from the Ministry downwards, are staffed with this generation; men and women who answered Fidel Castro's call to go to the people in 1961 and, subsequently, the call to take children from the towns into the country during the summer holidays to work and learn among the crops and the people—*escuelas al campo*. Cuba's educational administrators therefore have a direct and unique experience that can be equalled by few of their colleagues in the developed or the developing world.

And what they are administering is an amalgam of the old—mainly in the towns—and the new—mainly in the rural areas. The old is represented by the traditional elementary school, housed often in converted buildings, with makeshift furniture supplemented by newer, purpose-built equipment. This is still the physical context of primary schooling for those Cubans not living in new housing developments, where the schools go up alongside the apartment blocks, and are built to conform to the '*girón*' design, as are the new secondary schools in the country. It is also represented, by and large, by a standard 'European' academic curriculum of a type not very different from that to be found in, say, West Germany, Poland or Sweden. It is by no means innocent of Piagetian precepts about 'ages and stages'; but the teaching/learning mode is largely didactic, from teacher to pupil. In this it is not very different from the practice of most of the world—and of nearly all the developing world. The Cubans feel that the main achievement is to have got most of the nation's children into schools, sitting behind desks, learning to read, write and calculate by *any* method. It is a considerable achievement.

The new in Cuban education is represented by such impressive institutions as the V.I. Lenin Vocational High School in Havana, the new Technical University outside the capital, the various specialist schools attached to developing industries, like electronics and agricultural technology, and the dozens of *escuelas en el campo* (Schools in the Country) where young people from the cities spend their time during the week confronting the abstractions of an academic curriculum *and* the materiality of concrete labour among citrus and other crops, returning to the more sophisticated life of home at weekends and holiday times. The space and elegance of these '*girón*' buildings, with their marble walkways and stilt construction to allow the free flow of cool air during the stifling tropical summer, their rooftop social areas, their well-equipped kitchens and dining halls, would be remarkable in the developed world. The design—in common with other innovations in revolutionary Cuba—is named triumphantly and defiantly after the battle of Playa Girón, the Bay of Pigs, where

Kennedy's ill-judged adventure in counter-revolution was so decisively and ignominiously defeated. The buildings, whether housing new technological institutes or *escuelas secundarias básicas* (Basic Secondary Schools), stand in proud rejection of North American intervention, hostile or benign. They are an assertion of self-respect and confidence in the future of national regeneration, as well as political and economic dissidence from the erstwhile Pan-American order.

Also among the new ideas brought into practice in Cuba by the revolutionary generation is the notion of female emancipation. This is an idea particularly foreign to the Spanish element in the national culture, with its open challenge to the principle of *machismo*, the confident assertion of masculinity through unquestioned male ascendancy. The concept of female equality is no less problematic among that proportion of the population of African descent, since it runs counter to the strict role-divisions of traditional life. The Cuban revolutionary regime, however, while respecting tradition, European or African, is adamant in heralding a new age which will require new social practices. Cuban women, urban and rural, are encouraged to seek educational parity with men, an invitation which ordinary women in Cuba seem enthusiastic to accept, judging by the enrolment in day and evening classes, where men and women are to be found in equal numbers and where the spirit is one of good-natured *camaraderie*.

A specific aspect of Cuban female emancipation is the need for women's participation in the economy, requiring a changed attitude, particularly in the countryside but also in the towns, with the advent of light industry manufacturing consumer goods for which the country was hitherto totally dependent on the developed world. This is part of the conviction that national regeneration depends ultimately on self-reliance and the full participation of the whole population in production. Consequently there is, as in Eastern Europe, a considerable expenditure of resources on crèches and nursery schools which free young mothers for the productive effort and, incidentally, help towards social and personal emancipation. These nurseries and crèches in turn require trained personnel—the *asistentes* whose preparation is part medical and part educational. On the educational side these women are taught about child development, with an emphasis on social play rather than individual activity. The training of the *asistentes* is typical of the way Cuba copes with the acute shortage of specialist and technical skills in all areas of society, above all in education. They are, basically, ordinary women with elementary education who are trained 'on the job', rather than undergoing preliminary courses at colleges—though release to attend college-based courses is an important aspect of educational development in all sectors of the economy.

Some Cuban children, therefore, experience contact with systematic educational methods from a very early age. More are being enrolled in what the Cubans regard as 'pre-school' classes at age four or five. In these classes—as distinct from the compulsory elementary schools which begin at age six—the emphasis is on play and direct experience of materials, as it is in our own infant classes. The influence of Soviet educationalists in the Vygotsky-Luria tradition can be seen in the special equipment of these classes, most of which are physically housed in the buildings of elementary schools and come under the general direction of the elementary school principal who, as in British primary schools, is generally a man. It is to be hoped that female emancipation in the educational career structure will advance faster in Cuba...

Full-time compulsory education proper begins, as has been said, at age six. Just as in many of our own Junior schools, one's impression is that in Cuban Elementary schools play is regarded as a thing for break times and out of school activities. Its inclusion in the curriculum is seen as a characteristic of the 'pre-school' stage—in our terms, of the infant school. The impression one gains of Cuban classes of six and seven year olds is of a serious dedication to learning from teachers and textbooks—just as soon as the mechanics of reading have been mastered. The atmosphere, though by no means lacking in warmth and humanity, is one of quiet concentration and drill rather than 'activity' in the sense of the British/North American myth of 'modern' primary methods. It is a great deal closer to the expectation of most schooling throughout the world, whatever the economic-political complexion of the society in general. The excitement, in Cuba's case, is in the *presence* of all children in classrooms at the primary stage, rather than the nature of what goes on in them.

Not that *all* aspects of education for Cuban children are unexciting. Alongside some rather dull and wordy textbooks there are beautifully produced readers and song-books with traditional stories and songs besides colourful celebrations of more recent events in Cuban history, like the heroic, but unsuccessful, attack on Batista's Moncada Barracks in 1953. Many of the children's books are illustrated with children's own drawings. Examples of children's art, while lacking on the walls of the elementary and secondary classrooms, are paradoxically present on the public hoardings. At least one huge poster visible on a motorway in 1976 was a reproduction of children's work. The exuberance and vitality of such children's art reflects the exuberance, vitality and evident health of the children in the streets after school. It augurs well for the continuation of the Cuban flair for design, especially in graphic form, but it augurs well also for the continuation of a more general vitality. Passivity is certainly not a post-revolutionary Cuban characteristic.

Amid such self-assured exuberance it seems a little strange to note the conservatism of curriculum and methodology in the actual day-to-day business of learning. Part of this lack of methodological adventurousness is no doubt an official distrust of bourgeois educational adventurism: the standard response of Soviet and East European educationalists to Western 'progressivism' is quite certainly reflected in their advice to the Cubans—and the help, material and pedagogic, of Soviet and other advisers is fully acknowledged by Cuban administrators. But perhaps a more fundamental source of caution is the afore-mentioned dearth of trained personnel. Partly due to the exodus of the petty bourgeoisie to the United States, in the wake of Castro's proclamation of the socialist nature of the Revolution, partly as a result of the massive increase in the physical provision of schools, there is an absolute shortage of teachers in Cuba and a relative absence of *experienced* teachers. This has called forth the typical Cuban response—on the job training.

In the 1970s thousands of sixteen year old boys and girls have come forward in response to Fidel's appeal for help in the schools. They formed the *destacamentos pedagógicos*, educational shock-troops, who filled the breach at a time of desperate need. Leaving basic secondary schools, they undertook to work in the elementary classrooms and in the understaffed departments of the basic secondary schools themselves. Clearly, with such raw recruits, untried methods and unfamiliar curricula were out of the question. Though undergoing courses of lectures at the pedagogical institute, they were not trained teachers. Even now the average age of primary and secondary teachers is very low by the standards of the developed world, and initial training of teachers as the general rule is only just getting under way. In this respect Cuba is no different from other developing countries. It seems to differ only in the energy with which the problem is being tackled. Perhaps some experiments in different classroom practices will develop pace by pace with an improvement in the availability of more experienced teachers. However, it cannot be denied that wider ideological questions are at stake here—a point that will be returned to at the conclusion of this essay.

Elementary education is now universally available in Cuba and a very high proportion of boys and girls in town and country in fact complete the sixth and final elementary grade—which in Cuba, as in most of the world, developed or underdeveloped, may mean more than six school *years*, since promotion from one class to another at the end of a school year depends on passing the appropriate tests. A high proportion, however, are recorded as passing Grade Six at twelve plus, which indicates at least that there is no pressure to keep this formal requirement for secondary schooling to a minimum to conform to the number of secondary places actually available —no 'twelve plus' selection in other words. However the provision of physical accommodation and trained teachers for successive levels of the education system becomes progressively more expensive and therefore represents a great problem in a developing economy such as Cuba's—and our own recent experience serves as a reminder of how expensive 'secondary education for all' is for *any* economy. In this context Cuba's achievement of three quarters of the 13-16 age group in schools by 1976 represents a considerable commitment of national resources.

In a situation of shortage of secondary provision there are two courses available to a country aspiring to 'secondary education for all'—to quote our own slogan of forty years ago. The one adopted in Britain in 1944 was to adopt a 'dual' system by upgrading some schools from the elementary system, filling them with youngsters of the appropriate age group and re-labelling them 'secondary' while limiting access to the established secondary schools by selective tests. The other, less underhand way is to allow a proportion of youngsters to leave school at puberty—or when they attain the notional equivalent of six years of elementary education, and take into genuinely 'secondary' institutions only those who show promise of definitely profiting society by making use of its scarcer resources. This is the alternative adopted by Cuba's politicians. Of course this, in turn, presents a difficulty: how to know when a youngster is 'showing promise'? The only obvious solution is to take into account his or her relative performance on grade tests over the primary years.

An additional problem is that, whereas capitalist societies can restrict the notion of 'secondary' schooling to one that is in practice a technical training for management and administration of a purely manipulative type, a society which aims at socialism clearly needs some other view of 'secondary'. Ideally this is one which takes all citizens beyond the possession of elementary, though vital, skills like reading towards some grounding in broad areas of conceptual awareness of the physical and social world. This would enable them to enter the productive workforce or higher education with a general level of consciousness adequate to genuine participation in the government and decision-making process of a free and equal community where classes of rulers and ruled have been abolished. Such is the vision.

The reality for a developing society is the need to stay afloat economically and therefore, in a hostile world, politically. This is exactly Cuba's situation. While there *are* schools called 'basic secondaries', these are necessarily preparatory to a tertiary stage of post-sixteen (and sometimes post-fifteen) institutions, specialist schools which will train technicians and technologists qualified to keep the economy viable and advance the technical base on which everything else materially depends.

This combination of necessities—the necessity of finding some fair and 'objective' means of deciding which young people should fill the restricted number of post-elementary places, and the necessity of providing specialists to develop the economy as a secure base for social advance—result in a familiar picture for socialist countries which historically have all been 'developing' countries at the time when political revolution settled the social and political decisions. In the Soviet Union and, after the ideological battles of the Cultural Revolution, in China, no less than in Cuba, 'secondary' has come to mean 'specialist preparatory'. In Cuba, as in Russia in the 1920s and China today, it is economic necessity not the ascendancy of a particular faction which determined the issue. The curriculum is settled not by ideology, but by the demands of survival as a revolutionary and developing society.

The difficulty in this, of course, is to separate expedient necessity from opportunism. Genuine and universal conceptual education like genuine socialism can be put off *sine die* in the interests of a comfortable *status quo* where the non-achievement of socialism in its transition to communism is delayed while ever-new levels of consumer 'development' are achieved. This is a danger against which any would-be socialist developing country must guard. At the moment the signs in Cuba are ambiguous. Clearly, different levels of physical comfort are experienced as between town and country—a situation of which the Government makes no secret and which the country is committed to overcoming. More subtly, however, different levels of life-style are visible *within* the cities and—worryingly —these are related, as they are in capitalist countries, to differential educational provision. Mention has already been made of the exceptional '*girón*' type buildings for schools in new housing developments.•Clearly the inhabitants of these new developments are already privileged. While they may have paid for that privilege to some extent by personal labour on the building at weekends, it is a basic socialist precept that it is the working class *as a whole* which really pays for the privileges of any section of society, including the majority in Cuba who cannot yet be housed in elegant new apartments.

If it should be the case that access to the prized *secundarias básicas en el campo* becomes, on the basis of performance on 'objective' grade tests, disproportionately drawn from children from comfortable home backgrounds and that access to higher education is further narrowed by social circumstances and lifestyle, then there is a considerable danger of bureaucratisation of the country's political and technical leadership. Of course, these things are by no means *inevitable* in Cuba, and an even narrower area of recruitment in the prerevolutionary society did not prevent the emergence and eventual triumph of radical and socially conscious leadership.

So far Cuba, in the school year 1976-77, has embarked on an ambitious Improvement Plan, aimed at rationalising present practice and increasing the inservice training of teachers. This is obviously a necessary first step. Let us hope that the determination and pride exhibited by working people in their adult classes and the quiet confidence and modesty exhibited by the staff of the new technological institutions is matched on the political front by the resolution to advance the Revolution towards the truly socialist and humane future envisaged by Marx, Engels, Lenin and others, including José Martí, to whose vision Cuba's leaders are committed.

Theatre as Revolutionary Activity: The Escambray

Marian Sedley

October 1971:

A lorry, bus and jeep make their way along mud tracks, through fields of high waving sugar cane, in the gathering darkness. As the light fades small groups of people can be seen, old and young, some on horseback and others on foot, pushing their way through the cane to the village of Cafetal to join the villagers for the evening's event. The event in question is a play—'a live film' as one peasant who had recently seen the Mobile Cinema refers to it.

As the vehicles bump round the last bend towards the village the sound of harmonica music and singing can be heard through the warm night air. A crowd of women, men and children, with babies held in brothers' and sisters' arms, can be distinguished in the darkness. The lorry and bus lurch and jolt into view, a cheer goes up and the people move onto the track led by a young boy playing a harmonica. The Escambray Theatre Group arrives at its venue in slightly more style than usual.

Everyone wants to help unload the equipment. Someone lights the Chinese lanterns and hands them out, to be carried gently across the rough ground to the space in front of the cottage which has been chosen as the backcloth. A crowd of over a hundred has already formed and more are drifting in. By

now it's pitch dark—no moon or stars—and people are trip-
ping over the ground and each other. The lanterns are set in a
semi-circle in front of the cottage and the crowd settles.
Children and old people sit at the front, the children on the
ground and the old on wooden chairs brought with them from
their houses. Ranks of people stand behind, with those perched
on horses, lorries and tractors at the back.

A member of the group introduces the evening: 'We're
going to do a play for you tonight. There's something a bit
special about this. Usually theatre is seen in a special building,
indoors. But because there aren't any theatres here and because
we wanted you to have a chance to see some plays we decided
to do something new and perform in the open air... One other
thing. After the play's over don't all rush away, because the
play itself is only part of the evening, and just as important is
for you to say what you think about it, so it's not just us
talking.'

The play on this particular night is called 'The Showcase',
which is also the name of the Dairy Plan being set up in the
region. It tells the story of an old peasant lying ill in his cottage.
Two men from the Land Commission come to visit him.
Although they have in fact come to ask after his health, he
assumes that they are there to take his piece of land from him
to incorporate it into the Dairy Plan. The titles to this plot of
land, which prior to the Revolution he had worked for a
landowner, had been granted to him only a few years before by
the Agrarian Reform Law. The worry is too much for him and
he dies of fright.

The wake that follows his death rapidly turns into something resembling a meeting. The neighbours have all packed
into his cottage and, while they temporarily forget their
recently deceased friend, heated debates ensue about the pros
and cons of collectivising the land, about the health risk to the
cattle which might arise if Pancho's dying wish to be buried on
his own plot of land is carried out, about the black market and
the inedibleness of Russian tinned meat. Some reveal to the
Commission their profound disagreements with the Dairy
Plan, while others defend it hotly. Ripples of laughter and loud
comment spread through the audience as gripes and grouses
usually restricted to the privacy of people's homes find public

expression through the characters in the play.

In the distance, on a raised plateau and visible to actors and audience alike, flicker the lights of 'La Yaya', a new town being built by the labour of brigades representing many people from the area, and which is to house those who move from their mud and wattle cottages to work on the Dairy Plan. This new town which forms part of the natural scenery behind the village of Cafetal is also referred to in the play itself. In the latter it is the subject of great controversy. There are those peasants represented in the play who hope they will be among the lucky ones to move there, and others who say that living in a four storey block of flats will be like living in a chest of drawers, and anyway if they've got to live in a town they want to live in a real one, 'Not a toy town in the countryside'.

The audience begins to get involved in the argument, actively taking issue with the various views expressed, and then the play carries on and draws to a close. The performers appear uncertain as to how to handle this audience participation, especially when an old man among the spectators gets into a heated row with one of the actors thinking that the actor's assumed stutter is done deliberately to mock him. But since the engendering of some sort of participation was a deliberate intention when writing the play, it will be a topic for much discussion within the Group over ensuing weeks.

After the play a performer steps forward and asks the audience for their opinion of what they've just seen. Some people are already leaving, but others seem more than ready to take up the arguments. The atmosphere, hilarious at times during the show itself, becomes quite tense as it polarises between the waged farm workers from the Dairy Plan and the peasants—or small farmers—with their different expectations and ambitions. Some of the farm workers voice strong criticisms of the peasants, accusing them of being backward elements, holding up the revolutionary process by clinging on to the old desire to own their own piece of land. The peasants are divided between those who are loath to leave the life and home they have always known, and others who say they can't wait to get out of 'this mud bath', which the area turns into in the rainy season, to move into La Yaya.

The evening finally comes to an end, and everyone makes

his and her way home. The following day the members of the Group will visit the villagers in ones and twos to talk more informally about what they thought of the play and the ideas in it, and generally to exchange experiences.

Origins of the Escambray Theatre Group

The Group takes its name from the mountainous region in central Cuba where it is based. It is in these mountains and foothills, wild and remote, that much of Cuba's history has been enacted, from the last century when the first War of Independence against Spain was halted here, to the 1960s when it became a base for many counter-revolutionary activities, with bandits operating amidst the population of small farmers. The assassination of a young literacy teacher from Havana gave further heat to what came to be known as the 'Struggle Against the Bandits'.

In December 1968 twelve actors and actresses from Havana arrived in the Escambray to carry out some preliminary research. They had come together earlier that year from a variety of backgrounds within the professional theatre, and shared a deepseated dissatisfaction with the state of theatre as it then stood, and with their own role as revolutionaries within it.

At that time 'theatre' was something that happened in Havana, and was seen at most by a few hundred regulars. Despite the fact that since the Revolution the doors had been thrown open to a wider public, the basic relationship between performers and audience remained the same—in other words, a passive audience watching material that usually had little or nothing to do with their own experience and lives. As Sergio Corrieri, the Group's director, puts it: 'Cuban theatre remained completely marginal to the nation's reality.'

More often than not the plays were imported from a developed country, a typical example of cultural colonialism. In addition the distance between audience and performers was partly sustained by an intervening bureaucracy, and by a level of organisation and technology likewise borrowed from a developed economy and totally inappropriate to the needs and possibilities of the Cuban people. As far as the content of the plays went, Sergio Corrieri described them as 'rarely having anything to do with the particular circumstances of the country'. They 'neither contributed nor challenged nor enlightened'. Furthermore, they were performed as if 'throwing pebbles in a river, without any thought as to where they'll land'.

How they came to choose the Escambray

The rejection of theatre as an end in itself led this group to seek out a totally new environment in which to work. Although there were proletarian neighbourhoods in Havana which would certainly have been virgin territory as far as theatre was concerned, the new group chose a rural area as their base. In their view 'it's in the countryside that the Revolution's most profound transformations are taking place.'

Unlike other rural zones which they considered, the Escambray had the advantage of a relatively stable and homogenous population, and a rich historical tradition. Furthermore it presented many specific political problems, such as the Struggle Against the Bandits mentioned above, which added a further challenge to the Group. Another reason for this choice is explained by Sergio: 'We felt that such a radical change of environment would force us to rethink many things, to start all over again, to face difficulties which would really unite us.'

Informal discussions with political leaders in the region were started, and soon the Group presented their project to the National Culture Council. It was well received. Practically speaking, this meant the Group had the go-ahead to work in this way, would receive their food and clothing rations like any other mobile work centre, but other than that would be left largely to their own devices. In other words the Group was set up autonomously, and whatever relation to the Communist Party might or might not develop was left to future practice to decide.

From the beginning however the Group found help and advice from members of the regional branch of the Communist Party fairly essential, and they solicited it from the start. When the first twelve members of the Group arrived in the Escambray at the end of 1968 to carry out the preliminary research, mainly to inform themselves about the region's economics, culture, history, present problems and so on, they tentatively divided the region into three zones with sub-groups of four people to cover each one. They would meet once a week to pool and discuss the information they had been able to collect. A member of the regional branch of the Communist Party was always present at these meetings. The Group felt that cooperation with someone who knew the area well was indispensible to their work: "someone," in Sergio Corrieri's words, "who could give us the information we might lack at any given moment, and with whom we could discuss fully anything which was new to us."

In addition links were established with the University of Havana, in order for the Group to gain help from people already experienced in this sort of investigation. The first work plan was thus developed from an overall picture of the area: from its centres of production and most important services, to the organization of family life, work, leisure and entertainment, and including countless interviews with combatants from the Struggle Against the Bandits.

This research element has been maintained consistently throughout the Group's history. Both the investigations prior to the putting together of a new show, and the recording of discussions with the audience after a play, and of conversations with them in their own homes, help to provide the basis for a more consciously evaluated theatre.

Performance cycle

Until 1972 when they built a permanent base camp, the Group would spend the rainy season at the Escambray's massive teacher training college at Topes de Collantes, contributing to the development of a cultural programme with the students and teachers. During the rest of the year, when the rain and muck no longer make road and tracks impassable, they tour from village to village, working for six weeks at a stretch followed by ten work-free days.

The Escambray Group prefer to work in small villages,

with between twenty and forty families, and they stay in each village for about a fortnight. The size of the village is important if they are to build any close relationship with the audience, huge audiences not being the most conducive to open and fruitful discussion. They never perform immediately on arrival, not wishing to create what they describe as a circus or country fair atmosphere, which would be unfavourable to what they are trying to do. First of all they set about making themselves known. Group members in pairs visit as many houses as possible to introduce themselves, to tell the people who they are and what they are doing, and invite them to the performances. Usually a puppet show is put on for the children of the village, perhaps in the school itself, and Group members explain to the children how they can make the puppets themselves with whatever materials are available. This often leads to invitations to the children's homes.

When not performing, the actors take part in the work of the village, in the fields, dairies and workshops. This they consider essential to establishing an organic relationship with the people they are performing to and to a real understanding of each other's work. A full subsidy from the State makes it unnecessary for them to place productivity, in terms of numbers of performances, above the political principles of shared work and living with their audiences. Time is not money in their case. So it is only after this preliminary period of getting to know each other that the Group presents its play—three different plays on three successive nights.

The plays

The nature and content of the plays performed by the Theatre Group since 1968 have been determined by the Group's insistence that theatre cease to be an end in itself, and become a vehicle for ideas, a tool for discussing and confronting vital issues. "One might think that by bringing the Symphony Orchestra to Magua", says a member of the Group, "we'd be doing important cultural work. It might be important for us, but not mean a thing to them. In other words, culturalisation can never be just offering a sum total of cultural knowledge, important as that knowledge may be. You have to give people the elements necessary to understanding their lives and surrounding, so they can work on those surroundings and thereby realize themselves. And this cannot be done by the simple accumulation of knowledge. The cultural information a person has in no way guarantees that he or she is better, freer or more fulfilled.''

The Group began to work out material consistent with this view. "Some Men and Others", for example, looks at the subject of the bandits who operated in the Escambray from 1960 to 1965. The play shows the problem of individual responsibility through the character of a young soldier who has to make the choice as to whether or not to be in the group that executes the bandits. Sergio Corrieri describes the soldier's dilemma: "The first part of the play depicts the hunting of the bandits, which is easy for the soldier. But in the second part of the play he can't make up his mind to shoot the bandit in cold blood. Then the two bandits fight amongst themselves and the young soldier listens to them discuss all they have done against the Revolution. Then the play ends, and there is a discussion and the audience is asked 'What would *you* do?'''

Another play in the early repertoire of the Group was an adaptation of Brecht's "Mother Carrar's Guns", originally about the Spanish Civil War. The Escambray has a particularly high concentration of Jehovah's Witnesses, who preach a philosophy of "non-involvement" and neutrality in politics. This version of the Brecht play is adapted to look at the position taken by the Jehovah's Witnesses to the US invasion of Cuba. Sergio said of it: "Its theme makes it very effective, but it has a structure that can't be broken through however much it's adapted to the Escambray...We feel that a theatre that assumes the right to give a single solution is insufficient... In this sense we are involved in absolutely political theatre where the actor puts forward hypotheses which he defends but doesn't cling to because they are susceptible to change within the play itself, generated by the constant exchange with the audience. Everyone's major problems need collective solutions, and that's the way theatre must deal with them. We need more plays that make suggestions, that are polemical, and although "The Guns" isn't exactly what we need in this sense, we've presented it in an area where there are still many

Jehovah's Witnesses and we've found that it has a great impact there". In 1973 the Group replaced this play with one entitled "Jehovah's Provisions", written by one of their own members.

By the early seventies they felt that the play that so far came closest to what they were looking for was "The Showcase", described at the beginning of this chapter. This play arose out of a study of the Dairy Plan of the Northern Escambray, carried out by the theatre group at the request of the Regional Communist Party. The fact that the Communist Party asked them to do this was considered very important by the Group. "It gave us a measure of how our own goals were complementary to those of the revolutionary agencies of the area, how we were really playing the role we'd proposed for ourselves: that of being a work collective at the service of the most urgent needs of the Revolution, specifically in that zone, and how the Group felt itself to be an integral part of that zone." In other words, from a situation in 1968 where they found help from local political leaders indispensable to gaining an understanding of the region, two or three years later, the need and ability of the Communist Party and other regional authorities to use *them* had become a measure for the Group of their own integration into the region.

The study took three weeks, during which time they did nearly 170 interviews with peasants in the Plan. The Plan was to cover 400,000 acres and include several thousand small farmers who would then collectively work the land that had previously been handed over to them in individual plots by the Agrarian Reform. This would of course mean a big change for the peasants, a change of class in fact, from small land holder to salaried agricultural worker.

The Group says of the play: "It's a complex problem and the peasants' reactions to it are very diverse. In the play we've tried to combine all the different aspects of the question. We've drawn on and used the vision of these people for whom, when you talk about a mechanical milking machine, you may as well be talking about the cosmos, for all the connection it has with their own lives. For these people, acceptance of the measures required by the Plan often means an extraordinary act of faith in the Revolution."

The views expressed by the peasants and farm workers

following the play often becomes incorporated into the play itself for subsequent performances. In fact before it was ever performed the Group predicted that when its run ended it might be a totally different play because of "the changes that will occur after contact with an audience for whom these problems are an essential part of their lives". Although some improvisation did take place during these performances, at the time they felt they were not yet ready to propose basic structures for improvisation.

The dramatisation of some short stories by Onelio Jorge Cardoso did open up more possibilities in this direction. They began to work with these stories because of a tradition in the region, which could usefully be taken up, of fifty or more people getting together to listen to someone telling a story. During the presentation of the three short stories the show is interrupted at the end of each unit. "The audience intervenes, they give their own interpretation of what's happened or begin to tell their own stories. This opens up endless possibilities for conceptual and artistic participation on the part of the audience and also for the actors who are forced to question the validity of the solutions they've found".

Working life

Two years after starting work in the Escambray the Group held a seminar during which they attempted to assess their work to date, and thus plan for the future. They discussed everything, from their relations with the Regional Party to what each of them understood by "cultural decolonization". They also talked about what the actors' and actresses' role should be in this area of work, what should be his/her aims and responsibilities, what should be required of those who want to join the Group. "Because it's not enough for someone to be a good actor. An actor in our group has to develop a whole range of activities other than acting...He's got to feel as creative in the villages, discussing people's problems with them or sharing in their work, as he does on stage."

This says something about the Group's attitude towards specialization, and the traditional division of labour between actors and the public. Clearly they reject this to a large extent.

They are all of them researchers of material, and any one of them can be a technician, performer, writer, director, or any combination of these. Furthermore the entire company turned builder for the construction of their base camp, which took eight months and more than an estimated 25,000 hours of physical work to complete. Like many such projects in contemporary Cuba, this arose from a mixture of practical necessity—shortage of skilled labour—and principles about the lessons and understanding to be gained from involvement in different sorts of work, especially if this includes both mental and physical work.

During the years since its foundation, the Group has grown from the original twelve members to numbers ranging between twenty and thirty. While on the whole the internal division of labour is fluid—the work of writing, directing, acting, puppeteering, technical work and so on may accrue to different people at different times—it is clear that Sergio Corrieri, the Group's director, acts as the principal spokesperson for the Group. The numbers also include a cook and a driver, the latter being essentially someone who knows the region, with its potentially dangerous tracks, like the back of his hand.

Life in this work is tough, and was so especially prior to the completion of the base camp in 1972. During the ten days off following each six week performance stint, most of the company would return to Havana to see friends and family. Many were separated from partners, and some even from their children. This was of course a conscious, but nonetheless difficult, choice, especially for those leaving children in the care of relatives whose political and social attitudes they might not share. This problem was a major factor in the predominantly male composition of the Group which the construction of a base camp sought to resolve. Now members of the Group can have their families with them, and their children can live with them and go to school in the area.

The way forward

Perhaps the most exciting development in the last few years has been the setting up of an amateur theatre group in the area in 1973. The new theatre group takes its name from La Yaya, the new town built as part of the Dairy Plan. Its members are the people who live in La Yaya, encouraged by an actress from the Escambray Group who now lives with her two children in La Yaya. The main difference between the two groups is that while the actors and actresses of the Escambray Theatre Group represent the peasants, the peasants of La Yaya represent themselves.

They choose subjects with which they feel intimately involved and which they regard as closely related to their everyday lives—male chauvinism, for instance, especially in relation to women working in the dairies against the will of those men who still feel that women should stay at home and look after their husbands.

Inspired by the success of this group, several other amateur peasant groups have emerged in other rural communities. This is perhaps the most logical and optimistic direction for the development of the work begun in 1968, where those involved described themselves as being hopefully "not the interpreters of peasant drama but a part of that drama".

Nino

Onelio Jorge Cardoso

Everybody went to the wake. The house was on the outskirts of
town, a long way from the last light-bulb. Even the Captain
came and the Mayor and a few soldiers. In the middle of the
room lay the coffin with the dead man inside. The face was
purple as it always is from death by asphyxia. A few weeping
women were moving about the room, and a child was sleeping
in an old armchair with its legs tucked up and its feet bare.

I went out into the yard, grabbed a stool, turned my back
to the moon and leaned back on the edge of the well. Old
Julián Barreras was there. Alone, difficult to talk to and as curt
as usual. Newcomers were already standing around in groups
nearby and making remarks:

"Hard labour for life, at least."

"Or they'll shoot him."

"Or they'll tell him to run and shoot him in the back."

"That's right, with him taking the law into his own
hands!"

They said all that and then started talking about women,
the Mayor and the Captain. But everybody was in agreement
about Nino's barbaric crime. Nino, from "La Carolina", had
killed Celorio Ramos. That was the news, and there was
nothing else to add except that he himself had gone to the
police barracks with the corpse over his shoulder and said
something that people weren't willing to repeat.

Old Ruperta, who had seen Corporal Ramos grow up, threw her shawl over her shoulders and went up to the widow:

"Have faith, my child. God remembers everything!"

And the Captain himself burst out, slapping his knee:

"You see those people alright and then they do this to you! I should string him up!"

The Mayor gave his total assent:

"Right away", he said.

In the meantime, the wives of the Captain and the Mayor were talking about fashions.

Lucio Bermúdez, a police clerk who had got leave to come to the wake, a most insignificant individual, resentful of his own lack of importance and with minor aspirations of his own, jumped up from his corner and spoke up furiously:

"I knew that Nino bastard would kill someone. He got half his land by stealing it, just imagine."

He said this in such a loud voice that it came over quite clearly to old Julián and myself, even though we were in the yard. I looked at Julián and heard him say:

"The things you hear!"

And once more I felt my usual respect for the old man when he spoke.

"What do you mean, old lad, don't you believe it?"

He turned his face towards me. I saw his hat pointing towards me, gleaming in the moonlights, and under the brim, in the shadow, I saw the red blob of his cigar.

"Well, you know that anybody who had to put up with what Nino did would do the same."

And then he told me the following story.

"Nino lived on his bit of land half a kilometre away from the police barracks. He was as tall and thick-set as a ceiba tree. Everything brought a smile to his lips. He had a good face and big, light-coloured eyes. Although he lived on his own in the middle of the cane, he always kept the front of his house covered with flowers all the year round, and people said he used to turn a blind eye when the kids started to come in, in May, to steal his mangoes. He spent the good times and the bad times bent over his land, keeping an eye on the phases of the moon and the signs of the weather. Everything there was in that place was his, from the black, damp earth with its hundreds of fat worms to the two teams of animals and the roads. It was all his by the sweat of his brow.

"Nino was like that, but you had to be polite to him and thank him for things because if you didn't a fierce light would come into his eyes. Unfortunately, Celorio Ramos didn't have much idea about what men are like, and he had too big an idea about what the police should be.

"One day the Captain told him to borrow an ox-team to do some work in the yard of the barracks. Celorio nodded three times even before the Captain had finished speaking. It was just bad luck that he went to Nino's place when there were so. many people round about without any fight in them. That evening Nino was taking advantage of "the cool" to plough up his land. The corporal arrived, took a look at the oxen and said, without taking his eyes off them:

" 'Unhitch them, the Captain needs them.'

"Nino wiped the sweat off his brow with his hand and said:

" 'I need them as well.'

" 'It's only for a short time', grunted the other man.

" 'I don't care whether it's for a short time or for a life-time, *nobody* is taking my oxen away from me.'

"The corporal made a gesture, nothing more, but he kept his temper and added: 'You see, they're for the Captain.'

"Nino looked up; the sun formed a triangle of light on his temple, and his eyes started glowing like two hot coals:

" 'I don't care if they're for God Almighty!'

"Celorio couldn't keep his temper any more. He stepped forward and:

" 'I'm either taking the oxen or you, you bloody fool!'

"Well, you have to know Nino. In one stride he had the policeman by the waist and lifted him over his head:

" 'You're not man enough for that', he said, gritting his teeth, and threw him down into the furrow. Then he turned his back as if he had just pulled up a dry and stubborn root. Turning his back was the bad thing. The other man drew his weapon and sank it into Nino's left shoulder. But he couldn't do anything else because Nino's right hand, gnarled and powerful, grabbed his neck and bent it down over the furrow.

"Just one hand, my God! Just the right hand. The soil had

only just been broken and was warm and moist. Celorio's skull struck it and his eyes, wild and almost bursting from their sockets, stared fixedly upwards at some vague point. His short arms drove their nails into the giant's body, his right arm over Nino's wounded shoulder, tearing savagely. But Nino could not be budged. It was just like a stone rolling down on top of an egg. Then Nino stood up and with his same right arm lifted the dead man onto his right shoulder, taking no notice of anything, either the pain or the warm blood, and set off towards the police barracks.

"He arrived at nightfall. The policeman on duty called halt, but he carried on walking up to the doorway, and when the light fell on him and the Captain came out, Nino said, sliding the corpse down off his shoulder:

" 'If you already have oxen, you don't try to take other people's.' "

That was what old Julián told me. And at about three in the morning, when Lucio Bermúdez came into the yard looking for a light for his cigarette, the old man stood right in his path with his lighted cigar, and when the other man asked him for the light Julián Barreras, looking at him all the time, took his cigar butt out of his mouth and threw it on the ground.

translated by Peter Turton

Onelio Jorge Cardoso, Writer of the Cuban Revolution

Peter Turton

Onelio Jorge Cardoso is one of the most popular of contemporary Cuban fiction writers. He was born in 1914, in Calabazar de Sagua (Las Villas province), and received his secondary education in the provincial capital of Santa Clara. On leaving school he turned his hand to an assortment of professions: schoolteaching, selling medicines, work in a photographer's darkroom and in radio broadcasting. In addition to his several volumes of short stories, he has produced scripts for documentaries and news programmes, plus a journalist's collection of pieces on peasant life entitled Gente de pueblo *(Village People, 1964). Although not a professional diplomat, in the early seventies he was appointed Cultural Counsellor to the Cuban Embassy in Lima.*

Despite his wide-spread popularity in Cuba, and the acknowledged quality of his writing, little of Cardoso's work has been translated into English. Comparatively little too, has been written about him, if one considers that he undoubtedly figures among the finest exponents of the Latin American short story. For example, in a recent study of Cuban fiction, Seymour Menton[1] devotes deserved space to the great Cuban novelist Alejo Carpentier and the rather esoteric work of a writer of the older generation, José Lezama Lima: but says little about Cardoso whose importance in Cuba is great. It seems fitting that in a book about Cuba today, so widely read a writer as Cardoso should feature with due prominence.

The scarcity of publishing houses in pre-revolutionary Cuba, the fact that literary culture was largely the patrimony of an elite, has meant that even such consecrated writers as Carpentier and Nicolás Guillén have in the past had to publish abroad. It fell to the present Cuban régime to enable Onelio Jorge Cardoso to come into contact with *his* public: the audience which appreciates his work fully and for which he principally produces—the rural and urban working class.

Cardoso's first collection of short stories, *Taita, diga usted como* or *Dad, Tell Me How* (1947) had to appear in Mexico. His only other volume to be published before 1959 was a collection called *El Cuentero* (*The Story-Teller*) brought out in '58 by the Universidad Central de Las Villas, although a few isolated short stories had been printed in magazines like *Bohemia*. Nowadays, however, Cardoso is very widely read, thanks to the facilities placed at his disposal by the Revolution. His *Complete Short Stories* have been published several times, the 1969 edition running to 50,000 copies. Many of these were acquired by working people who, thanks to the literacy campaign of the early sixties, form an entirely new reading public.

Cardoso's popularity has not come by chance and is just one more proof of the fact that, given appropriate stimulus, the working class can appreciate works of literary quality—especially when purely commercial fiction no longer circulates. Cardoso's intimate knowledge of the rural and urban workers and their problems, both in the pre-revolutionary period and since 1959, has played an important part in his success. More significant still is that Cardoso writes from the point of view of this social stratum, so much so that his literary activities appear almost as a series of dialogues with his working-class public. Much of his material is drawn from popular beliefs and modes of behaviour, and depicts popular characters who form part of the cultural heritage of ordinary people.

One of the marks of Cardoso's writing is indeed his creation of strongly individualized characters. It is around these individuals that he weaves his tapestry. Local atmosphere and social conditions are important, yet they never overlay the vital spark of the individual. In this he is very far from the naturalist manner of, say, the Chilean Baldomero Lillo or the Ecuadorean Jorge Icaza, whose personages, weighed down totally by adverse social conditions, usually become playthings of their wretchedness and tend to congeal into an acephalous mass of rebellious humanity destined to go under in the struggle for existence. Now and again one sees in Cardoso the odd character who does conform to this type—the Spaniard, Fernández, in *Isabelita* and *Along the River*— but these are rather exceptional. More frequent is the type exemplified in Julián Barreras (*Nino*), a difficult, granite-like personality who rejects any compromise with his principles.

As the Cuban critic, José Rodríguez Feo, has pointed out, Cardoso often structures his tales in such a way that the writer's own presence is hidden. The narrator of the action is a minor figure who takes part in and recounts events, with commentary, to an audience that appears to include the reader himself—as if he also formed part of the more or less chance group of listeners. This technique enables Cardoso to avoid direct judgements on what has happened. The writer here assumes the rôle of 'documentary director' whose task is merely to record reality as objectively as possible. Atmosphere is established at the outset of the story, then broadened and deepened through the use of significant, though unobtrusively situated detail, often picturesque or amusing in nature. This picturesque detail would in many lesser writers be simply gratuitous local colour. In Cardoso's work it forms part of the actual structure and therefore content of the narrative. It may appear as passing references to local customs, the odd colloquialism spoken by a character, an image which obsesses the narrator, or an action which because of its repetition draws the reader's attention, as in the case of the pauses taken by a village storyteller to wipe the sweat off his face and moustache. This detail, tellingly placed in the structure of the tale, creates an impressionistic effect, a rather subtle blending of different tones and hues, eminently suited to the patently non-manichean vision of the writer. There are very few total villains in Onelio Jorge Cardoso.

In order to gain a clearer appreciation of Onelio Jorge

Cardoso's talents, let us take a detailed look at two of his stories.

EN LA CIÉNAGA (IN THE SWAMP)

This tale revolves around the chance meeting of two anonymous individuals who have the misfortune to be tied to the terrible Zapata swamp in Cardoso's native province of Las Villas. We only know them as "el Gallego" (the Spaniard) and "the woman", who come into contact and are locked together for a time because the woman's small son is sick. The narrative skeleton of the story—a boat journey to get the child out of the swamp for medical attention—serves as a backcloth for illustrating a situation of hopeless poverty and misfortune which reduces the swamp people to the category of mere emanations of the disease-ridden atmosphere (both physical and psychological) associated with the region. The Spaniard, when requested to help the woman, at first refuses brutally, which in fact does not surprise her:

"She understood everything that the men of the swamp say, because she herself was from the swamp and had been kneaded together from the very slime of the earth, a treacherous soil which like them had been formed from the decay of dead years, plants that were never able to become plants, people that could never become people."

There is another reason for the Spaniard's bad temper: he, a charcoal burner, is worried that his charcoal oven will burn out if he leaves it. Thus his insulting reactions to her request— "Sod that! Am I supposed to be everybody's father?"... "What have I got to do with people who go wandering about this swamp? They shouldn't have children and if they have children and fevers they ought to have fathers as well." Such statements are not entirely unjustified from his point of view. But in the end he realises that the woman's bad fortune is due to the same grinding poverty he himself has to put up with and, leaving his oven, he goes away grumbling to fetch his boat.

Once he has taken the decision to help, and in spite of a whole chain of mishaps during the journey—an adverse wind forces him to spend hours rowing away with no prospect of advancing so as not to hole his boat on the banks of the channel, an oar breaks and he has to cut a piece of mangrove wood with a small knife to serve in its stead, they are constantly being bitten by blood-sucking mosquitos—he realizes that he has to push on and draw on his reserves of stoicism built up over long, hard years, in order to choke back his bad temper. So he rows all night, resentful at the woman and yet half-ashamed at his own bitterness, since he is well aware of the plight of the child.

In the end they reach a small settlement on the edge of the swamp, and by this time his hands are swollen and coagulated blood has formed round a wound in his arm. He irritably asks the woman why she is not happy at having arrived and why she has been silent for the last hours. She then tells him that the child has died, and this provokes in the coal-burner a terrible outburst of despair:

" 'Christ Almighty! I would have thrown it in the water!' And immediately he felt a deep shame, but she was looking at him with sincere gratitude, because when all is said and done, a man from the swamp is like the slime of the swamp, formed from the decay of dead years, plants which were never able to become plants, people who could never become people."

And there the story ends. The entire tragedy of the swamp-dwellers' lives has been made patent, and the figure of the Spaniard, so contradictory, has assumed the stature of a minor Prometheus struggling with an evil and implacable destiny.

By implication, the society which condemns people to this kind of existence stands condemned. Outside the swamp there is another life, for example that of the well-to-do, symbolized by the launch moored off the beach near the settlement and the man in holiday attire who appears on deck drinking a bottle of beer.

The Spaniard appears in two other stories, enabling the writer to present him in detail and show his incapability to take advantage of an event like the Revolution. By these means his contradictory nature is emphasized and the spectre of any possible Manicheism driven further away. In *Isabelita* he is shown as the brutal old husband whom a scarcely adolescent girl has been obliged to marry, and in *Por el río* he escapes from Cuba after the Revolution comes to power. He thus appears as an individual riddled by contradictions, most of them imposed on him by his environment. Cardoso's point is that such a character cannot be judged by conventional, "reasonable" standards. The swamp has infected his being at too many levels.

EL CUENTERO (THE STORY-TELLER)

The scenario of this tale is a hut inhabited by cane-cutters in the province of Pinar del Río, before the Revolution. The protaganist is Juan Candela, the "story-teller" of the title, who through the magic of his imagination has become a quasi-mythical figure in the region. More than a man, he is the personification of fantasy itself: his head is "full of rivers, mountains and men". Although initially the other cane-cutters do not realize this, his fantasies have come to form an integral and necessary part of their lives. As the narrator remarks: "In that place, where our wages were just bits of paper to be exchanged in the company store and where our backs were bent all day long in the sun, something inside us needed to listen to the things that might have been and weren't."

But the tensions arising from the contrast between the arduous and monotonous labour of these men in the cane-fields and the beauty which visits them at night in their shack through the story-telling of Juan Candela reach a point where they become unbearable, and the reader experiences the growth of a dull resentment in the audience, nurtured by the impossibility of harmonizing reality and fantasy. This resentment becomes sharper and sharper as Juan achieves ever higher flights of the imagination. For the reader the tension is further increased by the author's apparently chance allusions to depressing surroundings and daily problems.

At first nobody dares to contradict the weaver of words, silenced by the imposing gaze of finality with which he terminates his narrations. However, one particularly incredible episode—a dog is described as cutting itself in two after stumbling over a machete stuck in the ground—provokes a frankly sceptical commentary from the listeners. Soriano, the man most resistant to the magic of Juan Candela, declares straight out that it is a bare-faced lie and manages to win the agreement of the others for stopping Juan in his tracks, once and for all:

"The thing was to decide to break that power that Juan had in his body and that shone through his eyes... Really, we started thinking that we had to overcome Juan's power because you can stand a man lying to you if he does it once, and even a second time you accept it out of decency, but the third time it's like being slapped on the cheek, and then you have to slap him back at once."

In spite of this, such is Juan's way with words that even after another story where he has spoken of the possibility of journeying on foot from the Zapata swamp to Mexico City in six days, nobody feels confident enough to challenge him: "Then Soriano got up. He straightened up with his hands in his belt, but Juan caught him with his look. Soriano swallowed and sat down again."

The story-teller goes away, however, and Soriano finds concrete proof that the journey to Mexico on foot is not true when he sees an advertisement for a trip by boat. "My Christ, I'll speak up tonight, just you see!" While the men await this opportunity they sink back into the tedium of their daily work, and the writer mentions their having to fight a fire in a neighbouring cane-field, weed out the edges of theirs and solve the problems caused by plagues of insects, all of which tends to reinforce the barrier which has grown up between them and the poetry of the story-teller.

The latter, however, appears unaware of this hardening of attitudes, and in his next story tells of a snake forty yards in length which he has had to kill. Even now, nobody has the courage to attack him squarely, and the inevitable clash only occurs at the end when Juan refuses to give the slightest ground on being questioned:

"Juan fell silent and opened out his long, thin arms. Soriano was already on his feet, taking a deep breath to speak, but Juan stared at him. The fever had dried him up, but his eyes still preserved their power and he used all his energy to maintain it.

But Soriano remained standing with enough breath to say God knows what. Still, he kept silent and did not move.

Then I had an idea and I got up:

'Perhaps you didn't measure the snake right, Juan', I said, and he looked at me as he had looked at Soriano. His eyebrows stood out and we could see a spark in his eyes. I held his gaze as long as I could, until finally he stared at Soriano again and said:

'All right, perhaps you're right.'

'Maybe it was only thirty yards long!' Soriano almost shrieked, fixing his eyes on him.

'Maybe even a bit less,' laughed Miguel, and we all joined in his laughter.

But Juan crossed his arms, lifted up his chin and said calmly, looking round all of us,

'I'm sure it wasn't more than thirty, no mistake.'

'Go on, go on! Surely it wasn't more than six!' attacked Soriano.

Then what happened, happened:

Juan pulled out his machete and said, raising it over his head:

'I'll kill the one who takes off half a yard more!'. Nobody had the courage to move. His eyes were alight and his dark hand had turned white where he gripped the machete. We didn't say anything. Then he slowly lowered his weapon and said:

'You animals, you're just ungrateful animals!'

And he turned his back and was lost in the darkness of the shed.''

The cane-cutters lives return once more to the sordid drudgery of the off-season, the only relief coming when they have to weed out the fields. The pay is low and now, to crown it all, ''we had to fall back on our own poor memories, and the box where Juan used to sit was always vacant.''

But it is impossible for the gates of fantasy to remain closed:

''One hot night Don Carlos came and said something about the moon and the stars. He ended by declaring:

'The earth is round.'

'Well, it looks as flat as a board.' laughed Miguel.

Don Carlos puffed out smoke from his cigar and said, going off to his home:

'There are many things that are but don't appear to be.' Nobody spoke a word more, but I felt that those words depressed me, because I was beginning to realize that Juan was just that: something that was to do with the stars, *something that was, even thought it doesn't seem to be.* Something which was surely outside time, the shed and the world itself.''

This feeling has also taken root in another labourer , who declares: ''You have to believe in something beautiful even if it doesn't exist''. Even Soriano, with all his stubbornness, begs Juan to continue with his stories. The narrator concludes with the following words:

''And I myself caught them talking and I held my breath, hoping that Juan would say yes, because there was nobody like him, and he calmed you down and made you forget the dirt floor where we were living.''

Such are the stories of Cardoso. Written in everyday language, they can be read and fully appreciated by the cane-cutter, small peasant, fisherman and factory hand. Just as Nicolas Guillén is in the field of poetry, Cardoso is fully a people's writer. Furthermore, within the compass of the short story form, he is a master of many and delicate registers. The fact that he himself admits only to being a '*facilista*' or writer without complex ambitions, is typical of Cardoso's lack of pretention though perhaps not a just evaluation of his work.

He is basically interested in the day-to-day struggles and fantasies of the ordinary man, woman and child and does not embark on projects of larger, more ambitious and perhaps more abstract dimensions.

In *Tres tristes tigres*, Guillermo Cabrera Infante, self-exiled from Cuba since the mid-sixties and a man who displays an increasing bitterness toward the Revolution in his writings, has called Cardoso, somewhat ambiguously, a 'Chéjov del pobre': a 'Chekhov who writes (exclusively) about the poor', or a 'poor man's Chekhov'. Despite Cabrera Infante's slighting intent, Cardoso can indeed be seen as a Cuban Chekhov.

Chekhov tended not to take his short stories very seriously (he began by writing for humorous magazines), although as time went on he aimed at greater profundity. Likewise, Cardoso's self-deprecating remarks about his work, which, when applied to some of his tales, fall patently wide of the mark. Cardoso's *Ward Number Six* would be *The Story-Teller, In the Swamp* or *The Cat's Other Death*. Both writers are rooted in the provinces. Chekhov came from a small port on the sea of Azov in southern Russia. The Cuban was born in the modest township of Calabazar de Sagua in Las Villas province. Both were able to avoid the pomposity which membership of a literary clique in a large capital might have forced on them. Both are concerned to portray apparently insignificant people and adopt a minor key suited to the unpretentiousness of what they describe. Not surprisingly humour plays an important rôle in their stories.

These similarities may be partly explained by the fact that life in turn-of-the-century rural Russia and mid-twentieth-century rural Cuba (many of Cardoso's tales depict pre-revolutionary situations) ran on fundamentally the same lines for the working man and woman. Its basic components were poverty, hard work, exploitation and disappointment. Humour and fantasy provided necessary ingredients for mental survival.

A comparison with Chekhov should not suggest that Onelio Jorge Cardoso is unaware of the various modernist currents stemming from Joyce, Faulkner, Proust, Dos Passos, so favoured by Latin American writers. However, he has assimilated these experiments and used them, where appropriate, for his own ends. Cardoso is never interested in pyrotechnics for pyrotechnics' sake. Neither is there any question of his imitating anybody, as a few of the younger Cuban writers have tried to do. (One thinks of Norberto Fuentes, who consciously modelled *The Condemned of Condado*—a collection of short stories about the Escambray anti-bandit campaign which he had observed as a journalist—on Isaac Babel's renowned *Red Cavalry Tales,* about the Civil War in southern Russia and Poland after the Bolshevik Revolution. Fuentes was accused of falsifying the reality of the Escambray campaign by depicting revolutionary soldiers in the same light as counter-revolutionaries who had terrorised the area. His point, like Babel's, was that the violence of war necessarily brutalises both sides. But many of Fuentes' critics had themselves taken a far more direct part in the campaign than he had, and felt that he had libelled them. It did indeed appear that he had painted too lurid a picture for the sake of producing a startling book and emulating Babel's masterwork.)

Many of Cardoso's stories are in a genre sometimes associated with Russian literature: the *skaz* or tale narrated by a character who has taken some part in the action he describes and who, unconsciously, by his mode of telling, lets slip a great deal of information about himself, often to his detriment. The effect is one of sly comedy. Cardoso uses this genre in *En la caja del cuerpo* (*In the Frame of the Body*, an expression of José Martí) and in one of his best tales, *The Story-Teller*, where the narrator is just such a character, who may well have been drawn from reality.

The protagonists of many of Cardoso's stories are representatives of the pre-revolutionary poor from country areas: impoverished small peasants, cane-cutters, men from the Zapata swamp condemned to eke out a living from the production of charcoal, fishermen working in appalling conditions. Very few writers in Cuba have equalled him in depicting this type of setting. These people are, naturally, bound up with their local enemies: *guardias rurales* or country police, small-time political bosses and other exploiters. An intermediary type, who also appears, is the pre-revolutionary rural bandit, often driven to this kind of life through desperation.

Cardoso's later works show a greater preoccupation with urban dwellers and their problems, which are sometimes of a more purely psychological nature. One thinks of such collections as *Iba caminando* (*Out Walking*) (1966), *Abrir y cerrar los ojos* (*Opening and Shutting My Eyes*)(1969) and *El hilo y la cuerda* (The Thread and the String) (1974). Some of his stories belong to the sub-genre of children's fiction and usually have as their heart an Aesopian moral.

Perhaps the central theme in Cardoso's work — one to which he returns again and again — is what he terms man's 'two hungers'. Man has a need to satisfy his basic material wants. But he also has a longing to beautify the sordid world in which he exists, a pressing urge to illusion and fantasy. As with all writers of original genius, Onelio Jorge Cardoso has his own complex voice—a voice analagous to the subtleties of life itself. Perhaps the only fitting impression of his work may be conveyed by quoting a few lines from Pablo Neruda, another Latin American of indefinable resonances:

Os amo, idealismo y realismo	I love you, idealism and realism
como agua y piedra	like water and stone
sois	you are
partes del mundo	parts of the world
luz y rais del arbol de la vida.	light and root of the tree of life.

REFERENCES

1.   Seymour Menton, *Prose Fiction of the Cuban Revolution*, University of Texas Press, Austin, Texas, 1975. Invaluable as a reference work, this study is rather sourly and unfairly biased against the evolution of Cuba's cultural policies.

Three Poems

Nicolás Guillén
translated by Peter Turton

<table>
<tr><td>

SUDOR Y LATIGO

Látigo,
sudor y látigo.

El sol despertó temprano
y encontró al negro descalzo,

desnudo. el cuerpo ilagado,

sobre el campo.

Látigo,
sudor y látigo.

El viento pasó gritando:
— ¡Qué flor negra en
cada mano!
La sangre le dijo: ¡vamos!
El dijo a la sangre:¡vamos!.
Partió en su sangre,
descalzo.
El cañaveral, temblando,
le abrió paso.
Después, el cielo callado,

</td><td>

SWEAT AND THE WHIP

The whip,
sweat and the whip.

The sun woke early
and found the black man with
no shoes,
his body a mass of open
wounds,
over the canefield.

The whip,
sweat and the whip.

The wind passed screaming by
What a black flower in
each hand!
His blood told him: let's go!
He told his blood: let's go!
He set off in his blood,
with no shoes.
The canefield, trembling,
opened up for him.
Afterwards, the silent sky,

</td></tr>
</table>

y bajo el cielo, el esclavo	and under the sky, the slave
tinto en la sangre del amo.	dark red with the boss's blood.

Látigo,	The whip,
sudor y látigo,	sweat and the whip,
tinto en la sangre del amo;	dark red with the boss's blood;
látigo,	the whip,
sudor y látigo,	sweat and the whip,
tinto en la sangre del amo,	dark red with the boss's blood,
tinto en la sangre del amo.	dark red with the boss's blood.

El son entero, 1947

UN SON PARA NIÑOS ANTILLANOS

A 'SON' FOR WEST INDIES KIDS

Por el mar de las Antillas
anda un barco de papel:
anda y anda el barco barco
sin timonel

Sailing over the Caribbean sea
goes a little paper boat:
that little boat sails on and on
with no rudder.

De La Habana a Portobelo,
de Jamaica a Trinidad,
anda y anda el barco barco
sin capitán.

From Havana to Portobello,
From Jamaica to Trinidad,
that little boat sails on and on
with no captain.

Una negra va en la popa,

There's a black girl in
        the poop,

va en la proa un español:
anda y anda el barco barco,
con ellos dos.

and a Spaniard in the prow:
the little boat sails on and on,
with just those two.

Pasan islas, islas, islas,

Islands, islands, islands,
        float past

muchas islas, siempre más;

many islands, then more and
        more;

anda y anda el barco barco,
sin descansar.

the little boat sails on and on,
for evermore.

Un cañón de chocolate	A chocolate cannon
contra el barco disparó	fired at the boat
y un cañón de azúcar, zúcar,	and a sugar cannon,
le contestó.	all of sugar,
	fired back.
¡Ay, mi barco marinero,	
con su casco de papel!	Oh, my little sailing boat
¡Ay, mi barco negro y blanco	my little paper boat!
sin timonel!	Oh, my little black and
	white boat
Allá la negra negra,	with no rudder!
junto junto al español;	
anda y anda el barco barco	There goes that black girl,
con ellos dos.	all black,
	close by the Spaniard's side;
	the little boat sails on and on
	just with those two.

El son entero, 1947

BONSAL, 1959

	The wind brought Bonsal here.
	Bonsal's the ambassador.
Bonsal llegó en el viento.	An amimal.
Este Bonsal es el	with blue eyes, lead-coloured
embajador. Animal	hair, flesh-pink, whose English
ojiazul, peliplúmbeo, de	is lethal.
color rojicarne, que habla un	(How do you say it? *Bon*sal?
inglés letal.	Well, who cares?)
(¿Cómo se dice? ¿Bonsal? Oh,	
señor, es igual).	Smiles. His smiles
	burn like hard currency.
Sonrisas. Las sonrisas	Greetings. His greetings,
arden como divisas.	soft, silent gestures.
Saludos. Los saludos,	Promises. His promises
son suaves gestos mudos.	are a promise of long
Promesas. Las promesas	round-tables.
anuncian largas mesas.	And the imperial eagle.
Y el águila imperial.	

Y el dólar y el dolor.
Y el mundo occidental.
Bonsal. Este Bonsal
es el Embajador.

¿Qué quiere? Que Fidel
hable un poco con él.
Que la gente medite,
no que proteste o grite.

Que el campesino aquiete
su rifle y su machete.
Que vaya cada cual
a refrescar su ardor
con agua mineral.
Bonsal. Este Bonsal
es el Embajador.

Cuba por fin en calma.
* No Marti,*
no Maceo. Washington es
* mejor.*
¿El General? ¡Oh, no,
* la capital!*
Y continuar asi,
como quiere Bonsal,
que es el embajador.
Noche. Ni un resplandor.
Sopor. Guardia Rural.
¿De acuerdo?
* —No, señor.*

Tengo, 1964

And the dollar and the grief.
And the western world.
Bonsal. This Bonsal guy
is the Ambassador.

What does he want? Fidel to
    have
a chat with him.
He wants people to think it
    over,
and not complain or make
    a noise.

He wants the peasant to silence
his rifle and his machete.
Everyone should go away
and cool off
with a drink of mineral water.
Bonsal. This Bonsal guy
is the Ambassador.

No Martí,
no Maceo. Washington is
    better.
The General? Oh no,
    the capital!
And carry on like that,
as Bonsal wishes,
for he's the Ambassador.
Night-time. Not a glow
    anywhere.
Everybody asleep. Country
    police.
Alright?
            — No sirree.

Nicolás Guillén: People's Poet

Antoni Turull

'Every act or voice of genius comes from the people or goes towards it, whether directly or because it is transmitted through unending threads, by the pink smoke of bitter luckless passwords.' César Vallejo

Nicolás Guillén was born in Camagüey in 1902. Later in Havana as a student of Law he was introduced to the Afro-Cuban movement that was to influence his first published work Motivos De Son (1930). *Because of his negro origins he was able to imbue his poetry with a range of lived experiences denied to other followers of Afro-Cubanism.*

Motivos De Son *and his next collection* Sóngoro Cosongro *published the following year have predominantly negro and mulatto themes as well as poems sympathetic to the poor and the oppressed. In* West Indies Ltd. *published in 1934 he deals with the two themes of slavery and colonialism.*

Guillén's preoccupation with social and political themes continued. In 1937 he published España *on the theme of the Spanish Civil War and of the prospects for the future offered by communism. He was later to become a member of the Communist Party. Subsequent collections,* Cantos para soldados y sones para turistas *(1937),* El Son Entero *(1947),* La Paloma de Vuelo Popular *(1948) and* Tengo *(1964) all reflect his social concerns and political position.*

Nicolás Guillén is an important figure in Cuba in the 1970s. He continues to write poetry which reflects the changes and developments in consciousness of the Cuban people as well as entering fully into political life as President of Cuba's Writers Union, UNEAC, and as a member of the National Assembly of People's Power.

In 1937, Nicolás Guillén wrote of the two 'official' nineteenth century Cuban poets, Rubalcava and Zequeira: 'neither of the two stops to listen to the tone of his surroundings, of reality itself, which should provide a framework for their voices.' It is precisely to the tone of surrounding reality that Guillén himself has listened, and it is this which has made him the people's poet of Cuba.

By the age of 28, in 1930, Nicolás Guillén had published some post-modernist experimental poetry, led something of a vagabond existence, and worked as a journalist in the Ministry of the Interior. He had written nothing for five years, but had not succeeded in suffocating the poet within himself. For it was in 1930 that he, as he himself claims, literally 'woke' to the form in which he was to disover his poetic voice; a form which had always been around him—the *'son'* or dancing song. *Motivos de Son* (*Motives of Sound*) appeared in that year and caused a literary scandal in Cuba because of its subject matter: lower class life in Havana, not a subject previously made into poetry. Humorous, steeped in folklore and the ways of Cuban blacks, openly sexual and fresh with everday language, these poems made Guillén into one of the foremost of Latin American poets.

The *'son'*, a flexible form, became Guillén's model for future poetry. Afro-Hispanic, with its origins in the former province of Oriente, the *son* dates from the end of the sixteenth century and uses the so-called Extremaduran ballad form with repeated chorus. As Alejo Carpentier points out in his book on Cuban music, the *son* is, in effect, a song with a percussion (and not orchestral) accompaniment, where a plurality of rhthyms are enclosed in a fixed beat. The musical genre of the *son* reminds Carpentier of a primitive draft for Stravinsky's *Les noces*: 'The melodic material comes from the human voices and the rhythmic beat from the percussion instruments'.

Guillén's *Motivos de son* follow the scheme of the musical *son*. That is, the poem is divided into two parts which may overlap: first the motif or *largo* presents the theme or dramatic point, and then comes the chorus or *montuno*, repeated whenever the singers feel like it. This chorus speeds up the tempo and has a joking, sardonic character. To a certain extent, this last quality de-dramatises the whole, while at the same time pinpointing its drama. In this it resembles negro voices, of which Fernando Ortiz remarks, 'We do not know at any given moment whether they are joking or crying'. The duration of the second part of the musical *son* is indefinite, so that it may last until the public joins in or the singers get tired.

Here is a *son*, quoted by Carpentier, which was very popular in the twenties.

PAPA MONTERO	PAPA MONTERO
Señores,	Gentlemen,
Señores,	Gentlemen,
los familiares del difunto	the dead man's family
me han confiado,	have given me the task
para que despida el duelo,	of ending the wake
del que en vida fue	of the man known as
Papá Montero.	Papa Montero
Chorus	Chorus
A llorar a Papá Montero,	All weep for Papa Montero,
¡Zumba!	Go on!
canalla rumbero.	you rumba-ing bastard.
Solo Chorus	Solo Chorus
Lo llevaron al agujero.	They put him in the hole.
¡Zumba!	Go on!
Canalla rumbero.	You rumba-ing bastard.
Solo chorus	Solo chorus
Nunca más se pondrá	He'll never put on his hat
sombrero	again.
¡Zumba!	Go on!
Canalla rumbero. etc. etc.	You rumba-ing bastard. etc. etc.

And here is a sample of a *son* as written by Guillén;

TÚ NO SABE INGLÉ	YAH CAN'T SPEAK ENGLISH

Con tanto inglé que
   tú sabía
Bito Manué
con tanto inglé, no sabe
   ahora
desí ye.
	All that English
	   yah knew,
	Victah Manuel,
	all that English and now yah
	   can't even
	say yeah.

La mericana te buca *y tú le tiene que hui* *tu inglé era de etrai guan,* *de etrai guan y guan tu tri.*	The 'Merican dame's after yah yah English was just strike one, strike one an' one two tree.
Bito Manué, tu no sabe inglé, *tu no sabe inglé,* *tu no sabe inglé.*	Victah Manuel, ya don' know English, Yah don' know English, yah don' know English.
No te enamore má nunca, *Bito Manué,* *si no sabe ingle,* *si no sabe inglé.*	Don' yah evah fall in love again, Victah Manuel, if yah don' know English, if yah don' know English.

The *son* is a real poetic find, an unfixed form with well-defined characteristics: alliteration of a single letter or of groups of consonants, frequency of refrain, stress on the last syllable of a line, use of dialogue. It is an innovation which marries the two main strands of popular culture basic to Cuba: African and Hispanic. Guillén insists that his poetry is Afro-Hispanic, that is mulatto, just as he is. His book of poems, *Sóngoro cosongo* (1931) was subtitled, 'Mulatto Poems'. While Afro-Cuban elements, negro themes, are only one aspect of Cuba, the mulatto quality encompasses Cuba's entire essence.

Interestingly in *Motivos de son*, although Guillén uses negro themes and characters, he never mythifies the life and culture of the black community, so spurned by the Spaniards and Americans. The main characters to emerge in the poems are those blacks and mulattoes who were denied a leading role in any sphere other than that of ex-slave society. But these are neither held up as a norm, nor aggrandised as challenging examples to be followed.

In *Motivos de son,* there is already that simplicity of language that Guillén is to use throughout his poetic evolution. The attempt here to reproduce the phonetic peculiarities of Cuban Spanish through spelling is abandoned in subsequent books. However, there is much future use of *jitanjáforas* or nonsense words. In these words, the sound has more importance than the meaning, following African preferences 'for pure rhythm, for rhythmic structure in itself,' as Monica Mansour points out in *La poesía negrista.*

We also find in *Motivos de son* the popular humour of Cuba, evident throughout Guillén's work and also an aspect of his personality. This humour, ingeniously ironic, associated more with town than countryside, is what the Cubans call *choteo.* Guillén arrives at the purest form of *choteo* when he points a finger at the world of exploiters and their hangers-on.

Todos estos yanquis rojos	All those red yankees
son hijos de un camarón,	are sons of a shrimp
y los parió una botella,	and they come out of a bottle,
una botella de ron.	a bottle of rum.
'Cantaliso en un bar'	'Cantaliso in a bar'

This fragment comes from the poem, '*Sones* for tourists', whose main character is called, significantly, José Ramon Cantaliso or José Ramon Tell-it-straight.

Choteo is much in evidence in the 'Grotesque Little Litany on the Death of Senator McCarthy':

He aquí al senador McCarthy,	Here is Senator McCarthy,
muerto en su cama de muerte,	dead on his death bed,
flanqueado por cuatro monos;	flanked by four monkeys;
he aquí al senador McMono,	here is Senator McMonkey,
muerto en su cama de Carthy,	dead in his Carthy bed,
flanqueado por cuatro buitres;	flanked by four vultures;
he aquí al senador McBuitre...	here is Senator McVulture...

The nicknames given McCarthy, McGangster (a bourgeois bandit), McPlomo (McLead, a murderer), McVíbora (McViper, poison for the people), and so on, are only aspects of the totality of references suggested by Senator McCarthy.

Even when the literary clique of Havana finally granted

Guillén acceptance, he did not assume a personal attitude of intellectual seriousness and importance. Sardonic humour remains a personal trait and persists in his poems as one way of bringing out dramatic points. But another strain co-exists in Guillén's work. It is libertarian, justice-loving and lyrical. Side by side with the pleasure-seeking yankees in his work, the satires on McCarthyism, are Cubans struggling toward their own identity; themes of racial equality and of unity between the various peoples and classes of Cuba.

Baja el sol
nuestra piel sudorosa reflejará los rostros
húmedos de los vencidos
y en la noche, mientras los astros ardan en
la punta de nuestras llamas,
nuestra risa madrugará sobre los ríos y los pájaros.
     —(Llegada)

 In the sun
 our sweating skins will reflect the wet faces of the defeated,
 and at night, while the stars burn on the tips of our flames,
 our laughter will rise up in the morning over the rivers and the
  birds.
     —(Arrival)

In 'Guessing games' (Adivinanzas) the whole tragedy of an oppressed people is discernible.

Un hombre que está llorando	A man who is weeping
con la risa que aprendió.	with the laughter he learnt.
¿Quién será, quién no será?	Who can it be, who on earth
	can it be?
—Yo.	—Me.

Guillén is an innovator who—by using traditional structures, both popular and 'cultured', as the usual division has it, and free verse plus the *son* and *choteo*—constructs poetry which is both committed and lyrical, to express the very soul of Cuba while in *Caña (Sugar-Cane)* the history, geography and economy of the country are evoked:

El negro	The black
junto al cañaveral.	next to the cane.
El yanqui	The Yankee
sobre el cañaveral.	over the canefield.
La tierra	The earth
bajo el cañaveral.	beneath the canefield.
¡Sangre	The blood
que se nos va!	we are losing!

'Poema con niños' (Poem with Children) has as its theme racial equality:

La sangre es un mar inmenso	Blood is an immense sea
que baña todas las playas...	bathing everybody's beach...
Sobre sangre van los hombres,	Over blood go men,
navegando en sus barcazas:	sailing in their launches:

'La canción del bongó' (The Song of the Bongo), in turn, cries out with a plea for the rights of the black man: '¡que aquí el más alto soy yo!' ('cos here *I'm* the one who walks tallest!').

Social equality is heralded by a dove that flies singing by and wakes up a little black child: '¡Que muera el amo, / muera en la brasa! / Ya nadie duerme, / ni está en su casa' ('Death to the boss, / let him be burnt alive! / Nobody sleeps any more, / or stays at home').

There are references to the Spanish Civil War:

> ...*El camino sabemos...*
> ...*Los rifles engrasados...*
> ...*Están los brazos avisados...*
> *¡Y la canción alegre flotará como una nube sobre la roja*
>   *lejanía!*
>   (*La voz esperanzada*)

> ...We know the way...
> ...We've oiled our rifles...
> ...Our arms are ready...
> And the happy song will float like a cloud over the red
>   horizon!
>   (The Voice of Hope)

The history of Latin America, its reality and its future, are recalled in Guillén's verse. He mentions characters such as Lynch, Stroessner, Trujillo, Muñoz, Kennedy, Barrientos, Johnson, and also Bolívar, Washington, Martí, Fidel, Sandino, Che Guevara, to cite but a few of the names made famous in the history books. But Guillén also reveals what has been called *intrahistoria*, the history of everyday life of common people. And these ordinary people make their appearance in the centre of his poems. He always puts himself on the side of the oppressed to which he belongs. He takes part with the hopes of his people—who act as a symbol for all oppressed peoples—and against all those forces that have tried and are still trying to strangle movement toward emancipation. To celebrate the triumph of the Cuban Revolution—he was fifty-six at the time—Guillén wrote the poem *'Tengo'* (I Have), which concerns itself as much with economic questions as with social and racial equality, not themes common to European verse.

Having said this, it must not be forgotten that Guillén is also a master of the traditional forms of Spanish poetry: the *silva*, the sonnet, the *sonetillo*, the ballad, the *redondilla*, the tercet and the ballad-form called the 'romance'. Sometimes he keeps to the strictures of these classic forms, while at others he allows himself the freedom necessary for transforming them into Cuban 'expression'. So too, some of Guillén's themes are the traditional ones of love poetry, which he infuses with a new erotic tension. For example, 'Madrigal', a tour de force in which all the rhymes are masculine:

> *Sencilla y vertical,*
> *como una caña en el cañaveral.*
> *Oh retadora del furor*
> *genital:*
> *tu andar fabrica para el espasmo gritador*
> *espuma equina entre tus muslos de metal.*

> Simple and vertical,
> like a cane in the canefield.
> Oh how you challenge the fury
> of the genitals:
> your walk produces for the shouting spasm
> a froth of horses between your metallic legs.

Angel Augier has said that Guillén 'tunes his deeply popular sensibility to the historic process of his people and his era.' The two longings, the black and the white, end by fusing together. Guillén is a popular poet because he shares the aspirations and also the speech of the masses. He is himself an integral part of them, a committed writer in the deepest sense. As he told me: 'If a poet backs away from taking a stand with regard to public life, then public life may either catch him unawares or use him for its own ends. So it is necessary to have a clear-cut attitude. My poetry, I believe, is a dynamic process. It constantly supports and encourages the struggles of peoples against inequality and imperialism'.

Guillén is also popular in the sense that his work is known very widely. Not only are some of his poems recited by people who are possibly unaware of their authorship, but they have also been set to music by classical composers like Montsalvatge in Barcelona and a whole variety of folkloric and popular musicians in Spain and Latin America.

Nicolás Guillén stopped in his tracks and still does so to listen to the creative genius of his people. It is this which embraces his voice, his poetic voice. There is no better form of expression. And Guillén continues to write. 'Which part of your work do you prefer?' he was asked in 1972 when he had reached the age of seventy. Guillén replied, 'That which I still haven't written...'

REFERENCES

Guillén's works in English can be found in:

Man-Making Words: Selected Poems of Nicolás Guillén, edited and translated by Robert Marquez and David McMurray, University of Massachussetts Press, 1972.

Patria o Muerte: The Great Zoo and Other Poems, edited and translated by Robert Marquez, Monthly Review Press, 1973.

Tengo, translated by Richard Carr, Broadside Press, 1974.

The Collected Poems 1920-1972 are available in Spanish in two volumes prefaced by Angel Augier.

The Poetry of Nicolás Guillén, Dennis Sardini, New Beacon Books, London, 1976, provides a useful introduction.

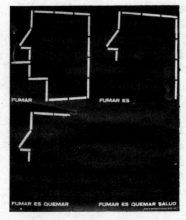

FUMAR   FUMAR ES

FUMAR ES QUEMAR   FUMAR ES QUEMAR SALUD

Poster Art

Chris Rawlence

In the mid-morning Havana heat they're busy preparing for the Carnival. Seven nights dancing, music, mass meetings, drinking—holiday—begins this evening. Beer and rum stalls are being set up. Six foot high barrels of white rum are manoeuvred into position; tankers full of beer back up; mountains of conical paper cups grow on the trestle tables. Around the corner some people are putting the finishing touches to their float: an oil derrick has been constructed on one end of the trailer; on the other platforms, decorated with streamers and strings of coloured electric light bulbs, rise at different levels; a steel band practises on the largest. A tractor backs up to the float and its couplings are inspected. This is Cuba Oil's float. Tonight it will join a hundred other floats for the grand parade: there will be floats from different sugar and tobacco plantations, from trade unions, from women's organisations—each with its steel band and dancers; and behind each float will walk and dance hundreds of carnival makers with conical paper cups, joined together in a snake of moving colour, sound and people. They are celebrating: for a week they will celebrate the completed sugar harvest and their Revolution, at the end of which, on the anniversary of Moncada—July 26th—Fidel Castro will make his major public speech of the year in Havana.

Carnival was celebrated in Havana long before the Revolution. The memory of its recent history—and of Cuba's recent history—lingers on in its forms. In the 1950s the floats would have been publicity for large Havana department stores: the bikinied dancing girls of those days now dance on the floats of a socialist economy. But it is a longer—and predominantly black—cultural memory and a socialist present that combine to create the exuberance of today's carnival.

Half way up a lamp-post a man is struggling to wire up a Tannoy. He makes the connection and Sinatra groans across the street: 'I'll do it my way'. Twenty miles out at sea a lone US warship surveys the scene, as it does day and night. High above US reconnaisance planes periodically leave their white wisps in the sky. While the imperialists keep their distance, strains of their ideology still penetrate, and live: someone has tuned in to a Miami radio station.

Midsummer light in Cuba is dazzling and intense. In the shadowed wall of a doorway to an old block of flats, multi-coloured ceramic tiles reflect the light, vividly articulating their drab architectural surrounds. High up on the end of the same building lurks another pre-revolutionary presence: Drink Coca-Cola. Twelve years after the Revolution this advertisement remains, blistered and bleached, but still there, slowly flaking away. The company left, and, unfortunately for the Cubans, took their formula with them: after twelve years of tooth destroying experiments, they have now rediscovered it. Socialist Cola lives. But its capitalist image is dying, its wallspace expropriated by the new imagery of the Cuban poster.

Brightly coloured images are everywhere, dancing in the light. On the road from the airport a series of ten hoardings, once the hunting ground of the Esso tiger, now proclaim José Martí's role in the struggle for the new Cuba. In a sequence of huge images, the face of this nineteenth century revolutionary grows to assume a central place in the development of Cuban socialism. The images are highly stylised: large flat interrelations of bright colour with a bold text. The style shows an awareness in the maker of the techniques of western advertising and of some recent developments in modern western painting. (The exhibition of Pop Art at the Salon de Mayo in Havana in 1967 was a seminal influence). Shop windows too have been transformed: in the absence of luxury commodities to display, and a prevailing ideology which promotes such value, many shop windows of the old Havana department stores are now glass canvases, painted from the inside for permanent exhibition to the street. In one of these stores, all windows but one have been painted to celebrate a recent event: the return of the fishermen. A few weeks back a small Cuban fishing boat was held by the US Navy in retaliation for the Cuban holding of a luxury yacht suspected of anti-Cuban activities. Its recent release was felt by Cubans to be a victory. The fishermen's return to Havana was greeted by an early morning meeting of 100,000 on the quay. In one window, a fish explodes in Uncle Sam's eye, in a style which suggests an intimacy with Marvel Comics and Disney. In another a Pinocchio-like fisherman gleefully suspends a drenched and sagging Uncle Sam from his rod, amidst a sky of brightly coloured stars. In the next, a monolithic M-O-N-C-A-D-A zooms at lightning speed into the winded belly of Uncle Sam. These paintings celebrate the joy of the fishermen's return. Their function is humorous: tongue in cheek, they affirm a victory. In the odd window out, Mogoyon is relaxing, grabbing a quick smoke. Mogoyon is a socialist Andy Capp with a regular strip in *Granma*. He is the loafer— polar opposite to the exemplary worker. He is what Cubans shouldn't be. His cartoon cut-out is sitting on a real trestle in the window which he is supposed to have painted. In the bubble he says: 'I've been told to clean these brushes, but they can wait till tomorrow.' The brushes next to him harden irretrievably into disuse.

Other painted shop windows are less explicit. They are less cartoons than paintings. The window of a CDR headquarters —once a shop—is filled with a barely figurative image of imperialist violence. The painting is reminiscent of *Guernica:* on the left a white dove-like shape is in the clutches of a suggested eagle; on the right, across what may be deep blue sea, a large red area ambiguously responds. There is no text, no slogan: a precise interpretation is not possible. In the sunlit street the painting makes the passer-by witness to a struggle between oppressor and oppressed. It evokes the heroism and suffering of liberation struggles, calling on you to take the side of the oppressed. Just round the corner they're redecorating the old Hotel Royal Palm. Its windows too are now occupied:

by the magnified decorative motifs of Chilean folk art combined into a large painting that announces pride and joy in Latin American culture.

But it is the posters which predominate. Pasted and pinned up on almost every available flat surface, they make the city vibrate with colour. Combined with the shop-window paintings, they decorate Havana. But they also speak directly.

Posters in Cuba have a number of functions. In *The Art of Revolution,* edited by Dugald Stermer, Pall Mall, (1970), Susan Sontag laid a misleading emphasis on the cultural posters—those publicising a film, the ballet, or some other cultural event. Together with a few anti-imperialist posters, these form the substance of the examples she chose. Admittedly many of the latter referred to the war in Vietnam, which for an intended US readership would have had a particular relevance. But to anyone who has visited Cuba and seen posters at work in their largely outdoor context, the more directly functional and internally oriented posters seem conspicuously absent from her selection. The overwhelming number of posters in the Havana streets, for example, are not about the ballet or a film; they are about the day to day business of pushing a revolution forward.

Cuban posters may be divided into roughly four categories: the 'cultural' posters referred to above; posters about the different national liberation struggles of the world—largely for 'export'; posters about the past and present political history of Cuba—mainly for 'internal' use; and posters about the day to day economics of life with socialism in Cuba: 'Save Empty Boxes' or 'Clean Your Machine' etc.

I am visiting a Jamaican friend in a suburb of Havana. It's a hot afternoon and we're having a cold drink in the shade on her small balcony. Pinned to her wall is a small poster: the words BLACK POWER are printed over the stylised face of a black panther. The poster's presence points to her identity with the struggles of black people in California. At this moment there are a number of Black Panthers staying in Havana: to escape arrest they took a Boeing 'home to Castro'. In the bottom corner of the poster are printed the letters OSPAAAL: Organisation for Solidarity with the Peoples of Asia, Africa and Latin America. Probably upwards of 40,000 of these posters have been produced on a 'litho machine' in Havana as a pull out 'extra' for *Tricontinental*—a journal exported to the three continents as an ideological component in the anti-imperialist struggle. One has found its way to her balcony.

OSPAAAL posters take as their themes the different liberation struggles of the world. Their images are often starkly simple and effective, with minimal text. One example celebrates an international week of solidarity with Vietnam. Apart from this information, small at the top, there is no text: a simple image of an orange sub-machine gun placed in a vertical plane over a dark green background. Superimposed over the machine gun is the traditional weapon of the Vietnamese—a crossbow. Another poster celebrates a day of solidarity with Zimbabwe. Again, there is no slogan: simply a white colonialist's hat against a black background penetrated by a vertical green arrow. These components—the stylised hat, arrow, gun—placed in simple juxtaposition, are elements of an accessible system of signs developing as part of a shared poster language in Cuba.

Yet another image portrays, at first glance, Christ; his face is encircled with a yellow halo rimmed in red; he wears a green top garment. Seemingly out of place, he has a rifle strapped over his shoulder—the gleam of its barrel as bright as the emanating halo next to it. His expression conveys a peaceful resolve to use the weapon if necessary. Closer examination shows that the poster is in fact a photograph of an oil painting: the texture of the paint is quite visible; ridges left by a palette knife reflect the photographic lighting used to illumine the painting. As a European, I have to have this image explained to me. It is a picture of Camilo Torres, the Colombian guerrilla-priest, who died fighting in 1970. Small oil-painted images of Christ are commonplace in Colombian homes. By integrating the image of the guerilla-priest with the form of an object of religious devotion, the poster aims to show that the revolutionary aims and tactics of Camilo Torres are reconcilable with the ethics and beliefs of Christianity. Such a message would not have been necessary in Cuba, where the Catholic church was never as dominant as on the main continent of Latin America. There, however, it is a very different story: this image would be shockingly direct, proposing a combination

TU TRABAJO
ES NECESARIO
EN EL TABACO

XVIII ANIVERSARIO
26
de JULIO

HOTEL HABANA LIBRE

JORNADA DE SOLIDARIDAD CON ZIMBABWE (17 de marzo)
DAY OF SOLIDARITY WITH ZIMBABWE (March 17)
JOURNEE DE SOLIDARITE AVEC LE ZIMBABWE (17 mars)

ANIVERSARIO

that would be instantly recognisable to most Colombian people.

Down in the street a queue is forming. People are standing with crates of empty beer bottles. A girl bends down to count her bottles knowing that she won't be allowed to buy more full bottles than empty ones she returns. Behind her, pinned to a bare wooden door, are two posters. One reads: 'Bring Your Bottles Back Clean'. The other reads simply: REVES. Against a vibrant orange background the word occupies a small space at bottom left. But its V grows out of the small word to fill the poster with a giant black and white victory V. Interpretation requires knowledge of recent Cuban events—with which the whole queue will be familiar, but not me. I ask my Jamaican friend. The poster refers to 1970's sugar harvest. The whole Cuban economy had been mobilised to achieve a ten million ton sugar crop. As each million was cut, huge posters went up on hoardings everywhere to signal the achievement: in monumental three-dimensional seeming letters, describing an arc in almost fluorescent colours, the word SEIS—SIX—the sixth million—and so on. But the target was not reached. This single-aimed concentration of Cuban resources failed to reach its target. The resultant criticism and self-criticism emerged with a slogan: 'Convert a Setback into a Victory'. And it is to this that the REVES poster refers: REVES means SETBACK. Up one side of the poster is printed COR PCC. These letters stand for Committee for the Orientation of the Revolution, Cuban Communist Party. COR is organised at a national and a regional level. It is responsible, among other things, for internal propaganda, for which it designs and produces posters.

REVES is one such poster. It is a large poster and unlike the OSPAAAL posters, it has been hand silkscreened. The paper it is printed on is closer to cardboard, buff and rough. The inks used are matt and gritty. The gauze of the screen was coarse: its weave is visibly imprinted, in places, on the set sludgy inks. The posters have been stacked before they had time to dry: the black ink of the letters has stuck to the wood pulpy back of the poster laid on top of it, pulling some paper away. The black letters have a white furry look. In every way the poster proclaims the process by which it was made. It also points to the very real constraints on certain kinds of production in an underdeveloped socialist economy: there are simply not the resources for enough printing machines, sophisticated inks, quality papers, vacuum-bed silk screens. They have to get by, in many cases, with what any western advertising company would regard as tenth best. Lack of resources dictates the making of most Cuban posters many of which are hand silkscreened in this way. Yet this apparent crudeness gives them a particular character. The thickness of the paper, the gritty quality of the inks, the traces of the process give them a tangible presence often absent in the sleek sophisticated surfaces of western advertisements. Some of them have five or six colours indicating several hand-pulled screenings. As each layer of colour goes on, the posters attain the quality of reliefs. They become almost sculptural in their presence.

COR and OSPAAL are not the only sources of posters in Cuba. The Nationalised industries each have their teams of designers and poster-producing departments. I met a black woman designer from Cuba Tobacco who gave me a few posters. We talked about them. The text of one read: 'Your Work is Necessary in Tobacco'. It was addressed to women. The top half of the poster—another hand-screened one—portrays the leaves and stems of tobacco plants in flat variegated greens against the plain coarse paper of the poster. Scattered over the leaves are the blue dew-drop-like stars with bobbles on their points, giving a sparkly, garden-like feel to the tobacco plants. Below the plants, next to the text, is the black and white image of a woman's face. From the shade of a straw hat she gazes at the spectator with a hint of sexual innuendo. Only one eye is visible, the other is in shadow. Its eyelashes are pronounced; it is a made-up eye with hints of eye shadow and mascara. It conforms to a fashion image. Her nose, mouth and bone structure are equally attended to. She is a woman's magazine ideal of beauty. Message: tobacco plantations aren't de-womanising, complexion-destroying places they're made out to be; if you work there you will retain your beauty and femininity. The poster addresses itself to a fear prevalent amongst Cuban woman that work in the plantations will turn them into the myth of what Soviet women have become through their revolution.

This poster points up some of the contradictions inherent in building socialism from underdevelopment. Where the needs of the economy come first it has publicised a half truth—that tobacco-plantations are garden-like—and projected an image of woman that perhaps builds on characteristics of women's oppression: she is, arguably, sex-objectified in the way she is presented: passive—a man's idea of women. A strong women's mass organisation coexists with such images in Cuba. The FMC (Federation of Cuban Women) has some two million members. At the time of my visit (1971) theories of women's oppression and exploitation, the double shift etc., were being argued over and discussed. A recent poster put out by the FMC was a simple hand screened image of Angela Davis. In sharp contrast to the Cuba Tobacco poster, in a style based on the simplification of a photograph, she is shown militantly, assertively, confidently fighting her oppression as a woman and a black. Yet the functions of the two posters both of which had mass circulation were different; one serving immediate economic needs; the other operating on a more directly political plane. Their coexistence simply underlines the uneven development in cultural, ideological and economic processes in building a new society.

It is not as if Cubans are unaware of these contradictions. They are discussed all the time. My friend from Cuba Tobacco showed me another poster. It was an anti-smoking poster, produced by COR. The outline of a head is arranged with cigarettes. Through four stages, one in each corner, the cigarettes are gradually removed: the head disappears. The text to the diminishing head reads: SMOKING... SMOKING IS... SMOKING IS BURNING... SMOKING IS BURNING YOUR HEALTH. Not surprisingly Cubans were used to being heavy smokers: tobacco is Cuba's second industry after sugar. Cigarettes are rationed now and in the process have become nicknamed Tupamaros: "Because everyone knows they're there but nobody knows where to find them". The encouraged growth of an industry so injurious to health, as is also, arguably, sugar, is another facet of the contradictions inherent in developing socialism from underdevelopment.

Some of Cuba's full time poster designers were graphic designers before the Revolution, working within the framework of capitalist advertising in Cuba or the United States. Trained in a language of advertising, their styles reflect this professional background. Often the slicker, more graphically stylised/abstracted images emanate from them, or those trained by them. Sometimes the degree of stylisation /abstraction goes too far.

In the School of Industrial Design in Havana, I sat in on a class of student poster designers who were examining the developing visual language of posters. They came from different class backgrounds: some were from middle class Havana families; others were the children of the Havana working class; and a growing proportion were the sons and daughters of plantation workers. They were discussing the results of a survey they had recently conducted in the streets of Havana: its purpose was to discover the response to half a dozen posters which were in circulation at the time. First they talked about survey technique—how to get a genuine response from those they had talked to—and then moved on to discuss the answers themselves. Their findings threw up important questions of when a designer had made an inaccessible image in his/her zeal to develop the visual language. One of the posters they discussed was CLIK.

Cuba has very few sources of natural power. There are no large rivers to provide hydro-electric power. There are no oil resources. Electricity is generated from oil-powered generators, and all the oil has to be imported. With the expropriation of Esso and Shell after the Revolution, access to oil imports became difficult. The relatively close oilfields of Texas and Venezuela were closed to Cuban trade. Consequently all oil had to travel half the world from the Soviet Union. Saving on electricity was encouraged to save on oil. The CLIK poster was the result of a long line of posters urging the saving of electricity and therefore oil. In previous posters, the image of a lightbulb was often used, sometimes stylised, sometimes a photograph. These design variations gave way in CLIK to the simple yellow letters C-L-I-K on a deep blue background. No more. In the discussion of the poster, it emerged that this poster was universally liked and understood. Its bare simplicity and inference were what was most appreciated. In fact, the CLIK campaign became so popular that groups of school children formed themselves into CLIK brigades who went round knocking on people's doors, asking them if that light on in the back room was really necessary.

Another poster used on the survey resulted in a more ambiguous response. Its intention and text are understandable enough: 'Everyone with Fidel on July 26th'. But the image, comprehensible to those familiar with photograph-derived visual abbreviation as a stylisation of a massing crowd, was read by one man in 'negative': he thought it represented the universe. The survey also involved questions of colour (people liked the brighter images), and of how Fidel was represented (he was most popular when the poster showed his crow's feet, the hairiness of his beard, the weathered texture of his skin).

The purpose of the class was to teach future designers about the processes of communication from the people to the designers to the people—in evolution of a shared poster language.

Other poster designers have been, and some still are, painters. Their pictorial background is often reflected in the more painterly, less graphic style of their products. It is interesting that it is painters who tend to be among the majority of those working on the culturally oriented film, ballet and exhibition posters. It is as if the evocation of the theme of a film or a ballet on a poster gives more space to the painterly imagination than a brief to encourage the use of more oil on machine tools. In fact, the Revolution threw many painters into extreme crisis. In a young society, struggling to rebuild itself, it was hard to justify the individual, often isolated, often—but not always—self-expressive character of many painters' work. Some have found a way through to big scale public painting, as described above. Others have become poster makers, and continue to paint in their spare time. Others have continued painting, alone, against all the odds: in a back street of Havana, I stumbled on one such artist. The themes of his paintings were not overtly revolutionary or socialist. They were portraits and landscapes. He seemed isolated in his studio, with a stack of completed canvases and severely depleted resources. He had no market for his work, and had no idea of what would happen. Not all painters find themselves in such a cul-de-sac but his position highlighted the central question of the role of the artist in a socialist society—a subject that is being continually debated and struggled over in contemporary Cuba.

By no means all Cuban posters came from the official organisations. Many are hand-painted, one-off jobs, produced by individuals interested in making a poster. An outlet for this activity is through the CDRs who provide a structure through which anyone can make posters. The CDR would supply paints, brushes and paper and the theme of the poster—which would then be painted and pinned up in the street.

Jose is a maintenance man at the Habana Libre hotel; he services the lifts. He also likes painting. One Sunday I was with him on the back of a truck with many other hotel workers and visitors, on the way to voluntary work in the Yucca fields about fifty miles from Havana.

After singing our collective way through everybody's repertoire—from Cuban revolutionary songs, through Elvis, to the Beatles and back—José and I got to talking. He made his posters in his spare time. His problem as always, in spite of sporadic supplies from his workers' committee, was materials. How was he to get more paint, new brushes?

A few days later he gave me some of his posters. Their themes were the commemoration of anniversaries—July 26th (Moncada) and the founding of the FMC. The components of his designs were recognisably the symbols and images of various 'official' posters: the castellated wall of the Moncada barracks; the stylised image of a woman with shouldered gun and embraced child—the symbol of the FMC; and other images taken from posters with which he was familiar. The arrangement of these components, the overall designs, however, were his own. On the bottom edge of the Moncada poster were the words HOTEL HABANA LIBRE. The hotel workers' committee had wanted a Moncada poster. This one had been pinned up in the hotel for some weeks and then come back to José. In the bottom right hand corner of each poster was an elaborate signature: his name enclosed by the outline of a palette with three brushes. They were his paintings.

Television and Radio

Diana Mansfield

National radio and television have played an exceptional role in the political information and orientation of our people. Today we have programmes for children, music, drama, information and audience participation programmes. They are aimed at fulfilling a social function, informing, entertaining, developing good taste. They influence the development of agricultural technology, stimulate production and higher labour productivity, promote good hygiene and nutrition habits, extend language teaching, deal with the complex theme of home education, provide preventative medical orientation, and develop artisitic capabilities...all of which contributes to economic and political development. Fidel Castro, 1975[1]

Effective communication has long been considered of prime importance for the successful restructuring of Cuban society. In February, 1958, before the rebel army had hardly any established territory, Che Guevara managed to set up a small radio transmitter in the mountains of Oriente which broadcast revolution for a few hours each evening to the surrounding peasants; and eventually across the whole island. *Radio Rebelde*, as it came to be known, played no small part in confirming the existence of the guerrillas, exposing the truth about Batista, and uniting those who opposed the government. Since then many different channels of communication have been used to further the aims of the Revolution—some (e.g. the mass organisations like CDR, FMC, ANAP) more directly than others. Television and radio are still regarded as important media for reinforcing political motivation, raising cultural awareness and supplementing educational resources. They are definitely a public service, with particular responsibilities towards their audience.

Fidel Castro was fortunate in inheriting a broadcasting service that was already well established by Latin American standards. Set up in the early 1950s by Goar Mestre (a Cuban-born, US educated businessman), it was the fourth largest service in the world by 1954, in numbers of receivers per 1,000 people. By 1959 there were an estimated 365,000 tv sets, for a population of 6,000,000.[2] Mestre first build up the CMQ radio network, and two local stations in Havana—one giving non-stop news and time-checks, interspersed with commercials, and the other broadcasting classical music. Then he started two national television networks which covered most of the country, except Oriente.[3] Modelled on American standards, the stations were privately owned, commercially oriented, and operated on imported equipment. The imported programmes consisted largely of trivial information and entertainment, and catered to the rich, urban minority.

When Fidel Castro marched into Havana with the rebel army he made immediate use of the CMQ studios to speak to the people, and, finding television an effective way of reaching the masses, he began a process of expropriation which led to his complete control of the media within two years. Stations that had been run by Batista sympathisers were the first to be confiscated, with people like Mestre eventually leaving of his own accord as the political atmosphere developed toward communism. In the early days Fidel Castro made weekly appearances on television, often speaking for more than four hours at a time, to ensure that people were informed about the rapid changes taking place. Broadcasters joked about his 'One Man Show', but the New York Times estimated that in this way he was reaching 95% of the people.[4]

The service was whittled down from seven channels to two (Channels 6 and 2), with a third set up (Telerebelde) to cover those areas of Oriente which had not formerly been reached.

Summarising the changes that took place after 1959, Castro said,

"A process of rationalising the facilities was started, the national radio and television network was set up, services were extended to the traditional zones of silence, the equipment was modernized and communication via satellite was introduced into our system. Programming at the service of the people was begun."[1]

An experimental project in Educational Television was immediately launched, in collaboration with the Ministry of Education. Daily programmes were broadcast to primary schools in Science, Maths, Spanish, Social Studies, and Music; written guidelines for teachers on how to use the programmes, and suggestions for follow-up activities, were published in the press. Similar programmes were subsequently prepared for secondary school children.[5] Results showed that besides fulfilling the original aim of supplementing teaching facilities, the programmes helped to bring the subjects alive, especially when they were able to broadcast from places such as scientific laboratories, the Zoological Gardens or the National Observatory. According to a survey done in 1960, two thirds of the 200,000 viewers of these programmes were teachers and children—the rest were adults not otherwise involved in any formal education.[6]

After the literacy campaign of 1961, which was also supported by teleclasses and live coverage of the *brigadistas*, the teleclasses were extended to adult education, to reinforce teaching facilities at the post-literacy level. Originally only in basic subjects, programmes for adults now include History of Music, Sewing, Cooking, French, Russian and English.

In 1966 a new educational programme was created, called the Popular Technical Institute, which reflected the shift in emphasis from industrial to agricultural development. TV programmes were an integral part of a two-year course on the importance of cattle-raising, plant growth, soil, animal nutrition, artificial insemination and livestock diseases. With the development of Schools to the Countryside, in 1968, further teleclasses were devised for students at that level, in Science,

English, and Teacher-training. These were first shown on Channel 2, and then repeated on Channel 6 after an interval of 60 days, to accommodate the school schedule of 45 days' practical work in the fields.[5] Nearly all of these programmes had to be broadcast live, owing to a shortage of videotape, and because of this constraint were usually of a straightforward, didactic style. Continuous evaluation studies on the effectiveness of these programmes for both teachers and students showed that they were valuable for the consolidation of known subjects, rather than the introduction of new ones. Stress was laid on the importance of accompanying written material, and the need for follow-up exercises to do after watching the programmes.[6]

"The importance of educational television as a powerful aid to the teachers can be clearly seen, in some cases to fill the gaps in their knowledge, and in others to provide instruction of a higher quality than would otherwise be possible."[6]

The first National Congress on Education and Culture in 1971 discussed the role of television amongst other topics, and concluded that it should be used to help develop vocational interest in specific careers, keep students aware of the latest scientific and technological advances, show them practical applications of the subjects taught in school, and should be regarded as a support, rather than a replacement, for normal teaching. The Congress emphasised that,

"Mass Media are powerful tools for ideological formation. They help develop social consciousness and their utilization and development should not be the result of chance improvization and spontaneity." The need was pointed out for close co-operation between the Ministry of Education and the propaganda agencies for the preparation of radio, TV and film programmes, newspaper articles, and literary and artistic works that will contribute effectively to the formation of children and adolescents.

Of the mass media, radio and television are those with the deepest and widest influence among the masses. For this reason, the Congress discussed with passionate vigour the problems related to these media. As a result of these discussions, the Congress decided to suggest that all cultural agencies co-operate more thoroughly in order to use radio and television as vehicles of the different cultural manifestations and achievements in their highest and most developed expressions. It was suggested that those media be more careful with the use of vocabulary, scenes and labels that affect the instruction and formation of students in a negative way, and that a careful review be made of programmes which might develop in the child certain erroneous and distorted ideas concerning courage, talent, love and work.'''

Other recommendations were that a news summary should be incorporated in the first two or three minutes of the morning and afternoon sessions, and that high quality actors should be used in Spanish and History teleclasses. Priority on the use of videotape should go to schools, which would greatly improve the scope of programmes, and the maintenance of TV sets in schools should also be given priority by the Ministry of Communications.

Following on from the Congress, a National Forum on Educational Television was held in May 1973, to look at the effectiveness of programmes in more detail, compared with the needs and goals of school education and curriculum. Because of the success so far, recommendations were made to retain TV as a permanent feature of education, though in recent years the number of programmes broadcast per week has been reduced, as more teachers become qualified.[8]

1968 was also the year when several programmes of a more indirect educational nature were introduced, such as *Nuestros Hijos (Our Children)*. The purpose of this programme is to give advice to parents on how to bring up their children, and viewers are invited to write in with any problems they may have encountered. In the first half, actors reconstruct the conflict, e.g. arguments between children and parents, trouble at school, or emotional disturbances. In the second half a panel of experts in psychology, health and child guidance discuss the scene that's gone before and suggest ways in which parents could deal with the problem.[9] Relationships are also the focal point of *Detrás de la Fachada (Behind the Facade)*. This is a situation comedy built round the daily life of one family (rather like "Till Death Us Do Part"), in which the children send up their parents' traditional attitudes and prejudices (e.g. father not helping with the housework) and point the way to more socialist values.

Films from all over the world are frequently shown on TV and one interesting idea involves the weekly appearance of a film critic from ICAIC. Before the start of a chosen film he talks about its subject matter (e.g. the socio-historical conditions in America at the time of the longshoremen's union dispute in *On the Waterfront*). Halfway through he makes a critical analysis of the film to that point, drawing attention to details of content, style, technique, etc., and he continues his analysis at the end.

Two American traditions—the soap opera and the thriller —remain a characteristic of Cuban Television, but are adapted to suit a revolutionary audience. Among the most popular programmes are those which serialise novels, both Cuban and foreign. These are genuinely chosen for their social or historical relevance to the revolution, such as *Cecelia Valdes*, an important 19th century novel which uses love, incest, jealousy and murder to highlight the problems of a multi-racial society in colonial times. Action is the main ingredient in the adventure series, *Aventuras*, but in contrast to its American counterpart —the police story—on Cuban TV it's usually the pre-revolutionary police who are the villains, as the stories are often based on real incidents from the history of the Revolution (such as the assassination of an official in Batista's government and the subsequent shoot-out between guerrillas and the police force).

There are numerous music and dance programmes, both traditional and modern, as well as art, literature, poetry and drama appreciation, which help to raise cultural awareness and foster a feeling of national identity. Here the local talent is fully exploited, and every section of society has its own 'variety show'. *All Together at Nine* is an outside broadcast from a different factory each week, in which the workers provide the entertainment (a sort of factory floor-show). The emphasis is on the fact that ordinary people are taking part, rather than star performers, and similar shows are generated from schools, army camps and rural communities. Peasant farmers have a special programme called *Palmas y Canas*, which consists of traditional music, folklore, and information that's directly relevant to them.

Live coverage of sports events is naturally well catered for, while *Ciencia y Salud* tackles all aspects of health education, from basic nutrition to practical demonstrations of how to construct a toilet in the countryside—an important consideration in a developing country.

Students at Havana Univeristy who are interested in a career in the media when they graduate are given a unique opportunity to train for television production by having responsibility for producing three hours' worth of programmes a week, broadcast on Channel 2 and usually of an educational nature. They are supervised by professionals from ICR (Instituto Cubano de Radiodifusion)—the State broadcasting body.

The production team at ICR normally consists of a writer, a director, and an *asesor*, who advises on the political content of programmes. ICR was inaugurated in 1962, and now produces 80% of programmes, the rest being imported documentaries and films from all parts of the world, though mainly socialist countries. Generally speaking the technical quality of broadcasts is poor, due to the age of the equipment (a BBC producer visiting studios in Havana in 1970 observed technicians with soldering irons on constant standby near cameras) and the fact that only one inch videotape is used (as opposed to the more usual two-inch). Outside broadcast units that were once British are now an international patchwork of electronics and an example of Cuban resourcefulness in the absence of spare parts. This helps to explain why the Cuban government is prepared to make the investment in a modern colour service, despite the fact that colour sets will be even scarcer than black and white ones. By 1976 the number of sets in use had doubled to an estimated 600,000[10], and the pattern of distribution was more in line with socialist principles: whereas before the Revolution they were mostly owned by the wealthy city dwellers, most new sets after 1959 went into schools (including a gift of 10,000 sets from China), the common rooms and work centres, and the new agricultural communities. Free sets were placed in the latter, as an added incentive for scattered peasants to join the new social groups, and as a means of providing additional links with the rest of society for those in most need.

The right of an individual to buy a new tv set is worked out on a system of merit—i.e. being voted an exemplary worker—to decrease the significance of the cost factor. They are, in fact, expensive items. An average set, usually imported from Russia or Japan, costs around 640 pesos (around £400 at comparatively meaningless rates of exchange, or eight times the minimum monthly wage) but instalment plans exist which are regulated according to salary, and so enable people to purchase something this big. As sets are becoming more plentiful, it is now possible to buy one outright without having to be an exemplary worker. When the system goes colour (probably in 1978, and probably the NSTC system) the first sets that are available will be installed in the common rooms of the largest manufacturing plants, to ensure maximum access by viewers.

In all, ICR broadcasts for approximately 130 hours per week, with the main programme areas falling into three categories: educational and cultural programmes (78 hours), news and information (33 hours) and light entertainment (25 hours)[11]. There are no commercials for material goods between programmes, but there are 'public information' slots—either news of forthcoming events, or 'consciousness-raising' cartoons which tell people not to drink and drive, not to spend too long on the phone (use of which is free for local calls), to take care of public property and so on. As with all programmes, comedy and drama are used wherever possible to put this social message across.[9]

Programmes for children have been produced in a special department since 1966. According to the Director of that department:

"Each programme has specific objectives. We try to have some message in each, without it being too heavy. We are convinced that TV aids in the formation of the New Man. Although sometimes a programme may seem like just entertainment, the words of a song, or the point of a sketch may have some healthy content. They may recommend habits of conduct, or stimulate love of family and humanity. For instance, in one we projected the idea of a large family composed of all the children in the world. All of the programmes, except the cartoons, are in some way educational and formative.''[12]

Some examples are *Caritas*, a half-hour programme for children between four and six, in which a girl dressed as a harlequin in a fantasy world sings songs, tells stories, and encourages good behaviour in young viewers. Actors, puppeteers, other children and illustrators also take part. In *A Jugar* (*Playtime*), a group of children from different schools each week take part in general knowledge quizzes, games and sports competitions. The winners and losers all receive a prize (sweets or a book) so children get used to the idea of winning for the satisfaction of it, rather than material gain. A seemingly widespread interest in journalism is encouraged in *Periodismo Infantil*, a weekly programme which has a newspaper editor, two reporters and a photographer (all children) who make up items from different schools about the activities there.[12]

News for adults is broadcast three times a day across both channels, and analysed from a Marxist-Leninist point of view. Besides the usual kind of coverage, anything which illustrates the development of Cuba is considered newsworthy, such as the opening of a new housing estate or factory, the reaching or surpassing of production targets, the arrival of delegations from socialist countries to take part in conferences, etc. There is extensive coverage of third world countries, particularly when Cuba is able to demonstrate its solidarity with movements against imperialism or repression, such as those in Angola or Ethiopia. Other kinds of aid, such as the medical or technical aid to Jamaica, are reported, and of course Fidel Castro's speeches or any kind of new legislation are covered in detail.

The sources of news are chiefly the correspondents of Prensa Latina, founded in 1959 with headquarters in Havana, branches in Moscow, Prague, Sofia, Paris, Mexico, a correspondent in Hanoi and London, and stringers in Latin American countries. There is a satellite link with Moscow, and the services of Visnews, Reuters and the Press Association are also utilised. Nearness to the USA means that selected news film can be rebroadcast in Cuba, with Cuban commentary dubbed over (as was done during coverage of the war in Vietnam). Copyright is not recognised. Other programmes broadcast in the USA are monitored by ICR for their interest to Cubans, such as a recent CBS documentary on the activities of the CIA, which included an interview with Fidel Castro. This was shown in Cuba, "Just as the viewers in the United States saw it", but followed up with an unequivocal statement by ICR condemning the CIA and emphasising the need for continued vigilance against counter-revolutionaries—an example of the support given by the media to matters of national security.[13]

The notions of 'balance' and 'freedom of speech' considered so important by most Western journalists, take on a different meaning in Cuban current affairs coverage, as Fidel Castro explained to Barbara Walters in an interview for American television:

Walters: Your newspapers, radio, television, motion pictures are under state control. The people can dissent in their meetings, in their congresses, but no dissent is allowed in the public media. Why, if you are so sure that everyone is happy with the way things are?

Castro: We don't allow dissent? Aren't 18 years of counter-revolution organised by the United States enough? Who says there's no opposition to the Revolution? It has been opposed by the United States—by its press, radio and TV and by thousands of counter-revolutionaries.

Walters: You tell me the people want socialism, they want the country this way. Fine, I believe you. Then why not allow dissent in the newspapers or an opposition paper, dissent on radio or television?

Castro: Look, Barbara, we don't have the same conceptions as you. Naturally our concept of freedom of the press is different from yours, and I tell you so honestly, since I have absolutely nothing to hide. If you were asked whether a paper against socialism could be published here, I will tell you frankly that the answer would be no. The Government, Party and people would not allow it. In that sense we do not have the freedom of the press that you do in the United States and we are pleased that this is the case. We do not have the scandals and commercial propaganda you have in the United States. Our mass media serve the Revolution. Now as long as the Revolution is developing and as long as there is hostility toward Cuba and counterrevolution supported by the United States—as long as this struggle persists, we will simply and categorically not allow any paper to be published that is against the Revolution.[13]

Radio programmes in Cuba operate along the same principles as television, and complete the network of mass communication. There are four nationwide stations, backed up by over 40 local radio stations, and in 1976 there were an estimated 2,100,000 radios in use. As in the capitalist days, *Radio Enciclopedia* broadcasts only instrumental music from all round the world, 24 hours a day, and *Radio Reloj* consists of round-the-clock news bulletins, punctuated by readings of the time every minute. *Radio Rebelde* is now the 'home service' station, with a variety of ingredients, such as traditional music, magazine items, drama, history, sport, interviews, requests, etc.

From the early days of the Revolution, Cuba has been subjected to anti-communist propaganda beamed from the USA. In 1961 *Radio Havana* was set up to broadcast Cuban propaganda to oppressed people in Southern USA and Latin America. The Russians moved an electronic jamming transmitter into Cuba in 1963, to shield their advisers and technicians from US propaganda via 'Voice of America', and the Americans subsequently jammed transmissions from Cuba. By mid-1965 Radio Havana was broadcasting more than 150 hours per week, mostly attacking dictatorships in Latin America. The external service was eventually extended to Europe, Africa and the Middle East, with programmes in Spanish, English, French, Portuguese, Creole, Quechua, Guaraní and Arabic. The English transmission can be picked up in the UK on a good day, with a strong receiver, between 2010-2040 hours GMT, on 19.5 metres shortwave.

Overall, radio and TV in Cuba are an example of how the media can be effectively co-ordinated with political aims, to promote and support fundamental social change. There is little

246   Culture and Media

audience research as we know it (except in the area of schools programmes, where their usefulness has been carefully evaluated) and so it is difficult to assess the value placed by people on broadcasting as an information/entertainment source, compared with other forms of communication. Reviews or articles on programmes occasionally appear in magazines like *Bohemia*, but these generally give further background information on content or presenters, rather than criticism. Viewers are, however, encouraged to write in with ideas or requests, and do participate in the sense that a lot of air-time is devoted to the activities of ordinary people working towards the development of the nation. Conversely, employees at ICR themselves participate in national development by doing voluntary agricultural or construction work whenever time allows. Given the massive contribution made by individuals towards social achievements, it's hard to imagine where anyone gets the time to watch TV, but when they do it's ensured that they see a reinforcement of revolutionary objectives in a popular format.

REFERENCES

1. Fidel Castro, Main Report to 1st Congress of Communist Party, December 29, 1975 *Granma Weekly Review.*
2. *Television Factbook*, 1960.
3. Timothy Green, *The Universal Eye,* Bodley Head, 1972, p.58-59.
4. Jerry Redding, "Castro-ating the Media", *Educational Broadcasting Review,* June, 1971 (now known as *Public Telecommunications Review,*).
5. Jorge Werthein, *Educational TV and the use of Mass Media for Education in Cuba,* MSS Stanford University, February 1976. Published in shortened form in *Mass Media Policies in Changing Cultures,* ed. George Gerbner, John Wiley and Sons, London, 1977.
6. Roberto Solis, *Educational TV International,* 4, 2, June, 1970
7. Report of 1st Congress on Education and Culture, 1971, MINED, Havana.
8. Report on 1st Forum of ETV, *Granma,* May 1973.
9. Extracts from Cuban TV, *Worldwide,* BBCTV, 3,11,75, produced by Maryse Addison.
10. *Europa Year Book,* 1977.
11. *World Communications,* UNESCO 1975
12. Karen Wald, *The Children of Ché: Childcare and Education in Cuba,* Ramparts, USA, 1977.
13. *Granma Weekly Review*, July 17, 1977.

Sport: The People's Right

John Griffiths

To many people outside Cuba, accustomed no doubt to the remote super-stars of sport in their own countries, Cuban sport is synonomous with two athletes: Alberto Juantorena, winner of the gold medal for the 400 and 800 metre events at the Montreal Olympiad of 1976; and Teofilo Stevenson, heavy-weight boxing champion at two successive Olympic Games, in 1972 and '76.

Both athletes are, in 1978, at the peak of their perfor-mance. They are, as Fidel Castro has described them, 'the standard-bearers'of Cuban sport. But, as was implied in that description, they are not unique. Like other Cuban athletes of outstanding calibre making their mark around the world, they are part of that generation who have grown to maturity during the short revolutionary period of Cuba's history. They have benefited from living in a climate, cultural as well as geo-graphic, conducive to sport. Here sport is regarded as every-one's right, no more and no less than any other element of the culture. It is also seen as a means of contributing to the development of a fit and healthy society as well as a balanced, unalienated one. In schools, where intellectual and physical effort is combined in an attempt to end the divisive distinction between different kinds of work, sport has a heightened role. Fidel Castro, a keen sportsman himself and an inspiration to others, has spoken about the importance of sport:

"Young people need sports to burn off the excess energy they have. Moreover, sports are a means of developing discipline, education, health and good habits. Sports are an antidote to vice. Young people need sports. And old people, too, not to burn off excess energy but to conserve what energy they have left and to safeguard their health which is necessary for a full life."[1]

This is in marked contrast to the actual role of sport in capitalist societies where it mirrors that society's class divisions, individualism, elitism, sexism, racism and commercial exploitation. Where, too, sport, because of the money-making opportunities it provides, is often associated with vice rather than acting as its antidote. In a socialist society, however, sport has the potential to be much more. It can act as a liberating force; as a weapon against racism and sexism, as a unifying part of the national culture at the service of all. And, where the commercial exploitation of sports no longer exists, the division, both physical and social, between sportsmen and spectators can be eliminated, resulting in a high degree of popular involvement. In Cuba this is certainly the case.

Sports and recreation are there, too, just for their enjoyment. The Cuban people, naturally, like to have champions of the calibre of Stevenson and Juantorena, but not at the expense of mass participation in and enjoyment of sports and other leisure activities. Fidel Castro has spoken very clearly on this point:

"It is important that we do not go wrong and neglect the *practice* of sports in our quest for champions. Everyone ought to practise sports, everybody, not only children in elementary schools. Adults and old people too—the old need it more than the young."[2]

One striking feature of Cuban society is the involvement in sports, by the young and old. Not just as vicarious spectators as is so often the case in the West, but as active participants in the range of sports and leisure pursuits available. In Cuba, the slogan of Britain's Sports Council, "Sport for All", means exactly that and not, as in Britain, for a predominantly middle-class patronage able to pay for the facilities at a sports centre. Although all areas of Cuba have access to sports and recreation facilities of some kind, there are few of the expensive sports 'palaces' found in the West. There are, for example, only two artificial running tracks in Cuba; one in Havana, the other in Santiago de Cuba (the latter only completed in 1977). Investment in such construction, especially because of its drain on foreign currency, has a low priority in a country building up its productive capacity.

That Cuba has been able to increase the amount of sport and leisure provision *at all* is a remarkable achievement. Most large centres of population possess their own purpose-built sports facilities, but where these have not been built, as in the smaller towns and villages, the people share the facilities of the local schools. With the high priority that has been given to education in Cuba there is no shortage of these. The sharing of these facilities has the advantage, too, of adding to the parents' involvement in their children's education and contributing to the sense of community. To use these facilities, or simply to watch, is, like all other cultural pursuits, completely free. At the larger baseball game, international athletics meeting, or boxing tournament, it is a case of 'first come, first served', whereas for local participation, or smaller events, everyone gets served.

At the local and provincial level, sports and recreation are co-ordinated through voluntary Sports Councils of which there are over five thousand throughout Cuba, served by more than fifty thousand volunteer administrators and coaches.[3] Working alongside the mass-organisations, activists from the Sports Councils work to stimulate interest and encourage participation in sports, fitness, and recreation. At a factory, for example, they would arrange team games leading to the selection of a baseball, volleyball, soccer, or basketball team to represent them. They would, in addition, provide special coaching for anyone wishing to specialise in a particular sport or keep-fit exercises for those simply wanting to keep in trim. Local groups of the FMC (The Cuban Women's Federation) working with their local Sports Council, frequently arrange exercise classes for their members, who are to be seen enthusiastically, and quite unselfconsciously, going through their exercise routines in the local park or square. Sports

Councils have no predetermined plan of work. Rather they must bend to the wishes of their workmates and neighbours, by providing support for whatever sport or recreation is required. A similarly flexible system has proved extremely successful in adult education; it is no less successful in sport.

The work of the Sports Councils leads to competitions involving industries, factories, farms, families and schools held at local, provincial, then national level. The degree of participation is staggering; 30,000 people in boxing, 300,000 in volleyball. For the 1976 Family Games there were 56,000 participants. In the same year the Workers Games drew on the two million trade union members of whom 600,000 took part, 105,000 of them women.[4] The final competition is preceded by hard-fought qualifying events; nine months competition at the local level, four months at the regional level, then three at the provincial level. A wide range of sports is offered so as to increase the likelihood of involvement; baseball, athletics, chess, table-tennis, volleyball, basketball, gymnastics and weight-lifting.

The body responsible for the overall co-ordination of these events, all other sports, and the work of the Sports Councils is the *Instituto Nacional De Deportes, Educacion Fisica Y Recreacion* (INDER). Founded soon after the start of the Revolution, in February 1961, it built on the preparatory work already begun in this field by the Ministry of Education (MINED), the Army(FAR) and an *ad hoc* body, the General Sports Council (DGD) set up to generate an interest in sport as a first step towards making it a natural part of the curriculum in education as well as everyday life. INDER's work was made all the more difficult by the relatively limited sports tradition existing in Cuba before the Revolution and the intrusion of commercial interests into what sport did exist. Jorge Garcia Bango, Director of INDER, has spoken of the tiny number of participants in organised sports before 1959. Just 1,500 out of a population of about 5 million. Coupled with this was the virtual absence of physical education in schools, although lip service was paid to its importance. What was important, however, were the commercial possibilities offered by sport. Basketball, baseball and boxing were almost entirely in the hands of the professionals. Boxers like Kid Gavilan, Benny

Paret, and 'Kid' Chocolate are examples of some of the boxers who made it to the 'big-time'. Baseball and basketball players were similarly creamed off by the US Big Leagues. Few professional athletes, especially the boxers, received any lasting material reward for their efforts. Most were discarded, broken and vulnerable, as soon as their decline set in.

What sports facilities did exist in Cuba were mainly located, like everything else, in the capital city, Havana, and were accompanied by the corruption and rottenness that were part and parcel of pre-revolutionary Cuba. Racism kept black athletes, the major source of Cuban athletic talent, out of the sports clubs that were used exclusively by members of Havana's, and the US's, 'high society'. Such exclusivity was to play no part in INDER's work. Working from the slogan, *Sport: The People's Right* INDER and MINED introduced physical education to the curriculum of every school. But education had clearly not been a priority in terms of provision for the mass of society before 1959 and it, too, had to be built up. As a part of the programme to eliminate the inequalities that existed between town and country, schools were built in rural areas as fast as resources allowed. To accompany them INDER launched its *Mountain Plan* to take sports to the country areas; sports fields were built and provincial baseball stadia constructed.

To generate interest in sports and, at the same time, to discover what talent existed, INDER began to organise *Listos Para Vencer* (LPV) (Ready to Win) tests. These were not competitions, except at a personal level, but standard sports ability tests. There were no prizes other than certificates or badges for successful candidates, but the interest generated throughout the country was enormous. To add to this interest the mass media provided increased cover on tv and radio, as well as in the press. The Postal Service played its part, too, in 1961 by issuing sets of stamps illustrating all the various sports it was possible to participate in. At the same time, the US blockade of Cuba threatened to curtail any expansion of sports by cutting off supplies of sports equipment which, like everything else, had previously been obtained from the US. This made necessary the formation of a domestic sports equipment industry. Today it represents an important and thriving sector of the Cuban economy, producing most of Cuba's own needs as well as some goods for export, like the official baseballs for the World Championship Series (which, incidentally, Cuba usually wins!).

The daily attention given to sports activities in all Cuban schools ensures a healthy, active, society as well as reinforcing the complementarity of physical and mental activities. Even before Cuban children start school, parents are shown, in booklets produced by INDER specially for this purpose, how to massage their children's young muscles so as to make them supple and aid their physical development.[5] Once at the *Circulos Infantiles* (nursery schools) children take part in some form of physical activity every day to further the development of co-ordination, balance, and muscle. These activities range from formal exercises, now out of fashion in most Western countries, to team games and free activities of the children's choice. The objective is the same in each case: to ensure that the physical development of each child proceeds at a pace along with its intellectual development. This process continues through Elementary School, the equivalent of the British Primary School, to Secondary and, even, Higher Education. At Secondary level the emphasis, as in the rest of society, is on participation, whatever the student's ability and whatever the sport. Chess has a place beside the more familiar physical sports, to enable students with intellectual, rather than physical, inclinations to take part like everybody else.

Baseball, though, is the game that has the greatest following in schools. Exported to Cuba by the US as part of its intense cultural penetration in the sixty years prior to the Revolution, it is now the national sport. But, like the West Indies at cricket and Brazil at soccer, the colonised assert their superiority in one field at least, over the former coloniser. Cuba, keeping alive this tradition, has been World Champion at baseball for the past seven years. The interest in the sport is reflected in schools. Every Secondary School has its own baseball diamond on which there appears to be always someone practising, whatever the time of day. Other sports are popular, like basketball and volleyball, with increasingly, an interest being taken in all athletics, due, no doubt, to Cuba's international successes. Few schools, outside of the prestigious

Vocational Schools or special Sports Schools, possess their own swimming pools, so children are encouraged to use the nearest local river, as Fidel Castro did as a child.

In addition to sports, schools are involved in constant, though friendly, competition with each other. Known as 'socialist emulation' it takes the form of competition, for which points are awarded, in a range of school activities; proportions of students passing examinations, production of agricultural and other goods, school attendance, care and maintenance of their facilities. There are no prizes for the winning school; the reward comes from having succeeded; though there is considerable pride taken in the achievement, and the competitions for 'Vanguard School' are hotly contested. The same goes for sport. All schools compete in local, provincial and national competitions. Practice is long and hard for the honour of representing the school. But the most important part is, first of all, to take part, then to put every effort into succeeding. Over two million school students are active participants in sports, from which pool of talents are drawn those with special abilities and commitment to sport. Students are given standard LPV tests throughout their careers to determine their athletic development and potential. Those showing special talents are, depending on their particular case, either eligible for entry to one of Cuba's special sports schools or given a tailor-made physical education programme to follow. The philosophy, and the practice, is just the same for those students showing special talents in the arts, music, or dance, as well as academic subjects. They are given, like the athletically inclined, every facility to develop their talents to the maximum. The net that is cast, too, is of a very fine mesh to ensure that not even the smallest fish gets through.

The model for sports development in Cuba is that every province—there are now fourteen—will possess its own special sports school. Thre are at present (in 1978) seven such schools. At the intermediate level are the *Escuelas De Iniciacion Deportiva Escolar* (EIDE) two of which were built, in Havana and Santiago, in 1977. These schools cover some twenty five different sports, practised by students attending on a daily or boarding basis from Elementary to Secondary level. Sports and the normal school curriculum are combined. In Santiago de

Cuba, the EIDE is known as the *Capitan Manuel Orestes School*. Here, about 1,500 students from Santiago and Guantanamo provinces receive their education and specialist training. The school has three swimming pools, one of which is of olympic size, and a diving tank. In addition, the school has two baseball diamonds, athletics facilities, a handball court and four tennis courts, with a cycle track planned for the future. The massive gymnasium provides facilities for a wide range of indoor sports and training. The staff support is impressive; sixty nine teachers take responsibility for academic subjects, one hundred and thirty nine coaches and other specialists for the sports.

Havana province's EIDE, *The Martyrs of Barbados School*, takes its name from the Cuban fencing team who were among the 75 people killed when a Cuban civil airliner was sabotaged and destroyed off Barbados in October 1976. The school is similar to the one in Santiago; there are 2,000 students enjoying similar facilities. Both schools are administered jointly by INDER and MINED, the latter being responsible for the academic part of the curriculum. All students attending specialist sports schools must, in addition to maintaining their athletic performance, also maintain a consistently high academic level as well as show a high degree of political commitment. This was pointed out strongly to the students by Fidel Castro at the *Capitan Manuel Orestes School:*

"You are not going to be professional athletes; you are not going to make a living at sports...you will make it from your *work*. You will be able to go as far as you wish in sports, but you will also be able to go as far as you wish as citizens and as professionals and technicians."[6]

To the Havana students he was equally to the point:

"One thing you must keep in mind at all times, one thing we will never let the greatest of champions get away with is not fulfilling their obligations as students. We can't allow an athlete in these schools to be a bad student. We'd rather lose that champion than violate these principles."[7]

Attendance at these schools in no way resembles the 'athletic scholarships' traditionally offered by North American universities that exploit the student's athletic abilities to the exclusion of everything else, leaving them vulnerable in society as soon as their skills, and bargaining power, have been exhausted. Stevenson and Juantorena are students as well as athletes, of engineering and economics, respectively. Their courses at the University of Havana, like those for the other athletes studying there, have been specially designed to take six years, instead of the normal four, so as to compensate them for the time spent in training and in competitions. Like the students of Sports Schools they, too, are expected to keep up with their studies and take an active political role in society. Both athletes have been elected as delegates to assemblies of *People's Power*, and their views on political matters are considered worthy enough to be printed in the national press.

Students with exceptional athletic abilities graduate to the *Escuela Superior De Perfeccionamiento Atletico* (ESPA) a single, national school, located in Havana, at the very top of the pyramid of sports specialisation where athletes are given the highly specialised coaching and attention necessary to the perfection of their sport. It is from ESPA that teams are selected to represent Cuba in international events; always more being selected than are required, to combat the formation of an elitist mentality. Nobody is unexpendable. This principle applies at all levels of sports activities; in school, factory, even neighbourhood competitions.

In the short time of their existence, INDER's sports schools have developed considerable expertise in sports and related areas. In the early 1960's INDER established the *Manuel Fajardo Physical Education High School* to train teachers of a high standard necessary to equip Cuba's schools and to provide the foundation for the future development of sport in Cuba. With the growth of similar institutions this school has been upgraded to university level as the *Higher Institute for Physical Culture*, with the function of producing teachers still, but at a much higher level.

The Institute for Sports Medicine is a further example of Cuba's expertise in the sports field. Set up in 1966 it is now a source of attraction for athletes and their coaches throughout the world. In Britain, a country with a long sports tradition, there is simply no counterpart to this centre nor for that matter to the special sports schools. In this one centre there are 42 doctors specialising in various aspects of sport; 6 dentists, 17 physiotherapists, and 7 psychologists. The last's function is not, as one might suppose, to motivate the athletes but, rather, their coaches.[8] Sports medicine, massage and physiotherapy have been developed in Cuba on a par with, if not superior to, most developed countries with infinitely more resources.

These developments, INDER readily acknowledges, would not have been possible without the fraternal support of other socialist countries; the Soviet Union, Poland, Czechoslovakia, and the German Democratic Republic. Juantorena, for example, was coached during a critical period of his development by the late Zygsmund Zabierzowski from Poland. In the period 1969-1972, 'more than 50 Soviet coaches helped to train Cuban athletes for the Olympic and Pan-American Games.'[9] Building upon that support, Cuba has now developed considerable expertise of its own, which is being shared, along with its medical, educational and economic know-how, with other developing nations like Peru, Panama, Jamaica, Guyana and Angola. The socialist countries have themselves developed a system of mutual assistance and exchange whereby expertise is pooled and shared amongst each of them. For instance, Enrique Figuerola, the Cuban sprinter was coaching Soviet athletes in Odessa and Minsk in 1972.[10] Similarly, the *Spartakiade of the Friendly Armies* (FASC); drawn primarily from the socialist countries, was held in Cuba in September 1977 and attended by over 1,300 athletes from Europe, Asia, Latin America, and Africa, who competed in a variety of sports and military events.

The positive developments that have occurred in Cuban sports over the last ten years can be clearly seen in the achievements of Cuban athletes in international events. At the Pan-American Games in Chicago in 1959 Cuba was placed 11th; in 1975 in Mexico it was second only to the United States. In the Olympic Games, Cuban successes have been no less dramatic. In the Rome Olympics of 1960 Cuba was 45th; in Montreal in 1976, eighth; ahead of most developed countries, it was only beaten by those, like the USSR and the United States, with a long sports tradition and resources to match.

Cuba's strengths are to be seen in areas like athletics and

boxing where, it could be said, Cuba has always had talent. Athletes like Juantorena in the 400 and 800 metres; Silvio Leonard and Sylvia Chivas in the 100 metres; Alejandro Casañas in the 110 metres high hurdles. Boxers like Stevenson, Herrera, Aldama, Soria, Hernandez and Duvalon; an array of talents. But what of other sports? In recent years Cuba has been making inroads into those sports traditionally associated with the rich, developed countries; sports like fencing, weight-lifting, judo, volley-ball, and water polo. Fidel Castro, aware of the areas in which Cuba has still to develop, has spoken frequently of the need to encourage participation in them. Swimming is just one example. Cuba shares with many other Caribbean countries the paradox of being surrounded by water yet having a small proportion of its population able to swim. Fidel Castro has urged students to do as he did and learn to swim in the local river. That may be fine for basic instruction, but it is not much use for anything else. More recently, however, he has spoken about the possibility of building 500 prefabricated pools so as to provide each locality with one.[11]

An attempt is being made to break out into new areas of sport, so correcting the bias that already exists in more traditional areas. When Ronald Pickering, the well-known British athletics coach visited the EIDE on the Isle of Pines in 1976 in preparation for his documentary film "Cuba: Sport and Revolution", he was able to see the priority given to all water sports. There, swimming, diving, water-polo (the Cuban national team is ranked 4th in the world), canoeing and sailing are the specialisms being taught.[12] Fidel Castro has spoken of the need for the mass media to provide more coverage of less-fashionable sports, like archery, which because of its high cost and association with the West tends not to have a large following and, hence, gets overlooked.

There is wide coverage by tv, radio, and the press of all sports events, from the Baseball League to the School Games and prestigious international events like the Barrientos Memorial Games held annually in Cuba. Daily sports news is carried by all the mass media, with the emphasis on informing rather than whipping up partisan support for local, or even national, teams, and athletes. This treatment of sport by the media is noticeably different from that which it receives in the West. In consciously *not* building up the image of one or other athlete, the problems associated with the formation of an elite are minimised. A further effect is to demystify the nature of sport.

By moving away from the idea of sport as the preserve of individual athletes with exceptional natural endowments, the elite, or the *aficionados*, sport becomes accessible to all. In Cuba *everyone* is the *aficionado*. The major coverage of sport, other than the daily national and provincial newspapers, is provided by magazines devoted entirely to the subject. *Deportes: Derecho Del Pueblo* (Sport: The People's Right) and *Listos Para Vencer* (Ready to Win) are produced weekly by INDER. They provide information about international sports events, especially when, like the Montreal Olympics, Cuban teams are competing. Internal events, junior events and general news are provided as well. Both magazines emphasise technique and performance, rather than personalities, which helps to put sports into the hands of the people by making them understandable. Chess, because of its enormous following, has its own journal, *Chaque Mate* (Check Mate). Jose Raul Capablanca, the great Cuban Chess Grand Master, inspires as many young people as Alberto Juantorena. Cuba has, in Amador Rodriguez, at 19, the youngest Chess Grand Master in the World.

In spite of the wide coverage of sports on tv and radio, for Cuban people *do* like to follow the major sports meetings and are already anticipating live coverage of the Moscow Olympics in 1980, most have not been reduced solely to the level of spectators of *The Big Match*, or *Match of the Day*. Attempts to get people out of their armchairs, which have been so ill-fated in Britain and other developed countries, are successful in Cuba. Why should this be so? Cuba's successes in the development of sport have to be located in the political and social context in which they occur. It is impossible to understand one without looking at the other. Sport is an important part of the Cuban culture available to all and, at the same time, a means of asserting Cuba's independence and evidence of the tangible successes that have been made in other spheres.

A further reason for Cuba's success is that the distorting influence of commercialism is absent from sport. In Cuba, athletes are no longer commodities to be bought and sold, as they were before the Revolution; nor to be nurtured as an elite to be packaged and displayed as freaks in advertising sideshows, as disposable as the products they sell. There are no pay-offs for athletes; they are just as privileged as any other sector of society. The compensatory extra diet they receive to make up for the energy expended in training is something they share with the only 'millionaires' now in Cuba; the canecutters, 'millionaires' in terms of what they produce, not what they gain. Nor are Cuban athletes an elite set apart from the rest of society by their style of life. Teofilo Stevenson has been constantly harassed by Western promoters to fight professionally. A fight between him and Mohammed Ali would have provided a rich prize for any entrepreneur as well as a luxurious life style for Stevenson himself. Yet when offered a million dollars to turn his back on Cuba and fight for money, he is reported to have replied: "What is a million dollars against the love of nine million Cubans?"[13]

When Cuban athletes do win awards, as Juantorena did at the Montreal Olympics, they are at pains to share them. To show his identification with the Revolution he dedicated his first gold medal to the 'Heroes of Moncada'.[14] Later, to the incredulity of the world's sports journalists, he gave one of his medals away, to Fidel Castro, for the whole country to share. Such an act was consistent with the personality of Juantorena, a modest, hard-working student and athlete, who seems quite unaffected by the attention and acclaim he has received. It was consistent, too, that he should have given one of his medals to Fidel Castro who has provided Cuban sport with such personal inspiration, and who, as a student, played basketball and baseball to international level and still misses no opportunity to don vest and shorts and get on to the pitch.

For a politician in the West such behaviour would, at the least, smack of opportunism and vote-catching. In Cuba, however, where sport is an integral part of the culture; where old and young, peasant and president join in ball games, such imputations do not arise. Sport is, of course, everywhere intimately bound up with politics. In most cases it is used simply as part of the armoury for propping up the status quo, at a professional and amateur level, by reflecting and reinforcing the prevailing ideology. In Cuba, too, sport has this function. Where it differs from capitalist societies is that it is at the service of the people, no more and no less than any other component of the culture. Such an ethos has resulted in a level of participation in sports equal to that achieved at the political, and international successes equal to those achieved internally in the economic, social and political fields.

REFERENCES

I am grateful to Ronald Pickering and James Riordan who read and commented on an earlier version of this paper.

1. *Granma Weekly Review*, 23.10.1977
2. *Granma Weekly Review*, 23.10.1977
3. *Granma Weekly Review*, 16.1.1977
4. 'Why Cuba Wins at Sports, *Cuba Review*, New York, Vol.VII, No.2, June 1977.
5. *Granma Weekly Review*, 23.10.1977.
6. I am indebted to Ronald Pickering for this information.
7. *Granma Weekly Review*, 23.10.1977
8. *Cuba: Sport and Revolution*, Richard Taylor/Ronald Pickering, BBC/TV, 1977.
9. 'Sovetsky Sport', 22,6,1973, quoted in *Sport in Soviet Society*, by James Riordan, Cambridge University Press, Cambridge, 1977
10. Riordan, op.cit., p.383.
11. *Granma Weekly Review*, 23.10.1977 and 12.9.1976
12. Pickering, op.cit.
13. Pickering, op.cit.
14. The Heroes of Moncada were those killed during the attack on the Moncada barracks in Santiago De Cuba led by Fidel Castro on July 26 1953 and which signalled the beginning of the armed struggle against Batista.

Other Works Consulted

"Sport and Physical Education in Cuba" by Ronald Pickering in *Sport Under Communism*, ed. James Riordan, Richard Hurst, London, 1978.
The Flowering of Cuban Sport by Tony Duffy in *Sunday Times*, 18.7.76.
Cuba: Sport En Revolution by Raymond Pioneau and Roger Fidani, EFR, Paris, 1975.
Manfred Komorowski, "The Development of Sport", *The International Journal of Physical Education,* Vol.XIX, No.4, 1977.

Sources of Information

John Griffiths

A Selective Bibliography

The following is a list of some of the major books that have been written about Cuba. It would be an impossible task to list every book and article; work that is already admirably done in *Cuban Studies*, published twice yearly by the University of Pittsburgh. Rather, I have selected those books that have been found most useful in research on Cuba, or for teaching purposes.

GENERAL

Barkin, David & Manitzas, Nita R. eds. *Cuba: The Logic of Revolution.* Warner Modular, Andover, Mass., 1973.

Bonachea, Rolando E. & Valdes, Nelson P. eds. *Cuba in Revolution.* Anchor Books, New York, 1972.

Selected Works of Ernesto Che Guevara. M.I.T. Cambridge, Mass., 1969.

Castro, Fidel. *Fidel in Chile:* Major Speeches During Fidel Castro's Visit to Chile. International Publishers, New York, 1972.

Gerassi, John, ed. *Venceremos:* The Writings and Speeches of Ernesto Che Guevara. Weidenfeld & Nicolson, London, 1968.

Goodsell, James Nelson, ed. *Fidel Castro's Personal Revolution.* Knopf, New York, 1975.

Horowitz, Irving Louis, ed. *Cuban Communism.* Transaction, New Jersey, 1970.

Huberman, Leo & Sweezy, Paul. *Socialism in Cuba.* Monthly Review, New York, 1969.

Karol, K.S. *Guerrillas in Power.* Cape, London, 1971.

Kenner, Martin & Petras, James. *Fidel Castro Speaks.* Allen Lane, London, 1969.

MacGaffey, Wyatt & Barnett, Clifford. *Cuba: Its People, Its Society; Its Culture.* HRAF Press, Newhaven, 1962.

Mesa-Lago, Carmelo. ed. *Revolutionary Change in Cuba.* University of Pittsburgh, Pittsburgh, 1972.
Cuba in the 1970s. University of New Mexico Press, Albuquerque, 1974.
Nelson, Lowry. *Cuba: The Measure of a Revolution.* Univeristy of Minnesota, Minneapolis, 1972.
Rius. *Cuba for Beginners.* Writers & Readers, London, 1977.
Roberts, C. Paul. *Cuba 1968: A Statistical Abstract.* UCLA, Latin American Center, 1971.
Ruiz, Ramon Eduardo. *Cuba: The Making of a Revolution.* Norton, New York, 1968.
Seers, Dudley, ed. *Cuba: The Economic and Social Revolution.* University of N. Carolina Press, Chapel Hill, 1964.
Suchliki, Jaime. ed. *Cuba, Castro, and Revolution.* University of Miami Press, 1972.

PERSONAL ACCOUNTS
Caute, David. *Cuba, Yes?* Secker & Warburg, London, 1974.
Chadwick, Lee. *A Cuban Journey.* Dennis Dobson, London, 1975.
Edwards, Jorge. *Persona Non Grata.* Bodley Head, London, 1976.
Hart, Richard. *The Cuban Way.* Caribbean Labour Solidarity, 10 Leigh Road, London N5 1AH., 1978.
Lockwood, Lee. *Castro's Cuba: Cuba's Fidel.* Vintage, New York, 1969.
Mankiewicz, Frank & Jones, Kirby. *With Fidel*: A portrait of Castro and Cuba. Ballantine Books, New York, 1975.
Nicholson, Joe Jr. *Inside Cuba.* Sheed and Ward, New York, 1974.
Reckord, Barry. *Does Fidel Eat More Than Your Father?* Deutsch, London, 1971.
Salkey, Andrew, *Havana Journal,* Penguin, Harmondsworth, 1971.
Sartre, J. P. *Sartre on Cuba.* Ballantine Books, New York, 1961.
Sutherland, Elisabeth. *The Youngest Revolution.* Pitmans, London, 1971.

HISTORY
Aguilar, Luis E. *Cuba 1933: Prologue to Revolution.* Cornell University Press, Ithaca, 1972.
Blackburn, Robin, *Slavery and Empire.* New Left Books, London, 1978.
Cardenal, Ernesto. *In Cuba.* New Directions, New York, 1974.
Castro, Fidel. *History Will Absolve Me.* Cape, London, 1968.
Farber, Samuel, *Revolution and Reaction in Cuba 1933-1960.* Wesleyan University Press. Middletown, 1976.
Foner, Philip. *A History of Cuba and its Relations with the United States.* 2 Vols. Monthly Review, New York, 1962.
The Spanish-Cuban-American War. 2 Vols. Monthly Review, New York, 1971.
Inside the Monster. The writings of José Martí on the USA and American Imperialism. Monthly Review, New York, 1977.
Antonio Maceo: The Bronze Titan of Cuba's Independence Struggle. Monthly Review, New York, 1978.

Our America: Writings by José Martí on Latin America and the Struggle for Cuban Independence. Monthly Review, New York, 1978.

Fraginals, Manuel Moreno. *The Sugarmill.* Monthly Review, New York, 1977.

Gellman, Irwin F, *Roosevelt and Batista.* University of New Mexico Press, Albuquerque, 1973.

Guevara, Ernesto. *Reminiscences of the Cuban Revolutionary War.* Monthly Review, London 1968.

Guerrilla Warfare. Monthly Review, London, 1961.

Huberman, Leo & Sweezy, Paul. *Anatomy of a Revolution.* Monthly Review, New York, 1960.

Lavretsky, I. *Ernesto Che Guevara.* Progress Publishers, Moscow, 1976.

Le Riverend, Julio. *An Economic History of Cuba.* Instituto Del Libro, Habana, 1965.

Martinez-Alier, Verena. *Marriage, Class and Colour in 19th Century Cuba.* Cambridge University Press, Cambridge, 1974.

Nelson, Lowry. *Rural Cuba.* University of Minnesota, Minneapolis, 1950.

Ortiz, Fernando. *Cuban Counterpoint: Sugar & Tobacco.* Vintage, New York, 1970 ed.

Perez, Louis R. Jr. *Army Politics in Cuba 1896-1958.* Pittsburgh University Press, Pittsburgh, 1976.

Thomas, Hugh. *Cuba or The Pursuit of Freedom.* Eyre & Spottiswoode, London, 1971.

POLITICS AND ECONOMICS

Acosta, Maruja and Hardoy, Jorge. *Reforma Urbana en Cuba Revoluciona-ria.* Sinteses Dosmil, Caracas, 1971.

Alphandery, Jean Jaques. *Cuba: L'Autre Revolution. Douze Ans D'Economie Socialiste.* Editions Sociales, Paris, 1972.

Bernardo, Robert M. *The Theory of Moral Incentives in Cuba.* University of Alabama Press, Alabama, 1971.

Blackburn, Robin. 'The Economics of the Cuban Revolution' in *Latin America and the Caribbean: A Handbook.* Claudio Veliz ed., OUP, London, 1968.

'Cuba and the Super Powers' in *Patterns of Foreign Influence in the Caribbean,* Emmanuel De Kadt, ed., OUP, London 1972.

Bonsal, Philip. *Cuba, Castro, and the United States.* University of Pittsburgh, Pittsburgh, 1971.

Boorstein, Edward. *The Economic Transformation of Cuba.* Monthly Review, New York, 1968.

Brunner, Heinrich. *Cuban Sugar Policy from 1963 to 1970.* University of Pittsburgh Press, Pittsburgh, 1977.

Draper, Theodore. *Castro's Revolution.* Praeger, New York, 1962.

Castroism: Theory and Practice. Praeger, New York, 1965.

Dumont, Rene. *Cuba; Socialism and Development.* Grove Press, New York, 1970.

Is Cuba Socialist? Deutsch, London, 1974.

Fagen, Richard R. *The Transformation of the Political Culture in Cuba.* Stanford University Press, Stanford, 1969.

Goldenberg, Boris. *The Cuban Revolution and Latin America.* Praeger, New York, 1965.

264 *Culture and Media*

Gillette, Arthus. *Cuba's Educational Revolution.* Fabians, London, 1971.

Gonzalez, Edward. *Cuba Under Castro: The Limits of Charisma.* Houghton Mifflin, Boston, 1974.

Green, Gil. *Revolution Cuban Style.* International Publishers, New York, 1970.

Gutelman, Michel. *La Agricultura Socializada En Cuba.* Ediciones Era Mexico, 1970. (Part translated in Stavenhagen, Rodolfo ed. *Agrarian Problems and Peasant Movements in Latin America.* Anchor, New York, 1970.)

Halperin, Maurice. *The Rise and Decline of Fidel Castro:* An essay in contemporary history. University of California Press, Berkeley, 1972.

Harnecker, Marta. *Cuba. Dictadura O Democracia?* Siglo XXI Editores, Mexico, 1975.

Isy, Joshua. *Organisations et Rapports De Production Dans Une Economie De Transition: Cuba.* Centre D'Etudes de Planificacion Socialist, Paris, 1968.

James, Daniel. *The Complete Bolivian Diaries of Che Guevara.* Allen & Unwin, London, 1968.

Che Guevara: A biography. Allen & Unwin, London 1970.

Lataste, Alban. *Hacia Una Nueva Economica Politica Del Socialismo?* Editorial Universitaria, Santiago, Chile, 1968.

Levesque, Jaques. *L'URSS Et La Revolution Cubaine.* Université De Montreal, 1976.

Löwy, Michael. *The Marxism of Che Guevara.* Monthly Review, London, 1973.

Mandel, Ernest et al. *Sur La Revolution Cubaine.* Cahiers de la Quatrieme Internationale, Paris, 1971.

Martinez-Alier, Juan. 'The Peasantry & the Cuban Revolution' in Carr, Raymond. *Latin American Affairs.* OUP, Oxford, 1970.
Cuba: Economia Y Sociedad.

Mathews, Herbert. *Castro: A Political Biography.* Allen Lane, London, 1960.

Meneses, Enrique. *Fidel Castro.* Faber, London. 1968.

O'Connor, James. *The Origins of Socialism in Cuba.* Cornell University Press. Ithaca, 1970.

Ritter, Archibald R. M. *The Economic Development of Revolutionary Cuba.* Praeger, New York, 1974.

Scheer, Robert & Zeitlin, Maurice. *Cuba: An American Tragedy.* Penguin, Harmondsworth, 1964.

Silverman, Bertram. ed *Man & Socialism in Cuba: The Great Debate.* Atheneum, New York, 1971.

Suarez, Andres. *Cuba: Castroism & Communism. 1959-1966.* M.I.T., Cambridge, Mass., 1967.

Williams, William Appleman. *The United States, Cuba and Castro.* Monthly Review, New York, 1962.

Wolpin, Miles D. *Cuban Foreign Policy and Chilean Politics.* Lexington, Mass., 1972.

Zeitlin, Maurice. *Revolutionary Politics and the Cuban Working Class. Harper, New York, 1967.*

SOCIAL STUDIES

Gillette, Arthus, *Cuba's Educational Revolution.* Fabians, London, 1971.

Blackburn, Robin. 'Sociology of the Cuban Revolution' in *New Left Review,* No.21, October, 1963.
Douglas-Wilson, I. & McLachlan, G. 'Cuba's Health Service' in *Health Service Prospects*, The Lancet, 1973.
Fagen, Richard R. *Cuba: The Political Content of Adult Education.* Hoover Institute, Stanford University, 1964.
Hagelman, Alice & Heaton, Philip E. eds. *Religion in Cuba Today.* Association Press, New York, 1972.
Huteau, Michel & Lautey, Jacques. *L'Educacion A Cuba.* Maspero, Paris, 1973.
Leiner, Marvin. *Children are the Revolution: Day Care in Cuba.* Viking Press, New York, 1974.
Randall, Margaret. *Cuban Women Now.* The Womens' Press, Toronto, 1974.
Wald, Karen. *Children of Che: Childcare and Education in Cuba.* Ramparts Press, Palo Alto, 1978.

CULTURE

Cohen, J. M. ed. *Writers in the New Cuba.* Penguin, Harmondsworth, 1967.
Desnoes, Edmundo. *Inconsolable Memories.* (Memories of Underdevelopment). Deutsch, London, 1968.
Guillén, Nicholás. *The Great Zoo and other poems.* Monthly Review, New York, 1973.
Man Making Words, University of Massachusetts, Mass. 1972.
Obras Poeticas, 2 Vols. Instituto Cubano Del Libro, Habana, 1972-73.
Menton, Seymour. *Prose Fiction of the Cuban Revolution.* Univeristy of Texas Press, Austin, 1975.
Myerson, Michael. ed. *Memories of Underdevelopment. The Revolutionary Films of Cuba.* Lorrimer, London, 1973.
Otero, Lisandro. *Cultural Policy in Cuba.* UNESCO, Paris, 1972.
Souza, Raymond D, *Major Cuban Novelists.* University of Missouri Press, London, 1976.
Stermer, Durgald. ed. *Art in Revolution: 96 Posters from Cuba.* Pall Mall, London, 1970.
Salkey, Andrew. *Writing in Cuba Since The Revolution.* Bogle L'Ouverture, London, 1977.
Yglesias, Jose. *In The Fist of the Revolution.* Allan Lane, London, 1968.

BIBLIOGRAPHIES

Fort, Gilberto V. *The Cuban Revolution of Fidel Castro as Perceived from Abroad.* University of Kansas Libraries, 1969.
Peraya, Fermin. *Revolutionary Cuba: A Bibliographical Guide-1967.* University of Miami Press, Florida, 1969.
Suchlicki, Jaime. *The Cuban Revolution. A Documentary Bibliography, 1952-1968.* Centre for Advanced International Studies, University of Miami, Florida, 1968.
Valdes, Nelson P. & Liewen, Edwin. *The Cuban Revolution. A Research Study Guide (1959-69).* University of New Mexico Press, Albequerque, 1971.

JOURNALS

Cuban Studies. Carmelo Mesa-Lago, Editor. Centre for Latin American Studies, University Centre For International Studies, University of Pittsburgh, PA 15260. Published twice a year.

Cuba Review. Cuba Resource Center, Box 206, Cathedral Station, New York, New York 10025. Published four times a year.

Britain-Cuba Scientific Liaison Committee Bulletin. Literature Secretary, BCSLC. c/o Writers & Readers, 9-19 Rupert Street, London W1. Published irregularly.

CUBAN PUBLICATIONS

All Cuban journals and periodicals—including *Granma*, the Cuban national newspaper—are available from: Collett's Holdings Ltd., Subscription Import Dept., Denington Estate, Wellingborough, Northants. NN8 2QT.

Books published in Cuba are available from: La Empresa De Comercio Exterior de Publicaciones, O'Reilly 407, Cuidad De La Habana, Cuba.

Books from Cuba—and the rest of Latin America— are available from: America Latina, 71, Fleet Street, London EC4 1EU. Tel: 01-353 6609.

The following are a tiny sample of some of the many interesting books published in Cuba during the last few years.

Cuba Today: 16 Years of Socialist Construction. Prensa Latina, Havana, 1975.

Cuba: Organizacion de la Educacion. Ministerio de la Educacion. Annual Report to UNESCO.

La Educacion En Cuba: 1973. Ministerio de la Educacion, Havana, 1973.

La Educacion En Revolucion. Instituto del Libro, Havana, 1974.

Fidel Sobre Deporte. INDER, Havana, 1975.

Los Asentamientos Humanos En Cuba. Editorial De Ciencias Sociales, Havana, 1976.

Revolucion En 1972: Construcciones. COR & Sector de la Construccion, Havana, 1973.

Segre, Roberto. *Diez Anos De Architectura En Cuba Revolucionaria*, Havana 1970.

Historia De Cuba. Pueblo Y Educacion & FAR, Havana, 1968.

Development And Prospects of the Cuban Economy. National Bank of Cuba, Havana, 1975.

Guillen, Nicolas. *Obras Poeticas.* Instituto Del Libro, Havana, 1972/3.

Annuario Estadistico De Cuba. JUCEPLAN, Havana, published annually.

....

OTHER SOURCES OF INFORMATION ABOUT CUBA
Contemporary Archive on Latin America
1, Cambridge Terrace,
London NW1 4JL.
Tel: 01-487 5277.

Hispanic and Luso-Brazilian Council,
Canning House Library,
2, Belgrave Square,
London SW1.
Tel: 01-235 2303.

Institute of Latin American Studies, London,
31, Tavistock Square,
London, WC1.
Tel: 01-387 5671

The British Library, The London School of Economics, and other specialist libraries, Glasgow University, Liverpool University, St. Antony's College Oxford, etc. all have large Latin American collections, including Cuban material.

The Latin American Newsletter published weekly carries regular information about Cuba.
Latin American Newsletter,
90/93 Cowcross Street,
London EC1:

The Cuban Embassy,
57 Kensington Court,
London W8.
has a Cultural and Information Department, which can supply films, posters and stamp exhibitions, photographs and other information.

....

FILMS FROM OR ABOUT CUBA ARE AVAILABLE FROM:

The Cuban Embassy,
57 Kensington Court,
London W.8.
Tel: 01-937 8226. List available.

The Other Cinema,
12, Little Newport Street,
London, WC2.
Tel: 01-734 4131.
"Born of the Americas", "Hasta La Victoria Siempre", "Fidel", (Saul Landau)
"Battle for the 10 Millions", (Chris Marker)

Contemporary Films,
55 Greek Street,
London W1.
Tel: 01-437 9392.

"Memories of Underdevelopment", "Lucia", "The First Charge of the Machetes", "Death of a Bureaucrat", "For the First Time", "LBJ", "Now", "Cyclone", "Hanoi Tuesday 13", "Hemingway".

Connoisseur Films Ltd.,
167 Oxford Street,
London, W.1.
Tel: 01-734 6555.
"Cuba Si" (Chris Marker), "The Last Supper."

....

SLIDES OF CUBA
Slides on the History of Cuba, The Economy, System of Government, Education System, and Culture are available from:
The Slide Centre,
143, Chatham Road,
London SW11 6SR.
Tel: 01-223 3457.

TRAVEL TO CUBA

Information on all aspects of travel to Cuba is obtainable from:

Regent Holidays Ltd.
13 Small Street
Bristol, BS1 1DE
Tel: 0272-211711/12

Regent Holidays Ltd
Regent House
Regent Street
Shanklin P.O. 37 7A E
Isle of Wight
Tel: 098-386 4212/24

British Overseas Trade Board
1 Victoria Street
London SW1
Tel: 01-215 7877
(Hints to businessmen — details of what to buy, living conditions, etc.)

TRADE WITH CUBA

The Commercial office of the Cuban Embassy, (167 High Holborn, London WC1, 01-240 2488), can provide information about Cuban products available in this country and opportunities for British trade with Cuba.

The Britain-Cuba Scientific Liaison Committee

The BCSLC consists of scientists and technologists from Higher Education and Industry. It was set up in 1971 with the following aims:

1. To assist in obtaining published materials relating to science and technology.
2. To advise and assist on academic courses and research projects with Cuban scientists and technologists.
3. To collaborate with counterparts in Cuba on specified projects or problem-solving.
4. To assist Cuban scientists and technologists visiting Britain.
5. To provide lecture courses of varying duration in Cuba.

In addition, the Committee set itself the task of informing the scientific and technical community about progress in these areas in Cuba.

The Committee has been active in all these aspects of its work. Committee members have taught in Cuban Universities and assisted with research projects. The Committee has provided much-needed literature in a wide range of fields; assisted with the visits of Cuban academics and scientists to Britain. Since 1973 it has published a Bulletin and organised day-schools about scientific, technological and cultural development in Cuba.

Increasingly, the information that the Committee provided is obtainable through more formal diplomatic, cultural and commercial links, at governmental and institutional levels. However, the BCSLC will continue to organise day-schools and to disseminate information in Britain about Cuban science and technology.

The Secretary, BCSLC,
c/o Writers & Readers,
9-19 Rupert Street,
London W.1.

Notes on Contributors

JOHN GRIFFITHS is a Senior Lecturer in Economic History at the Polytechnic of North London. He has visited Cuba frequently and lectured and broadcast widely on Cuban affairs. He is co-author of the forthcoming *Education: The Cuban Experience* and has contributed to the revised edition of *Cuba for Beginners*.

PETER GRIFFITHS is co-organiser of the ILEA English Centre for secondary school teachers. He is a founder member of *Teaching London Kids* magazine and has contributed to *Experiments in English Teaching* ed. D. Craig and M. Heineman. He visited Cuba in '76.

ANTONIO JOSE HERRERA is a Research Fellow at the Center for Latin American Studies, University of Pittsburgh. He visited Cuba in '76.

DOUGLAS HOLLY is Lecturer in Education at the University of Leicester School of Education. His books include *Society, Schools and Humanity, Beyond Curriculum* and the forthcoming *Education: The Cuban Experience*. He visited Cuba in '76.

CHRIS LAZOU is section head of the Compilers and Graphics Group at the University of London Computer Centre. He visited Cuba in '76.

CHRIS LOGAN is Research Associate at the Institute of Social Studies, The Hague and author of the forthcoming *Basque Workers Co-operatives*. He was in Cuba in '71 and '75.

RODNEY MACE is part-time lecturer in Architecture at the Polytechnic of the South Bank. His publications include *Trafalgar Square—Emblem of Empire*. He visited Cuba in '71 and '74.

DIANA MANSFIELD is a production assistant at the BBC and has worked in the Latin American Department and the Open University. She visited Cuba in '76.

J. R. MORTON is Lecturer in Animal Genetics at the University of Cambridge. He was in Cuba in '76.

CHRIS RAWLENCE is a Founder Member of the Red Ladder Theatre. He visited Cuba in '71.

HERNAN ROSENKRANZ is doing research on Cuba at the University of Liverpool and is a research Fellow at the Center for Latin American Studies, University of Pittsburgh.

MARIAN SEDLEY is presently doing research at Bradford University. She worked with the Red Ladder Theatre from '68 to '76 and visited Cuba in '71 under the auspices of the Federation of Cuban Women.

PETER TURTON is Lecturer in Latin American Literature at the Polytechnic of North London. He worked at the University of Havana in '70-71.

ANTONI TURULL is Lecturer in Latin American Literature at the University of Bristol. He was in Cuba in '75 and '77.

CYNTHIA COCKBURN is a freelance journalist and has done research on the construction industry, urban management and local democracy. She is author of *The Local State: Management of Cities and People.* She visited Cuba in '76.

JOEY EDWARDH is doing research into the care of the elderly in Cuba at the University of Toronto. She was in Cuba in '76 and '78.

MICHAEL EDWARDS is a Lecturer in the Economics of Environmental Planning at University College, London. He was in Cuba in '76.

Glossary

ANAP—
National Association of Small Farmers—both private and co-operative, provides support for small farmers at the agricultural level as well as social (education, health, etc.)

CDR—
Committees for the Defence of the Revolution were formed in 1961 primarily as security groups at local level in the face of internal sabotage and external attacks on the revolution. Now perform a variety of social and political tasks as well. *Public Health*—ensuring that every child on the block receives necessary innoculations, women cancer-screened, etc. *Social*—recycling card and paper, care of the environment, etc. *Education*—assisting allocation of school places. *Political*—discussion of current political topics, political study.

CTC—
Federation of Cuban Trade Unions protects workers' rights, stimulates increased production and productivity, reinforces all workers' political and educational development.

FMC—
Federation of Cuban Women. A mass organisation to contribute to the political and social development of Cuban women. Organises education programmes, fitness classes, health, hygiene and political study.

JUCEPLAN— *Central Planning Board,* was supported by JUCEI at municipal level.

PCC—
Cuban Communist Party was formed in 1965 from PURS, a combination of the PSP (Popular Socialist Party, the pre-revolutionary Communist Party) and 26th July Movement led by Fidel Castro.

ICAIC—
Cuba's Film production and distribution agency.